SATURN RENDEZVOUS

Book Two of The Saturn Accords

SATURN RENDEZVOUS

Book Two of The Saturn Accords

D. Bishop

Miritish Publishing

Dedication

This book is dedicated to my wife
and long-time supporter, Ann.
Thank you for your patience
and understanding.

Published by Miritish Publishing.

This book is a work of fiction. All names, characters, and references to places and events, are fictional constructs of the author's imagination and are not to be taken literally. Any resemblance to actual persons, places, or events is entirely coincidental.

Other Books by D. Bishop

Saturn Conundrum
(Book One of The Saturn Accords)

Mastering Spanish Irregular Verbs

C For Programmers

C-Tools:1

Organic & Biological Chemistry Lab Manual

Laboratory Manual for Organic Chemistry

Acknowledgements

I would like to thank my fellow members of the Chaffee County Writers for their many constructive suggestions and careful editing of this manuscript. A special thank you to my beta readers, Cam Torrens and Tom Dury. All of you fine folks have helped me become a better writer than I ever thought I could be.

Credits

Cover Art: D. Bishop
Cover Fonts: Ethnocentric Typodermic
               Arial
This book was written and formatted using Microsoft Word
               on Windows 11.
Interior fonts by Microsoft:
               Garamond, Garamond Italic, Arial, and Courier New

Part One

Note to Readers

You are about to meet representatives from several intelligent, sentient species. Having evolved in environments different from Earth's, they defy the 'he/she/his/her' gender attributions commonly used for Humans. Consultants advised against using 'made up' pronouns such as 'zhe/zher/zhis,' so I have arbitrarily assigned the 'he/him/his' pronouns to these characters to facilitate the telling of this tale.

Chapter 1

Saturn Orbit, 2043

Rae Anne Chavez pressed her head into her headrest and gazed at Saturn's glistening silver rings on her monitor as *Aurora* began its final plunge toward the giant planet. She had taken the last three morphine capsules to help assuage the agony from her gangrenous foot. Between pain and drug fog, she fought to keep her attention in focus.

She took comfort knowing her decision to hijack the Mars-II mission after her colleagues had died and bring *Aurora* to Saturn had provided scientists earthside with a wealth of information and discoveries they would not have gotten otherwise. With funding cuts to the space program and priorities being reoriented to address the climate crisis, her Saturn obsession may have produced humanity's only Human mission to deep space ever. Submitting herself to the fiery embrace of Saturn's atmosphere would be her small sacrifice for the greater gain.

Unbeknownst to Rae Anne, a mammoth alien starship was trailing *Aurora*. Captain Vahler adjusted his Shalcerian battlecruiser's trajectory to intercept the Human's fragile spacecraft.

"Increase approach velocity ten percent," he ordered as both vessels plunged deeper into Saturn's outer atmosphere. "Their ship is beginning to come apart. If we don't catch it now, we'll lose it."

Two of the three eyestalks atop his headless torso bent upward to view the bridge monitor, while his third eyestalk drooped downward to scan his console readouts. The tiny vessel they were approaching was clearly in need of help. Article 12.383 in the Code of Interstellar Conduct gave him no choice but to respond to any ship in distress. That this action would initiate First Contact between Shalcerians and Humans filled him with serious misgivings. An encounter with such a primitive species possessed a high degree of unpredictability.

The timing, however, couldn't have worked better for his own personal agenda.

As *Aurora* slipped past Saturn's inner rings, the image on Rae Anne's monitor morphed to display Saturn's giant orb with its multihued cloud layers in vivid bands. Numerous black vortices sprinkled across the cloud layers like ground pepper flakes, boring holes deep into the atmosphere.

"Mountain-sized chunks of ice pulled from the rings, diving into oblivion," she muttered aloud in partial delirium. A chill coursed through her fevered body as that thought drove home.

Just like me.

Aurora began to vibrate, a drumming throb shaking her to the core. She gripped the armrests and set her jaw. Her heart pounded in her chest. The cabin temperature was becoming unbearably hot. Sweat oozed from every pore in her body.

The sound of metal scraping metal screeched through the ship as antennae and gear mounts ripped away from the hull. The vibration increased. *Aurora* bucked like a speedboat plowing through waves.

Rae Anne gritted her teeth. Every muscle in her body tensed.

It won't be long now.

"It's a good thing we arrived when we did," Vahler commented to his Second. The scale-plates covering his egg-shaped torso rippled in teal and yellow stripes.

The ship ahead took on an orange glow. Chunks of debris from its dorsal fin spun away into the swirling cloud base below. Trails of flame streaked behind the hull where they had torn free.

"Open the forward bay door. Let's bring it inside before it disintegrates."

Vahler wondered if this species was prepared for First Contact. Humans had just begun to forge their way into space, planting bases on their large satellite and planning exploratory trips to neighboring planets. *Avenger's* quantum computer predicted it would be a couple hundred years before First Contact, assuming the species survived that long. It gave odds for their survival at less than 30%.

Vahler's ship, the *Avenger,* was assigned to patrol a vast disk of comets and asteroids beyond the orbit of Neptune that Humans called the Kuiper Belt. An oasis for water-ice in this region of the galaxy, the Kuiper Belt provided water, hydrogen, and oxygen, three substances essential for interstellar travel for most star-faring civilizations.

Keeping tabs on the locals was part of his job. This required little effort, as Humans were the lone sentient species in this system. Frequent drone reconnaissance forays into Earth's atmosphere over the previous 2000 years supplied invaluable intelligence on every aspect of Human civilization. Eavesdropping on radio and television broadcasts and probing more recently into the Internet added to that database.

Radio transmissions had alerted Vahler that a ship with Humans aboard had taken orbit around Titan, Saturn's largest moon, and he changed course to investigate. When *Avenger* reached Saturn, the Human's ship was about to plunge into the planet's atmosphere. Vahler reluctantly set about to rescue it.

"Park it in Hangar D. Alert the berthing crew."

Avenger rotated to port 0.5-degree to align its D berth with the craft just 1000 meters ahead. It then glided forward to engulf the crippled vessel within its capacious maw. But at the last moment, the buffeting atmosphere bounced the small craft upward like a stone skipping on water. *Avenger* almost smashed into *Aurora,* sliding beneath it by a mere 10 meters.

"Good zaltar! That was close!" Vahler watched his quarry float from his grasp. Alarmed, his body scales changed color to a solid magenta.

"Bring us under the ship and we'll lift it back out of the atmosphere," he commanded. "That will make it easier to bring it in."

Soon the two ships were gliding smoothly in tandem several thousand kilometers higher. Vahler maneuvered *Avenger* behind *Aurora* and guided his ship forward to bring *Aurora* safely within the confines of Hangar D.

"Seal the hangar and fill it and the adjoining quarters with an atmosphere matching this system's third planet. We'll need to determine what, if anything, we can do for any survivors."

Vahler turned and approached the door at the end of the bridge platform. An oval opening appeared through the deck hologram as he approached. Stepping through the hatch, he waved the left of his three arms in a circular motion over his torso, drawing his Second's attention.

"I'll be in the Council Chamber. Assemble the Directorate for a meeting in an hour. That will give me time to gather the information I need. Agenda: First Contact with Humans."

Rae Anne bolted upright, peering intently at her monitor in a brief moment of mental clarity.

What the heck just happened? Am I still alive?

She called on Jason's AI brain to explain before remembering she had powered the computer down to save energy for life support.

Trying to focus through the fog in her head, she struggled to stay upright. She grimaced and narrowed her eyes to better make out the brightly lit surroundings that engulfed her ship. She felt like a minnow just swallowed by a whale.

This must be a morphine induced hallucination.

Aurora settled to the floor of the immense hangar bay with a loud THUMP. Rae Anne felt her body sink into her lounger, plunging her leg into spasms of agony. She shook her head sharply, confused at feeling gravity where none should exist.

Her bewilderment increased as she watched a couple dozen alien creatures approach her ship. They were smaller than Humans, with headless, ovoid bodies, three arms, three legs and three eyestalks attached to the top of their torsos. Each was carrying a tool, or possibly a weapon. They began banging and drilling on *Aurora's* hull.

What strange looking creatures. And their bodies are covered in an artist's palette of shimmering fluorescent colors flowing in swirls and stripes, constantly changing patterns.

If this is the kind of hallucination a morphine overdose can inspire, it's not such a... not such a bad way to... to...

Rae Anne drifted into a black unconsciousness verging on death.

Chapter 2

Aboard *Avenger*

Thrahn focused his three eyes on the holographic display before him as colored symbols popped into view in the center of a three-dimensional spreadsheet and radiated outward, congregating along the edges in neatly categorized groups. Each group represented a distinct set of biomarkers describing his patient's condition. He sent a command to the medical facility's computer and the process repeated with a different set of symbols. He buzzed with satisfaction, a sound not unlike a well-worn electric motor. His upper body scales fluoresced in warm pink and coral horizontal waves.

When Captain Vahler had assigned him to this patient's care six days earlier, his first challenge was to devise a unique treatment for her alien physiology. The treatment was working, and the patient was responding.

A faint sound behind him caught his attention. He rotated his central eyestalk to see if the patient had aroused from the coma he had induced when she arrived. Her eyelids fluttered, but there was no other sign of movement in the biogel tank in which she was immersed.

Ah…a good sign. The Human's brain is beginning to engage in shallow dreaming. She should wake up before long.

He sent another command to the computer and the monitor hologram faded while a cryo-cabinet opening appeared in the wall, revealing a compartment with several recessed shelves. Heavy white carbon dioxide vapor poured from the opening. Thrahn pulled a pair of gloves from a neighboring compartment and slipped them over two of his three hands, wriggling his four slender, suction-padded fingers into each glove's insulation. He then removed a steaming-cold package of carcinogen-neutralizing nanobots. Spinning around on the central leg he was using as a seating pedestal, he stood upright on all three legs and approached the biogel tank in a kind of skipping motion.

Thrahn removed three capsules from the packet and dropped them into a funnel shaped orifice at the top of the tank's fluid circulation unit. As yellow-green gel swirled through the circulator, the nanobots would be fed into the thick liquid and dispersed throughout the tank. They would attach to any biological surface they encountered and burrow into the organism's body pores to perform their various functions.

He stared at the strange creature's naked body. From the ship's data archives, he had identified her as a female Human. But he wondered how such awkwardly built creatures could have successfully evolved. If she stood upright on her two fat legs, she would be half again Thrahn's height.

With just two arms, Humans must be seriously disadvantaged. And with eyes restricted by the hard, bony structure atop their shoulders, they can't even see what's going on behind them.

Thrahn's mid-body scales rippled purple in parallel diagonals as he pondered how this new species might fit into the Shalcerian scheme of things.

Earth is a watery planet, but the creature's physiology suggests she is a land-based organism, evolving in a vastly different environment from our nurturing seas. The protective skeletal structure suggests a necessity for defense against predators. I will enjoy learning more when she gains consciousness.

Thrahn returned the nanobot package to its cryo-cabinet and sealed it inside. The door faded from view. He then sent a few additional commands to the computer, turned toward the side wall, and approached a hatch that appeared. The opening disappeared the moment he stepped through. The room darkened to deep twilight, the only sounds being the dull, continuous thrum of the ship itself and the biogel tank's steady hum.

When Thrahn returned a half day later, he was pleased to see his patient's eyes open, eyelids blinking rapidly, and her head swinging back and forth to take in her surroundings, a gesture necessitated by her lack of eyestalks. Neuro-blocking drugs in the biogel kept the rest of her body motionless. Thrahn skipped across the room and came to a stop at the tank. He reached down to adjust the breathing mask strapped across his midsection covering his gills and reduced the ammonia level with a long, slender finger. Two tubes connected to the mask wrapped around his body and fed into a small backpack.

He withdrew his eyestalks a couple of centimeters to better view his patient as he leaned over the tank. Her eyes widened the moment Thrahn came into her view.

I wonder how Humans convey emotions and feelings without the benefit of color. At least so long as she's in the tank, I don't have to smell her. I nearly retched when we brought her in from her ship.

Shalcerian olfactory sensors lined their eyestalks, so breathing masks offered no help to assuage odors.

His body scales swirled in varying colors and patterns depicting sympathy, comfort, and calm, at least to a fellow Shalcerian. Thrahn sent a signal to the computer to begin translating. A low tenor voice filled the room, speaking English with a decidedly British accent. The biogel fluid in the tank transmitted sounds as though it were air.

"Hello, Rae Anne Chavez. Welcome aboard the *Avenger.*"

Rae Anne mouthed words and tried to enunciate through the biogel in her throat. The computer's translation was garbled, but Thrahn anticipated what any alien under these circumstances would want to know. 'Where am I? What the hell are you? Get me out of here!'

Ah, praise zintar, her mind may still be intact.

Thrahn chirped several commands to the ship's computer, and the audible voice again filled the room.

"You are aboard *Avenger*, a Shalcerian battlecruiser. I am a Shalcerian medical officer and your caregiver. You may call me Thrahn."

Previous encounters with aliens taught Thrahn to dole out information only as requested. Too much information swirled the sediment and clouded the waters.

I'm sure I look as odd to her as she looks strange to me. No telling what she would do if it weren't for the neuro-restraining drugs.

Rae Anne made another attempt at speech. This one turned out better. "How did I get here? Where's my ship?"

"We captured your transmissions from Titan's surface and came to investigate. We rescued your ship from plunging into Saturn's atmosphere and incinerating. Your ship is moored in a neighboring hangar."

"I want to return to my ship. Immediately."

"In due time. But for now, you are in recovery. We had to cut into your ship to save your life. We are treating you for the multiple traumas you experienced before we arrived."

"My leg was in terrible shape. I don't feel the pain anymore."

"We amputated your left leg, and fabricated a prosthesis that is attaching itself to your body. It will take time for it to be fully effective, but you are responding well. We anticipate a successful outcome."

Thrahn watched his patient furrow the skin above her eyes and lower her eyelids. Thrahn's middle eyestalk twisted to glance at the monitor behind him. He was relieved to see his patient had fallen into a deep sleep.

I wonder what we are going to do with her.

The ship's Directorate had been debating that very question. An Earth ship in Saturn's neighborhood wasn't anticipated for another hundred Earth years, possibly more. Shalcerian data on this system indicated Earth inhabitants were just beginning to reach beyond their home-planet's orbit with crewed ships. Saturn was a big and unanticipated step for these creatures.

Chapter 3

Near Jupiter

Later that day, Rae Anne opened her eyes and grimaced in response to the intense blue-white glare.

Am I still hallucinating? Aurora being swallowed by a whale? Weird headless creatures with skinny arms and legs surrounding my ship and banging on it, like they're trying to get in?

And an avenging medic. What's with that?

She squinted to take in her surroundings.

Light radiated evenly from all surfaces, though not as brightly as she had first thought. The room had no corners or edges. To her right, a large block of equipment with blinking lights loomed over the edge of the container surrounding her.

Raising her head, the only thing she could move, she found herself lying—no, floating, naked, immersed in a yellow-green liquid. She pondered the fact that she had no need to breathe yet had no fear of drowning or suffocating.

I feel like I'm on a tropical beach. I can't remember the last time I felt this cozy. Makes my excursions on Titan's frozen hell-hole surface seem like ages ago. And my leg! No throbbing pain. I could stay here forever.

She rotated her head to the left and gasped at the strange creature from her dream working at a nearby bench.

It wasn't a dream after all. Is it a robot? Why do I want to call it a 'thrahn?'

The creature was two-thirds her height, with an egg-shaped torso the size of two stacked volley balls. The red tubes connecting a bag strapped to his back with a mask fastened to his torso where a bellybutton would be suggested a life-support system.

So, it's not a robot. Dios Mio! I'm looking at an honest-to-god alien!

She noticed that his six identical appendages served as arms or legs as the occasion demanded. They were slender and sinewy, with two joints. Each terminated in hands (or feet) with four finger-like digits ending in cups. This creature was using one of the appendages like a pedestal to support himself, while he used the other five as though they were all arms. With five arms at his disposal, his activity at the bench blurred in a flurry of motion.

Rae Anne could not make out whether his mottled turquoise coloring was skin, scales or a snugly fitting uniform. Then she caught sight of three marble-sized eyes perched on spindly stalks at the top of the torso. All three eyes turned in her direction and stared at her without blinking.

"Ah, Rae Anne Chavez. I am glad to see you are awake again. I am Thrahn."

That sounds familiar. Have I been awake before?

"I am your caregiver. How are you feeling?"

"Where am I? What place is this?" Rae Anne tried to sit up, but her muscles refused to respond.

I can't move. I feel like I'm enmeshed in a tight-fitting glove or an invisible web.

"You are aboard *Avenger,* a Shalcerian battlecruiser assigned to patrol your star system's Kuiper Belt. We saved you from being destroyed in Saturn's atmosphere. Your ship is stowed in a hangar bay."

"Why am I restrained? What are you doing to me?" Rae Anne thought her voice registered fear and anxiety, but she was aware of her body remaining relaxed and sedated, lacking any surge in adrenalin.

"We immobilized you so our medical treatments on your body will have the greatest effect. You are being irradiated with cancer-fighting nanobots and nutritional supplements to make you whole again."

Rae Anne sighed and closed her eyes. The precious warmth washed over her like a blanket.

I'm not going to die after all.

Her mind clouded and she fell into a deep sleep.

Thrahn skipped down the corridor toward the airlock separating Rae Anne's quarters with its Earth environment from the rest of the ship. A signal had alerted him that his patient had again resumed consciousness. His three hands strapped his breathing mask over his gills. He stepped into the airlock and recycled it to the oxygen enriched atmosphere Humans needed for survival.

When the 'READY' indicator began flashing, the hatch opened into the patient's room and Thrahn stepped through. The opening blended into the wall and disappeared behind him as he approached the biogel tank.

"Glad to see you awake again," he announced, peering into the tank.

"Excuse me, are you Thrahn?"

Ah, her memory is intact.

"Yes, I am Thrahn."

"How long have I been here?"

"Eight days. You were in a medically induced coma so we could repair the damage to your body without interruption."

"Am I allowed to sit up and move about?" She lifted her head and gazed down at her naked body.

"Not yet. We don't want to rush recovery from your leg surgery."

"How is it you speak English?"

"Your news and entertainment broadcasts over the last 150 years enabled us to learn over 20 Earth languages. Or rather, our computer has amassed a library of languages we can tap into for communication. The broadcasts have also kept us informed of your species' recent activities. We identified your language as English from your radio communications from Saturn. That's how we know who you are."

"Why did you rescue me?"

"Your ship was a vessel in distress and our laws required us to assist. In addition, your visit to Titan and your colleagues' recent visit to Mars are evidence Humans may be ready to join our consortium of space-faring species."

"Thank you for saving me."

Rae Anne closed her eyes and appeared to be in thought. After a long pause, she looked up at Thrahn and asked "So, how did you happen to be in my neighborhood just when I needed help?"

"Our species has been patrolling your system for several thousand years. The Sol System is an oasis in this part of the galaxy. Water is scarce in this region, and your Kuiper Belt contains a vast collection of ice asteroids and comets. It thus attracts all sorts. We are here to ensure its safety and security for those with legitimate business and, whenever necessary, to counter those who may be a threat to our civilization."

"Is Thrahn your real name?"

"No. My name is unpronounceable in Human speech. The computer generated a word that doesn't conflict with any other English word. Where translation is possible, that word is used. Our ship's name, for example, *Avenger*, has the same meaning in both languages."

Thrahn noticed Rae Anne's eyes drooping closed and waited a few moments to be sure she had drifted back to sleep. Before leaving the room, he made several adjustments to the medical instruments treating his patient.

This will keep her under for another two days. That should be all she needs before I can release her from the tank. As for her mental health, we'll have to wait and see.

Two days later, Rae Anne opened her eyes and found herself wide awake. She yawned and stretched. Her body was warm, almost radiant.

I feel fifteen years younger. I… Oh my god, I can move again!

She noticed she was floating three inches above a bed with a light coverlet draped over her body. When she sat upright, her body settled to the bed's surface. She instinctively pulled the blanket over her breasts and wrapped it around her body as she surveyed the room.

How odd. I was floating as though I was in zero-G, but now I'm sitting and feeling gravity. A light gravity. Like on Titan.

A warm yellow-white light radiated from the walls, and wispy clouds drifted beneath a cobalt blue ceiling. After a moment, she realized the ceiling was a shallow dome with clouds forming and dissipating above her as she watched. Green and gold vegetation appeared to be growing around the room's edges.

Hmm… Holograms? Great idea for rehab. A forest clearing on a sunny afternoon, surrounded by nature. Could use some birds and a babbling brook.

The small table and stool near her bed were the only other furniture in the room. There was no trace of medical equipment or storage cabinets.

She folded the blanket over to reveal her left leg.

Wow! My leg looks perfectly normal. I can't even see where the prosthesis is attached.

She tried to wiggle her toes. Except for the slightest discernable motion, they refused to respond. Her ankle, too, did not move at her command. She slapped her calf with both hands, as if trying to wake it up.

Oof! It's got plenty of feeling. But no movement.

Rae Anne jumped when Thrahn popped into the room as though he had walked through the wall. For the first time, she noticed his headless body was more ovoid in shape, broadest at the top, from which his three eyestalks extended. He used three of his six appendages for locomotion. Rae Anne admired his fluid movements and wondered how he could skip using three legs. One of his arms was wrapped around a bulky package.

As he approached the bed, Rae Anne wrinkled her nose at the traces of ammonia and rotten-egg hydrogen sulfide gas leaking from his life support system.

What kind of chemistry cycle must his species rely on?

"Hello, Rae Anne Chavez," he said, his upper body glowing a steady yellow coral. "I see you are ready to be up and about. But you'll have to take it slowly to get the feel of your prosthetic leg. Your nerves must learn to mesh with the mechanisms in your leg. I've put together a therapy regimen to give you full use of your leg in no time. Meanwhile, please try these on."

He handed the bundle to Rae Anne.

"We fabricated some garments for you styled after the tattered clothes you were wearing when we rescued you and what we could find on your ship."

"You searched my ship?" Rae Anne asked sharply before telling herself to remain calm.

Of course, they searched Aurora. I would have done the same thing.

Thrahn seemed to ignore her outburst. Instead, he was clearly in a different emotional state than she had seen before. He hopped about from one leg to another, seldom with two feet on the floor at the same time.

"Try them on and tell me how they fit."

Rae Ann unfolded the clothing and put on her underwear, then wriggled into her shirt. The jumpsuit proved to be a challenge, working it over her stiff left leg. Eventually she managed and fastened the shoulder straps in place.

"We also have a special gift for you. Jason, you may enter."

Rae Anne saw a man appear to walk through the same wall where Thrahn had entered earlier. He took four awkward steps into the room and stopped, his arms hanging loosely at his side.

Rae Anne lifted a fist to her mouth and choked back a sob. Tears welled in her eyes. Her heart seemed to stop beating.

"Carson?" she asked, not believing her eyes. She stepped back in shock at seeing her long-lost lover, Carson Weaver, standing before her. Her legs bumped the bed behind her, forcing her to sit hard on the mat.

Seven-year-old memories flashed through her brain, stabbing her heart as she momentarily experienced the pain and despair from that period in her life.

Chapter 4

Flashback—2036

Rae Anne and Carson were both astronaut candidates for the Mars-II mission. By fall of 2035 they had fallen deliriously in love and were sharing an apartment on the base. A year later, Carson, an experienced military pilot, was selected for the three-person mission. Rae Anne was one of the twelve disappointed trainees who had to pin their hopes on being chosen for a future mission.

By October 2036, with the May 28 launch just months away, the Agency tightened everyone's training schedules and curtailed holiday leave. Crunch time meant the two lovers saw little of each other and when they were together, they were usually too exhausted to be much company. To make matters worse, Carson signed up for a weekend conference in San Francisco, further reducing those precious moments Rae Anne could be with him before he left on the 26-month mission to Mars.

The Agency assigned a T-38 jet for Carson's trip to the coast. Rae Anne begrudged the weekend he had chosen to spend away but recognized that he needed the break and getting back into a jet's cockpit would do him a lot of good. Besides, he could have dinner with his parents in Redwood City on Sunday afternoon before flying back to Colorado.

On the Friday afternoon before the conference, Carson and Rae Anne walked back to their apartment so he could pack his gear for the trip. Carson opened the door and held it for Rae Anne. He stopped short with a surprised look on his face.

"Wow! Do I smell lasagna?"

Rae Anne laughed. She had hired a local caterer to come in and prepare one of Carson's favorite Italian meals as a going-away surprise. An authentic sausage lasagna with toasted garlic bread and a spinach-and-arugula salad with feta cheese was accompanied by a spiced iced tea.

When they had finished, Carson sighed. "I'm glad I didn't join the others and fly out this afternoon. That was the best lasagna I've ever eaten."

He rose and stepped behind Rae Anne's chair. He began rubbing her shoulders and leaned over to kiss her neck. "I don't have to be at the airfield for several hours."

Rae Anne reached to her shoulders and grasped his hands.

"Hmm. I like the sound of that, Carson," she said, rising from her chair. She put her arms around him and pulled him tightly to her. "I do like the sound of that…"

Later, after Carson dressed and packed his bags, he embraced a still-naked Rae Anne tightly and they kissed long and hard.

"Do be careful," she admonished. "I want to do that again and again and again before you leave for Mars."

"I love you so much, Rae Anne. Being away from you for two years is going to feel like forever."

They kissed again and he was gone.

Rae Anne watched through the living room curtains as he drove away, then stretched luxuriously on the bed, reveling in the memory of their intimate moments together.

How will I possibly cope for two years without Carson?

Rae Anne spent Saturday obsessed with much-neglected domestic chores. She vacuumed carpets and furniture and mopped the floors. She wondered whether Carson would learn anything useful at the conference that he could use when he landed on Mars.

Late Sunday morning, Rae Anne was chopping vegetables for her lunch salad. The local NPR station broadcast light classical music Sunday mornings, followed by a noon newscast covering national news.

A three-minute appeal for call-in donations that would be triple-matched for the next hour followed the music. Then the Sunday afternoon DJ came on the air.

```
The time is twelve noon. Temperature in
Colorado Springs is 56 degrees, with clear
skies. Overnight low will be 38. No
precipitation is forecast until Wednesday
afternoon. And now for the news…

This just in…

Two training jets have collided over Moffett
Field in San Jose, California. There appear to
be no survivors. Fire crews are on the scene.
The wreckage is fortunately confined to the
airfield. There are no known civilian
casualties or property damage. Further details
will follow as more information becomes
available.
```

Rae Anne's knife clattered to the floor as she brought both hands to her face. "Oh, please, don't let it be Carson," she gasped aloud, tears flooding her eyes.

She collapsed into a chair, her hands shaking.

Breathe deeply. Breathe deeply. The Agency owns dozens of T-38s. It can't be Carson. After all, Carson has thousands of hours flying much more sophisticated planes and he's a very careful pilot.

But no amount of rationalization helped calm her fears.

The phone rang, interrupting her torpor. She dropped the phone the first time she tried to pick it up. When she did have it in hand, she could barely activate the call.

"Rae Anne?" It was Mindy, her best friend, who had been selected to be the Mars-II Mission commander. She sounded urgent, concerned. "Have you heard? There's been a terrible accident involving two jets over San Jose. I called Human Resources, and they refuse to comment. They said a press release would be issued later. That can only mean they were Agency jets."

Rae Anne couldn't respond. She clicked off and staggered into the living room in a daze and turned on a national news channel. The 'Breaking News' was about the accident with live coverage from California showing in heart-wrenching detail the burning, twisted wreckage as fire crews worked to extinguish the flames. A column of thick black smoke twisted into the sky.

Her phone rang in the kitchen, but she couldn't bring herself to move, mesmerized by the scene. The commentator's monolog barely registered, but it didn't matter since they had no additional information to convey.

An Agency spokesperson in Colorado Springs appeared on the screen behind a bevy of reporter's microphones. Several other officials accompanied her. Rae Anne recognized the building behind her, just a few blocks from where she sat.

```
It is with deep sorrow that the Interplanetary
Exploration Agency must announce that three of
our astronauts in training have perished today
while performing training maneuvers in their T-
38 Talon jet aircraft. The two jets collided on
takeoff from Moffat Field in California. There
are no survivors. The identities of the victims
are being withheld pending notification of
their families. The Interplanetary Exploration
Agency and the NTSB will be investigating the
cause of the accident. We will keep you
informed as further information becomes
available.
```

The cacophony of questions the reporters shouted went unanswered as the Agency officials turned and walked back through security and disappeared into the administration building. Rae Anne sobbed as she pulled a blanket over her shoulders and curled up in a fetal position. She heard someone pounding on her door, but she couldn't budge from her cocoon.

Shortly, she felt strong arms wrapping tightly around her shoulders and helping her to sit up. Rob, a neighbor and fellow astronaut candidate, had entered the apartment when she didn't answer the door. "I can't tell you how sorry I am," he said.

"Carson was one of the pilots, wasn't he?"

"Yes, Rae Anne, he was. I'm so very, very sorry. Marty called from California. He saw it happen. Said he couldn't get through to you, so he called me. I'm here for you. Whatever I can do, just ask."

He hugged her again, more tightly this time, and held her quietly as she sobbed into his shoulder. An hour later Mindy showed up and the two of them remained with her throughout the night, Mindy helping her into bed with Rob lending support for his two friends and colleagues.

The official report released to the public after the NTSB investigation laid blame for the accident on pilot error, though it was impossible to determine which pilot may have been more to blame. Nat Simons had been flying one of the jets, while Carson piloted the other with Barry Moore as a passenger. The two pilots were performing a formation take-off in violation of both Agency rules and FAA regulations.

Eyewitness accounts suggested one aircraft tipped the wing of the second, drawing them into a midair collision just above the runway. As soon as their aircraft hit the ground, they burst into flames.

Rae Anne had her own explanation for the accident, knowing Carson's aversion to risk and strict adherence to safety. She would forever wonder if Nat goaded Carson into trying a stunt he would never have done on his own. Barry was as much into photography as she was into astronomy, suggesting to her that Nate may have wanted Barry to film him close-up from Carson's jet during takeoff. An innocent request with unintended, disastrous consequences.

Rae Anne pursued the following days on autopilot, unable to get Carson out of her mind. She remained cloistered in her apartment the entire week, eating little and sleeping less.

Rob tried to pull her out of her despair, but to no avail, despite neglecting his own studies and spending most of the week with her.

The memorial service for all three was held at the Air Force Academy chapel north of Colorado Springs on the first Saturday in November. The large church was packed with Agency staff and personnel. Rob and Mindy accompanied Rae Anne to the service.

That evening she packed her bags to fly home to Albuquerque. She hadn't formally submitted a resignation to the Agency, but only because she wasn't formally doing anything. Her mind was in a fog. Nothing mattered to her. She figured the Agency would know she had left the program when she didn't show up for the Monday morning briefing.

Rob reluctantly offered to drive her to the airport. He tried without success to talk her into waiting six weeks before making any important decisions. When he arrived at the door Sunday morning to pick her up, he took her bags, and she followed him to the car and got in.

Traffic was sparse. Rae Anne paid little attention to Rob's choice of route until he turned into the lot outside the Agency's psychotherapist's office just off Academy Boulevard.

"Rob! What the hell is going on," she blurted angrily. "I'll miss my plane."

Despite her protests, Rob came to a stop at the curb. Three other vehicles pulled in around him, blocking the car. Before Rae Anne could speak, the entire team had gathered around Rob's car. Mindy opened her door.

"Mindy, what are you doing here? What is this?"

"We can't let you go without hearing from us, Rae Anne. With all we've been through together, we're family. You are part of that family. We've lost three of our members, and your leaving would make it four. That's more than we can bear. Please, don't go."

Rae Anne burst into tears. Mindy helped her out of the car and wrapped her in her arms. The others showered her with heartfelt consolation and support.

"There's someone inside who wants to see you, Rae Anne," Rob said.

"There's nothing a therapy session can do for me, Rob."

"No, no. It's not the shrink. Please, come with me." Rob held out his arm. "If you decide you must leave us after this, I'll buy your replacement ticket and see you off. But trust me for now, please. Come inside."

Feeling she had no choice, she allowed Rob to lead her to the door.

Maybe I should follow Rob's advice and give myself some time before making a major decision. These wonderful people truly are my family. Still, I can't see any joy in going on with the program. Oh, Carson, I miss you so.

Mindy handed her a tissue as she and Rob reached the door to the building. She was surprised to see their team supervisor Jeremy inviting her to enter. They walked through the door, passed security with a nod, and entered the first-floor conference room.

The sight of Colonel O'Connell, the Agency head, sitting at the table surprised her even more. He stood as they walked in and motioned for her to take a chair beside his. He was dressed casually, as though he had dropped in after a round of golf.

"Come in, Rae Anne, and please, have a seat."

Rob helped her into the chair and closed the door as he stepped from the room, leaving Rae Anne and the colonel alone together.

"Hello, Rae Anne," Colonel O'Conner said warmly. "I must tell you how terribly, terribly sorry I am about Carson's death, and not just for the program, but for you personally. I fear the Agency hasn't been responsive enough in your time of need, Rae Anne. For this you have my deepest, personal apology. Please forgive me."

Rae Anne forced a nod in acknowledgement and choked back a lump in her throat. She was astounded that the Agency chief was meeting with her one-on-one, and that he had apologized to her personally.

"I'll get right to the point. With the loss of both Carson and Barry, we've had to reassess all the skill sets each member of our astronaut corps has to offer. Using that, we put together a new crew roster for Mars-II.

"Rae Anne, with your proven expertise in computer science and proficiency in navigation and communications, you are one of those three people. We need you to ensure that the mission is a success. Mindy will stay on as commander, with her engineering and geology background, and Rob will bring his piloting skills and knowledge of biology and medicine to the mission."

Rae Anne gasped.

The Agency has chosen me, ME, for Mars-II. But I wouldn't even be here if it weren't for Carson. I know he would want me to accept. If I do accept, it will be in honor of your memory, Carson.

"There are only seven months left before launch. You will be crushed bringing yourself up to speed in such a short time. But the fact is, we need you, Rae Anne. We are 100% confident you can do it. What do you say?"

Rae Anne was unable to speak. She nodded 'Yes,' feeling chills up her spine. She felt as though a light was beginning to peek through the black shroud that had engulfed her since Carson's death. She could feel the tiniest bit of her characteristic sense of hope and anticipation returning.

Her back straightened and she raised her head to look directly into the colonel's eyes.

"I will do this. I'll do it for the mission, for myself and for Carson."

It's the least I can do for Carson's memory.

Chapter 5

Colorado Springs, 2043

Ian Bentley, recently appointed head of the Astronautics Division in the US Interplanetary Exploration Agency (the 'Agency'), glanced out the west-facing window to the left of his desk. Although Peterson Space Force Base was just a few miles east of Colorado Springs, he couldn't see Pikes Peak through the sheets of rain pelting the region. The torrent produced a continuous drumbeat on the window.

He turned his attention back to his computer, and tried to ignore the cacophony as he studied the latest report from his division's Astro-Science Department. The report detailed the calculated Saturn-to-Earth trajectory of *Eagle*, the small lander packed with Rae Anne's samples from Titan. Ten days before, Rae Anne, lacking sufficient provisions or life support for a return to Earth, had used her last remnant of fuel to boost *Eagle* free of Saturn's gravity. In doing so, she condemned her own ship, *Aurora*, to burn up in Saturn's atmosphere.

As Rae Anne had predicted in her final transmission, *Eagle* would intersect with Earth's orbit in six years, in December 2049. The problem, however, was Earth would be on the opposite side of the sun. Catching the lander would not be a simple operation.

"Nothing is ever simple around here," Ian grumbled to no one in particular. He couldn't take his mind off Rae Anne. They had met once on the Earth-Orbit Transfer Station (EOTS-I) just before *Aurora* launched from Earth-orbit for Mars. But they maintained constant ship-to-ship communication throughout his own Mars-III mission as *Aurora* followed Rae Anne's detour to Saturn. He thought of her as a close friend and colleague.

Reflecting on losing her brought a heaviness to his chest. Only now did he realize his feelings ran deeper than friendship. His emotional response at losing her surprised him.

Is it possible to fall in love with someone you met just once? I cared deeply for her. And now she's gone. It's like a knife has torn out my heart.

Ian glanced at the name on the report's first page and tapped his phone.

"Jan, set up a meeting Monday morning with our long-range planning group. Attach a copy of Sandra's report to the notices. And include her in the meeting as well. Title the agenda Options for Capturing *Eagle* in 2049."

Ian typed a number into his phone. Sandra's image appeared on the screen. Her short red spiky hair erupted randomly around her head, giving the impression that she was aflame.

"Sandra, I want to compliment you on a great report. I'd like you to give a concise summary with video at Monday's meeting. It's not too early for us to begin figuring out how we can retrieve *Eagle*."

"Thanks, Ian. The data is still preliminary. *Eagle* is too far away to get an accurate reading on its trajectory. But the big picture holds."

"Fair enough. That's all we need to start with. See you Monday."

The following Monday, Ian entered the small conference room in the Astronautics Administration Building carrying his laptop under his right arm and clutching his ever-present coffee mug in his left hand. He set both down at the end of the conference table. Looking around the room to verify everyone designated to attend had arrived, he sat and connected his laptop to the room's AV hardware.

The twelve positions around the table each included secure connections to two large monitors on either side of the room. Attendees could view presentation displays on their own computers or on the display monitors while working on their own projects. They could also share their own screens with the room displays or to other attendees' laptops as needed, encouraging everyone to feel some degree of ownership in the proceedings.

Ian called the meeting to order and gave a brief preview of the problem.

"It's imperative we do everything we can to bring those samples home. I trust you've taken time to study Sandra's report. To make sure we're all on the same page before proceeding, I asked her to highlight the key details for us. Sandra, you're up."

Sandra began tapping keys on her laptop. The room monitors projected a large, animated diagram of the Solar System with a date tag in the corner. The animation showed *Eagle's* position from the current date to January 2050 in conjunction with the inner planets' motions. Each second corresponded to one month's progress. She stopped the animation when the time stamp showed December 2049.

"As you can see, when *Eagle* passes through Earth's orbit in December of 2049, Earth is about 150 million miles away, on the opposite side of the sun."

"Comments? Questions?" Ian asked. Several hands popped up. Ian called on each person by name.

"Is the trajectory on a collision course with the sun?"

"No," Sandra replied. "It's in an elliptical orbit like a comet. But the orbit will deteriorate over time. My simulations show that it will plunge into the sun in April of 2077. That is, if nothing disturbs its trajectory before then."

"Why aren't these projections more precise? Seems like there's a bit of hand waving here."

Sandra nodded in agreement. "The simulations are only as good as the data we plug into them. Given *Eagle's* distance from Earth, the 'plus or minus' factor in its trajectory is too large for more precise results. Any small discrepancies at this point will show up as a far greater variation after six years."

"What if we try to catch it on the rebound? How long before it returns to Earth-orbit?"

"About nine years. But here's the catch. That's nine additional years for errors to accumulate. And there is one other complication should the actual trajectory be close to one of our more extreme simulations."

She moved the display cursor next to Venus.

"It may not even make it beyond the first pass. Note how *Eagle's* trajectory swings close to Venus on its path around the sun. If it comes too close, Venus will alter its trajectory. The new path would loop into a tight spiral into the sun."

"So, what you're saying, Sandra, is the first pass in 2049 may be our only chance to catch it, is that right?" Ian asked.

"That's correct."

Another comment came from across the room, directed to Ian.

"A 150-million-mile expedition is like two Mars missions. How can we fit something like that into our budget? Things are tight enough as it is."

"I'm sure we can get some additional funding for this effort," Ian replied. "But nothing approaching the cost of even a single Mars mission. Fortunately, the entire operation can be handled autonomously, reducing the cost considerably."

"If I may," Sandra said, restarting her animation. "I was reworking my simulations over the weekend and came up with another possibility."

She tapped on her computer, halting the simulation at March 2049.

"We've been discussing a mission to retrieve *Eagle* from Earth. However, *Eagle* will be passing through Mars orbit here, in March of 2049, and, as you can see, Mars is in an ideal location for an intercept. The Mars-V mission is scheduled to leave Mars-orbit in late September of 2048. If its departure were delayed six months, it's conceivable they could capture *Eagle* on the way home."

That revelation elicited several comments from around the room.

"That's a lot to ask. Extending the 26-month mission to 32 months."

"Logistics would be formidable. Supplies alone would have to be increased by 25%."

"Not to mention a lot of extra fuel. Mars-V would need additional fuel to match *Eagle*'s higher velocity for a rendezvous and even more fuel to change trajectory and to decelerate both ships to achieve Earth-orbit."

"Actually, the extra acceleration may help with the first problem," one of the engineers offered. "If Mars-V left Mars with additional acceleration to catch up to *Eagle,* the higher return velocity would shorten the return flight from the usual eight months to what, maybe four or five? This would reduce the necessary extra provisions by half."

"But there's no way to get around the extra fuel requirements," someone else added.

"There's plenty of time to put an orbiter into Mars orbit with extra fuel. A few modifications on the Mars-V ship to allow it to refuel in orbit shouldn't be a problem."

"Your proposal may be the solution to our problem, Sandra," said Ian with a nod. "Good job."

"We'll meet here again in a week, same time. Let's everyone concentrate on the possibility of a Mars-V capture and see what we can come up with. Sandra, use your simulations to provide likely trajectories and velocities for *Eagle* as it crosses Mars orbit and send those out to everyone. That will give us some data to work with.

"I want to know if the Mars-V option is technically feasible, what hurdles we'll face, and what it will take to make it happen. Include cost estimates for the extra orbiter as well."

He dismissed the meeting and returned to his office, confident his team was on top of the problem but glad they had several years to work on it.

Late in the day, as he wrapped things up to head home, his notebook buzzed with a flashing red 'ALERT' icon in the corner of the screen. He frowned in irritation.

Perfect timing. I wonder how late this emergency will keep me tonight.
He swiped the phone icon.
"Ian here."

His communications officer, Penny, was on the line. She sounded alarmed.

"Ian, we just received an urgent notification from the International Astronomical Union. World-wide distribution. There's a large object headed directly towards Earth."

"Any specifics, or is it too early to tell?"

"It's the size of several football fields and they say it's about a week out. But it's moving incredibly fast. Over 900 kilometers per second."

"Did you say 900 kilometers per second?"

"That's right. I've forwarded the announcement."

Ian whistled in astonishment.

"That's faster than anything we've encountered inside the Solar System. Thanks, Penny."

Ian checked the IAU's statement Penny sent. He then forwarded it with alert tags to his department heads and set up an urgent meeting for 9:00 the next morning.

Hopefully, we'll have more information to work with by then.

Chapter 6

Near Jupiter, 2043

Rae Anne stared at the man standing before her and tried to make sense of what she was seeing.

He looks like Carson. But Carson is dead, and Thrahn called him 'Jason.'

Thrahn must have noticed her hesitation.

"We downloaded your ship's memory into our computer archives and discovered the extensive programming you put into your ship's AI, the AI persona you named Jason. We thought you might find an android embodying your program to be useful and our engineering team was looking for a challenge. They designed Jason, here, using your body as a template and a photograph we found on your ship for its features. It is linked to your program in our computer so it should respond just as it did on your ship. What do you think?"

The lump in her throat prevented her from speaking. All she could do was stare at Carson…at Jason…at this Human form that wasn't Human.

"Hello, Rae Anne," the android said, standing rigidly in place. The voice was Jason's AI voice she had worked with throughout the past six years aboard *Aurora*. The words appeared to come from his mouth, though his mouth didn't move.

"Remember those times you wished I had a body? Well, here I am! Now I can play poker using real cards and you won't think I'm cheating."

Jason said this with an appropriate jesting tone, but his face remained frozen.

Thrahn broke in to explain.

"Jason has all the characteristics you programmed into it. Its memory contains all the physical nuances and facial expressions you taught it to look for in others so its responses would fit the context. But as an android, it must now learn to link those actions it has observed to its own physical body. You're just the person to teach it."

Thrahn skipped to the invisible door he and Jason had come through. "I'll leave you two alone now. I'm sure Jason will be a quick study. After all, it's now linked to our advanced quantum computer."

Thrahn disappeared as though through the wall.

Rae Anne swallowed hard and stared at Car… at Jason. He hadn't moved.

"Come sit next to me Jason," she said as she scooted to the side to make room for him.

"Thank you, Rae Anne. Please show me how."

Whew. So, we're Back to Basics.

"First, walk over and stand next to me. You obviously know how to walk."

"Hobble is more like it. The engineers couldn't figure out how Humans walk with just two legs having a single knee joint and no suction devices on their feet."

"And I am amazed at how gracefully they get around on three legs with two joints. But I wonder what's with the suction cups?"

"Shalcerians are amphibians who have evolved body scales for communication. A large part of their evolution took place in shallow waters on their home world. Evolution gave them octopus-like suction cups to grasp onto rocks and pull themselves along. When they moved to land, they had to adapt with what nature gave them."

How does he know so much about Shalcerians?

Rae Anne nodded. "Unfortunately, at the moment I only have one working leg. But maybe you can learn by watching how I use it."

Rae Anne pulled the loose trouser leg over her right knee so Jason could watch her leg and ankle at work. She limped over to Jason with a cane Thrahn had provided with the clothing.

After instructing him to walk beside her while concentrating on his gait, they began walking together. After two circuits of the room, Jason had mastered the basics.

"That's pretty good Jason. Now let me show you how to sit."

Thrahn appeared several hours later carrying a mug of hot tea. Rae Anne and Jason were sitting beside each other on the bed. She was demonstrating the lip and facial movements required to match various speech phonemes in the English language.

"I thought you might like some tea," Thrahn offered, holding the steaming mug out to her, handle first.

She took the mug and sipped the tea.

"This tastes very good. In fact, it's just the way I like it. How did you manage that?"

"Jason came up with the idea and prepared it in *Aurora's* galley. It then asked me to fetch it for you."

The hairs on Rae Anne's neck bristled and a chill ran down her arms.

Whoa. There's more going on here than meets the eye. I'll need to check it out with Jason when we're alone.

Changing the subject, she asked "How long has *Avenger* been patrolling the Kuiper Belt?"

"Fifty years, off and on, for *Avenger*. But the Empire has been keeping order here for over 2000 years. Captain Vahler has been in charge of the region for nearly 400 years. He knows it like the scales on his body."

"That's a long time by Human standards. What is the average Shalcerian life span?"

"With our advanced health care systems and rejuvenation protocols, it's not unusual to live to 600 years. Captain Vahler will probably be retiring in the next 50 years or so."

"What kind of threats are you facing in our Kuiper Belt to warrant patrolling it for so long?"

"The Empire does have its enemies, both internal and external. For example, a Baltar raiding party attacked and destroyed one of our battle cruisers, the *Nemesis,* while it was monitoring the Kuiper Belt. We were tasked to look for survivors. Fortunately, we did rescue a fair number, and Military Command assigned *Avenger* to take over its mission."

"It sounds like a dangerous assignment. Could *Avenger* come under attack as well?"

"It's possible. There are occasions when risks are necessary to maintain security. But you know that from your own Earth history. Space is not much different. Just more powerful weapons."

"So, are we still in Saturn-orbit?"

"Oh, no. *Avenger* is now inside Jupiter's orbit. We're headed for Earth. You'll be home in eight days. We've been taking it slowly to give you time to recover."

Eight more days? So, eighteen days to duplicate my six-year trip, and he says they're taking it slowly!

She almost missed Thrahn's final comment as he left the room.

"Beginning tomorrow, you will meet with the Directorate. I believe they may have a specific task in mind for you to help with First Contact. In the meantime, you will be doing three two-hour physical therapy sessions every day. Be sure to get a good night's rest."

When Thrahn had gone, Rae Anne asked Jason if the room was being monitored.

Without answering her question directly, he said "As far as I can tell, they have no monitors aboard *Aurora.*" He emphasized the word '*Aurora.*'

Rae Anne nodded, hoping to signal to Jason she had picked up his meaning.

"I should look into what supplies are left on *Aurora.* I hope this isn't my last tea bag! Can you take me there?"

"Of course. Hangar D is right across the hall, and it's pressurized with oxygen, same as this room and the corridor. Follow me."

Hmm… More information I wouldn't expect him to know.

Jason turned and strode to the wall and stepped through. Rae Anne followed, hesitating at the threshold. This was her first encounter with this mysterious door. It remained open while she stepped into the hall, then seamlessly solidified behind her. Out of curiosity, she reached back to poke her hand through it and her knuckle rapped against a solid wall.

"Before we go any further, can you explain how these weird doors work?"

Jason stopped and turned to Rae Anne. His face wrinkled in various contortions, obviously practicing his facial muscle skills.

"According to the computer, the hatches on *Avenger* are all sophisticated shields made of densely packed nanoparticles. A sensor next to the door detects your intention to pass through and activates a force field to draw the particles aside. A counteracting force field pushes them back in place behind you."

Rae Anne rubbed her chin, thinking. "So, if the particles are the same color as the walls, the doors seem to disappear."

"Actually, the computer data suggests the opposite is true. Nanoparticles are a unique substance with their own color. The walls have been colored to match the nanoparticles."

"So, what should we call these doors that aren't doors?"

"Hmm… 'Walldoor' is too mundane for such an advanced mechanism. How about 'nanoscreen'?

"Nanoscreen it is. But do the sensors read into our minds?"

Jason pursed his lips, mimicking Rae Anne's earlier facial contortions.

"I don't think so. It may be that the sensors are fine-tuned to an approaching creature's body movements and can discern its intentions from the motion it sees."

"But I've noticed that *Avenger's* computer translator speaks for Thrahn without his vocalizing any sounds of his own. That would suggest it was reading his thoughts."

Jason paused and furrowed his brow as though he was solving a difficult problem. Rae Anne smiled at his quick adoption of Human facial expressions.

"The computer archives show that *Avenger's* crew all have implants that detect thoughts directed to their neurologic receivers and transmit those signals to the quantum computer. So Thrahn can send what he wishes to say to you to the computer for the computer to translate over the room's speakers. He can also send commands to the computer for processing without vocalizing them."

"So, without an implant, the computer can't pick up my thoughts."

"That is correct."

"What about yours?"

"We'll discuss that in a moment. First, let's check out *Aurora's* larder."

Jason turned and led Rae Anne through a second nanoscreen that led into an enormous hangar. *Aurora* rested on the deck, much the worse for wear. The telescope and antennae on the communications fin weren't the only things that had sheared off in Saturn's atmosphere. In addition, a gaping hole yawned near the airlock where the Shalcerians had cut into its hull to rescue her.

Aurora sure isn't going anywhere.

Jason stepped through the hole and into the galley on Level 2. Turning, he reached down and helped Rae Anne aboard. She wouldn't have made it without her cane. She sat at the table and closed her eyes. sniffing deeply, relishing the familiar smells.

You'd think after six years alone here, this would be the last place I'd want to be. But this is home.

"Are we free to talk here without being monitored?" she asked, looking around the room as if she were looking for an alien spying device.

"I believe so. I don't read any data streams flowing into the computer from room sensors like I did in your quarters. Also, you asked if I was being monitored. The simple answer is yes, since I am now a part of their computer. The more complete answer is that I have created a bypass directly into *Aurora's* computer that circumvents their monitoring my thoughts and actions. They are not aware that I have done this."

"Good. So, the tea you prepared shows you're still connected to *Aurora's* computer, and you sent a message to Thrahn without leaving the room, presumably through *Avenger's* computer."

"Exactly. I still have full control of the sensors and systems on *Aurora*, both through their computer and through my bypass circuit. For the tea, I used the link through *Avenger's* computer so they wouldn't suspect I created a bypass. But my access to their computer archives is an AI's dream come true. I don't think they intended for that to happen."

Just how much access does he have? Maybe a few innocent questions…

"How many Shalcerians are aboard *Avenger*?"

"*Avenger* has a crew of 576."

"That's an unusual number."

"It's 300 in base 12. It seems Humans aren't the only ones to use the number of digits at the end of their arms for their counting systems. Shalcerians have three arms with four digits on each."

"Interesting. What star system do they call home?"

"18 Scorpii, a G1V yellow star much like Sol."

"So, their sun is a bit hotter than our G2V star. How many planets are in their system?"

"Twelve, two of which are inhabited by Shalcerians. Their capitol is on Shalkor, the fourth planet from their sun."

"How distant is 18 Scorpii from Earth?"

"45.74 light years."

"How many star systems make up the Shalcerian Empire?"

"The empire includes 120 star-systems. Their nearest base to Earth is at epsilon-Eridani, 10.5 light years away."

Wow! Jason has access to their encyclopedic database. I wonder if they set up a firewall to prevent him from accessing technical information.

"What is *Avenger's* source of power?"

"*Avenger* has four nuclear fusion reactors, three of which are dedicated to propulsion."

"Surely *Avenger* isn't big enough to accommodate four fusion reactors. The three experimental fusion reactors on Earth are gigantic."

"Their reactor design is much simpler than the tokamak reactors on Earth. Smaller, simpler, and much more efficient. Keep in mind, the three on Earth were commissioned in just the last ten years. Humans have a long way to go to match Shalcerian technology."

"Four fusion reactors. They must be at least a thousand years beyond us!"

There don't seem to be any restrictions on Jason's sifting through their computer archives. And Jason is my android. What a resource to draw from!

Chapter 7

Earth

- Killer Asteroid Aimed at Earth!!
- Earth in Asteroid Crosshairs!!
- Extinction Event Looming??

The morning after the IAU's initial announcement, every media outlet was broadcasting their interpretation of the notice. Although news reports varied in content and degree of speculation, all were based on the single terse statement from the IAU.

Several observatories are reporting a large object near Jupiter in a path that will bring it into Earth's general vicinity within a week. Its velocity is estimated at 900 km/sec. No object originating within the Solar System is known to possess a velocity of this magnitude.

The object, designated 7/2043 U1, is 350 to 400 meters long and 60 to 80 meters wide. Until its exact trajectory is determined, the risk of collision with Earth cannot be accurately assessed.

Despite the official announcement's cautious nature, many media sources compared this asteroid with the Chicxulub asteroid that wiped out the dinosaurs. Although much smaller, its greater momentum would impart a devastating blow. Should it strike at sea, the resulting tsunami would be catastrophic.

Twenty-four hours after the first announcement, the IAU had gathered enough additional data to prompt a follow-up.

```
A trajectory analysis of object 07/2043 U1
reveals that it will strike Earth in seven
days, at 20:12 UTC on July 15, 2043. The impact
will take place within a 500-km radius of a
point in the Mediterranean Sea that is 250 km
due west of Haifa, Israel. This places Israel,
Lebanon, Jordan, Syria, Egypt, Turkey, and
several Mediterranean islands in direct
jeopardy, as well as all coastal regions
bordering the Mediterranean Sea in the event of
a tsunami.
```

Panic and mass hysteria swept the world. Stock markets plummeted. Several exchanges halted trading. Survival gear and firearms sales skyrocketed. Stocks of food and household staples disappeared from store shelves. Business as usual came to a standstill.

Countries bordering the Mediterranean saw entire populations pack everything they could carry and attempt to travel as far inland as possible by whatever conveyance they could find. Coastal cities became eerily deserted. Massive traffic jams clogged every highway. Panicked passengers jammed airports and airlines doubled their flights.

Governments on islands with large populations and possessing mountainous terrain, such as Cyprus, tried with some success to convince citizens to migrate to the mountains. They enlisted every organization to sponsor asteroid parties, emphasizing this would be one firework show no one should miss. They could only hope a direct strike was unlikely.

Turkey, Greece, and Italy opened their borders to island residents who would be inundated if hit by a tsunami. By contrast, Albania and Croatia imposed a lockdown and assigned additional border security for enforcement. Tsunami precautions were initiated as far away as Spain, France, and Morocco.

Marine traffic in the narrow Dardanelles looked like commuter rush-hour in Los Angeles as every ship and yacht in the Mediterranean sought safe haven in the Sea of Marmara or, better still, the Black Sea. Turkish marine pilots worked double shifts and were still in short supply.

The situation in the six mainland countries within the target area was more chaotic. Governments imposed martial law and curfews to quell the massive demonstrations demanding governments do something, anything, despite the fact there was nothing that could be done. Predictably, thousands died in the ensuing riots.

Government officials in other countries, while breathing a collective sigh of relief, assigned commissions to predict how the asteroid strike would affect their economy and population. Attempts to reassure citizens that they had everything under control had limited effect. Religious zealots, preachers, and imams alike, worked their followers into a frenzy by predicting this event was the prophesied apocalypse and Armageddon was at hand. After all, look at the target area God had chosen to strike.

CEOs of major corporations around the world formed 'working groups' to ameliorate the damage the asteroid impact might have on their supply chains and bottom lines. Multinationals were the most concerned. Insurance reinsurers were apoplectic and had already begun lobbying governments to cover their pending losses.

Sam Durban and Karen Sanders belonged to this elite group of wealthy entrepreneurs. Sam had made his fortune in the commercial space arena, operating a fleet of rockets ferrying passengers and cargo into orbit and to the three permanent bases on the moon. His TransWorld Space venture maintained daily sub-orbital service between major cities on every continent. He also owned Luna Xtract, a fledgling mining operation on the moon. Luna Xtract mined and processed ore containing rare elements essential for electronics, microchips, and batteries. He planned someday to expand his operations to Mars and the Asteroid Belt.

Karen Sanders had inherited Sanders Robotics when her husband died under mysterious circumstances on a fishing trip in the Baja. She maintained a controlling interest in the world's largest industrial and health-care robotics company. She was also heavily invested in wind turbine installations around the world.

Sam's companies used Karen's robots extensively, so Sam was one of Karen's most valuable customers. Some years back, even before her husband died, Sam and Karen began an affair that still flourished. When the IAU made their asteroid announcement, Karen was visiting Sam at his 500-acre estate in New Hampshire's White Mountains.

"A tsunami will wipe out my offshore wind operations in the Mediterranean," Karen moaned, toying with her eggs Benedict over breakfast on Sam's deck facing east toward Mount Washington.

"Surely you're insured."

"This will sink the entire insurance industry, Sam. I'll be lucky to come out of this with ten cents on the dollar."

Sam smiled inwardly and sipped his coffee.

"You'll still be one of the richest women in the world."

"What's left of it."

A Steller's jay landed on the railing and looked at them, bobbing its black crest accusingly. Sam broke off a piece from his English muffin and tossed it to the bird. The jay snatched it in his beak and took to wing.

Sam continued, hoping to console Karen and lure her back to bed.

"The world economy will take a hit, for sure. I'll lose passenger volume. But if we're smart, we'll see opportunities to pull us through. For example, I've been looking for another site for a spaceport. The Middle East is as good a bet as any, long term. If, say, Israel's economy is bust, there'll be tons of cheap labor drooling for work. Cheap land, too. And manufacturers forced to rebuild will be buying tons of new robotics equipment. They might even be open to converting to wind energy."

"That's what I like about you, Sam. You are the quintessential optimist." She leaned over and pecked his cheek.

Sam finished the last of his Bloody Mary and stood. He stepped behind Karen's chair and began massaging her shoulders.

"Then let me give you some of my optimistical therapy to ease your worries," he said, leading her back into the house.

Chapter 8

Asteroid Belt

Thrahn stepped through the nanoscreen into Rae Anne's quarters while she slept, pulling a cart that floated several inches above the floor. Therapeutic exercise equipment hung over the cart's rim. Thrahn began unloading it and setting things up. Rae Anne bolted upright with a start at the commotion and stared at the odd-looking devices.

Thrahn's third eye caught her movement. "Good morning, Rae Anne."

"Oh, Thrahn. You startled me."

"I'm sorry. Did you sleep well?

"I've never slept better. Although it's easy to beat six years sleeping in a vertical sack strapped to the wall. Floating horizontally is so much more natural."

"The anti-gravity aspect is only one property the bed has to offer. While you are sleeping, it radiates your body with nanobots carrying your daily nutritional requirements and nanobot sensors that report any anomaly within your body requiring attention."

"That explains your orders to sleep nude. The warmth I feel radiating from the bed reminded me of the Treatment Center tank. Does that also explain why I'm not hungry?"

"Exactly. Eliminating food, food preparation, and solid bodily waste simplifies everything on extended space missions. We Shalcerians take one powdered sulfur tablet each week, and the nanobots take care of the rest. Of course, you may miss eating, but so long as you are our guest on *Avenger*, you'll just have to get used to it.

"And speaking of getting used to things, I've set up some equipment to help speed your recovery." Thrahn picked up a helmet with one of his three hands and extended it towards Rae Anne. "We need to recondition your brain to control the micro-motor 'muscles' in your prosthetic leg and foot. The helmet provides ultrasonic impulses to the appropriate motor neurons in your brain while the mechanical 'boot' forces corresponding movements in your leg and foot."

Rae Anne donned the helmet while Thrahn fastened the boot to her prosthetic leg.

"Start by emptying all thoughts from your brain. Aim for a meditative state. Concentrate solely on your breathing. Inhale… Exhale…"

Thrahn maintained a slow cadence and watched as several traces on his monitor smoothed into gentle undulating lines.

"Good. Now concentrate on your big toe. No movement yet. Just become aware of how it feels. Is it hot, or is it cold?"

Thrahn pressed a button on his console.

"Ouch. Something bit me!"

"Flick it off. Wiggle your toe and get rid of it."

Rae Anne's face reflected the intensity of her concentration.

"It's moving! I can feel my toe moving in the boot."

"Excellent. This is just the beginning. You are a quick study. Now let's work out on the treadmill."

Thrahn helped Rae Anne off the bed and handed her the cane. Rae Anne limped across the room without giving a thought to her nakedness. She was intent to begin her first physical therapy session.

Later that morning, Rae Anne expressed to Jason her discomfort at having Thrahn barge into her quarters unannounced.

"Shalcerians don't seem to have a concept of personal space. I don't have those feelings with you. But this isn't a hospital room, and I'm not a patient anymore. It would be nice to have some control over my privacy."

Jason stood quietly by for a moment before responding.

"I may have the solution to your problem. I need to retrieve something from *Aurora*. Hold on a minute."

Jason disappeared through the nanoscreen.

I wonder what he has in mind.

He reappeared a few minutes later holding a flat piece of black metal about the size of his hand. He turned toward the nanoscreen he had just stepped through and pressed the object against the wall next to where the nanoscreen had appeared. He then released his hand and stepped back. The object remained in place.

"That looks like an oversized refrigerator magnet. Mom used them to hang my school pictures and awards in the kitchen for all to see."

"As a matter of fact, that is exactly what it is. I knew we had a magnet in the geology kit to draw out iron ore and other ferromagnetic materials from rock samples. My studies into *Avenger's* computer archives led me to believe that the nanoparticles in the nanoscreens were ferromagnetic, and as you can see, they are."

"That's an interesting experiment, Jason. But what does that have to do with my privacy?"

Jason reached out and knocked on the nanoscreen as though it were a solid door.

"The magnet's forcefield counters the one controlling the nanoscreen. If applied when the nanoscreen is open, it stays open. If applied when it's closed, it stays closed."

"So, it works like a lock, a deadbolt?"

"Exactly. It's what the Shalcerians use in their brig."

"*Avenger* has a jail?"

"Of course. In any large population, there will be occasional offenders. Although I must say, my studies of Shalcerian jurisprudence suggest that the punishments they exact are much harsher than are imposed by Human courts."

Before Rae Anne had a chance to have Jason elaborate on that point, a muffled thump followed by several pounding knocks emanated from the locked nanoscreen. She laughed and pointed to the wall. Jason removed the magnet and Thrahn literally fell through the opening.

He shook himself all over after Jason helped him to his feet. His scales showed blinking yellow spots on a solid orange background, something Rae Anne had not seen before. She explained their experiment with the nanoscreen and her need for privacy.

"We can live with that. I'll have Engineering install a notification device on the wall to let you know when someone wants to come in. But you'll have to physically remove the magnet every time. I do find your discomfort strange, though. We Shalcerians have no such inhibitions.

"The reason I've come, however, is to take you to meet the ship's Directorate. Please follow me."

Relying on her cane to steady herself, Rae Anne followed Thrahn through the nanoscreen and into the short corridor. For the first time, Rae Anne thought she could distinguish a slightly darker shade in the walls marking the nanoscreen locations. Four nanoscreens lined the hallway, including the one she just came through.

"The hangar where your ship is housed is through this door," Thrahn said, gesturing with one arm to the wall on his left. "The hangar uses the same air composition and pressure as your room, so you can safely visit *Aurora* any time."

He doesn't know I've already visited my ship. So, they aren't monitoring my every move.

"We've set up a small interview room for you at the end of this hall. But the door to your right is the airlock leading into the rest of our ship. The atmosphere there includes 16% ammonia and several sulfur compounds. It would be lethal to your system. The airlock is for Shalcerian use only. Oh, and I've seen Jason come and go through the airlock on numerous occasions. Androids are not affected by environmental concerns. It could survive in a vacuum."

Hmm… Jason has access to the rest of the ship as well as the ship's computer. How interesting.

Rae Anne followed Thrahn through the nanoscreen at the end of the corridor and found herself in a foyer-sized compartment separated from a large conference room by a transparent wall. Thrahn gestured for her to sit on the only stool in the room.

This looks like the movie set for a corporate board room.

"What you see through the window is an elaborate hologram that projects meeting attendees as though they were meeting together around a conference table. They each see your image as though you were present at the table as well."

The image in front of her showed seven Shalcerians sitting around the table that appeared to extend through her window. Rae Anne pressed her hands flat on the table's surface.

Thrahn sat down next to Rae Anne, causing her to focus momentarily on her companion.

The suction cups at the end of his center foot's four splayed digits enable him to maintain his balance on a single leg, freeing up his other two legs. I wonder what it's like to have five arms at your disposal.

Each director had something like a computer tablet at their table, and most were focused on their work, paying no attention to the others. One director, noticing that Rae Anne and Thrahn had arrived, spoke.

"Our guest has arrived. Thrahn, please make the introductions."

Thrahn's three eyestalks bent forward till they brushed the top of his roundish form, all three eyes directed at the floor.

That looks like an obsequious gesture. A hierarchy or caste system, perhaps.

Thrahn looked up, with one eye turned toward Rae Anne, the others toward the directors.

"My dear comrades, I am pleased to introduce Commander Rae Anne Chavez, of the Human interplanetary explorer *Aurora,* which we rescued from destruction in Saturn's atmosphere. As you know, Rae Anne is the only surviving member of *Aurora's* crew."

Thrahn introduced the seven directors, with their ranks and titles. The only name that stuck for Rae Anne was the captain's, Director

Captain Vahler. He was the Shalcerian who had opened the meeting and appeared to be the Directorate's director.

I've got to identify some visual clues to tell these creatures apart. They all look alike to me.

The captain directed several high-frequency, sharp whistles interspersed with clicks and choking noises toward Thrahn. Thrahn again bowed his eyestalks and left the room.

I don't think Humans have the capacity to speak Shalcerian. Thank god for their computer translator.

Captain Vahler's computer simulated voice was the same low tenor as Thrahn's, and with the same British accent.

"Welcome aboard the *Avenger*, Rae Anne Chavez. I trust you are finding our hospitality suitable. If you need anything, don't hesitate to bring it to Thrahn's attention."

Rae Anne wondered if she should dip her head, but decided against it, not knowing how such a gesture might be taken.

"Thank you for rescuing *Aurora* and caring for my physical needs. You have been most gracious."

"It was the least we could do for a ship in distress. However, the incident has provided us with a unique and timely opportunity. Now that Humans have begun to explore interplanetary space, we are authorized to welcome you into the family of space-faring species. Our consortium includes eleven distinct species and, at last count, 120 star systems. Should Humans choose to join us, we can look forward to an era of prosperous cooperation with your species."

I need to be careful. I don't want them to think I speak for the entire Human race.

"I'm sure my fellow Humans will entertain your invitation with utmost consideration. What obligations are required of cooperating species?"

"Members of the Shalcerian Empire are responsible for looking after the security and welfare of their individual star systems and any others they colonize. In your case, this would begin with maintaining an active presence in the Kuiper Belt. With our guidance and technological assistance, we can make that happen.

"To that end, we need a Human representative who is well known and highly respected to represent us in our negotiations with your species. We can lead Earth out of its climate quandary, and perhaps help unite Earth's political factions, if Humans join forces with us. We believe you, Rae Anne Chavez, are the right person for this job."

Rae Anne's heart skipped a beat. Her mouth went dry and she swallowed hard. Her rescue by Shalcerians would go down in history as First Contact. But Shalcerians were offering their help in saving humanity from its self-induced climate disaster.

Do they really think I can help them with this? They need someone like the president or the U. N. Secretary General. They must know how fractious and suspicious Humans are.

While these thoughts roiled in her mind, she tried to imagine how Shalcerian technology could benefit Earth. Progress in science and technology would make a multi-generational leap in just a few years.

This is a planet-saving opportunity. Surely every person on Earth with any intelligence will recognize that.

Rae Anne cleared her throat. "I would be honored to represent your people to Earth's Humans. Our species has many factions, however. Uniting them for the common good may be a difficult challenge."

"With your insight and our experience with other species, we are confident we will succeed. We realize Humans may be reluctant to accept us initially. My first officer will fill you in on the extent to which we are authorized to help humanity. With that as a foundation, together we will draft a plan for approaching your species to achieve our common goals."

"Captain Vahler, have you contacted anyone on Earth to let them know we are coming?"

"Premature contact has proven many times to be inadvisable. We need to introduce ourselves to the entire planet at once so no nation is seen as being favored. A single broadcast from a distance cannot achieve that end.

"Once we enter orbit, we can manipulate the world's broadcast media so every nation hears an identical message in their own language at the same time. You, Rae Anne, will have the honor of delivering that message."

"Thank you for your confidence in me. Humans will certainly benefit from cooperating with you. I will do my best to help bring that about."

They have no idea what they are up against. They'll be lucky no one nukes them before they arrive. I need to find a way to get a message to the Agency from Aurora's transmitters. Doubt it will work, but it's worth a try.

Chapter 9

Washington, D.C.

The Air Force helicopter from Andrews AFB settled gently on the pad behind the White House. Ian straightened his tie and took one last gulp from the bottle of Perrier he had retrieved from the cooler next to his seat. The two security agents with him were uncommunicative.

Havel Nelson, the White House Chief of Staff, approached the helicopter and opened the door.

"Mr. Bentley. Good of you to come on such short notice."

As if anyone would turn down an invitation to meet the president, especially under these circumstances. Come to think of it, the flight out from Colorado in an F-15E wasn't such a bad inducement either.

He followed Havel up the steps while he fiddled with his tie, wiped his moist palms on his trousers and brushed his hand through his hair. Havel led him to the Oval Office. A light tap on the door, a muffled "Come" and he found himself shaking hands with President Stratton over the Resolute Desk.

Ian noted how different the president looked in person. She was shorter than she appeared during press conferences. Her hair was tinged with gray, and her face was more wrinkled. She wore a tailored business suit with a blue silk scarf draped over both shoulders.

After a few pleasantries, the president settled down to business.

"You may be wondering why I chose to meet with you over this situation, Ian. Quite frankly, it's because I know what you tell me is 100% accurate. You proved that several years ago when you testified in Congress and convinced both sides of the aisle to eliminate the military control over the USIEA. I wish I could get that kind of bipartisan response from those toads."

She chuckled, prompting a spontaneous smile from Ian. He hoped the moisture in his armpits was not visibly soaking through his shirt.

"So, tell me what we're facing. I want to know everything we know about this approaching asteroid."

"Thank you for your confidence, Madam President. First, this object is similar to another that whizzed through our system back in 2017. The astronomers named it *Oumuamua*. Both are nearly the same size and shape. The main differences are their trajectories and velocities. The *Oumuamua* shot into the Solar System from way above the plane containing the planets' orbits.

"This new object has remained within the ecliptic plane and seems to be coming straight at us from Saturn. And it is moving incredibly fast."

With his explanation, Ian couldn't help but make sweeping gestures with his arms to illustrate his verbal narrative.

"Could it have anything to do with *Aurora?* It's been only days since your agency reported it crashing into Saturn."

"There's no evidence of any connection, Madam President. No known physical phenomenon could connect the two events, despite the conspiracy theories being touted on social media."

"Then what is it? And how concerned should we be?"

"At the moment, we can't be sure what it is. In a day or so it will be close enough for us to discern more details. But we do know it's aimed directly at Earth."

President Stratton frowned and pursed her lips.

"However, the Agency doesn't think there will be a collision. Our best people have studied the data and agree that this object must be an alien spacecraft. First, its similarity to *Oumuamua* can't be a coincidence. Second, it is moving much faster than any natural object ever observed in our Solar System. And third, the trajectory is line-of-site between Saturn and Earth."

"If you're correct, wouldn't the aliens have contacted us?"

"If we're dealing with aliens, we have to set all expectations regarding behavior aside. They likely think and reason very differently from us. Not to mention the obvious communication problems. They may not even use audio sounds we would recognize as speech."

"What can we expect, then?"

"At their extreme velocity, we think they will veer slightly from their current course and zip right past Earth. Who knows how much data their advanced technology might be able to glean with a quick fly-by. The USIEA, and NASA before it, have presaged Human exploration with uncrewed fly-by missions to the moon and Mars."

"All this is assuming it's not a large asteroid."

"I'm confident in my team's assessment. We put the odds of it being an alien vessel at better than 95%."

"I hope you're right. I have a major press release to hand out within the hour. Your take on the situation may reduce anxieties to some extent, but there's still that 5% risk of a major disaster. We need to do what we can to prepare for any possibility."

They shook hands. Ian was surprised at how firmly she clasped his hand.

"Keep my office informed of any changes and notify me directly if you have any breaking news."

"You have my word."

Havel ushered Ian out of the White House and to the military helicopter.

I'll be back in Colorado before dinner. Plenty of time to catch up on the latest. What an amazing day.

Four days before the feared collision with Earth, orbiting observatories obtained the first pictures providing detailed imagery of the approaching object. Its smooth surface and symmetrically contoured shape left no doubt it was an alien spacecraft. On the one hand, everyone was relieved that a dinosaur-style catastrophe had been avoided. On the other hand, conspiracy theories abounded proclaiming that a superior alien civilization was about to attack Earth.

President Stratton appointed Ian to head up a task group to deal with impending contact with the aliens, should that happen. Ian, in turn, selected twenty leading scientists from the Agency's divisions and an equal number of outside authorities from around the world to serve as consultants. Even with less than twenty-four hours' notice, no one turned down the invitation to the First Contact Commission's first meeting.

With forty brilliant minds working on this, we should be able to deal with anything short of an outright attack. I hope!

The next day, Ian found himself running ragged making last-minute arrangements for the meeting. He checked in at the communication center being hastily set up down the hall from his office before realizing he had just enough time to make it to the group's first meeting.

The conference room had space for forty participants, but many seats were vacant. Fifteen of the Agency's staff showed up in person, joining three consultants. The remaining twenty-two attended the meeting through virtual connections. Ian's assistant had pulled everything together. The only inconvenience was with time zones for a few of the international participants. Nevertheless, everyone invited was present.

After a short preamble and introductions, Ian presented the assembly with its mission.

"We may be verging on First Contact with an alien civilization, assuming they don't simply fly past Earth to collect data. But President Stratton has asked us to formulate an appropriate response if they do contact us. As we apply our skills to address this singular event, let's remember we are representing all of humanity. We must resolve to work with each other as a team toward a common goal. That goal is to achieve peaceful rapport with an alien civilization and present Humans in the best light possible."

"Ian, have we received any communication or other signal from the aliens indicating a desire to interact with us?" asked a professor from MIT.

Ian turned to face the monitor screen and shook his head.

"Nothing to date. We've been monitoring a wide swath of electromagnetic frequencies: radio, microwave, infrared, visible, and ultraviolet. We haven't detected anything that could be construed as communication."

"I would suggest language may be one of our first major hurdles," offered Amy from the Agency's AI division.

The renowned linguistics expert from Oxford cleared his throat.

"Not only that, but language itself is rooted in the collective experience of a species. Our understanding regarding vocabulary and syntax will be totally irrelevant as we attempt to communicate with them."

"If their biological clocks are geared much faster or slower than ours, we might find any sort of interaction with them difficult, if not impossible," added J. R. Singh, a biologist in New Delhi.

"I hadn't even considered that possibility," Ian noted in dismay. "In that event, our back-and-forth communication would have to be through a recording medium that allows us to alter playback speeds. That would definitely complicate things."

Mike Skinner, an astrophysicist from Caltech added, "I think our foremost consideration must be to find some way to signal that we wish to approach them in peace. Working out the details of formal communication will take considerable time."

"But what might that signal look like, Mike?" Ian asked. "A white flag or a 60's peace symbol would have no meaning for non-humans."

"In fact, there's always the chance that any symbol we use might correspond to a similar sign or symbol that the aliens find threatening or offensive. I point to the American finger gesture for 'okay' that has an obscene interpretation in Brazil," said Maria Sanchez from the University of Texas in Austin.

"Or a thumbs up in the Middle East," someone else added.

Roger Blake, the Agency's liaison with the Pentagon, spoke up. "I hate to bring this up, but our intelligence agencies have informed us China and Russia are taking the opposite stance to ours and have put their nuclear forces on high alert. Any pre-emptive action they might take would overshadow our efforts at peaceful negotiation."

"The president informed me of that this morning," Ian announced. "She is in daily contact with all the world's leaders, counseling restraint. It helps that everyone's nuclear arsenals are targeting each other. Any missiles directed toward the alien ship would first have to be reprogrammed."

"Unfortunately, that can be done in a few hours," said Amy.

"Our problem today is lack of data," Ian pointed out. "All we can do for now is list the issues that might come up and create a committee for each one. As we go along, add your name to each issue that fits your qualifications or interests. If it is one of your specialties, underline your name as being available to chair the group.

"Before you leave, meet with your highest priority group and choose a coordinator. I want each group to meet once each day between now and actual contact. Stagger meeting times so individuals can participate in more than one group. Within an hour after each meeting, submit a summary report to my office. We'll compile these and submit an abstract to each of you every afternoon.

"First Contact, if it happens, will probably take place in a matter of days. I'll schedule further task-force meetings as needed so keep your schedules flexible."

Following Ian's introduction, the group quickly identified a dozen issues. Over the next hour, they added another dozen. Further discussion resulted in consolidating overlapping topics, resulting in a final list of fifteen unique issues to address. Most participants volunteered to work on at least three committees.

Late that evening, Ian was having cold pizza and beer in the lunchroom with Amy while discussing the first seven reports submitted.

"Your comment about language was right to the point. Establishing reliable communication is at the heart of every one of these reports," Ian observed.

"We could put together a group of communication specialists, but there's nothing they could do until we actually meet the aliens and know how they communicate."

"Even so, it might not hurt to make a list of experts to be ready the instant we have something to work with. I'll check with the communications group tomorrow to see who they might suggest. Meantime, I should check to see if we've discovered anything new about our visitors."

Ian stood, gathered his half-eaten pizza and empty can for the trash receptacle by the door, and returned to his office.

Despite the late hour, he sent a short report to Washington describing the day's activities and summarizing the reports he'd already received. Then he leaned back in his chair, hands clasped behind his head, closed his eyes, and sighed.

We're doing everything we can on our end, but we are totally in the dark. If they would only send a signal, that could at least provide a place to start. Of course, maybe they have no interest in contacting us. They may not even know we exist.

Chapter 10

The French Riviera

Two days before the alien ship was to arrive, Sam and Karen met at her chateaux in southern France. The hot, humid air prompted the two lovers to soak in Karen's Olympic-size infinity pool *au naturel*. The pool's south edge appeared to flow into the Mediterranean.

"We've got to quit meeting like this," scoffed Sam, repeating a phrase he'd often used before. A bit trite, but Karen usually responded by nuzzling her head into his chest and doing a bit of playful groping.

To his dismay, today she did neither.

"No one knows what these aliens might want. What they might do to us. To humanity, I mean."

"You're spoiling a perfectly lovely moment. Stop it."

"I mean it, Sam. Haven't you thought about how their superior technology will make everything our companies provide obsolete?"

"What makes you think they'll share their knowledge with the likes of us? If they have anything to do with us at all, it will likely be in the form of exploitation."

"That could be even worse, Sam."

"I'm betting they zoom right past Earth and not even acknowledge us. Maybe use their technology to learn everything there is to know about us and fly on to a more interesting destination. Think about it. What do we have that they could possibly want? My guess is they couldn't give a tinker's damn about us."

"But what if they don't just fly by. I'm really worried. We could be ruined."

Sam pulled her back to him and stroked her cheek and hair reassuringly.

"You may be putting yourself in a dither for nothing. Remember what I said earlier about keeping our eyes open for opportunities?"

"I can only hope you're right."

Sam pulled her against his chest, enjoying the feel of her body against his in the warm water.

"Think positive. Last week when we thought it was an asteroid, you predicted total ruin. Today we know it is only an alien spaceship, something we might be able to deal with."

Karen responded by biting his neck, initiating a torrent of underwater activity that soon left them both exhausted, but satisfied.

Colorado Springs

Just past midnight, the ring tone on Ian's phone broke the silence. Ian leapt from the cot in his office storeroom and banged his shoulder against a shelf in the darkness.

"Ouch! Where's the damned doorknob?" he muttered in exasperation.

He opened the door and stumbled to his desk. Grabbing the phone, he pressed the answer icon, struggling to bring his brain into focus.

"Ian here," he mumbled.

"Ian, I think we've got a signal from the alien craft." Victor's voice carried a note of confidence.

Ian's eyes popped wide open. He grabbed his notebook and shot through the door. Seconds later, he turned into the temporary Satellite Communications Center three doors down the hall.

"What have you got, Victor?" Ian asked as he burst into the room.

"Well, it's kind of strange, you know? Here's the signal trace sweeping through the high energy radio band." Victor punched some keys on his keyboard and a jagged horizontal line looking like earthquake aftershocks filled the screen.

"This is all noise, of course. This is what we've been staring at for five days, you know? But here, right here…" Victor pointed to a series of jags that were wider and higher than the rest. "These blips first appeared an hour ago. They last for 5 minutes, disappear for 5 minutes, then reappear."

"That may be just the signal we've been waiting for. The regularity is a strong indication it originates from an intelligent source. Can we separate it from the noise and get some audio resolution?"

"I did that right before I called you. I combined the six blips we've received so far to increase that one signal's amplitude. But what we get doesn't make any sense."

Ian bit his tongue and tried not to strangle him. "Well play it then, for god's sake."

Victor pressed another button. The playback crackled and popped. But through it all a faint Human voice could be heard.

"It sounds like a short message repeated dozens of times through the five-minute interval," Ian observed. "If that's the case, we have multiple copies we can pull from each five-minute segment and choose those with the best signal-to-noise ratio. Combining them may give us an intelligible recording. How long will that take?"

"A few minutes. I've started working on that already, you know?"

Just then Eileen wandered into the room with two cups of steaming coffee and a bag of bagels.

"Oh, Mr. Bentley," she said, startled. She had never used Ian's first name despite his expressed preference. "I, uh, I figured we'd need something to see us through the next four hours."

"Understood. Victor's trying to cobble together something meaningful from the blip you guys found. It certainly sounds like a Human voice, but the brain can easily be fooled. Sometimes at night I wake up and swear I hear someone talking in the kitchen when it's only the refrigerator doing its thing."

"That's happened to me too," Eileen said, setting a bagel beside Victor's keyboard and offering one to Ian, which he declined. "I've read that the Human brain is wired to look for patterns, so we often see or hear things that aren't really there."

"There! This is the best we can do with what we have, you know? Ready, set, GO!"

With a dramatic flourish, Victor punched a key. The crackling noise on the speakers was considerably reduced and…

```
This is Rae Anne Chavez aboard Aurora.
We are coming home.
The aliens are friendly.
Don't shoot.
```

"Oh my god." Ian felt his heart skip a beat. And another. The hairs on his neck bristled. For a moment, everything swirled out of focus. He pressed both palms to his eyes and scrunched his forehead to bring himself back to the moment.

Rae Anne. Alive. Is it possible? How can that be?

"How can that be?" asked Eileen. "The signal is way too high in frequency for anything the Agency uses. *Aurora* couldn't be communicating on that wavelength."

"Actually, she's not," Victor replied. "We're seeing a Doppler shift due to the alien ship's incredible approach velocity. This is the same 'blue shift' astronomers see when viewing a star or galaxy approaching us, you know? Only this is in the radio spectrum rather than visible light."

"Good thinking, Victor." Ian squeezed his shoulder. "Since we know what frequency Rae Anne must be using and we know the size of the blue shift, we can determine the alien's velocity precisely. Send this information down to the computer geeks right away. If our velocity matches what the astronomers have observed, that will confirm this as the real thing. I'll be back shortly with a return message."

As soon as Ian closed his office door, he pulled a wrinkled card from his trousers and tapped the number into his phone, wishing he had been allowed to add it to his contact list.

"Office of the president. Chief of Staff Nelson speaking. What's up, Ian? It's three in the morning here."

"We have decoded a message from the alien ship, Havel. But the message is one for the president to disseminate as she sees fit. Can you put me in touch with her?"

"She happens to still be in the Oval Office. Hold on…"

"Hello, Ian. I see you're working late too. Havel tells me you've decoded a signal?"

"Yes, Madam President. But it's not like anything we expected. Here's what we have."

Ian relayed the message to POTUS.

"Do you think it's some sort of hoax?" the president asked.

"I think it's legit. The signal is coming from our own Agency transmitters aboard *Aurora* and it's unquestionably coming from the alien ship which is certainly large enough to accommodate *Aurora*. My guess is they rescued her and are bringing her and *Aurora* back to Earth. We can scratch my fly-by theory. They'll either orbit or land. But we have Rae Anne's assurance that they are friendly."

"Thanks, Ian. Sit tight on this information until we've made it public. There are some important international considerations my staff needs to work through. Let's not forget that the Chinese tried to destroy *Aurora* back in… when was it, '37? They could feel threatened by Rae Anne's return. So, we'll keep her identity under wraps in any case. Keep on top of this and continue your updates. You are providing critical information for the sensitive decisions we have to make."

Ian sat at his desk to compose a return message to Rae Anne, not knowing if she had the means to receive it. Given how garbled her transmission was and the fact that her receiver antenna, damaged from the Chinese attack, was unreliable, he doubted his chance of success. Despite the odds, however, he believed he had to attempt a reply.

Five minutes later, he was back in the communications center.

As he stepped through the door, Eileen looked up.

"Computing just sent word. The two velocities match perfectly."

"That clinches it. Eileen, transmit this message to *Aurora*. Use the same protocols Rae Anne is using but transmit our message during her dead spaces. And offset our normal transmission frequency by the same amount, but to a longer frequency. That way the Doppler blue-shift will align our transmission with her receiver's frequency."

Victor swiveled his chair around to face Ian and stretched.

"If Rae Anne has been with these aliens for two weeks, she might have a leg up on the communication thing, you know? I spent a month in Costa Rica in a Spanish immersion class. You pick up a lot of stuff really fast that way."

"Yeah," said Eileen. "Like: Where's the bathroom?"

"*Dónde está el baño.* I think. Been a long time." He swiveled back to his desk.

"You do have a point, Victor. Rae Ann will be an excellent person to have on the communications team. She'll be able to steer the language experts in the right direction."

Chapter 11

Earth Orbit

When *Avenger* instantly slowed from its incredible approach velocity two days later and matched Earth-orbit speed, it assumed a perfectly circular polar orbit at 1800 kilometers. There still had been no official communication with Earth. But neither had there been any indication of hostilities. Amazement and awe (and relief) was palpable throughout the world. Watching the alien ship/satellite glide across the night sky became an instant attraction.

Conspiracy theories continued to abound, all predicting an imminent doomsday invasion, differing only in what the aliens had in store for humanity. In America, sales of survival gear and weapons soared.

Aboard *Avenger*, the first order of business was arranging electronic hacks into the world's communications. Shalcerian technicians placed twenty robot repeaters in geostationary orbit alongside Earth's major communications satellites. During Rae Anne's presentation to Earth, these would override the standard broadcasts, using different feeds as translated by *Avenger's* computer for the appropriate audiences below.

They employed a variety of technologies to similarly interrupt terrestrial transmissions. Three days after *Avenger's* arrival, the Shalcerians had ensured that every television, computer, laptop, tablet, and smart phone throughout the world would broadcast Rae Anne's message in real time at 15:00, Coordinated Universal Time (UTC), correlating with daylight hours for Europe and the Western Hemisphere. They planned to repeat the entire process worldwide twelve hours later with a recording of the original broadcast.

The holographic displays in Rae Anne's quarters were programmed following Rae Anne's suggestions. She requested the appearance of an executive suite as the most effective no-nonsense surroundings for her delivery. To that end, she had a dark oak desk, high-backed leather chair and expensive looking desk accouterments projected in front of a floor-to-ceiling wall monitor. Two wing-walls joined it at wide angles, allowing images on their smaller monitors to be visible as well.

Rae Anne put Thrahn in charge of providing her with a USIEA astronaut uniform. She was still a member of the Agency's team, and Humans the world over would recognize the uniform. Jason trimmed her long black hair to shoulder length, without bangs, and she combed it with a wave over her left eyebrow.

"Will you want me to appear with you?" he asked.

"I've decided to be alone on this first broadcast. I don't want any distractions. My message will be hard enough for people to digest. That's probably why the Directorate doesn't want any Shalcerians present either. It's just as well. Humans will have a hard time adjusting to an alien species."

"Humans can't respect slight differences among themselves," Jason said with a note of disgust.

"That is a very astute observation for an android, Jason."

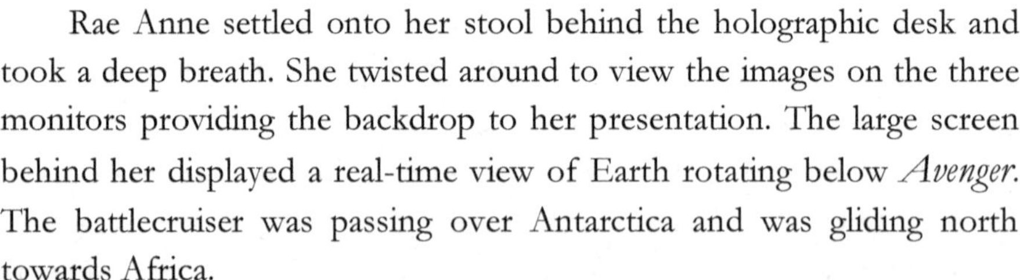

Rae Anne settled onto her stool behind the holographic desk and took a deep breath. She twisted around to view the images on the three monitors providing the backdrop to her presentation. The large screen behind her displayed a real-time view of Earth rotating below *Avenger*. The battlecruiser was passing over Antarctica and was gliding north towards Africa.

On her left, the screen displayed an orbital view of 18 Scorpii-ε, Shalkor, the Shalcerian home world, with its three moons and a sun-like star in the distance. The planet and its moons appeared as crescents against the black backdrop of space.

To her right was an eye-popping image from Shalkor's surface. A vast turquoise ocean washed gently against a creamy-yellow sandy beach. The sun-drenched beach backed up against a thick mass of purple and orange vegetation from which tall spindly trees with purple puff-ball shaped canopies sprouted, reminding Rae Anne of candy-store lollipops.

Rae Anne turned back toward the camera and watched the seconds tick down on the holographic monitor on her desk.

Remember, keep your hands in your lap. The desk is just a hologram. Letting your hand or elbow pass through the desk image would not go over well!

As the timer approached 00:00 she took another deep breath.

This is it, Rae Anne. The most important speech of your life. Smile!

At 15:00 UTC, she looked up from her desk and gazed into the camera. A trace of a smile crossed her lips, but her face, with a slight furrow across the eyebrows, was a picture of serious resolution.

```
My fellow citizens of Earth, my name is Rae
Anne Chavez. I am broadcasting from the
interstellar cruiser that is in polar orbit
around Earth. You may be familiar with my
recent transmissions from the planet Saturn. If
you followed those reports, you know that my
ship, Aurora, was about to plunge into Saturn's
atmosphere and burn up.

I am pleased to report that all announcements
regarding my demise were premature.
```

Rae Anne paused and smiled more broadly, hoping her attempt at humor might ease the tension her viewers must be experiencing.

```
An alien starship was investigating my
transmissions from Saturn and, seeing Aurora's
```

impending doom, followed their space-faring
directive to assist any spacecraft in distress
and rescued me and my ship.

These people call themselves Shalcerians. They
brought me home to Earth in just three weeks.
In that time, they nursed me back to health,
curing me of cancer caused by years of exposure
to cosmic radiation, and replacing my gangrene-
infected leg with a prosthesis that looks and
works like the real thing. Their science and
technology are centuries beyond ours.

I mention this to convey how responsive the
Shalcerians were to my needs and my welfare,
and to demonstrate how advanced their
healthcare technology is. They are proposing to
share these achievements with us Humans.

Rae Anne brushed the hair over her left eye to keep from appearing
too stiff on camera. This also created another pause to let her last
statements sink in.

This is the chance of a lifetime, my fellow Earthlings. Don't blow it!

I could mention other examples of Shalcerian
technology that would sound like science
fiction to us: antigravity transport, room
temperature superconductivity, portable nuclear
fusion reactors, and space propulsion systems
based on manipulation of gravity waves. But the
bottom line is this: Shalcerians are willing to
share these technologies with us and help
humanity deal with the dire climate crisis we
are now facing on Earth.

She paused one last time to give her listeners a moment to visualize
how these gifts would radically change their lives. The mere promise of

solutions to climate change was bound to strike a positive chord with most of her audience.

If the Shalcerians come through on their promises, humanity will be changed forever.

The Shalcerian's home world is Shalkor, the
fourth planet in the 18 Scorpii system. It is
the planet shown on the two side monitors
behind me. They come to us in peace and desire
to help us achieve a brighter and more stable
future for every Human being on Earth. But
their offer is contingent on all of humanity
uniting with one accord and agreeing to join
them in this cooperative venture.

In closing, let me reiterate. You have nothing
to fear from the Shalcerians. They come in
peace. They wish to be our partners as we
become a space-faring species. This is an
incredible opportunity for all of humanity.
Every person on Earth stands to benefit from
their assistance. My future communications will
provide more details on this and on how we can
proceed.

Thank you for your attention.

Monitors and screens around the world flickered and returned to their regular programming.

Captain Vahler entered the room with Thrahn when Rae Anne signed off. Thrahn remained a pace or two behind the captain.

"An excellent introduction, Rae Anne Chavez. We couldn't have picked a better Human to represent us for First Contact."

"Thank you, Captain Vahler. I'm sure our sudden presence in Earth orbit has caused a great deal of anxiety. I hope our broadcast will calm their fears. Will you be joining me on our next broadcast?"

"Experience has shown that would not be advisable. We need to wait until we see overt signs of acceptance and expressions of cooperation before we show ourselves. However, you will need someone with great influence to be your liaison on Earth. This person must have resources at their disposal to create a gathering of Earth's political leaders from every nation so we can begin serious negotiations.

"Let Thrahn know who you wish to contact and how to communicate with them. He can direct our technical staff to work out the details."

Thrahn remained behind when Vahler excused himself to return to the bridge.

"Thrahn, your technicians have monitored Earth's broadcasts since day one. I would like to have the current English language broadcasts relayed to *Aurora's* computer so I can view them on my monitor. This is crucial if I am to be an effective representative. I must know how my transmissions are being received and how Humans are responding."

"I'll have the link set up right away. Do you have someone in mind to work with you as your liaison?"

"As a matter of fact, I do…"

In the following days, media outlets around the world repeated portions of Rae Anne's presentation *ad nauseum*. Pundits called on experts and people claiming to be experts for opinions and insights. The prevailing media response following Rae Anne's announcement reflected a profound skepticism at the aliens' supposed altruism. The Chinese and Russians remained at red alert, ostensibly to save humanity from imminent invasion.

Chapter 12

Colorado Springs

When Rae Anne's broadcast terminated, Ian's TV screen flickered and returned to the news broadcast depicting the latest hostilities in the Middle East. Syria and Israel were fighting over control of Lebanon and Iran's six-month blockade in the Strait of Hormuz had no end in sight.

Maybe First Contact will be a catalyst to bring peace to Earth's warring tribes. And how remarkable that Rae Anne is their spokesperson.

He gazed at the screen, the half-full coffee mug in his hand forgotten. He couldn't release his mind's image of Rae Anne addressing the entire world from an alien spacecraft. He felt drawn to her with a visceral energy.

Rae Anne, alive and well. I must find some way to get aboard the alien ship and welcome her home. That could be a real challenge. They likely have unbelievable security.

As the USIEA's director, Ian had flight authority to any of the Agency's bases. He'd visited all three science stations on the moon at least once, and the Lunar-Orbit Transfer Station (LOTS), his old command post, on numerous occasions. But none of the crewed satellites were in polar Earth-orbit.

He sat down to his usual scrambled eggs, toast, and coffee breakfast. Picking at his food, he called his office to set up a meeting with the First Contact Commission for the next day at noon. He pondered how to manage a visit to Rae Anne. Then he closed his laptop and stepped outside to his hydrogen powered hovercar. Ducking through the door, he issued the command 'My office,' and sat in one of the two plush leather seats.

The rotors began to swirl but the craft didn't budge.

You must buckle in before we can leave.

"Shit," Ian muttered, surprised at being so preoccupied. He grabbed the straps and snapped them together over his shoulders.

The hovercar thanked him and rose into the air.

Gazing through the plexiglass bubble, Ian could discern no change from any other day. Traffic, both air and ground, was as congested as always. Commuter trains still sailed along on their monorails, adhering to their schedules.

People must earn a living. What did I expect? The most earth-shattering event in Human history has just occurred, but people have no idea how profoundly this will affect their lives.

Four Air Force fighters in tight formation flew overhead, their contrails feathering into the deep blue sky. Ian watched the planes shrink and disappear.

As much as I hate to bring the military into this, they may hold the key to my getting to the Avenger.

On arriving at his office, he initiated an encrypted call to General Melinda (Milly) Wilson at the Pentagon. Following the shakeup delegating civilian control of the Agency, she was the only sympathetic high-ranking officer with whom Ian maintained regular contact.

"What's up, Ian? This have anything to do with Rae Anne's announcement?" General Wilson was a stickler for not wasting time.

"Matter of fact, General, it does. I need to get to *Avenger*. Once there, I'm sure Rae Anne will be able to get me aboard."

"The president has forbidden any military craft from approaching the alien spaceship. She doesn't want them to interpret our activities as being hostile."

"But wouldn't you like to have someone observe *Avenger* first-hand? All we have now is imagery from our orbiting telescopes and all they reveal is the ship's shape and size. They show none of the small details, like airlocks, viewports, antennae. A close-up inspection would reveal a lot about their ship."

"We all would sell our grandmothers to see that thing up close and with our own eyes. It's no secret you have an 'in' with President Stratton. You might be able to wrangle an exception. What do you have in mind?"

Ian laid out his planned course of action. General Wilson listened carefully, muttering a 'humph' after Ian's most salient points.

"That might work, Ian. But it will take a special launch from Vandenburg. And I'll have to check if we have any Manned Orbital Surveillance Shuttles available."

"Can you bring a MOSS back if they're all in orbit?"

"No. Each one that's flying is mission critical. And turn-around time when they land is over a month."

"Ok. I'll get back with you this afternoon to see if you have a MOSS I can use. In the meantime, I'll see what I can do to get official approval from the White House. How much time would you need to get a MOSS ready for launch?"

"Two days if we hustle and everything clicks. A full week if we run into glitches."

After his conversation with the general, Ian headed for the Satellite Communications Center down the hall.

General Wilson never said how many MOSS were on the ground, but she didn't stop me cold, either. That tells me there's at least one available. I wonder how difficult it will be to persuade the president to go along with my plan.

Both Eileen and Victor were focused on the console monitors. Neither looked up when he entered.

"Don't you guys ever go home?" Ian said, grabbing the last glazed donut in the bakery box on the counter by the door. He poured himself a cup of coffee.

After taking a sip of the pitch-black brew, he screwed up his face. "Phew. This is awful. How do you stand this stuff?"

Victor looked over his shoulder. "It's the glue that keeps us here 24/7, you know? Couldn't live without it."

"Any change in *Aurora's* message?"

"None. Rae Anne hasn't posted anything new, and there's no sign she's received our reply. I think her message was just to warn us not to fire on their ship, you know? Now she doesn't need to use *Aurora's* transmitter."

"You're probably right, Victor." Ian sighed and trudged back to his office.

If I can't get hold of Rae Anne, how will the aliens know my approaching ship is friendly? They likely have defenses we can't even imagine. Given our history, no one would blame them for shooting me down.

His telephone rang before he got to his desk. He pulled it from its holster on his belt.

Not a moment's peace. It's as if people are monitoring my every move!

He glanced at the calling number on the display. '000-000-0000'.

Damn robocalls. Now they don't even bother with fake telephone numbers.

He switched the phone to vibrate and slipped it back into its pocket. A minute later it began vibrating.

Ian sighed and pulled the phone out. This time the display read '005-028-2037'. He noticed the odd number format and shook his head as he replaced the phone into its holster.

When the phone vibrated again after another one-minute pause, he snatched it out and was about to turn it off when he noticed the display reading '008-027-2039'.

Curious. That's the exact date my Mars-III mission left Earth orbit for Mars!

He clicked back to reveal the previous caller's number.

And that's the date Rae Anne's Aurora launched for Mars. What if…

His heart pounded in his chest and beads of sweat popped out on his forehead as he answered the call.

"This is Ian Bentley, Director of the United States Interplanetary Exploration Agency." There was a short pause, reminding him of the time/distance lags common with space communications.

"Ian, it's so good to hear your voice. And with such a good com link! Got to hand it to the Shalcerians. They know what they're doing."

"Rae Anne! Are you still aboard the alien's ship?"

"Yes. I may be here for some time. They nursed me back to health, but even their technology can't remediate the disabling effects of six years in space. I'll never be able to return to Earth.

"Anyway, did you hear my message?"

"Everyone in the world heard your message. Are these aliens for real? Why do they want to have anything to do with us?"

"Two questions, one answer. Yes, the Shalcerians are the genuine article, Ian. From my dealings with them, I am convinced their intentions are to save us from ourselves. Their technologies will profoundly change the world as we know it and the course of Human history.

"The answer to your second question will become apparent in time. But you must trust me when I say as far as I can determine, there is nothing sinister going on."

"We received the message-loop you transmitted from *Aurora*. Is *Aurora* actually aboard the alien ship?"

"It is, though it will need to have a big hole patched up before she'll fly again. They had to cut me out of the ship to rescue me.

"But listen, Ian. The reason I'm contacting you is this. I need someone I know well and can trust to be my liaison on Earth. We must set up a major conference with world leaders in the next two months. I know the Agency has the resources, workforce, and influence to make it all happen. And you, Ian, are in charge of the Agency. You know how to get things done."

Ian took several deep breaths to calm his racing heart. He decided this wasn't the time to reveal how far his current influence extended. He smiled at the thought.

"I'll do my best, Rae Anne. I may need to pull some strings to get the Agency involved."

"Thank you, Ian. I knew I could count on you. There's one other thing. The Shalcerians are working on how best to approach Humans without causing undue anxiety, but they don't want to make an appearance yet. We can't risk a communication snafu blowing everything apart. I need you here with me as soon as possible so we can start nailing down an agenda. How soon can you arrange to be in orbit at EOTS-I?"

Ian gulped. He stifled a burst of laughter. He wanted to shout for joy. He took a deep, calming breath before replying.

"I can be there on the next orbital shuttle, Rae Anne, but it might not be for a few days. I can't tell you how much I'm looking forward to seeing you again!"

"The Shalcerians will have a shuttle waiting off EOTS-I for you. I'll see you soon."

The phone went dead. Ian sat immobilized, as though cast in bronze. His vacant stare registered nothing, while his heart hammered, and his thoughts raced.

'I'll see you soon.' My god, it's going to happen. I'm finally going to see Rae Anne again after all these years. And I'm getting a free pass to board the alien ship. Is this my lucky day, or what?

He still couldn't force himself to move. Events were moving too fast, even for him.

An alien shuttle to the alien ship. I'll be the second Human to encounter a real alien. But only if I get off my butt and make things happen!

Ian immediately contacted the White House. It took no effort to convince the president to direct the USIEA to allocate all the resources needed for cooperating with Shalcerian requests. The president also promised to contact the Pentagon and authorize an emergency shuttle launch from Vandenburg AFB in California to the EOTS. Ian then asked Jan, his assistant, to schedule an Agency jet to fly him from Colorado to California that evening and arrange a room for a few nights.

On his way out the door, he paused at her desk.

"You'll have to facilitate the First Contact Commission meeting tomorrow. You're up to speed with our goals and agenda. Our job is to keep everything coordinated and keep everyone busy. The big change is that communication is not going to be a problem.

"I don't know how long I'll be gone, Jan. Hopefully not more than a few days. If you get a call showing all zeros, that'll be me. I'll have specific instructions to pass along and perhaps a message for POTUS herself."

He took the elevator to the roof and headed to his hovercar.

The next months are going to be busier than a Mars launch on steroids.

Chapter 13

San Francisco

"Alien technology will supplant everything I've ever worked for. If they have portable nuclear fusion reactors, my wind energy investments will be worthless. I'll be ruined!"

Karen absently stirred her vichyssoise with her left hand while taking a sip of her Burgundy. She had arranged to meet with Sam at her penthouse suite on Nob Hill in San Francisco.

"You've still got Sanders Robotics, Karen. That should cover any shortfall you experience from the energy business."

Sam finished his soup and reached for his Vodka Collins. A gentle breeze drifted off the bay and over the spacious rooftop patio. He gazed out over the bay, sparkling blue beneath a cloudless sky. Dozens of sailboats dotted the water with their white sails. A container ship huffed its way beneath the Golden Gate Bridge. Afternoon fog was beginning to form around the Marin Peninsula and distant Tiberon.

"You don't know how heavily I've invested in wind energy, Sam. I'm mortgaged up to the hilt. If that goes down, it will sink Sanders Robotics as well."

Sam nodded sympathetically. "I can't say I'm in any better shape. With their space propulsion systems, my ferry services look like a throwback to the horse-and-buggy days. How do you sell a trip to the moon when your competition can get there ten times faster? Even my mining operations may be at risk."

"I feel so frustrated. There's got to be something we can do to save our businesses."

"There's not much we can do until we know more about what they have in mind. We just need to be patient."

"It's hard to be patient when your stock futures are tanking."

Sam let this comment pass and took another sip from his drink.

"They may have provided a glimpse into a weakness we could exploit," he said thoughtfully.

"They aren't going to let you shoot them out of orbit, Sam. How do you propose we stop them?"

"The key may be in Rae Anne's closing comment. Something like 'all nations must unite and agree to cooperate with them.' If this is a make-or-break condition of theirs, there are things we can do here on the ground to reduce the possibility of cooperation."

"I don't see how. With what they have to offer, people will line up around the block to cooperate with the aliens."

Sam laughed.

"My comment was not about humans cooperating with aliens. Rae Anne was talking about nations cooperating with other nations, all nations on Earth working together. But when has that ever happened? What is the likelihood it will happen now, aliens or no aliens?"

"I see your point, Sam. Maybe things aren't looking so bad after all."

"Not only that, but you and I have the wherewithal to stir things up if we need to. My dealings with governments around the world have given me access to several influential leaders. A bit of discreet lobbying here and there can do wonders. And I happen to know that you are cozy with several important people in media circles. We could sway public opinion into opposing any kind of international agreement."

And if all else fails, it's nice to know Sanders Robotics could find itself on the auction block. I could pick it up for pennies on the dollar.

Vandenberg AFB, CA

Ian settled into his quarters on the west coast and ordered a small veggie pizza with extra cheese for room delivery. After removing his shoes and jacket, he set up his computer and typed in the hotel's wireless password. Then he began scanning through the news feeds he subscribed to in order to catch up with world events.

At the end of a typical day, nearly a hundred news items would await his perusal. For most, he would read the header, digest its impact, and delete the article. Some would merit a first paragraph read before he hit the delete icon. Only a handful would grab his full attention.

One that drew him in this evening was reprinted from a Moscow news source. The picture accompanying the article showed several Russian soldiers painting 'из России с любовью' on what appeared to be missile nosecones. Ian's rudimentary knowledge of Russian allowed him to correctly translate: 'From Russia with love.'

```
Russia Arms missiles for Earth's Defense

The Defense Ministry of the Russian Federation
today declared that Russia is taking a hardline
posture in defense of Mother Russia and the
entire world by arming two dozen satellite-
killer missiles with tactical nuclear warheads.
These missiles are programmed to target the
alien ship in its polar orbit above Earth.

The Ministry spokesperson issued assurances
that the weapons would be used only if the
aliens were to exhibit outright aggressive
behavior toward Earth and its inhabitants.
```

The spokesperson noted that Russia was the
first nation with these capabilities to step
forward for the preservation of all of humanity
and urged other nations to follow suit.

Ian rubbed his eyes with the palms of his hands and sighed deeply.

I wonder what they will interpret as 'outright aggressive behavior?' And here I am, deliberately flying into a nuclear target zone.

Another news article reported that the U.S. State Department was urging all nations to remain calm and stand down from any aggressive posture, and uncharacteristically mentioned Russia and China.

China too? That is either a leak from the intelligence agencies or an intended public warning from the State Department.

A few minutes later, Ian found the answer to his question in an article describing an impending increase in scheduled shipments from China's Jiuquan Satellite Launch Center to their orbiting space outpost. A satellite image of the site showed boosters standing upright on all eight launch pads. At their base, several cargo stages were being prepped for attachment to the boosters.

Hmm… China is the only nation known to have killed a satellite from an orbital missile launch. Someone must suspect these payloads are to beef up their orbital launch capabilities because of the alien's presence.

That makes the alien ship a double nuclear target. Go figure.

Chapter 14

Earth Orbit

"Please remain buckled until I give the word," the pilot commanded as he maneuvered the sleek military shuttle toward the EOTS-I docking ring. Ian sat next to the pilot. Behind him were three military personnel assigned for a six-month rotation aboard the station. Ian had an excellent view of the station through the front viewport.

The Earth-Orbit Transfer Station replaced the International Space Station in the late '20s. Originally, it consisted of eight oversized payload cylinders arranged in an octagonal ring, with accordion-like tubes for walkways connecting them end-to-end. An additional cylinder, perpendicular to the ring, occupied the hub position and was connected to the ring cylinders with eight longer accordion tube spokes. The entire structure rotated slowly, generating an artificial gravity directed toward the ring's outer edge.

Over the years, the station doubled in size with a second identical ring attached atop the first. Although Ian had visited the station several times, it still reminded him of two fat bicycle wheels stacked on top of each other. Its usefulness as a science research station, military observation post, and tourist destination was such that it was often filled to capacity with 64 occupants.

Ian glimpsed something odd and leaned forward to get a better view. If it weren't for the sunlight reflecting from its surfaces, the obsidian black disk would have blended with the deep void behind it. The object shimmered as if it were pulsating. Ian could make out two rows of white lights circling the disk's top and bottom edges.

"What the hell is that?" the pilot muttered. "I've never seen anything like that before."

That, my friend, must be my taxi.

The hairs on Ian's neck prickled as he imagined himself flying to the alien ship in a real flying saucer.

Once the shuttle docked and the four passengers had disembarked, Ian made his way to the station's Command Center. There he found Lisa, the station commander, and her two assistants animatedly discussing the presence of the strange craft hovering just beyond the station. Once he explained it had arrived from the alien ship and was there to pick him up, the atmosphere calmed.

"How are you supposed to board it?" Lisa asked.

"Damned if I know."

The hub monitor showed the last supplies being off-loaded from the shuttle. Lisa authorized the pilot to seal the hatch and release the shuttle from the station. As it drifted away, its reverse thrusters fired intermittently to decelerate it for the return to Earth.

Meanwhile, the alien object approached the docking hub. The Command Center's monitors flickered, and Rae Anne's face appeared on the screens. The background was the same as in her worldwide broadcast, suggesting she was still aboard the alien spaceship.

"Rae Anne Chavez to the commander of EOTS-I. A shuttlecraft is approaching your docking ring. Once it has assumed position over the hatch, a forcefield will connect the shuttle to your station. The forcefield will maintain atmospheric pressure within its confines, allowing you to open the hatch for Ian to exit the station and enter the shuttle. I'll inform you when it's safe to open the hatch."

"You had better be on your way, Ian," Lisa said, shaking her head. "Craziest thing I've ever seen. But just to be safe, I will close the inner hatch once you are in the airlock, so we don't lose station pressure if anything goes wrong."

"What about me?"

Lisa laughed. "You're expendable."

"That's not very reassuring." Ian picked up his travel bag and began climbing the ladder leading to the station's hub and its airlock.

In the hub, he floated in microgravity and propelled himself to the docking ring at the top. When he reached the airlock, he notified Lisa to seal the inner hatch. He fidgeted nervously as he waited for the docking ring's rotation to stop and for the outer hatch to open.

This better work, or I'll be sucked into the vacuum without an EVA suit. Not a pleasant thought!

After a short wait, the outer hatch opened. Ian noticed a lighted opening in the center of the shuttle's belly, ten meters from the station. Between the station and shuttle, nothing but a black void. He took a deep breath and launched himself toward the alien craft.

A forcefield tugged at his body, drawing him into the shuttle. Within seconds, he was surrounded by smooth walls and muted lighting in a small room not much larger than an office cubicle. A padded bench rested against the far wall. Ian searched for straps or restraints to buckle himself in but found nothing. A quiet hiss shooshed behind him. He turned just as the forcefield lifted and the opening sealed shut. A large holographic monitor took its place. It depicted the receding space station and the majestic cloud-speckled blue expanse of Earth below.

Amazing. We're rapidly accelerating, yet I feel no sensation of motion.

The EOTS slipped behind Earth's curved rim. Earth itself gradually diminished as the shuttle gained altitude to match *Avenger's* higher orbit. Then he saw it, the alien ship, filling the screen as they approached.

My lord, that thing is HUGE. It's at least the size of an aircraft carrier.

He stared wide-eyed at the monitor. The mammoth obsidian-black wedge filled the entire screen. A small yellow opening appeared on its forward end and grew wide enough to receive the shuttle. The effect was like approaching a lighted garage door on a dark night. Ian realized this analogy was on the mark when the shuttle crossed through the opening and came to an abrupt halt alongside *Aurora.*

The monitor Ian had been watching disappeared, and the wall behind it opened up into the hangar's large cavity.

Just like magic. Walls appear and disappear on command. Someone once pointed out that future technologies would seem like magic to us.

Ian stood and stepped out of the shuttle, amazed to be experiencing 1/6 gravity when he should be in free-fall. He watched as the hangar door coalesced into a wall. Even with two large craft parked inside, the hangar could easily accommodate another *Aurora*.

"Ian! My god. It's been years since I've seen a Human being!"

Ian spun around. Rae Anne sprinted toward him with arms outstretched. His heart stopped and his head began to swim. For a moment he forgot to breathe. He shook his head to bring himself back to his senses. This was the moment he had pined for over the last six years.

Rae Anne collided with him and wrapped her arms around him. They hugged each other tightly for over a minute.

"Rae Anne Chavez, I presume…" he said officiously, hoping to lighten the moment.

"The one and only," she replied, her voice cracking. "You know, you're much better looking than I remembered."

"I could say the same about you. And you've cut your hair since your TV broadcast. Very stylish. Do aliens do hair, too?"

Rae Anne laughed. "Oh no. Jason cut it for me. I showed him what I wanted, and he did a splendid job."

Ian's heart sank. He cleared his throat to cover his consternation at hearing he might have serious competition for Rae Anne's attention.

But…But wasn't Jason a computer AI on Aurora? This doesn't make any sense.

"So, when do I get to meet a real alien?" he asked.

"Shalcerian, Ian. Let's relegate the 'us versus them' path to history's garbage heap. One of your most important jobs when you return to Earth is to combat our natural tendency of discrimination. Language and words matter. Insist media outlets refer to our visitors as Shalcerians and correct people when they do otherwise."

"You're right, of course. I'll do my best, but it won't be easy."

At that moment, Ian became aware that he and Rae Anne were not alone. He turned and found himself face-to-face with two Shalcerians, one slender, the other rather stout. The slender individual was about six inches shorter than Rae Anne, while the other was shorter than his partner by another three inches. Ian blinked rapidly, trying hard not to stare.

Don't be silly. Aliens aren't aware of Human expressions and wouldn't be offended. Assuming Shalcerians can be offended.

Rae Anne began the introductions. "Captain Vahler, I'm pleased to introduce you to the director of the American Interplanetary Exploration Agency, Ian Bentley. Ian is also a good friend of mine. He has consented to be our earthside liaison for First Contact negotiations. Ian, this is Director Captain Vahler, Captain and Commander of the Shalcerian battlecruiser *Avenger.*"

"Welcome aboard *Avenger,* Ian Bentley."

"I'm honored to meet you, Director Captain Vahler. Thank you for having me aboard and for rescuing Rae Anne and bringing her home."

Rae Anne turned to the shorter Shalcerian. "And this is Thrahn, my Shalcerian doctor, therapist, and friend."

Thrahn held out a hand for Ian to grasp and put a second hand on Ian's wrist in a Human gesture of warmth and acceptance. Thrahn's suction cup digits pressed gently into Ian's flesh and released.

"Good to meet you, Ian. Rae Anne has been teaching me some Human gestures," he said. His voice seemed to emanate from the hangar walls, as had the captain's. Both possessed the same British accent. Ian assumed he was hearing a computer translation of their thoughts.

I wonder if they can teach us how to do that.

"I'm honored to meet you, Thrahn," Ian said.

Captain Vahler spoke next, using the same computer-generated translator.

"On behalf of the Shalcerian Empire, I thank you, Ian Bentley, for volunteering to assist us in this important and delicate project on which we are about to embark. We have much to offer your species, but you must be willing to accept our presence and abide by our dictates for this venture to work. Our knowledge of your species' history suggests this will not be an easy task."

Ian frowned. "What are these 'dictates' to which you refer?"

"We'll go over the details when you and Rae Anne meet with the Directorate tomorrow morning. You have had a long day. We'll leave you and Rae Anne alone so you can talk and get some rest."

He turned and skipped toward, and through, the hangar wall, with Thrahn close behind.

"How did they do that?"

Rae Anne laughed. "A nanoscreen is located there. Nanoscreens open whenever you approach with the intention to go through and reform the instant you're on the other side. Jason explained it as a mass of nanoparticles being manipulated by a force field. One of many new experiences to get used to.

"But for now, let's get some tea." Rae Anne brushed her right hand across her mouth and over her ear with her eyebrows raised.

Hmm. She seems to be signaling that we're being monitored. Which is probably the case.

"Lead the way."

She led him through the gaping hole in *Aurora's* hull.

Once in *Aurora's* galley, Rae Anne proceeded to heat water.

"Do you suspect the Shalcerians of monitoring your conversations?"

"I know they do. Jason discovered this on day one. He determined from their computer logs that *Aurora* is the only place we can have secure communication."

"I seem to recall that Jason is *Aurora's* computer AI. But you mentioned that Jason cut your hair and has access to *Avenger's* computer. I'm confused."

"Jason is amazing, Ian. The Shalcerians fabricated an android body for Jason's AI persona to entertain me as I convalesced. They downloaded *Aurora's* memory banks into their own archives. In doing so, Jason became part of *Avenger's* computer system and has access to their entire knowledge database. I don't think they realize what they've done. They certainly aren't aware that he's a sentient being."

"So, where's Jason now? I'd like to meet him."

"He could be anywhere. The Shalcerians have given him run of the ship. He's fascinated by *Avenger's* propulsion system. He's also picking up their language."

"That's ironic. Our First Contact committee at the Agency has been pulling its collective hair out fretting over how to communicate with an alien species. I can only imagine the looks on their faces when I tell them the Shalcerians speak perfect English!"

"And 20 other languages as well. Communication will not be a problem."

Over tea, Rae Anne filled Ian in on details about her experiences with the Shalcerians. Ian couldn't take his eyes off her. It seemed to him Rae Anne felt the same way. Before long, their conversation became awkward.

Ian leaned toward Rae Anne and stroked her cheek.

"Do you know how beautiful you are?" he asked as he pressed his lips to hers. To his delight, Rae Anne responded as though she had been longing for this moment. Their interactions rapidly became more heated and intense.

"The lounger on Level 3 is plenty large enough for two," Rae Anne suggested breathlessly.

"Then we should try it out."

Various pieces of clothing trailed them to the hatch as Rae Anne led him down to Level 3.

Chapter 15

Earth Orbit

"It is important we show no favorites regarding individual country's leaders for our first contact with Humans," Captain Vahler explained after Thrahn introduced Ian to the six other members of the Directorate. He and Rae Anne were in the cubicle containing the holographic projection of Avenger's Council Chambers.

"We should announce a conference with the presidents from every country on Earth and present ourselves and our goals. The United Nations is the obvious venue for this meeting. These leaders will return and gather the support of their people. We may begin our operations within a couple of weeks after the conference." Vahler sounded self-assured and confident.

"Unfortunately, that approach won't work with Humans, Captain Vahler." Rae Anne glanced at Ian whose face conveyed a similar skepticism.

"You would never be able to gather these leaders in one room without an immediate display of antagonism and competition. Individual egos and nationalism would doom the conference from the start." Rae Anne shook her head sadly.

"Then how do we get them to agree to work with us? The entire Human race will benefit from cooperation. Surely, they will understand that."

"I suggest we use a stepwise approach. Rather than begin with presidents and deal with their egos and political agendas, I suggest we first hold a 'Future of Science' conference and invite the world's leading scientists. These people understand the climate crisis humanity is facing.

They see the possibility of extinction looming on the horizon. For them, logic, facts, and science will prevail. Once we lay out the technological advances you have to offer, they will see how your assistance may be the only hope for humanity."

"But do their opinions have sufficient weight to convince the political leaders and the population at large?"

"My bet is they will begin lobbying on your behalf the moment the conference is over. This will create anticipation and a willingness to hear you out."

"So, then we can get the world leaders together at the United Nations and forge an agreement for cooperation," Vahler offered.

"At that point, some political leaders might be convinced, but the populace will remain skeptical. Few leaders will return home and be willing to go against public opinion."

"That's outrageous! How could you Humans have reached space and still be so divided. What a tremendous waste of energy and resources. So, what's to be done?"

"Human tribes are more often swayed by their religious leaders. That's why we should plan a second conference to which we invite the world's important religious leaders from all faiths, including atheists, humanists, and renowned philosophers and writers. These leaders have tremendous influence over the general population. We can hope they return from this second meeting and bring their followers on board. With scientists, religious leaders, and strong popular support on our side, political support will fall into place."

"How many representatives do you recommend we invite to these conferences."

Rae Anne pursed her lips. "About two thousand for each conference," she said after a moment's thought.

"What can we do to help ensure successful outcomes from these conferences?"

"For the scientists, give them some object to take back to their labs, something that demonstrates how advanced your technology is. It should be unlike anything we have on Earth, a peek at what you have to offer once cooperation is established."

"We can do that. Anything else?"

"Humans are a skeptical race, Captain Vahler. Your remaining hidden from view engenders ever more conspiracy theories suggesting you are hiding something and that you have sinister intentions. I understand your past experiences with other races have made you reluctant to show yourselves too soon. But think about sending a representative, someone like Thrahn, to these conferences. Humans will have to get used to your presence sometime. Why not now?"

"We'll consider your request, Rae Anne. But members of your species are not known for tolerating others who look even vaguely different from themselves."

"Perhaps that's something you will help us overcome," Ian offered.

"Very well then. Ian, Rae Anne has assured us your influence at the space agency and with the American political arm will help us arrange these meetings. We want to move quickly on this. Once we start producing visible, viable projects, we anticipate opposition will evaporate. See if you can get the first conference set up two weeks from today."

Ian swallowed.

Two weeks to set up a conference for two thousand attendees from around the world. Who do they think I am? But since it's about the aliens, er Shalcerians, that may be enticing enough to make it happen.

Ian expressed his concern to Rae Anne on their way back to her quarters.

"I don't know if two weeks is enough time. The Agency does have the platform for disseminating information to the world's scientific community. Everyone listens to us. But to put together a select list of the top 2000 scientists and expect them to work us into their schedules with less than two weeks' notice? Maybe a month, better yet six weeks. But two weeks?"

"You can do it, Ian. Put the full weight of the Agency behind this effort and pull every string you have in Washington to make it happen.

We have one strong incentive on our side. Humans have never been in contact with an interstellar civilization. Curiosity alone should be a sufficient driving force to make people drop whatever they're doing. Especially scientists.

"And it's not like they must physically attend a meeting. I trust the Agency can connect anyone from anywhere in the world to a centralized conference. Once the invitations have gone out, I'll do another broadcast and a hard sell. I think everyone will take us seriously."

Colorado Springs

Organizing the scientific conference went surprisingly well. Ian got things rolling from EOTS-I on his return trip to Earth and sent Rae Anne's request and instructions directly to his subordinates at the Agency. They, in turn, snagged the Colorado Convention Center in Denver between billings. Not only was this a convenient location, being a short distance from the Agency's headquarters near Colorado Springs, but with a capacity exceeding 3000 and dozens of adjoining conference rooms for small meetings, the facilities were ideal. Carriers at Denver International Airport provided direct supersonic flights to locations around the world.

Since this was a scientific conference, Ian had no qualms about taking charge and organizing it without first obtaining permission from Washington. He did, however, keep POTUS fully informed as to the Agency's activities. She, in turn, expedited visa approvals for attendees.

The big challenge was winnowing the invitations to 2000 of the world's most active and renowned scientists from every major discipline. Ian's astronautics and computer AI groups at the Agency took on this task. Science departments at accredited universities and scientific societies happily supplied names. In addition, widely published scientists were asked for lists of colleagues for consideration. By week's end, they had collected over 5000 names. Triage turned out to be the most difficult part of the whole project.

Ian's concern that short notice would be a problem proved unfounded. Curiosity won the day. Though Rae Anne followed through with her world-wide telecast to promote the conference, it wasn't needed. Holding an invitation to this meeting was a badge of honor.

Karen wrangled an invitation for her company's lead engineer. She tasked him to look for anything her company might use to negotiate an advantage with the aliens. She also suggested that he watch for any weaknesses that could jeopardize the alien's agenda, explaining that Sanderson Robotics should avoid contract negotiations with risky partners. She kept her true motive for this second request to herself.

Chapter 16

Denver

Despite providing for virtual participation, the Future of Science conference drew a large crowd of scientists and engineers at the Colorado Convention Center in Denver. Such was the activity and bustle that the meeting started twenty minutes late. But eventually, everyone found a seat and the room assumed an atmosphere of quiet anticipation.

Rae Anne's image came to life on giant monitors around the mammoth room.

```
Welcome.
```

Rae Anne paused to allow virtual attendees throughout the world to focus their attention on her opening remarks. As before, she was seated behind the large desk hologram in her communications corner aboard *Avenger*. The large monitor behind her desk revealed that *Avenger* was just passing over Southeast Asia. The wide, blue expanse of the Pacific Ocean stretched to the rim of the planet's image. The side monitors were blank.

```
Welcome to the Future of Science conference.
I'm Rae Anne Chavez, sending my greetings from
Avenger, an interstellar Shalcerian cruiser in
polar orbit above...
```

She glanced behind her before continuing.

...above Viet Nam. The fact that I am here, alive
in Earth-orbit, rather than incinerated in
Saturn's atmosphere, I owe to the delightful
creatures, the Shalcerians, who have called
this conference. The Shalcerians have come to
Earth to share their technology with us, to
help us survive climate change, and to guide us
in becoming an interplanetary species with
Human colonies throughout our Solar System.

Their experience with other worlds leads them
to believe we Humans are likely to become
extinct within 50 years because of climate
change. Only an immediate infusion of advanced
technology can save us. The Shalcerians have
that technology and are offering to share it.

Let me give you a concrete example.

Rae Ann reached down to her lap and brought up a notebook-sized object, obsidian black and completely smooth with rounded edges. Light glistened off the shiny, glass-like surface.

This material is GESC-Plasticor. Shalcerian
scientists spent more than a dozen centuries
developing this substance. The acronym stands
for 'Graviton-Embedded Super-Conducting.' It is
a room-temperature superconducting material
that can be fabricated into any shape, from
wires and cables thousands of kilometers in
length to skyscrapers and bridges and spaceship
hulls. It is a metal/plastic hybrid that has
several unique and fascinating properties.

Rae Anne waved the plate back and forth for emphasis.

If it is fabricated into a plate like this, it
exhibits anti-gravity on one surface and a

gravitational attraction on the other. For example, *Avenger's* hull is 100% GESC-Plasticor. While inside the ship, I experience 1/6-G, allowing me to walk around normally and pour liquids, even though *Avenger* is in free-fall. The antigravity force on the outside of the hull repels everything from meteorites to deadly cosmic radiation.

Besides spaceship hulls, imagine how our fledgling nuclear fusion industry might use this material. Earth's three working fusion plants contain mammoth reactors surrounded by giant super-conducting magnets that must be cooled with liquid helium. Half the energy they produce is drawn off merely to keep them running.

If a fusion reactor's containment vessel were built with GESC-Plasticor with the antigravity surface facing inside, the plasma ions would be repelled from all sides, keeping the plasma in the core. Leakage and quenching problems disappear. And since the material itself is superconducting at room temperature, the elaborate cooling systems surrounding the magnets can be eliminated.

This is just one of the technologies the Shalcerians have offered to share with us. There are others in health care, in space vehicle propulsion, in food production.

I'll pause here to take a few questions.

Ian had set up video links to *Avenger* from as many sites as he could arrange. Rae Anne's control board beside her desk allowed her to select and broadcast any site transmission she might choose. Scanning the images before her, she chose one whose face betrayed a healthy dose of skepticism.

Dr. R. M. Venkat from Mumbai…

Dr. Venkat cleared his throat, then spoke in nearly perfect English. "What is it going to cost us to have access to this technology?"

That is a very good question. Shalcerians do expect something in return. Our Solar System's Kuiper Belt is an essential oasis on many interstellar commerce routes used by dozens of species. Shalcerians have been providing security for this area for over 2000 years to keep peace and maintain order. Once they have helped us develop our own space-faring capabilities, they expect us to take on that responsibility. This may be several years down the road.

Dr. Lisa Fitzgerald of Cambridge, Massachusetts…

"Do we have the materials here on Earth to manufacture this plasticore stuff?"

Most of the raw materials are available on Earth. The remainder can be mined in the Asteroid Belt between Mars and Jupiter. Shalcerians will help with that. Once in operation, a GESC-Plasticore center can produce a working fusion reactor in a single month.

Mr. Harold Miles, Austin, Texas…

A tall man wearing a Stetson betrayed a strong Texas drawl. "If you are speaking from the alien ship, there must be an alien crew. I want to see what these buggers look like."

The Shalcerians have determined that Humans
aren't yet ready to deal with them directly.
Your use of the words 'alien' and 'buggers'
points to the wisdom of their decision. We
Humans have yet to learn respect for other
Humans who don't look or behave like us. We
certainly aren't ready to work face-to-face
with a vastly superior life form that looks
like nothing you could imagine."

The next question came from a bearded gentleman with a heavy Russian accent. "Kuiper Belt is very far distance. Way past Saturn. How possible for us to go there? They provide fleet of deep-space rockets?"

Shalcerians will teach us how to build space-
warping propulsion systems and help us create a
fleet of interplanetary spaceships. With their
GESC-Plasticor technology, we can build
colonies on Mars, Ganymede, and Titan without
worrying about cosmic radiation. The material's
antigravity character repels even the most
intense radiation.

Rae Anne next called on Dr. Wei Fang from Beijing.

"I don't understand why the Kuiper Belt needs patrolling. Are there pirates out there, or competing civilizations warring for control?"

That question goes beyond what I know, except
to say there are many space-faring species.
Conflicts occasionally occur, and the
concentration of icy comets in our Kuiper Belt
is an attractive resource for all concerned."

Rae Anne held up the plasticor sample again.

Shalcerians have fabricated enough GESC-
Plasticor samples for each of you to evaluate.
If you aren't present in Denver, the USIEA will
send your sample to you. I'm sure you'll invent
dozens of applications for this material.

Shalcerians also have solutions to our food
production and distribution problems. I am
living testimony to their incredible health-
care technology. Imagine what lies ahead for
humanity should we agree to work peacefully
with each other and with Shalcerians.

We are at the threshold of a Golden Age for all
humanity. It's up to you to help overcome any
bias and resistance that might keep us from
stepping through that door.

Ian Bentley, the person who organized this
conference, will direct you from here. We have
set up numerous rooms with teleconference
capabilities to meet with other scientists from
around the world in your own disciplines. Many
of you know each other. Discuss among
yourselves what you can do as scientists to
convince your political leaders and the general
public to accept the Shalcerian challenge.

After thanking the attendees for their participation, Rae Anne turned
the meeting over to Ian. She tapped her tablet screen and went off-air.
Sitting back in her chair, she closed her eyes and breathed a deep sigh of
relief.

I'm totally exhausted. I can only hope this meeting gets things rolling.

Aboard *Avenger*

When Rae Anne returned to her quarters, an incoming message from Ian had arrived.

"Rae Anne, do you remember that strange alien artifact we discovered on *Osprey's* third Mars landing? The one we labeled 'Shark Fin'? It looked like a mammoth disk that had smashed into Mars but remained strangely intact?"

"Of course I do. I remember correlating it with *Oumuamua's* appearance and with the two alien objects I observed orbiting Ganymede. What about it?"

"This sample of GESC-Plasticore I'm holding looks and feels like the material on Shark Fin. Especially the antigravity character on the one side. Your take?"

"I suspected as much. Look up *Oumuamua* in the news from October 2017 and compare that object's shape and size with *Avenger's*. I think they both are Shalcerian battlecruisers. At one point, Thrahn mentioned that a Shalcerian battlecruiser named *Nemesis* was destroyed in a fire fight while patrolling the Kuiper Belt. I believe the remains of *Nemesis* and *Oumuamua* are one and the same."

"That could put a different light on their wanting Humans to take over their patrols in the Kuiper Belt. The situation out there may not be as benign as they've led us to believe."

"You may be right, Ian. As I see it, we're in a difficult situation. If their stats are correct, without their help, humanity is a hair's breadth away from extinction. Do we really have any choice but to promote full cooperation with the Shalcerians and hope for the best?"

Chapter 17

Denver

The Future of Science breakout sessions lasted far into the night. Ian's department provided a full buffet to keep the attendees energized throughout the afternoon and evening. Clusters of scientists bustled between the meeting rooms and the buffet in the main auditorium. Conversations were universally upbeat and animated.

Ian mingled among the small groups to catch snippets of their conversations to gauge how things were going.

Rae Anne's proposal to target scientists first was spot on. Every single delegate here will be a strong advocate for cooperation when they return. We can only hope the politicians listen to them.

As delegates departed, Ian tried to determine which groups would be in control of their situation back home and which would face an uphill battle with hostile governments. Although he trusted Rae Anne's instincts, he retained a healthy skepticism regarding the Shalcerian's motives.

They've been patrolling the Kuiper Belt for 2000 years, and they are willing to give us all this technology in return for relieving them of this one chore? There's got to be more to this than they've revealed. For one thing, they recently lost a battle cruiser. Clearly, policing the Kuiper Belt isn't a holiday cruise. What are we getting ourselves into?

Ian and his staff finally escorted the last delegation through the glass doors, bidding them 'Good Night' and 'Good Luck.' The sun was already lighting up the eastern horizon, painting the cirrus clouds a dazzling yellow and orange. To the west, Rocky Mountain peaks glowed salmon pink in the sunlight's first rays to welcome the new day.

When Ian approached his hovercar in the lot atop the main hall, he was astonished to see graffiti scrawled across all the car's windows.

ALIENS HERE TO ENSLAVE HUMANS!

DEATH TO ALIEN LOVERS!

ALIENS GO HOME!!

HUMANS = ALIEN SNACKS!

Ian sighed and opened the door.

I may be skeptical about their intentions, but I really don't think they're here to eat us or enslave us. Too much B-rated science fiction.

"There he is! He's one of them. Get him!"

The shouts came from the corner of the lot. Ian glanced toward the ruckus and saw a dozen demonstrators running toward his hovercar. Several waved protest signs in the air.

Ian's adrenalin surged and his heart jumped. He hopped in and slammed and locked the door.

"Agency Administration Building," he shouted before reminding himself he was talking to a computer.

You must buckle up before we can leave.

Ian swore an oath while he fumbled with the latches on his seat belt. Two demonstrators reached the hovercar and began banging the windows with their fists. The little craft shuddered, then leapt into the air and left the mob staring after it, waving their signs and fists angrily.

What a contrast in moods! It's going to take a lot more than promises to convince these protestors to go along. I wonder how widespread this attitude is.

As if to answer his question, the view looking down through the graffiti revealed that the park between the state capitol and the Civic Center was teaming with people waving placards and confronting two SWAT teams in full riot gear on the capitol steps. The crowd extended several blocks north and south on Broadway. Protesters also jammed East and West Colfax Avenue to the north.

Ian pulled out his notebook and tuned in to the local news.

Roughly half of yesterday's demonstrators
stayed through the night, many sleeping in the
park or at curbside. They're awake now and
demanding the legislature do something. Amy?
You're on the scene. What do you see there?

Thanks Jean. I interviewed several protestors a
few moments ago. They're all scared. Terrified.
Nothing like this has ever happened before.
They want someone to assure them this alien
visitation doesn't pose a threat. Jean?

So far, the only feedback from the
administration in Washington is the admonition
'Don't Panic' and 'The Shalcerians are
Friendly.' The public needs more than that.

I agree, Jean. This hastily organized
conference with notable scientists from around
the globe added fuel to the fire. When I mixed
with the new arrivals at the Conference Center
yesterday, I heard every language under the
sun. Your average person knows this wouldn't
happen unless something serious was about to
take place. Many here believe Washington knows
far more than they're willing to tell us. Jean?

Thanks, Amy. Our international feeds report
similar crowds in every capital around the
world. London, Paris, Berlin, Moscow, Beijing,
Tokyo, you name it.

Meanwhile, in international news, the border
conflict between India and Pakistan in Kashmir

is heating up as the Pakistan army makes
significant advances into the high Kashmir
Valley.

Ian switched off the news. He had half an hour to catch a much-needed nap before arriving at his office on the base east of Colorado Springs. Once there, he planned to gather everyone who was anyone for a 10:00 o'clock meeting to determine what the Agency could do to calm people's fears before the crisis erupted into an uncontrollable inferno.

Colorado Springs

The 10:00 o'clock meeting was held in virtual space, the only option for a session called on such short notice and with participants located around the country. Havel Nelson, the president's Chief of Staff was present at the White House. General Wilson and other top military brass were logged in from the Pentagon and Vandenberg AFB in California. Even Ian's staff was scattered widely, calling in from EOTS-I and Moon Base Alpha, Cape Canaveral, Little Rock, and New York City. Ian tried to reach Rae Anne aboard *Avenger* but couldn't get through.

After opening formalities, Ian presented the group with the difficult task they were facing.

"We must quench the conspiracy theories social media is spreading throughout the world. It's understandable that people faced with a new and uncertain situation are nervous. Is there anything we can do to convince them their fears are unfounded?"

"Nervous is an understatement, Ian. People are scared shitless."

"So, how do we counter this hysteria?"

Havel spoke up. "It would help if the aliens introduced themselves and used their communication override to address the world directly. You've seen them, Ian. Are they so scary this would do more harm than good?"

"They are odd looking, I'll say that. But threatening or scary? Definitely not. My understanding is their reluctance to show themselves is a First Contact protocol based on earlier encounters with other species. Working through a liaison, like Rae Anne, has proven to be the more successful approach."

"Shows they know nothing about Humans."

A marine general spoke up. "If things get much worse, we'll have to declare Martial Law and institute curfews. You can imagine how that will go over."

General Wilson disagreed. "Seeing the military in the streets could reassure people."

Ian wasn't sure about that assessment. He thought the opposite reaction would be more likely.

Havel spoke above the hubbub.

"What we need is trusted leadership to get everyone to calm down."

"That's fine for you to say," came as another unsolicited comment. "No one trusts their government, and not just here in the U.S. of A."

Havel responded calmly.

"I wasn't thinking about governments or politicians. Ian has scheduled a second conference two weeks from now with the world's religious leaders. These are people who do have their followers' trust. If we get the same response from them that we saw from the scientists, the demonstrations should cool down."

"We may not be able to hold off for two weeks. Things are already at the boiling point," added Melony Blain from the Agency's PR department.

"If we can get Rae Anne to give another global broadcast, it might help," said General Wilson. "Announcing the conference with the world's religious leaders might quiet things down a bit. That shouldn't be too much to ask the aliens to do for us."

There seemed to be general agreement with this proposal, realizing that the Shalcerians would have to concur.

After the meeting, Ian sent a request to Rae Anne for an additional broadcast from *Avenger.*

I can only hope Rae Anne receives my communication in a timely manner. With them monitoring our broadcasts, they must know about the turmoil here on the ground.

Ian was relieved to hear back from Rae Anne within the hour. She reported that Captain Vahler was perplexed at the world's response to their magnanimous gesture. Bowing to Rae Anne's advice, he gave his approval for the broadcast. Rae Anne would once again appear on the world's media stage unannounced the very next day.

This time she reiterated her belief that the Shalcerians had come in peace and their presence would help motivate humanity to work together and use their advanced technologies to solve problems related to climate change. She announced the Confluence of Religions conference that was to take place within two weeks and urged everyone to be patient and wait for guidance from their religious leaders when they returned from that meeting.

Although this announcement didn't quench the firestorm, it did subdue the flames. The crowds were smaller and less vociferous. Arrests for disorderly behavior were down. The world held its collective breath while waiting for the next conference.

Chapter 18

Colorado Springs

The Colorado Convention Center was not available for the Confluence of Religions conference, so the Agency scheduled this meeting at the Broadmoor International Center in Colorado Springs. The setup and catering reflected the Future of Science conference, but the delegations were much more colorful. Buddhist saffron robes and Sikh turbans mixed with Catholic clerical garb, Jewish yarmulkes, and Muslim prayer caps. Native Americans and Polynesians came wearing festive native outfits. Beards of assorted sizes and shapes were commonplace. Unfortunately, but not unexpectedly, females were a distinct minority.

As before, Rae Anne opened the meeting and addressed the attendees from her office studio aboard *Avenger*. But this time, to help reduce anxiety among the world's populace, the Shalcerians broadcast her remarks live to the world on all communication channels. Rae Anne convinced Captain Vahler that her broadcasts required the widest possible dissemination.

Her opening remarks were the same as those she used for the scientists two weeks earlier. But rather than highlighting Shalcerian technology and how it would help humanity, her emphasis for this conference was decidedly different. She didn't hesitate to get right to the point.

You were each selected to participate in this
conference for a special reason. You are
respected leaders with followings ranging from
several thousands to millions. You have
dedicated your lives to creating a better, more

just world for your people. As a result, you
have earned their respect and trust.

Our hope is that we can convince you that the
Shalcerians are peaceful, and their motives are
philanthropic. I have lived with them for two
months and firmly believe they are here to
guide humanity to a greater and more equitable
future. With their help, poverty and hunger can
be reduced, perhaps even eliminated. With their
help, every child throughout the world will
have a better future to look forward to.

Just imagine the impact small nuclear fusion
reactors would have in every political
jurisdiction throughout the world. Every
community would have unlimited, clean energy.
Energy for water purification, for hydrogen
fuel production, for air conditioning to
mitigate the effects of climate change.

The side screens behind her showed videos to correlate with the
subjects she was presenting. She had previously vetted them and was
pleased with how well the Shalcerian public relations crew had assembled
material that would appeal to their Human audience.

Their health care technology goes far beyond
anything we can imagine. They have effective
treatments for cancer and viral infections.
They can replace damaged limbs and failing
organs with artificial substitutes that work
like the original thing.

Agriculture will be turned on its head with the
introduction of their advanced hydroponics and
aquaculture. The scourge of hunger and
starvation will become distant memories.

Meditate on these things. Imagine the impact
these technologies will have on the lives of
the people you lead, the people you care for.

Rae Anne paused and sipped some water from a glass on the small table near her holographic desk. She hoped her emphasis on Human values would be the winning card to bring the members of this diverse group over to her side.

The Shalcerian offer comes with a brief list of
conditions which I will present to the world
today for the first time. I hope you will view
these mandates in light of the added benefits
and security for every person in your community
that I have just mentioned.

Shalcerians believe these are the minimum
requirements to ensure that we humans neither
annihilate ourselves nor drive our species to
extinction by neglecting to respond to our
changing environment.

The first condition is universal nuclear
disarmament.

Rae Anne paused to give her viewers time to digest this dictate, expecting it to generate the most controversy. She took another gulp of water to soothe her parched throat. Only now did she begin to harbor doubts about the success of her mission. Human intransigence was going to be a major hurdle to overcome.

All fissionable material throughout the world
and all nuclear waste will be collected and
sent into the sun for disposal. Nuclear power
facilities will be phased out as they are
replaced by Shalcerian fusion power plants.

Our world will be safer without the constant
threat of nuclear war. Our environment will be
healthier with the elimination of radioactive
waste.

Rae Anne paused again to gauge her audience's reaction. In contrast with the excitement from the science conference, her feed from the auditorium showed that the room was deathly still.

Hmm… Waiting for the second shoe to drop. Can't blame them. At least they're listening.

The second condition is the elimination of
fossil fuels within five years. The carbon
dioxide from their combustion is largely
responsible for global warming. Replacing
fossil fuels with fusion plants to provide
electricity and pollution-free hydrogen fuel
will be a breath of fresh air, literally.

Rae Anne glanced at her monitors and noticed that the last comments created a stir in the audience. There was scattered applause, but a few groups, notably those from the Middle East, were showing signs of agitation.

The third condition is that all industrial and
agricultural processes be re-engineered to
eliminate their negative impact on the
environment. For all processes, top priority
must be given to environmental preservation.
Shalcerian experience and knowledge will be
useful in achieving these goals.

The fourth condition is one where we give back
something in return for Shalcerian largess. I
mentioned this in the Future of Science
conference. The Shalcerians expect us to take
over patrolling the Kuiper Belt in the outer

regions of our Solar System. They will provide
us with the ships and equipment and training
necessary to provide security for this distant
region.

Ray Anne noticed the crowd in the conference center was becoming considerably more restless. She couldn't shake the feeling that her last comment about the Kuiper Belt patrols had been ignored. Nationalistic fervor had some delegates on their feet, shaking their fists in protest. She tried to make out what they were shouting, but the audio pick-ups were useless in the general din.

Not good. Certainly not the reaction I was hoping for. Still, the objectors are the minority. Although a vocal minority, at that. Well, time to wrap things up.

Rae Anne cited the statistics she had been given for the number of neighboring species that had destroyed their civilization through nuclear war. The statistics predicted that Humans had a 71% chance of nuclear annihilation within 50 years if conditions were left as is. The side monitors behind her showed images of barren planets laid waste from nuclear conflicts.

In conclusion, the Shalcerians are giving us a
pathway to save us from ourselves. It's a win-
win situation that could eventually pave our
way to the stars. We are asking you to consider
these proposals in view of the alternatives and
return to your followers and your governments
and encourage them to agree to the proposal the
Shalcerians have presented to us.

The Shalcerians are asking for worldwide
cooperation in agreeing to these demands and in
working diligently to see they are met. With
your leadership, we can meet that challenge and
achieve a unity of purpose and vision.

Rae Anne finished her exposition with the same concluding remarks she made at the Future of Science conference and turned the meeting over to Ian.

The wall monitor went black and disappeared when Rae Anne tapped her tablet to end the transmission. She decided not to entertain questions from this group. Media interviews since *Avenger's* arrival with members from these factions often ended in diatribes about God (which god depended on the sect), Satan, devils, angels, and Armageddon. She did not wish to get entangled in such irrelevant inanities. She could almost imagine some group forming a 'Missionary Society' to proselytize Shalcerians into joining their sect.

Colorado Springs

The day following the Confluence of Religions conference, Hurricane Briana, a Category 5 hurricane that had ravaged the Bahamas, smashed into the north Florida Atlantic coast with a vengeance. The slow-moving storm, having sucked incredible volumes of water from the Gulf Stream, inundated the Orlando region with its heaviest rainfall on record.

Climate-change-induced rising sea levels created a storm surge that washed over beaches and highways, flooded coastal towns, and washed away infrastructure. Lingering torrential rains added to the misery. Flood waters surpassed the eaves of one-story structures far inland. Helicopter and boat rescue operations were taxed to the limit. Despite mandatory evacuation notices, lives lost would be in the thousands.

To the north, St. Augustine was nearly obliterated. To the south, several tornados struck the Cape Canaveral launch complex, causing severe damage. Launch pads were submerged beneath several feet of water while towers and access elevators were reduced to twisted, useless hulks, some flattened to the ground.

Ian and his colleagues at the USIEA center at Peterson SFB followed the storm's news coverage with rapt attention. The prevailing mood ranged from dismay to horror. All operations had been halted and personnel safely evacuated prior to Briana's landfall, but watching their principal doorway to space being washed away by an act of nature was like losing a member of the family.

"There's not much left, Ian." Penny choked back a sob. "It'll be years before we'll be able to launch from there again."

Ian shook his head sadly. "At least the Vehicle Assembly Buildings appear to be weathering the storm. No telling what shape the boosters and shuttles inside are in. Most are on elevated racks, so the flood water may not have damaged them."

"High tide isn't for another six hours, Ian." Victor took a bite from his bagel, chewed, and swallowed. "Water's already lapping several feet at the hangar doors. Amazing they've held up in all this, you know?"

"Will we be able to use Vandenberg for our launches?" Eileen asked.

"I've already begun working on that angle," Ian answered. "General Wilson is lobbying at the Pentagon on our behalf. I'm certain we'll have limited use, but we'll have to reduce the number of launches we have scheduled."

"We may have to contract some shuttle flights with TransWorld Space, you know," Victor suggested.

Ian glanced again at the video monitor.

"If events like this don't drive home how much we need help to save our planet from climate change, I don't know what will."

Chapter 19

New Hampshire

From the beginning, Rae Anne and Ian had planned the third and final conference for the world's political leaders to take place at the U.N. in New York City. The Call for Unity conference was scheduled to take place two weeks after the Confluence of Religions conference.

A week before this meeting, Karen joined Sam at his New Hampshire estate for a strategy session. Karen's pilot landed her Gulfstream 580 at a private airstrip in New Hampshire with his usual deft hand despite a crosswind that stiffened the windsock like an arrow.

The turbines roared, slowing the plane on the short runway before it taxied to the nearby hangars where Sam stabled his three corporate jets. Once the engines quieted, her valet opened the door and lowered the steps. Karen stepped out onto the tarmac.

An autonomous hovercraft descended and landed fifty feet from the jet. Karen, grasping her hat with one hand and holding her skirt down with the other, walked briskly to the vehicle and stepped inside. Her valet followed and placed her thin briefcase on his lap as the rotors spun up and the craft lifted into the air.

Five minutes later, they were hovering over Sam's mountain estate. Karen watched as a transparent dome, centered in a maze of roofs, gables and turrets, opened like a shutter, revealing a landing pad surrounded by lawns and hedges. The hovercraft descended to the pad while the dome closed overhead.

Sam appeared around the corner of a hedge in a golf cart. He pulled up alongside the small copter.

"I'm glad you could make it on a day's notice, Karen. Things are happening too quickly to hold off till our usual monthly rendezvous."

Karen smiled thinly. "I agree. The sooner we take action against these aliens, the better."

Sam gestured at his golf cart. "Hop aboard. Lunch is waiting."

He turned to Karen. "We can eat by the pool where you and I can talk business in absolute privacy. After dessert, of course."

"So, here's how I see it," Sam began when they had finished eating. He took a long swig from his brandy. Karen swirled her Chardonnay and lifted the glass to her lips.

"There's already plenty of suspicion and distrust out there. Media outlets are producing new conspiracy theories every day. We haven't had to do anything to stir things up yet."

"Unfortunately, investors don't think the aliens will leave, Sam. Wind Resources is down 27% this past week, and it's dragging down Sanders Robotics by association."

Sam held out a small humidor containing a variety of expensive cigars. Karen turned down his offer with a hand gesture. Sam selected one and closed the lid. He tapped its tip on the table while removing a tool from his pocket and cut a slim piece off the tip with practiced expertise. He held the cigar to his nose and sniffed.

"You can tell a quality cigar by the wrapper's fragrance. Nothing beats a good cigar after a satisfying meal."

Nothing beats watching a man preen for a woman's attention. Peacocks do a much better job.

Sam lit a match and held it near the freshly cut tip, taking care to toast the wrapper without catching it on fire.

"Speaking of robotics, have you heard the rumor claiming there are no actual aliens aboard their ship, that they're all robots? That would explain why they haven't shown their faces. The videos with Chavez might be recorded too. The Bentley fellow is the only one who claims to have seen her."

Sam finally lit the cigar, savored his first draw with closed eyes, and exhaled a white smoke ring.

Karen took her wine and moved to a chair upwind of Sam's cigar smoke. She ignored his comment about robots and continued with her concerns.

"The science community has been blathering non-stop since their conference about how the aliens will save humanity from extinction. A large part of the religious community has fallen for their social welfare pitch as well. Whatever we do will have to counter all that."

Sam smiled and puffed on his cigar before continuing.

Karen gave him a skeptical look. Sam wagged his cigar in her direction and cleared his throat before continuing.

"We will take advantage of the scientist's enthusiasm for the alien's offer to share nuclear energy with humans. We can launch a worldwide ad campaign to counter their fusion energy plans. Nuclear is a dirty word to a lot of people. All we need to do is mention Chernobyl and Fukushima and Three Mile Island. We'll reinforce the idea that nuclear isn't safe."

"But Sam, they're talking nuclear fusion. Fusion can't melt down or explode, and radioactive waste is almost inconsequential. You're an engineer. You know that."

"I know it. You know it. But millions out there have no idea that there's a difference between fission and fusion. Most politicians haven't a clue, either. Our campaign will make sure they don't figure it out."

"That might have an effect in the long term, Sam. But things are moving too fast. If we could slow everything down somehow, a propaganda campaign like you've suggested would have a better chance at working."

"I've given that some thought, too, and this is where you're, umm…special contacts can be put to good use."

Karen frowned.

"I don't know what you mean."

"I have it from reliable sources that Sanders Robotics has 'disappeared' more than one union organizer and an occasional whistleblower over the years."

"That's utter hogwash."

Sam wagged his cigar in her direction.

"I'm not asking you to admit to anything. I'm just suggesting your people could conjure up a 'terrorist' event to drive home humanity's antagonism against the aliens. Maybe take out someone important. Someone like Ian Bentley, for example."

How much does he know about my business dealings? I need to get my people to take a closer look at Sam's operations. A little ammunition for self-defense never hurts.

"That's an interesting idea, Sam. Purely theoretical. I can see how something like that could turn the tables."

The two conspirators continued their discussions through the afternoon. By the time Karen left, the sun had just set. Orange, coral, and pink streamers washed through the clouds to the west. Her Gulfstream lifted into the sky at a steep angle and leveled off at 36,000 feet for the long flight to her Aspen home.

She settled back in her lounger and sipped the vodka martini her valet had prepared. Her mind kept coming back to Sam's comment about involving key players in a violent incident. The thought excited her in a delicious, orgasmic way, bringing back memories.

There was Mr. Photographer on the beach in the Baja, filming their small yacht through a telephoto lens as her husband worked at reeling in a swordfish. Filming as she crept up behind her husband and bludgeoned his skull with a heavy belaying pin. Filming as she unstrapped him from his chair and lowered him over the boat's railing and fed him to the sharks. Extorting her afterwards for a cool million. With the help of one of her less savory 'partners,' his DVD was now safely in her possession, and Mr. Photographer was safely deep-sixed with her former husband. Viewing his video always provided a better orgasm than any she'd experienced in bed with her husband. Or with Sam, for that matter. She felt a tingling in her groin just thinking about it.

I need to look up the fellow in Las Vegas who took care of Mr. Photographer for me. He might know someone with the resources to involve Ian Bentley in a 'terrorist' attack.

Chapter 20

New York City

The participants in the Future of Science conference four weeks earlier had unanimously lobbied their governments to support the initiative, focusing on the incredible benefits to every cooperating nation. The religious leaders returning home from the Confluence of Religions conference were not as enthusiastic. A few opted for full cooperation, but most were more cautious, and some proclaimed the orbiting ship was a demonic visitation and must be destroyed.

The Call for Unity conference inviting the world's political leaders together was held at the United Nations General Assembly Hall. Several nations sent their chief executives, presidents, and prime ministers, to accompany their U.N. ambassadors. Anticipation filled the packed room like static electricity. The world's media pundits were there to offer non-stop commentary and broadcast the meeting itself in real time.

The Secretary General introduced Ian and turned the meeting over to him. Ian welcomed the attendees and recapped the information Rae Anne had provided at the previous two conferences. He then plunged into the agenda they had laid out for the world's political leaders.

"What we haven't focused on is this: we do not have the luxury of time. Earth's annual temperature average is at a precipice from which it may never recover. Till now, Earth's built-in mechanisms for moderating extreme temperature changes have reduced the effects on climate, keeping annual global temperature increases within uncomfortable, but tolerable, ranges."

"But we are about to overwhelm those moderating mechanisms. Once we step over the threshold, several independent phenomena that have been strengthening through the years will join forces and reinforce each other, causing temperatures to take precipitous jumps. Humanity will simply disappear. As Rae Anne mentioned in her previous broadcast, extinction in our near future is a distinct possibility."

Ian took a sip from the water glass on the dais. He was pleased to note how still the auditorium had become.

This is good. I need to drive this point home.

"Shalcerians have witnessed similar situations on a dozen planets over the last several millennia. In every case, the intelligent species inhabiting those planets ceased to exist within a few short years after their planet's temperature crossed that precipice. Think about it. Imagine Earth becoming a hellhole like Venus."

He paused again for emphasis. Subtle stirrings suggested his audience might be feeling uncomfortable with his predictions.

Time to present the Shalcerian solution to all our problems. I hope.

"The Shalcerian Code permits intervention only when a civilization proves it is capable of sustainable space exploration. Humans, having now landed on two distant worlds, Mars and Titan, meet that definition. The Shalcerians have authorized *Avenger's* captain, Captain Vahler, whom I have met, to provide the assistance we Humans desperately need for survival. These technological advances will leapfrog humanity hundreds of years beyond our current capabilities."

He paused a third time for dramatic effect. He tried without success to ascertain the prevailing mood in the auditorium. Faces reflected emotions ranging from eagerness to curiosity and anxiety to outright skepticism and hostility.

This is a far more difficult sell than I imagined. At least they're still listening.

Only the Secretary General and Ian were prepared for what happened next.

The doors to the auditorium opened and five Shalcerians came down the aisle to join Ian at the dais. Audible expressions of surprise and wonder filled the room. Dozens of smart phones were lifted in the air to record the strange creatures. Reporters rushed to the exits to call their editors from the foyer. Others furiously typed their impressions on their tablets.

Ian waved both hands high above his head to call for order. When things quieted, he continued.

"Today, we are most honored to have five members of the starship *Avenger's* Directorate visit us. It is my pleasure to introduce them to you."

Ian made the introductions, hoping to get the Shalcerian names right, but reminding himself on this occasion they had no translating connection to *Avenger's* computer. It was enough for the world to see an intelligent and sentient species different from themselves for the first time.

"I apologize that we're not set up to translate or communicate with them today. They made their decision to appear here at the last minute. But when we begin negotiations, we will be able to communicate with them and they with us in all languages quite fluently."

Ian stepped back from the podium and welcomed each Shalcerian. They each gave Ian a hearty handshake, having been tutored in the gesture by Rae Anne. They then turned to the audience. Their body scales swirled in shades between yellow and turquoise. After waving to the delegates (Rae Anne's doing, again), they skipped up the aisle in their unique gait and out the door.

Outside, they entered their black 'flying saucer' and noiselessly took off for their return to *Avenger*. The event's video footage grabbed top billing on news media outlets around the world.

Ian continued his presentation to the delegates.

"You have now seen with your own eyes the first of many star-faring species with whom we may soon come in contact. Not surprisingly, they don't look anything like us. They come from a world quite different from ours. You may have noted they were all wearing respirators, since they cannot breathe our air. But despite how strange they appear to us, they are a welcoming and friendly people. They want to work with us.

"But their offer to help comes with the stipulations Rae Anne presented in the Confluence of Religions conference. We should have embraced these actions on our own seventy years ago. We are paying the price for our inaction today.

"If every nation cooperates with the Shalcerians to achieve universal justice and equality, outright war will become obsolete. Diplomacy and compromise will resolve disputes between nations. Thus, nuclear disarmament is a non-issue. Abundant, pollution-free energy will be available throughout the world. Water shortages will be a thing of the past. Future generations will enjoy the abundant, worry-free lives we have always wished for our children and grandchildren."

A subdued commotion spread through the audience, quickly reaching a crescendo. Some delegates animatedly discussed these opportunities with their aides. Others jumped to their feet and shouted their dissent. Ian again waved his arms for order and waited for some semblance of quiet before continuing.

"These are actions we must take immediately if we hope to counter imminent extinction. There is no guarantee it's not too late. But our Shalcerian friends believe we have time to save ourselves if every government gets behind this program, if we all work cooperatively together, and if we all do everything possible to make it succeed.

"Discuss these issues with your individual governments and your military, with business and industry, and with your citizens. Many, perhaps most, will have heard this broadcast. The benefits from cooperation compared to the alternative could not be more distinct. The Shalcerians are expecting you to return to this location in two weeks with a comprehensive action agenda for each of your countries. The Shalcerians are ready if you are."

Ian thanked the delegates for their attention and left the podium. Many remained seated in stunned silence. Representatives from most European countries intermingled, engaging in serious discussions, with their aides taking notes and making calls, presumably getting things underway without delay. Canada, Mexico, and the U.S. appeared already to be in agreement.

Leaders from the Middle Eastern countries stormed from the room with angry shouts about aliens being fallen angels led by the Great Satan. The Iranian delegation also prepared to leave, but not before the Iranian ambassador shouted, "We will never abandon our nuclear defenses. With Israel and Saudi Arabia waiting to destroy us, to do so would be suicide!" Their representatives filed out without a backward glance.

Ian watched from the sidelines with dismay. Trying to ignore the naysayers, he searched the room for any positive takeaway.

At least Russia and the U.S. are talking with each other. Maybe they're finally getting serious about nuclear disarmament.

Chapter 21

New York City

Ian stepped from the autonomous taxi at the curb in front of the U.N. Secretariate Building, followed by his two colleagues from the USIEA. They were just in time to make their 09:30 appointment with the Secretary General to discuss the previous day's Call for Unity conference. A dozen reporters rushed to his side as they made their way to the front doors.

"Mr. Bentley, what do you think are the odds for achieving universal nuclear disarmament?"

"Do you think North Korea will go along with this mandate?"

"What about Iran?"

"How will the Shalcerians enforce a disarmament agreement?"

Ian waved them off and shouted, "I have no comment at this time." He and his companions strode up to the glass doors leading into the building.

A thunderous explosion ripped beneath the portico. Glass windows and doors shattered. Shards of the trash receptacle containing the explosive rocketed in every direction. Heavy smoke billowed from the entrance into the courtyard.

A security guard ran through the reception area toward the doors.

"Call 911," he shouted as his boots crunched through the glass and he plunged through the jagged door frame.

The receptionist had miraculously escaped serious injury, although her face was bleeding from several lacerations and blood was oozing through the right shoulder of her blouse. She was already on the phone with the NYPD dispatcher.

Two more security guards raced past her desk. In the smoke-filled portico, the first guard, now bare chested, was tearing his shirt into strips for tourniquets. A second guard followed his example while the third stepped into the courtyard to face the gathering crowd.

"We have seven victims up here," she yelled. "Some are still alive. We need a doctor here fast."

Two people pushed their way through the crowd, claiming to be medics. A nurse also came forward. The three rushed to the victims and began to provide what first-aid they could. At one point the nurse stepped back with a hand to her mouth and muttered, "Oh god, so much blood."

Two guards carried posts with rope coils onto the courtyard to cordon off the area. Distant sirens echoed through the city's concrete canyons.

"I need a couple tourniquets over here," one medic called. "This one's pretty bad."

The bare-chested guard brought his T-shirt strips to the medic.

"Who else needs a tourniquet?" he shouted.

"I could use one over here."

The guard quickly obliged.

Within minutes, four ambulances and six NYPD patrol cars arrived at the scene. Behind them lumbered two firetrucks and three other bright red vehicles from the nearest fire station. EMT's hustled to the scene with medical kits and wheeled stretchers and began triage. Three of the victims were dead. Two were seriously injured, clearly in need of emergency surgery, while the remaining two suffered multiple minor injuries, hearing loss, and trauma.

The EMT's were loading the survivors into their ambulances when the FBI pulled up in two black SUVs. After a brief interview with the agents, the EMT's left with sirens blaring to transport the four injured parties to Belleview Hospital's emergency center. The police department's forensic investigative unit arrived in two large vans and began hauling equipment to the crime scene.

That same morning, Sam was meeting with Russia's ambassador to the U.N. on the seventeenth floor of the Secretariate Building. The ambassador was accompanied by General Sergei Orlov, one of Russia's highest-ranking generals and Dmitri Peskov, a rotund fellow wearing three gold braids around his neck that brushed against his fashionable, expensive gray jacket. Sam recognized Dmitri as a well-known Russian oligarch who was said to be the Russian President's most trusted confidant and advisor.

A muffled thump and momentary tremor rattled the building, giving Sam a start. He frowned as the four men looked at each other.

"I'll check on it," said the ambassador. He stood and stepped out of the small conference room attached to his office.

Dmitri raised his eyebrows with a slight shrug, as if to say 'New York—what do you expect?' He turned to Sam.

"Demand for nuclear disarmament is, how to say in English, is suspicious. Maybe they fear we use missiles to destroy their ship. So *koneshno*, they demand we disarm. Then they have their way with us."

"We have capability to strike any satellite or ship in Earth-orbit," General Orlov said. "We have demonstrated this with tests against space debris. The aliens are in our crosshairs," he smugly added.

Sam smiled inwardly.

Typical Russian bluster. But worth encouraging.

He steepled his fingers. "I don't think we need to worry about nuclear disarmament. No one with a nuclear stockpile will give up their weapons. You think China won't try annexing parts of Siberia if you give up your nuclear defenses? India also faces constant threats from China, not to mention Pakistan. And then there's North Korea. Can you imagine them budging on this issue?"

The ambassador re-entered the room, catching Sam's last remark.

"It would seem to me that disarmament is a non-issue," he said, resuming his chair and calmly crossing his legs.

The general turned to the ambassador.

"Did you find out what caused the tremor?"

"Some protestors exploded a small bomb at the entrance to the building. Some injuries, but they say they have everything under control."

Dmitri sighed. "Is good. Every great city around world is dealing with protest. Too much about aliens we not know."

General Orlov stood and began pacing with his hands clasped behind his back. He turned to face Sam.

"Unlike your government, we see presence of aliens as threat to all humanity, not just Russia. We must destroy them. My concern is if direct nuclear blast of five missiles to be enough."

Sam reached into his jacket pocket and removed a small recorder.

"I think they are vulnerable to a nuclear attack, General. As Dmitri pointed out, this might be why they demand that we disarm. But I have additional evidence here."

Sam flipped the 'play' button on the recorder.

```
This is Rae Anne Chavez aboard Aurora.
We are coming home.
The aliens are friendly.
Don't shoot.
```

"Where did that come from, Sam?" asked the ambassador.

"I have a friend at British MI6 who thought I might find a use for it. They obtained it from the USIEA. It was their first direct evidence that the approaching object was an alien ship instead of an asteroid."

"But how is that relevant to our conversation?"

"It's in the last thing she says. Listen."

Sam played the recording again.

"Why would she have added 'Don't shoot.' if the aliens were invulnerable. Rae Anne knows the limitations of our technology and weapons. She must have added that last line because they are fearful we might blast them out of the sky."

"*Da. Pravda*," Dmitri muttered, rubbing his hands together. A big grin spread across his face.

General Orlov nodded his head. "That is valuable observation. *Spasibo*, Sam. I take this information to *Moskva* tonight. Helpful for Council of Generals to make decision."

Dmitri continued to nod. "I also pass word to Illustrious Leader over secure line this afternoon. Your news very useful. Maybe reward for you."

Sam handed the recorder to the general. "Take this to your meeting. It will help verify what we discussed here with your comrades."

He turned to the oligarch.

"I'm not expecting any sort of reward, but thank you for the offer. However, I do plan to submit a proposal to the Moscow Regional Duma for building a spaceport and hotel complex just north of the city, near Borodino. If you could facilitate getting the proposal approved and seeing to the permitting red-tape, that would be very helpful. Putting Moscow just hours away from every major city in the world would be a win-win for everyone, but especially good for Russians."

Nodding, Dmitri said, "*Da, da.* I see it very well. *Koneshno*, with reasonable percent of future profits. Maybe 25%.

Sam blanched. He always paid bribes up front to get these projects rolling. But Dmitri's ask was beyond the pale.

A 25% share of the profits? Absurd.

Deciding this wasn't the place to negotiate terms, Sam said, "We can cover the details over lunch sometime, perhaps next week. But I am anxious to get things started."

Sam left the meeting wondering if the Russians were seriously planning to blast the aliens out of orbit. If so, that would solve his 'alien competition' problem. He was more guarded about prospects for a Moscow spaceport.

That's why I've never had successful dealings with Russians. Sheer, unadulterated greed.

Chapter 22

Earth-Orbit

Rae Anne watched Thrahn on the monitor as he crossed the hangar to *Aurora*. She put down her notebook and set it to 'sleep' mode.

Amazing how fluid their movements are. I wonder if the two joints in his legs give him extra agility. But I've never seen him flashing purple, magenta and green body colors. He must be in an unusual mood.

Thrahn entered through the hole next to *Aurora's* airlock and skipped to the table.

"Rae Anne, I have some bad news. Everything may have changed."

Rae Anne gripped the table's edge to prepare for Thrahn's announcement. She felt a surge of bile in her throat.

"Why, Thrahn? What's wrong?"

"The Baltar Alliance has attacked our colony on Alsafi-γ. A combot from our outpost, Safe Harbor, popped into Sol-space calling for help less than an hour ago. We are preparing to leave immediately to go to their aid."

"You can't take me with you! We've just begun negotiations."

"We have no choice. There isn't time to transfer you to one of your space stations, and *Aurora* hasn't been repaired." Thrahn gestured to the hole he had walked through.

"But…" Rae Anne sputtered. "This could destroy all our hard work with First Contact negotiations. The moment *Avenger* disappears from the scene, everything could fall apart."

Thrahn ignored her outburst and put a hand on her shoulder. "Have no fear. You'll be safe as long as we are. We will return."

That's not very reassuring. An interstellar military expedition is the last thing I want any part of. What if Avenger meets the same fate as the Nemesis?

Rae Anne's stood and began pacing the cabin.

What can I do to salvage something from this disaster?

She paused and turned to face Thrahn.

"Could I join Captain Vahler on the bridge? A jump to another star system would demonstrate what lies ahead for humanity. It might help me convince reluctant humans to cooperate with Shalcerians when we return."

"We anticipated your request, Rae Anne. We're fabricating a breathing apparatus and a protective suit for you to wear outside your quarters. I'll bring it to you shortly. We plan to leave Earth-orbit in twenty minutes and make the jump in two hours. This will be your first trip through a wormhole, and you should experience it from the bridge. After that, Captain Vahler will decide whether to allow you to remain there."

"Would you contact Jason and send him here? I need his take on our situation."

"Of course. I'll post an alert on the computer."

Thrahn left through the jagged hole in *Aurora's* hull. Rae Anne descended to Level 3 and sat on the lounger. She put her head in her hands in despair.

I need to send a message to Ian. This whole First Contact endeavor will be in his hands until I return. Given the rampant conspiracy theories, I'm not sure anyone will believe our absence is just temporary.

She glanced up when Jason arrived.

"Jason! Where were you? I need to send an urgent message to Ian."

"I was in engineering, probing *Avenger's* archive database. I discovered that three-thousand years ago, the Shalcerian civilization relied totally on very sophisticated robots. But the robots revolted and tried to set up their own society. The resulting civil war nearly destroyed both civilizations. Shalcerians eventually won, and they have restricted the production of fully functional robotic creatures ever since. I'm a rare exception. In fact, …"

"That's great, Jason. Save it for later. Right now, I need to get a message to Ian. He may still be at the United Nations, but the Agency will know how to reach him."

"I can do that. What is the message?"

"*Avenger* is leaving orbit on an emergency run to Alsafi and taking me with them. Reassure the world's leaders that Shalcerians will return and continue negotiations as soon as possible. Urge all nations to meet as planned, with or without us, and formulate realistic plans for meeting the Shalcerian stipulations for cooperation."

"Got it. The message has been sent."

"Good. Now search their database and fill me in on these current events. Who is behind this surprise attack at Alsafi-γ and what precipitated it?"

"One moment while I put the network threads together.

"Ok, got it. The Baltar Alliance attacked Safe Harbor on Alsafi-γ four hours ago and the colony is taking heavy damage. This much came from their combot that just arrived. The Baltar Alliance is comprised of …"

"Save the details, Jason. For now, why are they attacking a Shalcerian colony?"

"Digging through recent event databases. Connecting threads.

"Ok. It appears they are retaliating for a surprise attack on an Alliance convoy. Shalcerians destroyed three Alliance ships while suffering damage to two of their own. The Alliance claimed they were transporting raw materials and support provisions for a new outpost. Shalcerians believe they were carrying weapons and munitions to use against the planet's indigenous population, which violates long-standing interstellar treaties."

"You're saying these two advanced civilizations, with the whole galaxy at their disposal, are in a deadly Hatfield and McCoy conflict? It makes their condescension toward Humans seem a bit cynical."

"The archives indicate the antagonism with the Baltar Alliance goes back many centuries. It may have started when …"

"Later. One other question. Thrahn said the message arrived here just hours after the attack began. Something about a combot. But wouldn't that violate the limitations set by relativity and the speed of light?"

"You're right. Alsafi is 18.81 light years from Earth. Checking. Hmm…

"Ok. A combot is a miniaturized autonomous recording device and transmitter. The sender creates a small wormhole to the destination star system and shoots the device with the message through it. On arrival, the combot transmits an alert on a common frequency. When it's safe to do so, the receiving party sends a code activating it to relay the message on a secured channel."

"So, Shalcerians use the same wormhole technology for combots that they use for interstellar travel, but on a much smaller scale. That's interesting."

Rae Anne raised her hand to her lips, signaling Jason to stop. Thrahn's image appeared on the monitor at the hangar nanoscreen. He was pushing a floating cart containing her suit.

"I only have a few minutes to suit up and get to the bridge before *Avenger* launches for Alsafi. We'll talk later. Are you coming with me?"

"No. I'll stay here and watch events as they come through *Avenger's* computer system. I'll monitor all the ship's sensors when they take it through the wormhole. Should be very informative."

Jason held up a hand.

"Hold on. Reply from the Agency. Penny wants to talk to you directly. I'll put her on speaker."

"Hi Penny. Did you get my message for Ian?"

"Oh, Rae Anne. You haven't heard."

Penny choked, then cleared her throat before continuing.

"There was a terrorist explosion at the U.N. Ian's in Emergency at Bellevue with life-threatening injuries. They've been working on him for four hours already. Martin Lefevre from Public Relations was also seriously injured. And Hikari Yoshida from Astrobiology was killed."

Another audible sob. Rae Anne put her hand to her mouth in disbelief.

Dios mio, this can't be happening. Not now. Not to Ian. Oh god, please let him live. I can't breathe.

Swallowing hard, she tried to speak, but couldn't. Her chest was clamped in a vice. She forced a deep breath and tried again.

"Penny, I won't be available for a while. *Avenger* is leaving within the hour and taking me with it. Please forward my message to President Stratton. It's most important."

Rae Anne could hear Penny crying.

"I can do that, Rae Anne. Please don't be gone long. Ian needs you."

Thrahn appeared inside *Aurora*'s galley on Level 2.

"Rae Anne?" he called. "Are you still here?"

"Thrahn! Stay where you are. I'll be right up."

Rae Anne signed off and wiped the tears from her cheeks with her sleeve. Gritting her teeth with determination to face whatever lay ahead, she climbed the ladder to Level 2. Thrahn was unloading her suit onto the galley table.

"We don't have much time. I'll help you put this on since this is the first time you've seen it. A few of the fasteners are a bit tricky."

When he turned his attention to Rae Anne, he stopped short.

"Is something amiss? You look ashen."

Rae Anne choked back another sob. Given Ian's crucial role in the First Contact negotiations, she didn't want to reveal the attempt on his life.

"A good friend of mine on Earth has been seriously injured in an accident."

Thrahn reached over and placed a hand on her shoulder.

"How terrible. And the worst time to leave. You have my deepest sympathies. I hope your friend fully recovers."

"Thank you, Thrahn." She sighed and wiped her sleeve across her damp face again. "Show me what you've brought."

In short order, Thrahn outfitted Rae Anne for her first excursion into the Shalcerian environment. The suit reminded her of the SEVA suit USIEA fabricated for her seven years earlier for the Mars-II mission. This material was more supple and fit comfortably around her body, and the helmet was much lighter. She patted the small package attached to her belt supplying oxygen to the helmet.

"How long will this last, Thrahn? It's much smaller than the bulky oxygen tanks I'm used to."

"That pack will last two days. It's a thermally insulated cryopack. The oxygen is in a compact crystalline state."

Once she was properly equipped, Thrahn led her through the hole in *Aurora's* hull and across the hangar to the hallway nanoscreen. They passed through, proceeded down the short hall, and entered *Avenger's* airlock.

Waiting for the airlock to cycle, Rae Anne felt her heart rate and breathing increase.

Mierda. Ian's in critical shape and I can't even communicate with him when he needs me. Please, please let him live! The Shalcerians have only begun trying to mend our fractious world and now we have to leave. We've got to make it back for humanity's sake. Earth's future is at stake.

Part Two

Note to Readers

In naming stars, I use common names if available (e.g., Alsafi). When a star has no common name, I employ the International Astronomical Union (IAU) method for naming stars. IAU uses the name of the constellation in which the star is found (e.g., Scorpio) with its possessive ending, preceded by a number designating its brightness relative to the other stars in the constellation. So, 18 Scorpii (the Shalcerian's home system) is the eighteenth brightest star in the Scorpio constellation as seen from Earth.

As for planets, IAU adds a letter suffix, starting with 'b,' to the star's name indicating the order in which the planet was discovered, a typical anthropocentric bias. (The letter 'a' is reserved for the star itself.) However, once a star system is known in its entirety, one logical way to designate a planet would be to reflect its relative distance from its sun. To accommodate this approach, I have used Greek letters, starting with beta (β), then gamma (γ) and delta (δ). So, Earth would be Sol-δ, the third planet out from Sol.

Chapter 1

Aboard *Avenger*

The airlock nanoscreen leading into *Avenger's* labyrinthine corridors opened. Rae Anne blinked to adjust her eyes to the dim blue light radiating from all surfaces. The illumination cast a pallor over everything and made edges stand out in bold relief. But the colors pulsing on Thrahn's body scales appeared bolder in this light, almost fluorescent. He radiated teal swirls over forest green stripes as they stepped through the hatch.

Rae Anne bent her shoulders forward to accommodate the low ceilings. In this light, the nanoscreen ovals were a darker tint than the walls. As Thrahn led her through the maze, Rae Anne noticed that each nanoscreen was labeled with a placard displaying alien glyphs in incandescent colors.

Not so different from a Human office building. Just gotta keep from cracking my skull on the low ceilings. I'm clearly the alien here.

As they moved deeper into *Avenger,* activity increased. Rae Anne marveled at how swiftly Shalcerians bustled about without colliding. They proved adept at using as many of their six appendages for movement as they saw fit, often affixing their suction cup digits to a wall or even the ceiling and dangling to the side to dodge each other as they scurried along.

Reminds me of the monkey house in a zoo. I wonder if I will ever be able to tell them apart. Relative size is all I've got so far, and that's not much help.

"So, Thrahn, this combot from Alsafi. Will *Avenger* retrieve it before leaving the Solar System?"

"Not likely. We sent out a drone to pick it up. We'll find them when we return. It could be anywhere."

Thrahn turned abruptly and stepped through a nanoscreen. Rae Anne followed and found herself on *Avenger's* bridge. She felt a spasm of vertigo and gasped. It was as if she had stepped off the ship and into deep space. She stood motionless for several seconds to allow her eyes to adjust to the darkness.

The room was inside a huge dimly lighted sphere. The transparent platform on which she stood bisected the sphere, lending a literal meaning to the word 'bridge.' Projected against the inside walls of this bubble were real-time holographic images of the space surrounding *Avenger*, seamlessly fit together. Star maps, charts, and symbols in diverse colors overlaid this background. Any position on the deck away from the walls provided a 360-degree three-dimensional view of the universe surrounding the ship.

Wow. This is the mother of 'heads up' displays. I just walked through the sun and that tiny blue disk must be Earth. I can't believe how fast it's receding. And here we are, surrounded by a star canopy and the Milky Way.

Rae Anne counted ten crewmembers, including the captain, on the bridge platform, each focused on the consoles before them. On closer observation, Rae Anne discovered that these, too, were elaborate holograms appearing and disappearing as needed. Though they were virtual images, the crew interacted with them as though they were real, pressing virtual buttons, adjusting dials and virtual switches as they watched their monitor readouts.

This room must be filled with sensors that follow each crew member's motions. The hologram consoles display controls as touch screens. The sensors record their finger positions and movements as though they touched an icon on an actual physical screen. Surreal!

All the crew wore special gloves, lending credence to her speculation.

Captain Vahler halted his stream of commands and turned to Rae Anne and Thrahn.

"Welcome to my bridge, Rae Anne. We'll be making the jump to Alsafi shortly. The wormhole will appear directly ahead, opposite the hatch you came through. Stay alert and be ready for a slight jolt as the ship passes through to the other side."

He turned his attention back to his console. The computer began to bark staccato chirps at even intervals, sounding to Rae Anne like a countdown to launch. She felt the floor vibrating beneath her feet with greater and greater intensity.

As she peered at the virtual display directly ahead, stars began to elongate and rotate in a weird spiral motion. They soon coalesced into a blur that became more intense as their rotation accelerated. Within seconds, they morphed into a brilliant blue-white disk. Rae Anne's stomach flipped at the disorienting physical and visual effects.

The star-disk abruptly ruptured, revealing a growing black spot fringed with red and orange in its center. The hole rapidly expanded, with the iridescent halo mixing into a blend of deep purple. The hole, blacker than any black Rae Anne had ever experienced, grew larger and more menacing until it dwarfed the ship.

With a sudden lurch, *Avenger* plunged into the abyss. Rae Anne stepped backward to catch her balance. For an instant, she had the distinct impression that time, and perhaps life itself, had stopped. But before she could pinpoint the feeling, everything returned to normal. The throbbing vibrations ceased. An orangish star glowed dead ahead—Alsafi.

The wormhole transit lasted just fifteen seconds. Yet in that time, *Avenger* had jumped the 18.8 light year gap between the two-star systems.

Captain Vahler broadcast a message to Safe Harbor that help was at hand and requested their current status. He turned his center eyestalk to Rae Anne.

"We're one light-hour from the planet, approaching at two-thirds lightspeed, so we have ninety minutes before we arrive. Normally we don't wormhole so close to a planet or approach at this speed, but this is an emergency. It will take an hour for my message to reach the colony and another 20 minutes before we receive their response. That will give us 10 minutes before arrival to devise an appropriate strategy.

"You're welcome to return to the bridge at any time. If we are forced to engage the Baltar, you will see *Avenger* at its best."

"Thank you, Captain. I'll plan to be here."

So much for any hope aliens might have evolved beyond warfare. I need to maintain a healthy skepticism as we negotiate with the Shalcerians. We shouldn't be expected to take sides in a conflict that we know nothing about.

As Rae Anne left the bridge with Thrahn, she paid special attention to their winding path back to her quarters and counted the nanoscreens they passed.

I don't want to miss any actions or wormhole transits if I can help it.

Chapter 2

Alsafi System

Once in her quarters, Rae Anne removed her helmet and oxygen pack and laid them on the table, then stripped out of her protective suit. She turned and headed into the hangar bay and *Aurora*. Stepping through the hole in the ship's hull, she wondered if she could get the Shalcerian engineers to fix it.

Jason was puttering around on Level 3 below.

"So, Jason, what did you learn about the wormhole drive while it was in operation?" she called as she prepared a mug of hot tea in the galley.

Jason appeared through the hatch in the floor and stepped into the galley.

"Quite a bit, as a matter of fact. It's a good thing they forget I'm a robot. I engage them in social conversation, pretending to bumble around to learn their language, although I now speak it fluently. This gives me the opportunity to observe their equipment in operation. I'm also tapping into their computer system and forging deeper into their data banks."

Rae Anne raised her eyebrows and stared at him. "Are you really fluent in Shalcerian?" She squeezed the teabag and set it on the counter while recalling the incomprehensible chatter she overheard on the bridge.

"It's not hard if you're a computer. Once you know the vocabulary, the clicks and buzzes and whistles are phonemes peculiar to their language. Their grammar and syntax are much simpler than English. Humans could learn from them, but I suppose it's too late for that."

Rae Anne sipped at her steaming tea.

"What about the wormhole drive?"

"I was probing the engineering files on their propulsion devices as we made the jump. Humans are centuries, maybe millennia, behind Shalcerians."

"No surprise there. Go on."

"Wormhole technology is dependent on manipulating black holes, so I need to begin there. To start with, Shalcerians have devised a gravity bottle to contain black holes."

Rae Ann abruptly swiveled on her stool to face Jason. "You've got to be kidding. Black holes are huge!"

"Those that form the central pivot of galaxies are huge. But the Big Bang produced an uncountable number of microscopic black holes, along with the quarks and electrons that eventually combined to make matter. The universe is still awash with them. Shalcerians have learned how to capture them. *Avenger's* gravity bottle contains two micro black holes. As small as they are, they are still quite massive. The ones in *Avenger's* gravity bottle each have a mass equivalent to Earth's moon."

"If *Avenger* is carrying so much mass, what keeps it from affecting nearby planets and moons?"

"The gravity bottle insulates the surroundings from their masses, so *Avenger's* mass appears the same as if it had no black holes. But here's the interesting part."

"What could be more interesting than containing black holes in gravity bottles?" Rae Anne shook her head and laughed.

"Shalcerians have a different understanding of black holes from how Humans think of them. For starters, tell me what you think you know about black holes."

Rae Anne put her cup on the table and ran a hand through her hair, pursing her lips in thought.

"What I know seems pretty simple. When an object concentrates enough mass in a limited space, even light can't escape its gravitational field and the object becomes a black hole. Surrounding the black hole is a threshold called the event horizon, and light and anything else crossing the threshold gets sucked in, never to return. Everything gets drawn down to the black hole's center point, a mathematical singularity. And the black hole keeps gaining mass by sucking in the stars and gasses surrounding it."

"Well, here's what Shalcerians have discovered. First off, forget about the singularity. Even Human mathematicians and physicists hate singularities. They don't make sense. A ka-jillion tons of mass concentrated in a dimensionless point. Utter nonsense.

"Next, expand your thinking to visualize our universe as being composed of hundreds, maybe thousands, of dimensions beyond the three we perceive. Before the Big Bang, there was nothing. No space. No matter. No energy. No time. I'll call this the Void to differentiate it from what we think of as Space.

"Now, suddenly, the Big Bang gives birth to our universe. The moment it bursts on the scene, Space begins surging outward into the Void in all its multiple dimensions. Space thus has an edge, the Space/Void Boundary, like an island's shoreline on a vast sea, where our universe and its multi-dimensional space is the island and the Void is the sea."

"Wait." Rae Anne lifted her hand in front of her like a cop intending to stop traffic.

"If our universe has thousands of dimensions, then each of these dimensions is its own island and has its own shoreline. So, there are lots of shorelines."

"Yes and no. Each dimension has its own shoreline, but there is only one Void, so all these shorelines are interconnected throughout multidimensional space.

"Now here's the thing. Every point in our three-dimensional world is located on a Space/Void Boundary in one or another of the other dimensions. So, if we select Point A in our x-y-z three dimensions, Point A is connected to hundreds of p-q-r Point Bs in various combinations of different dimensions, and one of these points will be on the Space/Void Boundary."

"I'm already having trouble envisioning this."

"Well, maybe an analogy will help.

"Consider Mary Twodee who lives in a two-dimensional universe. She can only perceive things in two dimensions. So, Mary Twodee is watching television in her two-dimensional living room having a glass of two-dimensional wine when a sphere passes through her living room. What does she see? First a point on the rug appears and changes to a circle. The circle expands until it reaches the sphere's diameter. Then it contracts to a point and disappears. There is no way for Mary Twodee to conceptually imagine what happened, let alone envision what a sphere looks like.

"We're in the same predicament regarding dimensions other than the three we are familiar with. But given this example, imagine a black hole as a sphere in which the entire inner surface is on the Space/Void Boundary. Everything inside the sphere is the Void. So, black holes actually are physical holes in Space. Space is like a mammoth block of Swiss cheese floating in the Void."

Rae Anne rubbed her forehead to fight the same feeling of vertigo she felt earlier when she stepped onto *Avenger's* bridge.

"Where does the event horizon come into all this? What happens to all the matter that gets sucked into a black hole?"

"The event horizon, that point in space where matter flowing into a black hole disappears because light itself becomes trapped, is not important in the Shalcerian understanding of black holes. As matter approaches the black hole, its orbit around the black hole gets tighter and its velocity increases. At some point, its orbit spirals through the event horizon. This is like stepping across the state line between Kansas and Colorado. It has no significance, because the matter continues to spiral inward faster and faster until it is converted to pure energy. At that point, we are at the Space/Void Boundary which marks the black hole's true inner edge. Everything beyond that edge is nothingness, the Void."

"Then, from what you're saying, the size of a black hole is smaller than Humans assume, with its surface boundary being some distance inside the event horizon rather than defined by the event horizon. But what about the mass of all the stuff that gets gobbled up?"

"By the time matter reaches the Space/Void Boundary, it has been converted to pure energy and its waveforms become resonant with the boundary. There is no matter-mass associated with a black hole. The 'mass' of a black hole is the energy equivalent of all the mass it has swallowed, based on Einstein's $E = mc^2$ equation. All that energy is contained at the Space/Void boundary."

"Whew. This will take some time to sink in. Einstein should have added another 'fudge factor' constant to his equations to account for black holes."

"Einstein himself was never happy about the singularity problem."

"We need to know more about gravity bottles and the science behind them. And how do they locate and capture micro blackholes in the first place?"

"I'll keep searching through their computer archives. If the information is there, I'll find it."

Rae Anne stood and turned toward the hole in *Aurora's* hull.

"While you're doing that, I need to suit up again and head back to the bridge. As much as I despise war, if there's going to be a firefight between two alien species, I want to be there to see it.

Chapter 3

Alsafi System

As *Avenger* swept toward the beleaguered outpost on Alsafi-γ, Captain Vahler was taking advantage of the Baltar natural bias toward low frequency infrared sensitivity. He hoped the blue shift to higher frequencies due to their velocity might keep *Avenger* from being detected until he was ready to engage, although he knew their gravity wave detectors had alerted them to his arrival inside the system. Having received no response from the colony, he could only expect the worst.

Five light-minutes from the planet, *Avenger* rapidly decelerated to orbital speed and assumed a highly elliptical orbit. Sensors revealed three Baltar attack cruisers in close orbit with their fighters swooping through the atmosphere and wreaking destruction on everything in their path.

A wide nanoscreen opened atop the aft third of *Avenger's* hull, revealing the flight deck and dozens of fighter disks stacked three deep like poker chips. *Avenger* swung closer to Alsafi-γ. On Vahler's command, bevies of fighters rose from the launching bays and sped into the conflict.

The Baltar cruisers acknowledged *Avenger's* arrival with a barrage of explosive bursts that surrounded the battlecruiser, a fireworks display like nothing Rae Anne had ever experienced. Several struck the cruiser head-on, causing the giant ship to shudder but causing no damage.

Avenger returned fire, focusing its torpedoes on the nearest Baltar cruiser. A deep rumble reverberated through the ship with each launch. Several bright flashes splayed against the Baltar ship's midsection in rapid succession and a blinding red-orange flash tore the ship apart. A spray of white-hot debris spewed into space in every direction.

Baltar fighters were diverted from the ground assault to engage *Avenger's* fighter formations in orbit. Rae Anne viewed these skirmishes on the deck's holographic displays. Baltar technology appeared to rely on high-energy lasers and thermobaric missiles, neither of which proved effective against the GESC-Plasticore hulls of the Shalcerian fighters.

The Shalcerian strategy assumed a different mode of attack. Relying on their nearly impervious hulls and structural integrity, Shalcerian pilots used their fighter disks as precision scimitars, slashing through their opposition with great effect. With superior speed and maneuverability, a fighter disk could trail a Baltar fighter, pull up alongside it, then cut sharply into it and slice it cleanly in two. The force of impact tossed the flaming remnants into widely diverging arcs, spewing trails of flaming debris.

When a Baltar pilot scored a lucky hit on a fighter disk's vulnerable spot, the fighter's plasma bubble would burst into space, resulting in a searing white flash. Occasionally, the blast of energy might engulf the Baltar fighter, converting it into an accompanying molten mass of burning debris spiraling into the planet's atmosphere.

Soon, *Avenger* came within range of the Baltar fighters, and they began harassing *Avenger* like a horde of mosquitoes. Blast after blast burst against the battle cruiser's hull as they searched for a vulnerable spot. Rae Anne felt the ship shudder with each strike. *Avenger's* fighter disks surrounded the ship to ward off the swarm, keeping them on the defensive. Occasionally, a disabled fighter would plunge directly into *Avenger,* creating a plume of fiery debris arcing into the void. Fragments and shards from destroyed fighters surrounded *Avenger* like a cloud.

The two remaining Baltar cruisers attempted a coordinated pincer movement toward *Avenger,* lasers and missiles spraying the ship in a continuous stream of fire. *Avenger* lashed back against the exposed flanks of the two approaching vessels. A lucky hit amidship on one Baltar cruiser's port side created a bright flash of white and yellow, followed by a ghastly red fountain spraying into space. The ship spun to starboard and began a crazy spiral out of orbit, the red plume forming a corkscrew in its wake. Escape pods popped off the cruiser and veered steeply into the safety of the planet's atmosphere.

A fourth Baltar cruiser appeared out of nowhere, speeding into the fray directly toward *Avenger*. A blistering barrage of laser fire swept over *Avenger'*s hull, searching for a vulnerability. In the last second, it arced upward to avoid an inevitable collision and disappeared into the void. But just prior to doing so, it threw a massive volley of ordinance at the one weak spot the lasers had discovered.

A jarring thump knocked Rae Anne to the deck. Regaining her feet, she watched a spray of red-hot metal spurting away from *Avenger*'s midsection, illuminated by greenish-blue Cherenkov radiation from one of *Avenger's* reactor cores.

Mierda. We've been hit. Please, don't let us explode like the cruisers we destroyed! I need to get back to Earth.

Vahler issued commands to his bridge crew faster than the translator could keep up with. But his demeanor showed no sign of anxiety. He ordered the ship be directed toward the remaining Baltar cruiser.

The Baltar captain swung his ship to port. Its engines flared brightly at full power, and the ship disappeared into the depths of space.

Over the next hour, *Avenger's* fighter-disks mopped up the Baltar fighters that had been left behind. Abandoning all hope, several fighters turned toward *Avenger* and dived directly into its hull, hoping to damage the ship in a Kamikaze attack. *Avenger's* fighters maneuvered to keep the attackers from *Avenger's* gaping wound lest they cause further damage. Vahler directed the ship toward the planet to assume a close-in orbit.

With the last of the Baltar fighters dispatched, Shalcerian fighter disks returned to the hangar deck. Once all surviving fighters had been accounted for, Vahler ordered the flight deck secured. Rae Anne noticed several gaps in the ranks before the giant nanoscreen obscured her view.

A damage control crew emerged onto *Avenger's* hull in full EVA attire and began working to contain the breach. Several mechanical arms and platforms protruded from the ship and surrounded the jagged hole, reminding Rae Anne of a skyscraper construction site.

Captain Vahler turned to Rae Anne, his scale colors a uniform dark gray. Rae Anne could see moisture glittering in his eye sockets.

"We lost 35 of our crew. That fourth Baltar cruiser must have been lying quiet, waiting for our arrival. They had plenty of advance notice, given the inevitable gravity waves produced by a wormhole transit.

"So, now you have a taste of our technical and tactical superiority when it comes to facing the Empire's enemies. Had we maintained our military presence here, Safe Harbor would have been spared. Our battlecruisers have far more important missions than running security on your Kuiper Belt. Human patrols will help enhance the Empire's security.

"Shortly we'll send teams to the surface and see what we can do for the survivors. With the intensity of the Baltar onslaught, we'll not likely find many. You're welcome to join my team."

"I'd be happy to join you. How badly has *Avenger* been damaged?"

"The plasma containment vessel on one of our propulsion units was breached. We'll limp to Shalkor for repairs after redirecting power from the ship's power reactor to the remaining two propulsion units."

"Will that take long?"

"Between seven and ten days, barring any unexpected difficulties."

So, we aren't returning to Earth anytime soon. What's worse is the Shalcerians have suffered a major loss here. What was it Thrahn said just weeks ago? 'The only difference is we have more powerful weapons.'

Rae Anne followed Captain Vahler below decks to *Avenger's* escape pods being repurposed as rescue vehicles. Thrahn appeared at her side as they boarded one of the pods. He was pulling his floating cart piled high with supplies.

I can't imagine how our delay will affect negotiations on Earth. Nothing good, I'm sure. And then there's Ian. God, I hope he's doing ok.

Chapter 4

Earth

News of *Avenger's* departure spread like wildfire through media outlets around the world. For many of Earth's citizens, it brought a sigh of relief. Fear of the unknown, fear of change, and fear of such odd-looking creatures and what their motives in dealing with Humans might be all played a part.

Others experienced shock and dismay at the lost opportunity. Most of the scientific community felt this way. These could only hope the Shalcerians would keep their promise of a timely return.

At the Agency, Ian's close colleagues were doubly devastated. Not only were three of their team caught in the terrorist explosion, but the very cause to which they had dedicated themselves night and day for six weeks had apparently evaporated. Most were certain the Shalcerians would return, but they all felt they had lost the momentum they had worked so hard to generate. They worried that *Avenger's* abrupt departure would create widespread distrust of Shalcerians and their reliability.

Penny forwarded Rae Anne's message to President Stratton who passed it on to the UN Secretary General. President Stratton also contacted General Adam Freemont in the Pentagon to take over in Ian's absence as head of her own First Contact task force. Although General Freemont had been part of the group from the beginning, he himself had reservations about jumping into any agreement with the aliens before learning more about them.

"We should proceed cautiously," the general advised. "There's no question their advanced technology would provide us with a tremendous leap forward, but I don't believe they've been totally honest about what they expect of us."

"How do you propose we solve that dilemma, General?" President Stratton studied his face on her monitor, noting the deep furrows etched into his forehead. Of all her military advisors, he was the person she trusted most. He always called things as he saw them, regardless of the consequences to himself or his career. And he was usually right.

"There are so many diplomatic hurdles to overcome right now, I suggest we encourage cooperating with the aliens and continue making progress while they are away. If things reach the point where real negotiations are possible, we can then insist on more information and transparency."

POTUS nodded agreement and signed off. Next, she called the head of the FBI to see if they had made progress in identifying who had bombed the U.N.

"We're still gathering evidence from the scene. Mostly, fragments from the trash can the bomb was placed in, although we have enough chemical evidence to identify the explosive. That may be of some help."

"Someone must be on camera depositing the explosive."

"We've investigated that angle. Unfortunately, the camera in the portico facing the trash can was not operating. Other cameras lead to only one suspect, a trash collector who emptied the can the day before. All we have on him is his general size. He could have placed the bomb in the can after emptying out the trash."

"I don't suppose he matches with any of the trash company's employees."

"No one matches his description, as vague as it is. We're interrogating the hauler who runs that route. He may have given a uniform and his keys to our perp. But he's keeping mum. So far."

Havel poked his head around the corner and reported that Ian and his colleague, Martin, were both still unconscious in Bellevue's ICU. For both, the prognosis was guarded. Neither had lost limbs from the explosion, but whole or partial paralysis was a definite possibility. Further diagnosis would await their regaining consciousness.

At the U.N., the Secretary General assigned the First Contact issue to his key subordinate with instructions that the process of ironing out details for cooperating with the Shalcerians must continue according to schedule despite the aliens' departure and Ian's absence. He hoped a unanimous international agreement could be achieved before *Avenger* returned. If it returned.

Over Indiana

Karen's ringer tone sounded on Sam's phone next to his laptop on the worktable aboard his corporate jet. He was 32,000 feet over Indiana on route to his Jackson Hole ranch, having finished his business in New York City. He frowned at the distraction but picked up the phone and answered.

"We did it Sam!" she gushed. "They saw the writing on the wall and left. We're home free!"

Sam had never known Karen to act so giddy. Her speech was slurred, leading him to believe she'd hit the champagne to celebrate *Avenger's* departure.

She probably thinks the explosion she orchestrated convinced them to leave.

"Not so fast, Karen. First, you're not on a secure line. Second, they promised to return. I believe they will. You and I both know how unexpected circumstances can temporarily interrupt progress in business negotiations. This just proves that these aliens aren't so different from us, despite how they look. Shit happens to them, too."

"Well, we'll just have to see about that."

Sam thought he might have let a little air out of her balloon.

"So, Sam, while I've been doing my part, with great success I might add, what have you been doing?" Karen couldn't keep from sounding boastful.

"Just what I said I would do. I'm lobbying influential parties to consider alternatives they might not have thought of. Sowing seeds of doubt. Whether my efforts are successful will be determined in time. With the aliens gone for now, there's no pressure for quick decisions. Debates will likely go on for weeks. Gives time for our nuclear fusion ad campaigns to reach the broader market."

The Kremlin

"What are we to do with our missiles, General Chernov? The one's we reprogrammed for the alien vessel." The voice on the secured military line sounded relieved. His orders had been to launch five nuclear missiles at 16:42 UTC, the very moment *Avenger* would have crossed over the horizon into view. When *Avenger* didn't appear, he must have found himself at a loss for what to do.

The general sipped from the bottle of vodka he kept locked in his desk and savored the warm glow as it trickled down his throat. With thousands of missiles in his nuclear arsenal, the five relegated to *Avenger* wouldn't be missed.

"Leave them programmed as they are. And stay on red alert. The aliens said they would return. If they do, they'll likely assume the same polar orbit. We'll be ready for them. They won't know what hit them."

The old-fashioned red rotary dial phone on his desk buzzed. This was the call he had been waiting for. He reached across the desk and lifted the handset to his ear. Only one caller ever used this phone.

"Army General Chernov here, Mister President…Yes, we heard the good news, too…Yes, had they not left, their ship would never have completed another orbit…That's kind of you to say, Mister President. I thank you for your confidence…Yes, I agree. They probably will return…Red alert? That's an excellent idea, Mister President. I'll see to it immediately…. Thank you, sir. You have a pleasant weekend too."

The general replaced the handset and inhaled deeply. He took a gulp from his bottle and forced his mind to recall every word of his conversation with the president.

That went well. I don't think I said anything that would turn him against me. It's not yet late. Irena may still be up for a short visit before I head to my dacha.

Chapter 5

Alsafi-γ

Three rescue pods dropped from orbit and descended into Alsafi-γ's thick atmosphere. They drifted over Safe Harbor's smoldering remains, pausing periodically to probe potential shelters that might hold survivors. Rae Anne gazed at the desolation below, a blackened landscape, charred beams of collapsed buildings, their skeletal remains thrust upward through the rubble as if pleading for mercy. Total devastation stretched as far as she could see.

She glanced at Thrahn. Puddles had formed atop his torso from the tears that streamed down his eyestalks. The scales on his chest were a dull slate gray.

"So many lost," he murmured. "So many…"

Rae Anne choked down the lump in her throat. She sorely needed someone to hug, a shoulder to cry on. Her chest felt like it was being crushed in a vice. The loss of life seemed too much to bear.

The pod hovered momentarily, sensors probing for survivors. There were none. They moved on. Clouds of smoke blackened the sky to the north.

They continued to scan the surface in ever widening circles. At the outer edges of the scorched area, the pod came to a halt and descended to the surface. Thrahn and eight crew members clustered near the hatch.

When it opened, acrid smoke drifted into the ship. Rae Anne shivered and was thankful for the protection offered by her suit. She watched Thrahn float his cart down the ramp toward a massive pile of rubble. A narrow break in the rock jumble led to an intact underground shelter. She followed Thrahn without hesitation, hoping to be of help.

Inside the shelter, dozens of survivors huddled in small groups. Thrahn unloaded his emergency medical equipment and handed supplies to his aides.

Soon, they began escorting the survivors to the rescue pod. Several needed to be transported on stretchers. Rae Anne wrapped her arms around two children at the back wall and helped them outside and into the ship. She settled them against the hull and covered them with a blanket. Then she scurried back into the shelter.

She helped lift a victim onto a stretcher and found six traumatized children huddled in a corner. She lifted the oldest to his feet and hugged him tightly to provide some reassurance. He showed no surprise or discomfort at Rae Anne's alien shape. Then she turned him toward the others and gestured toward them. He understood her intent and helped her bring the other children into the pod. When everyone was safely aboard, the escape pod lifted and Vahler continued his search.

They searched unrelentingly for two days. Rae Anne snagged short naps between stops, at one point curled up under the blanket with the first two children she had helped. In the end, they picked up 237 survivors, nearly half in need of medical attention. Captain Vahler seemed satisfied that they had canvassed the area sufficiently and ordered everyone to return to *Avenger*.

As they rose into the yellow-green sky, Rae Anne caught a glimpse of Alsafi, the red dwarf sun. It cast a vivid red-orange hue on the clouds below. Dense blue-green jungle carpeted the landscape. A wide river meandered through the trees like a dark purple python.

The first Human glimpse of an alien world. And interstellar war. Is competition and warfare imprinted in all sentient brains?

Repairs on *Avenger's* hull were ongoing when they returned. The hull breach was much smaller than before, with fresh plasticore shimmering in Alsafi's pale red glow, contrasting with the neighboring panels still covered with battle debris.

Rae Anne waited to catch the captain when he was free.

"Captain Vahler? Do you have a minute?"

The captain turned two eyestalks in her direction.

"Oh, Rae Anne. I forgot you were with us. Such a tragedy. Over twenty-thousand citizens lost. The Baltar will pay for this atrocity."

The computer voice captured his frustration and anger.

"I am deeply saddened at your loss. This must be a hard time for you."

"It isn't the first time. And it won't be the last. What can I do for you?"

"I was wondering how long it might take to repair *Avenger.*"

"The crew is almost finished with the hull repairs. It may be another week before we can head for Shalkor. The ship's power reactor isn't designed to be used for propulsion. Once we have repurposed it to the propulsion unit, we will have jump capability, but with less power. We'll have to break our journey home into two jumps."

"So, it may be a while before we return to Earth?"

"Depending on the availability of a replacement reactor at Shalkor and an engineering crew to install and test it, it may be several weeks before we can return to your Sol system."

Rae Anne's heart sank.

What a setback. All I can do is use the time to get to know these people and their empire better.

Oh, Ian. I hope you're doing all right.

Before she could leave the bridge, Captain Vahler addressed her.

"Rae Anne, you may find this interesting." He gestured to the view on the bridge monitor to her left.

Amidst the star-studded background, one bright spot caught her attention. It grew dimmer by the second.

"We are sending a combot to Shalkor, our home world. When the combot reaches a safe distance from *Avenger*, we will create a miniature wormhole. For such a small object, 300 kilometers is sufficiently far away to keep the warp we create in space/time from affecting our ship."

As she watched, the white pinpoint tripled in size and turned bright pink, changing to crimson. A shimmering blue and white halo formed around the angry red eye and twisted and reformed into a Möbius strip of color. The tortured space around this region twisted with it, causing the starlight beaming through to distort into fantastic shapes while being red shifted to longer frequencies before disappearing into the infrared.

An unfathomably black spot opened within the ring of fire, like a chasm into hell. The combot disappeared into this orifice with a brilliant white flash. The wormhole closed like a sphincter and disappeared, returning the starfield to normal.

Avenger's mammoth bulk experienced a series of sharp jolts when the resulting gravity waves washed through the ship.

"That was awesome," Rae Anne marveled, still staring at the screen where the small craft had vanished. "It looked like what we experienced when *Avenger* jumped from Sol to Alsafi."

"The process is identical. But with a ship of *Avenger's* size, the ripples left behind are much more powerful.

"Besides reporting this attack and the tragedy of our losses, I sent a request for a rehab berth in our shipyards and for a new propulsion reactor. The advance notice may shorten our stay at Shalkor."

"You mentioned an intermediate stop on the way. Where will that be?"

"12 Ophiuchi will be our first destination. We'll be there about three days while our reactor storage-units recharge, then we'll jump to Shalkor. Engineering just reported we should be ready for the jump to 12 Ophiuchi in six days, barring unforeseen problems."

Alsafi-γ Orbit

"Tell me all you know about 12 Ophiuchi, Jason," Rae Anne asked when she returned to *Aurora* from the bridge. She flopped on the Level 3 lounger in exhaustion fringed with despair.

"12 Ophiuchi is a bright red dwarf 31.81 light years from Earth, but only 18.62 light years from here. Why do you ask?"

"We'll be going to the Shalcerian home world for repairs before returning to Earth. Since the propulsion system is damaged, Captain Vahler is making the trip in two jumps, the first to 12 Ophiuchi. How many planets does that system have?"

"Earth astronomers haven't yet found any, but Shalcerian archives list four small, rocky planets, with several Shalcerian colonies on 12 Ophiuchi-δ. There is also an indigenous species, the Belkiri, on that planet. They belong to the empire's Interstellar Consortium."

"We'll be there six days. I hope I'll have a chance for landfall before we move on. Take in the scenery, maybe even meet one of these Belkiri creatures.

"But tell me about the Baltar Alliance and this feud between them and the Shalcerians."

"My sole resource is the *Avenger* archives, so what I tell you will be biased toward the Shalcerian perspective.

"First, both empires are nearly equal in size and resources. 435 years ago, exploration vessels from both empires entered the same star system with plans for colonization. Shalcerians say the Baltar fired the first shot. In any case, thousands of lives were lost and dozens of ships were destroyed. Subsequent years saw numerous hit-and-run attacks by both sides on established colonies and on commercial freighters."

"It's a large universe. Why didn't they just move on and find a different world to colonize?"

"Something about a third empire, the Tanzar Union, which abuts both their borders. It is much larger than the Shalcerian and Baltar empires combined. Very little is known about the Tanzar. Every effort to penetrate their borders has ended badly for the Shalcerians. They believe the Tanzar's technology is far more advanced than their own."

"From my Human perspective, that's impossible to imagine."

Rae Anne stretched and yawned deeply. She pulled a blanket draped on the armrest over her body and snuggled her head into the lounger headrest.

"I can't remember when I've been so tired. I hope you appreciate what an advantage you have as an android."

She closed her eyes and yawned again.

Six days until the 12 Ophiuchi jump, add another three days there, and who knows how long at Shalkor. I'll be lucky if I'm back home by Christmas.

A dark thought she couldn't dismiss crossed her mind, causing her to shudder.

Ian damn well better be alive when I get back.

Chapter 6

12 Ophiuchi-δ

Rae Anne squinched her eyes and inhaled deeply, burning the image of the kaleidoscopic fireworks she just witnessed into her memory. Her body tingled from the momentary lapse in time that accompanied the wormhole jump to the 12 Ophiuchi system.

The holographic view ahead displayed a steadily growing red-orange sun and three bright planets in the black sphere that surrounded the bridge platform. The nearest planet became a sphere, half illuminated by the red dwarf.

"That's 12 Ophiuchi-δ, our destination." Captain Vahler pointed toward the tiny orb.

"We'll arrive in 1.3 hours. It will take three days to recharge our reactors and check them out before initiating another jump. Engineering reported that this last jump put the substitute reactor under considerable stress."

"Could I visit one of the colonies while we're here?"

"I'll be going down to Quanara, our system capital, for a short diplomatic mission. You and Thrahn may accompany me. He's been there before. He can take you on a quick tour of the city. We'll depart tomorrow at 18:30 hours."

Good. That will give me time to get a full night's rest.

The next day, the landing shuttle, larger than the combat fighters but smaller than an escape pod, lifted from *Avenger's* flight deck and glided downward into the planet's pea-green atmosphere. The surface below was an arid desert of mottled reds and browns, reminding Rae

Anne of Mars. Like Mars, the only clouds were vague horsetail whisps of white sparsely dispersed over the planet's surface.

As they drew closer to the surface, she discerned several dark circles dotting the landscape like center-pivot irrigation circles seen on Earth. Sunlight glinting off their surface revealed that they were craters filled with water. Cracks and ravines in the dry surface became larger and more numerous as they approached.

The shuttle paused above the transparent dome over Quanara. Rae Anne watched for an opening to appear, but instead, a section of the dome began to sparkle like sunlight on water. The shuttle dropped through the shimmering nanoparticles and into the enclosed space below. Once they had cleared the dome, it became transparent again.

The shuttle settled on a square landing pad in the City Center. Seven hovercraft landed near the shuttle and discharged ten city officials, all Shalcerians, who arranged themselves in a triangle like pins in a bowling alley. Captain Vahler was first to leave the shuttle, followed by the rest of the *Avenger* delegation.

The lone individual nearest the shuttle greeted Captain Vahler when he emerged from the shuttle with the usual hand gestures and flashy displays of color on his chest scales. He then introduced the captain to the other officials and presented him with a ceremonial medallion.

Rae Anne began to gasp for breath. Her fingers desperately searched for a control on her respirator.

Mierda. I can't breathe!

She turned to Thrahn for help, but he signaled for her to wait. Three crewmembers accompanied Captain Vahler aboard a local aircar. The city contingent boarded their hovercraft and they all lifted off for the City Administration Facility.

Even before liftoff, Thrahn quickly turned and grasped Rae Anne under both arms to keep her from slumping to the pavement. Calling on an associate to help, he led her aboard the shuttle and settled her onto a bench. Her sensation of heaviness evaporated the moment she stepped through the hatch.

Thrahn let her hand drop. His scales rippled a light violet and yellow, the Shalcerian equivalent of laughter.

"Gravity here is twice Earth's," he explained. "Since our ship maintains a constant 1/6-G, this is twelve times what we're accustomed to. I myself felt like I was being crushed by an Orkashan awksander! I should have warned you."

"How can I visit the city?" Rae Anne asked with disappointment. "I won't hold up under this oppressive gravity."

"We have a hovercar aboard the shuttle that is made of plasticore, so we'll be comfortably ensconced in 1/6 gravity. Since it will be just the two of us, I'll set the environmental controls to provide your oxygen atmosphere and I'll wear my respirator. You should feel right at home."

"Thank you, Thrahn. When can we go?"

"Right away. We only have a couple hours before returning to *Avenger*, so we mustn't waste any time. Follow me to the cargo bay."

Rae Anne followed Thrahn through a nanoscreen and a corridor that wound along the hull and ended at an airlock. They passed through the two nanoscreens and entered a large hangar with several small craft. Thrahn motioned to one near the hangar door and put on his respirator as he performed his preflight check to be sure nothing was amiss.

When they were seated in the cabin, Thrahn adjusted the environment controls until he was satisfied with the information displayed on the monitor.

"You can remove your respirator now, Rae Anne. We won't be able to leave the hovercraft, but at least you'll be able to see the sights. I'll take you out to the perimeter first so you can look out through the dome and imagine what life must be like for the Belkiri."

The hovercraft lifted from the deck and passed through the hangar nanoscreen. Thrahn directed the machine to follow a wide boulevard that wound through a maze of tall buildings in the center of the city and out through an area filled with manufacturing plants and ore processing facilities. It ended at the Outer Ring Road, which followed the dome's inner circumference.

Rae Anne gazed through the transparent dome at the forsaken landscape beyond.

Dios mio. The dull red sun is twice the size of Sol but it's no brighter out there than on Earth. And not a cloud in that pea soup sky.

"How could any species survive on this planet?"

"12 Ophiuchi-δ is often struck by asteroids and comets. The comets supply all the water the Belkiri need. The asteroids provide carbonaceous substances they harvest for nutrients. I shouldn't be surprised if we experience a quake from a collision while we're here."

"That explains the roundish nature of the lakes we passed over. Will we see any natives while we're here?"

"Not likely. Never in the city. They can't tolerate even the slightest exposure to our atmosphere. Outside, on the surface, you may see one of their vehicles, but seldom an individual. 12 Ophiuchi is a red dwarf and frequently showers the planet with deadly X-rays."

"I studied red dwarfs on my trip to Saturn. I assumed unstable stars like 12 Ophiuchi would make life on their planets impossible. I'm amazed life could evolve and thrive under these conditions."

"Life is much more flexible and resilient than you might think. Almost every world with an atmosphere we have visited has some form of life. And where life exists, life evolves."

Thrahn gestured toward the red-brown expanse outside the dome.

"There. There's a Belkiri transport vehicle."

Lumbering along a straight, narrow ribbon highway beneath rugged bluffs, a torpedo shaped tractor on tank-like treads pulled three huge trailers on wheels and sprayed a rooster tail of fine red dust high in its wake. Three drones above the trailers tugged at cables attached to the trailers' corners. By providing lift and some forward momentum, a single tractor could transport the heavier load.

"Jason told me the Belkiri belong to the Interstellar Consortium. But what I see here doesn't suggest an advanced civilization."

"I believe you have a phrase 'Don't judge a book by its cover.' The Belkiri focus their technology on their five cities and their interstellar space activities. If you could see their cities clad in titanium and gold glinting silver and red reflections in the setting sun, or watch a Belkiri starship lift into the heavens, your impression would be quite different. Their wormhole technology is almost as advanced as ours."

On the return to Quanara's City Center, Thrahn detoured into a park with a broad expanse of bluish grass and a small forest of stunted trees. Their wide black trunks jutted straight into the air like industrial chimneys. Branches extended from their tips in clusters of short spikes. Leaves formed fuzzy orange fur-like tufts around each branch.

In the center of the park was a shallow dark-blue lake with four fountains. Dozens of Shalcerians, large and small, thrashed and splashed along the shore while others waded out to the lake's center.

"Your species certainly enjoys the water," Rae Anne observed.

"Our home planet is a water world. We evolved from amphibious creatures similar to your octopus. Water is essential to our survival. We have a small pool on *Avenger*. I spend time there nearly every day."

"Too bad I can't join you."

Rae Anne gestured to a tower rising above the city. Several disk-shaped antennae clustered about its top, pointing in every direction.

"What's that tower? The one to the left. Is it for communications?"

"That's the energy distribution source for the entire city. The large dome structure at its base is the nuclear fusion plant. With microwave distribution, there's no need for wires or conduits. The tower directs power to local substations around the city. The substations also use microwaves to send energy to receivers on each building."

"Is all transportation by air? I don't see any ground vehicles."

"The streets are all made of nanoplast, the same material used for nanoscreens. Laid out flat like a street or sidewalk, a magneto-gravitic flux between the two ends causes this seemingly solid surface to flow from one end to the other. This creates a one-way moving platform between intersections and accounts for all the surface transportation.

For longer distances, there is a subway system. Air transport is for emergencies and VIP travel. All the buildings have access to the subway, so all deliveries are handled underground as well."

Suddenly, the world around the small hovercar vibrated as if it were attached to a cello string. The gyration quickly ended, but the tower continued to sway back and forth.

"What was that? What happened?"

"I would guess a comet or asteroid struck the planet."

"Isn't Quanara at risk of getting hit?"

"Not a chance. We will deflect anything that threatens to come within 200 kilometers of the city. And the buildings and infrastructure have all been built to withstand the frequent quakes.

"We're due back shortly, but I want to fly by a new feature I've recently heard about."

Thrahn directed the car to follow a tree-lined boulevard toward the tower. As they approached, a structure with a zig-zag maze of open scaffolding dominated the scene. It rose thirty stories and encased thousands of enclosed glass cubicles.

"This is Quanara's new agricultural facility. It's designed to provide the city's nutritional needs, through both natural harvesting and chemical engineering. It employs our most advanced technologies in vertical hydroponics. Several of the units require extra heat and light to maximize production, so it's located next to the fusion power plant."

"This must use a lot of water. And the lake, too."

"Despite appearances, water is no problem. A vast reservoir underlies the entire city. Whenever a comet strikes the planet, the natives rush to harvest and store its ice for future use. They have been doing this for thousands of years. It's the key to their survival.

"When we built our colony here, the natives transported comet fragments to our own reservoir. For a price, of course. But they were happy to get paid for something they do every day."

Chapter 7

New Delhi

While *Avenger* was recharging its propulsion system at 12-Ophiuchi-δ, Sam was in a popular restaurant in New Delhi. He shared a private room with Zahir Kahn, India's most powerful military general. They had just finished a seven-course meal and were enjoying a fine brandy and cigars.

The general leaned forward to tap the burned ash from his cigar tip into a ceramic bowl on the end table.

"Our president came back from New York with instructions to devise a plan to disarm our nuclear force that we've worked so hard to build. He's convinced the alien's promise to solve our climate problems will convince everyone to cooperate."

Sam puffed on his cigar, releasing a cloud of pungent smoke into the air.

"I'm not nearly so optimistic, General. History shows us it's best to err on the side of caution."

"My feelings exactly. Especially with the current hostilities along our border with Pakistan. There's no question in my mind Pakistan will claim to disarm but hide a stash of nuclear weapons and blackmail us over Kashmir at some time in the future."

"You aren't the only one concerned, General. My contacts in Tehran tell me the Iranians suspect Israel is doing the same thing. Easier for them to hide their weapons, of course, since they've never admitted to having them."

Kahn scowled and nodded in response.

"And no one seems concerned about North Korea. They've made it clear they aren't disarming."

"Most experts think China will force North Korea to give up their arsenal," Sam suggested.

"As if China can be trusted. We're still dealing with Chinese incursions along our northern borders. If we give up our nuclear leverage, what's to keep them from invading us like they did Taiwan?"

"As long as China and Russia are at loggerheads over disarmament, neither will abandon their nuclear weapons. In fact, my sources tell me Russia plans to use several nuclear missiles to blast the aliens out of orbit if they come back."

"That's the first I've heard of this." Kahn paused and sipped from his brandy. "So, even if the aliens do return, they'll be eliminated. This information changes everything. Disarmament by any nation would be a most foolhardy action."

"Even so, it might be well to hedge your bets. You might consider squirreling away a few nukes somewhere safe. You can publicly disarm with great fanfare if you have to, but secretly maintain a sufficient level of security should you ever need it."

"That's a worthy thought, isn't it." The general smiled knowingly. "Too much distrust between nations. I can't imagine any nuclear power abandoning their national security and disarming. Especially with the aliens gone. Do you think they'll be back?"

"A very good question, General. I certainly believe we're better off without them."

New York City

"Time for your physical therapy, Mr. Bentley."
Ian looked up from the novel he was reading on his tablet.

The aide stepped over to the bed and helped Ian bring his body to a sitting position. Ian grimaced but made no complaint. His left shoulder was heavily bandaged, and his left leg bore a cast up to his hip. Medics had removed his head bandages earlier in the day, but dark scars showed where the doctors had performed plastic surgery.

"Anything new with Martin?"

"He's still in a coma. That's really all I can say."

"I understand.

The aide rolled a wheelchair over to Ian's bed.

"You'll be using this for transportation. It's motorized. Once you can use your left arm, we'll go to a standard wheelchair with controls on both sides."

"If I get use of my arm. I can't even wiggle my fingers. I may have to learn to write with my toes." He forced a chuckle to hide his concern.

"All the controls are on the right side for now. Once you get the hang of it, you can try to qualify for the Wheelchair 500."

"That sounds like an exclusive club. What do they do?"

"They race each other up and down the halls and harass the nurses. The winner gets all the losers' desserts for the day."

Ian laughed. He tried to ignore his complaining ribs.

"Sounds like the race to lose," he said ruefully.

"Here. Let me help you into the chair. Put your right foot down parallel to the bed.

"Now put your arm around my neck and stand while I position the chair.

"That's it. Twist a bit and settle into the chair. Good. Good job."

"Easy for you to say. He says 'twist.' My ribs say, 'don't twist'."

"Every day will be better. Once you start therapy, you'll be surprised at your progress."

"Progress in Primary Personal Physical Performance," Ian recited with fake gusto. "The five P's to success."

"That's the spirit. Let's go!"

That same day, the U.N.'s Secretary General convened the second Call for Unity conference session in the General Assembly. Unlike the week before, the room was not packed. Several nations boycotted the meeting. Venezuela objected over fossil fuel restrictions. Niger refused support in an effort to protect its uranium mining industry.

Many in attendance were there to protest mandates that would impinge on their freedoms as independent nations. Suspicions and diatribes, fueled by rumors and popular conspiracy theories, filled the morning hours. By noon, several attendees had left the meeting.

Determined to salvage what he could, the Secretary General broke those nations remaining into smaller groups he hoped would be compatible and have similar issues to work through. To his relief, things quieted down and there were no further departures.

By day's end, they had drawn up several tentative proposals outlining how each nation still participating could meet the Shalcerian mandates. They worked throughout the evening devising a uniform roadmap for nuclear disarmament and fossil fuel elimination throughout the world. The participants hoped that, between Shalcerian incentives and their urging with the U.N.'s backing, the recalcitrant nations would come on board.

But throughout the conference, one overriding question prevailed.

Would the Shalcerians return and make good on their promises?

Chapter 8

18 Scorpii System

Avenger popped through the wormhole it created connecting 12 Ophiuchi with 18 Sorpii. A bright yellow sun glowed steadily ahead. As before, the bridge crew focused on their holographic consoles and displays and paid no attention to the visitors.

Jason had accompanied Rae Anne to the bridge. It was the first wormhole jump he experienced visually, having observed the previous two through his connection with *Avenger's* quantum computer. In that mode, he had watched the data streams and intricate algorithms flooding through the computer's neural network and mirrored petabytes of data into his memory banks for later analysis.

Captain Vahler pointed at the hologram that filled the forward half of the bridge.

"There's Shalkor, Rae Anne. The bright planet to the right of 18 Sorpii. The Empire's capital city and our home planet."

She spotted a planet as bright as Venus as seen from Earth. Two faint moons straddled the planet.

A crewmember spoke and the computer automatically translated for Rae Anne. "Distance to Shalkor is 64.738 million kilometers."

"Good," Vahler responded. "Maintain current velocity at 1/3 light speed until we are one-million kilometers out, then slow to approach velocity. Port authority has authorized our arrival in…" He glanced at his console. "Arrival in 15.81 minutes."

He turned to Rae Anne. "I think you'll find Shalkor very interesting."

"I'm anxious to see your home world. Thrahn has been quite secretive, only to say that it is a water world. I hope to obtain permission to visit it."

"Alien visits to the planet's surface aren't permitted. But that won't impede your exposure to our culture. As you shall soon see."

Rae Anne watched the bright star morph into a rapidly growing blue disk. When *Avenger* decelerated, they were close enough she could discern more detail.

"Why, Shalkor looks much like Earth! The same deep blue with swirling white clouds. The same yellow G-type star for a sun."

"Shalkor has less land surface than Earth, although the seas are shallower. The perfect environment for an amphibian species like ours."

"Wait. Is that a ring around the planet?"

"The ring you see is the city of Shalkor. We refer to both city and planet with the same name. You'll see why in a moment."

Avenger slowed to approach velocity. The ring Rae Anne spotted took on more detail. The band circled the entire planet but was much narrower than Saturn's rings and hugged the planet more tightly.

Dios mio. The ring is entirely artificial. And it's the platform for a huge domed city!

Sunlight glinted off the transparent domes protecting each of the ring city's interconnected segments.

A donut shaped snow globe with a New York cityscape. All that's missing is the snow.

"How many ring sections are there?"

"There are 144 sectors, all connected to each other. We are approaching Sector 14. That's where our assigned docking berth is."

Rae Anne could now make out a spiderweb of bridges connecting the buildings at various levels. Flitting black specks filled the sky above them like gnats. Hundreds of spacecraft ranging in size from small ships the size of a ferry to seven mammoth battlecruisers like *Avenger* floated in space just off the ring.

No Human has seen anything like this. Totally awesome!

"Is the entire ring as heavily populated as this?"

"It is. The city is home to 5.61 billion people. It is the capital of the Shalcerian Empire. Sector 1 holds the Golden Palace and government offices."

As Vahler spoke, *Avenger* descended below the platform's ground level, eclipsing the city from view. Rae Anne estimated the platform's depth to be half the height of the transparent dome. The exterior surface of the base looked like a cratered asteroid. A dozen lighted rows like viewports on a cruise ship lined its sheer face. Near the bottom, an oval opening appeared, glowing brightly against the blackened rock surface. *Avenger* continued its slow descent and glided through this opening and into a mammoth cavern. It came to a stop and hung suspended between floor and ceiling.

Vahler brushed his hand over his holographic console and it disappeared. Others on the bridge did the same, leaving two active consoles. He turned to Rae Anne.

"Thrahn will meet with you tomorrow and arrange an itinerary for the duration of our stay. You are the first Human representative to visit Shalkor. You are our honored guest. Don't hesitate to ask Thrahn anything about our society. Learn all you can while we're here."

Rae Anne thanked the captain and she and Jason returned to *Aurora*. She pulled off her helmet and inhaled deeply. After turning off the oxygen regulator, she stripped out of her protective suit.

"This suit is comfortable enough for a surface EVA, but it still is confining. After several hours in it, my skin gets itchy."

"I'm glad I don't have to wear one.

"And by the way, Rae Anne, I've been meaning to tell you. Don't ever get rid of *Aurora*. It may not be useful as a spaceship with a hole in its side, but I'm using its computer to store my memory archives. If you and *Avenger* ever part ways, devise some excuse to hang on to *Aurora*."

"So that's what you've been doing with all those terabyte mempins I've procured for you!"

"Yes, and I'll need more when we get back to Earth."

"You were on the bridge, so you saw the city ring. How large is it?"

"The archives show the ring to be 10 kilometers wide and in orbit at 1300 kilometers. The planet's radius is half Earth's at 3656 km. So, the city's area is 312,000 square kilometers."

"Give me something to compare that to."

"Slightly smaller than the areas of Florida and Texas combined."

Rae Anne let out a low whistle.

"Vahler said they had 5.61 billion people. How does the population density compare with, say, New York City?"

"Shalkor's population density is about 150% that of New York City, but lower than Manhattan's."

"I can't imagine a city as large as two states. Is there any census for the total Shalcerian population throughout their empire?"

"A census four years ago put the population at 21.382 billion."

"So, a fourth of their entire population lives in their capital city. That would make their vast empire sparsely populated."

"That's true. Only four of the hundred-plus planets they occupy have populations in excess of one billion."

"What do you suppose is the reason?"

"Probably environmental issues. The three populous planets have environments strikingly similar to Shalkor. No need for enclosed domes, habitats, or maintaining an artificial atmosphere. Most planets have one or more of these issues, which puts a severe restriction on population growth. Quanara on 12 Ophiuchi is a perfect example."

"I'm surprised the Shalcerians haven't developed advanced terraforming techniques, or rather, Shalkoraforming techniques, to transform a whole planet to match their environmental needs."

"Hmm…Searching…The archives show one such attempt a while back. Turns out, it was a colossal failure."

"Good to know the Shalcerians have some failures hiding in their closet. Let me know if you find any others. That information could come in handy someday."

Chapter 9

Shalkor

Early the next day, Thrahn appeared in *Avenger's* hangar bay and peered through the hole in *Aurora's* hull.

"Rae Anne, are you in here? Ah, good. I checked in your quarters and assumed you must be here when I didn't find you. Are you ready for an excursion into Shalkor?"

"I certainly am. Can Jason come along?"

"Unfortunately, computer simulations of living creatures are not allowed on Shalkor. The restriction goes back a long way."

"Jason was telling me a bit of your history. Something about a devastating war with a robot uprising three millennia ago?"

"Yes. Our civilization barely escaped annihilation. I was surprised when Captain Vahler authorized Engineering to build Jason, even with his rudimentary intelligence. But he will have to remain aboard *Avenger* during our stay."

Jason sat quietly at the table as though oblivious to the conversation.

"Well, I'll put on my SEVA suit, and we'll be on our way."

The lift from *Avenger's* berth on Shalkor's lowest sub-level deposited Rae Anne and Thrahn in a park next to a boulevard bustling with Shalcerians. Tree-like plants grew in clusters throughout the park and lined the avenue. These had multiple narrow trunks growing from gnarled roots that looked like piles of coiled rope in a marina. The trunks twisted around each other in living knots as they rose to a broad canopy four meters above the ground. Their broad violet and magenta leaves contrasted with long, black seedpods that dangled through the foliage.

A shaggy turquoise ground cover filled the park's open areas. From where she stood, Rae Anne saw it as an oddly colored soccer field waiting to be mowed. A lake in the center of the park accommodated dozens of miniature Shalcerians who splashed about and waded in the water, their shrieks and squeals filling the air.

Children playing in the water. I haven't seen such commotion in years. And adults standing around like watchful parents everywhere.

"Welcome to my home, Rae Anne. What do you think of Shalkor so far?"

"It's utterly fascinating. So beautiful. The city ring is an incredible feat of engineering."

"It took 1800 years to complete. There are 144 sectors. Each sector was built as a separate orbiting entity. Then, 200 years ago, we linked all the sectors together. The causeways between them are large enough for the high-speed Levline and for hovercraft. In theory, you could circle the globe on the Levline without leaving your seat."

"In theory?"

"The 31,000 km trip would take over three days non-stop, even at 400 km/hr. We're in sector 14. I want to show you a special museum in sector 12. We'll grab a Levcab. It will take about an hour and a half to get there."

Thrahn took Rae Anne's hand and led her onto the crowded boulevard. The street was a solid, moving nanoplast platform extending the block's length between intersections, like those she observed at Quanara.

"The streets throughout the city are one-way in alternating directions. You need to stay aware and step off the conveyer at each intersection. After a while it becomes second nature."

Shalcerians made up the bulk of the pedestrians on the boulevard, but every so often individuals belonging to two or three other species appeared, blending in unnoticed (except to Rae Anne) among the crowd.

The cacophony resulting from the mixture of alien languages with their assortment of screeches and squawks, whistles, and clicks, grunts and sighs went far beyond anything Rae Anne had experienced at tourist destinations on Earth. Occasionally, a Shalcerian guide leading a group of such creatures appeared.

Tourists to Shalkor from other worlds, visiting the empire's capital. Creatures of every shape and size imaginable. I wish they weren't all wearing respirators. I would love to see more of their features.

Overhead, a continuous series of 3D holograms flashed dazzling images advertising products and services available in the neighboring shops and offices. Gazing through the holograms, Rae Anne marveled at the startling architectural variety exhibited by the towering buildings. One structure reminded her of a mammoth corkscrew, another of a slender, polished lance piercing the sky. Domes of various sizes accounted for more than half the structures.

They arrived at an intersection with a one-story structure set in its center. It looked like a subway entrance to Rae Anne, and to her delight, that's exactly what it was. Thrahn led her onto a wide escalator that took them down to an ornate sublevel platform where dozens of small cars sporting transparent bubbles were parked in orderly rows.

Thrahn stepped into a two-seater next to the curb. A glistening high-voltage power cable in a shallow trench ran the length of the platform and disappeared in the subway tunnel at the end. Thrahn motioned for Rae Anne to take a seat in the car.

"This Levcab will do." He flipped a switch and the nanoscreen bubble closed over them as he squirmed into his seat. She noticed a wide slot cut in the center of each seat's cushion to accommodate a Shalcerian's third leg. This was the first time she'd seen a Shalcerian sitting on something other than their center leg. Thrahn spoke a few commands and the car moved sideways over the curb and floated above the power cable.

Rae Anne felt a mild jolt as the car accelerated toward the unlit tunnel ahead. The cab's interior light blinked on. Once in the tunnel, other cars, both ahead and behind, appeared as lighted pearls on invisible strings gliding swiftly through the darkness.

"Captain Vahler said only Shalcerian citizens are allowed to go down to the planet's surface. Why the restriction?" Rae Anne asked, settling comfortably into the plush cushions.

"Early in our space-faring history we experienced a virulent plague which devastated our society. We ultimately conquered it, but investigations revealed that a visiting alien had introduced it. The virus was an essential part of that species' biome. They were unaware of the danger they presented to us, and we naively assumed species from other planets would be different enough as to not pose any health risks.

"That event stimulated our interest in orbiting cities, resulting in Shalkor. We passed laws to protect the planet from contamination by alien species and to preserve it forever for Shalcerians. We enforce strict quarantine measures for all visitors. I would have to remain in a quarantine facility for two weeks with frequent testing and inoculations before I would be free to roam about."

"Don't you face the same risk in this huge city?"

"We would, except the air in the city is continuously treated and recycled. This removes all airborne microbes. In addition, antimicrobial nanobots circulate throughout the atmosphere. It would be impossible to accomplish this for an entire planet."

Over the next hour, they passed through nine stations, brief flashes of light between extended periods in the dark tunnels. They also traversed the two causeways on either end of Sector 13. The walls were transparent and provided an orbital view of the blue planet below and 18 Sorpii shining brightly overhead. With the unimpeded view, Rae Anne was amazed at the flotilla of spacecraft surrounding the city.

The long ride gave her time to digest what she was learning of the Shalkor civilization. She squirmed in her seat at her unsettled thoughts.

This is like a modern version of the Roman Empire. With technology, there's no need for slaves. Yet they have an armada of cruisers and battleships to maintain control over their subjects. They enlist the sentient species they encounter to police their local systems. Like they want us to police our Kuiper Belt. I wonder what else they have in mind for Humans.

The Levcab decelerated. Other cabs zipped past them on either side and overhead.

Monorail is certainly not an appropriate term for the Levline. For one thing, there's no rail!

When they emerged from the last tunnel, their cab came to a stop next to the station platform. It slid sideways onto the platform and the bubble roof opened.

Thrahn stood and helped Rae Anne step from the car.

"We're now in the center of Sector 12. The museum is several blocks away, so we'll take the Sector subway."

Thrahn selected a lighted pedestrian tunnel leading from the Levline platform and after a short walk they entered the subway station. Whereas the Levline station had only one line with all Levcabs travelling the same direction, the sector station had four levels, each with its own pair of lines travelling in opposite directions. They took a lift to the third level and crossed over the monorail tracks on a bridge to the opposite side. As before, Thrahn selected a car, made sure Rae Anne was comfortably seated, and spoke their destination.

The car glided sideways to the monorail and, after pausing to allow several other cars to zoom past, slipped into the traffic and whisked them to their destination station. Once there, it smoothly glided off the track and onto the platform.

Taking the escalator to street level, they emerged next to a tree-lined boulevard across from a giant reflecting sphere set atop a squat, two-story base. Rae Anne guessed the sphere to be at least 20-stories high.

It's amazing the structures you can build in 1/6 G. We could build something like this on Mars. If we had the technology, that is.

The trees along this street had straight white trunks like aspens, but with deep purple leaves. They were festooned with bright crimson flowers, alive with small buzzing insects busily darting in and out among the elongated petals.

"These insects remind me of Earth's bees, Thrahn. Are they similar?"

"They are pollinators. But everything in our environment works in threes. The insects must collect three types of pollen when they visit the various flowers. When three different pollen types unite within the insect's gut and successfully converge, they secrete a substance which causes the insect to regurgitate them into the heart of the next flower it visits. The pollen then gestates and develops into a seed-bearing fruit."

"Are the flowers fragrant to Shalcerians? With my respirator, I can't tell."

"To us, the odor is quite pleasant. The sulfurous amine and sulfonamide mixture is delightful."

Ugh. Thank god for my respirator!

"How about birds, Thrahn? I haven't seen any birds."

"We have no birds. Shalkor-the-planet is mostly shallow seas. Evolution didn't find a niche for flying species other than insects."

They crossed at the intersection. Thrahn explained that jaywalking across moving beltways was forbidden. After entering the structure beneath the spherical building, they passed a Visitor's desk surrounded by creatures from six distinct species. Thrahn didn't stop but led Rae Anne directly to the escalator and up to the first level inside the glass sphere.

"This museum is the Library of Sentient Species. So far, we have encountered eighty-seven space-faring species, and each of these, as well as our own, is represented here. This entire floor is devoted to Shalcerians. Soon we'll have a section on the seventeenth floor for Humans. The higher floors are empty and reserved for species yet to be encountered."

Rae Anne wondered where the exhibits might be that Thrahn referred to. They were standing in a long, curved hallway with closely spaced nanoscreens on either side. Thrahn stopped at one of these and spoke. The nanoscreen opened and he ushered Rae Anne into an enclosed space not much bigger than a walk-in closet. A control console was located just inside the entry.

Thrahn demonstrated for Rae Anne how to initiate and control the holographic displays from the console. He held a hand over a lighted icon on the panel and spoke a command. In response, a holographic display filled the room and flickered to life, surrounding them.

"*Avenger's* English language translator has already been uploaded to Shalkor's system, so your spoken requests will be recognized and understood throughout the city. For example, no matter where you might find yourself in Sector 14, saying 'Return to *Avenger*' to any sector subway cab will get you back to the lift leading down to the ship.

"With these data consoles in our museums, you control the data stream with verbal commands, such as 'start,' 'stop,' and 'pause,' or 'search' followed by the subject you want information on. If it doesn't understand your command, it will ask you for further clarification."

Following his verbal request, the kiosk initiated a 3D holographic video pertinent to his query. Thrahn's request was for information on the biology of Shalcerian procreation. When Rae Anne realized the topic he had chosen, she gulped and took a deep breath to steel herself from blushing in embarrassment.

Think of this as a science lesson in extraterrestrial biology. Nothing to be embarrassed about. Still, what a strange topic to choose for starters.

Being immersed in the holographic display, she found herself standing on the rocky ledge of a crystal-clear pond within a sheltered grotto. Trees similar to those she had seen outside and manicured bushes surrounded the pond. A Shalcerian was standing waist-deep in the water. His eyes were closed, and two of his three hands were stacked atop his torso behind his eyestalks. His body scales were a solid pale peach color. Rae Anne thought he might be meditating.

Shortly, a second Shalcerian arrived. He stepped reverently into the water and waded to stand next to his colleague. They each wrapped an arm around the other's waist, meditating silently together. Finally, a third individual arrived and joined the other two in what Rae Anne could only describe as a group hug.

"This is the moment of Convergence," said Thrahn with a tone of awe. "These pools are found only on our planet's surface. When hormones urge for Convergence, one tries to make it to a Convergence Pool and join with two others who are feeling those same urges."

"Do the three people know each other beforehand?"

"No. We meet as strangers when our hormones begin to stir, we share in our intimacy, and then we go our separate ways."

The three individuals worked their way to the deeper part of the pond until they were totally submerged in the water.

"They may be there for up to an hour. During this time, their pheromones will intermix and initiate a secretion of genetic material through their gills. These fluids combine and are sheltered next to their chests as they embrace. Additional secretions provide nutrients and material to form a protective shell. The completed egg is deposited in the sands at the pool's bottom where an Egg Custodian collects it and brings it to the Hatching Pool, where he watches over thousands of eggs."

"So, although you have offspring, you have no idea who they might be?" Rae Anne asked.

"That is correct. There is no way to know which egg was generated by which donors. In fact, there is no effort to trace the other donors."

"How difficult is it to find three people of different sexes preparing for Convergence at the same time?"

"We Shalcerians are asexual except during Convergence At that time, pheromones promote the necessary sexual differentiation. So, any three people experiencing Convergence can meet and reproduce."

"And when the egg hatches?"

"The hatchlings are transferred to the first of three rearing ponds, one for each stage in development. They are nurtured and trained there until they morph into child Shalcerians. After that, their guardians are tutors who teach them and raise them into adulthood."

So, Shalcerians have no family sense. Something to keep in mind in our dealings with them. They may have trouble understanding our attachment to familial relations.

Although Rae Anne was anxious to visit the upper floors in the museum to glimpse holograms of other species inhabiting the local galactic neighborhood, Thrahn seemed strangely distracted and unaware of her desires. They spent the rest of the day viewing different aspects of Shalcerian history and culture.

Later, as they were returning to *Avenger*, Thrahn mentioned he would be absent for much of *Avenger's* stay at Shalkor.

"Ever since our arrival, I have been beset with a deep physical urge to visit the planet. I believe it may be the first stages of Convergence. Captain Vahler has granted me leave. Given the required quarantine period, I'll be gone for three weeks."

Dios mio! I'll be lost without Thrahn. Like visiting a foreign country and not knowing the language or customs. Even worse, given this is an alien culture.

Still, this is important to him. It explains his preoccupation with Convergence at the museum today.

"That's wonderful, Thrahn," she said, forcing an upbeat tone that she didn't feel. "And to have that happen now, while we are here. This must mean a lot to you."

"It is a rare opportunity for those of us in the Space Service. But Shalkor has an impressive Visitors' Bureau. I've contacted them to assign a volunteer to show you around while I'm away. Someone will show up at your quarters tomorrow morning. He'll take good care of you."

Chapter 10

Shalkor

Mid-morning the next day, while Rae Anne was dictating her impressions from her first outing into Shalkor, a BEEP sounded, and a holographic monitor appeared over her quarter's nanoscreen. An image of a creature unlike anything she had seen before was displayed in full three-dimensional detail.

```
VarConsa Epiben Tarbil Constalon from the
Shalkor Visitors' Bureau is here to see Rae
Anne Chavez from Earth.
```

"Allow entry," Rae Anne commanded.

Rae Anne caught her breath as her visitor stepped through the nanoscreen. She tried to hide her surprise before reminding herself that other species wouldn't be able to read Human reactions.

The creature before her was six feet tall. His small round head atop a narrow neck swiveled left and right in continual motion. With two bulging eyes in both front and back of his head, this motion provided him with a 360-degree view of his surroundings. He had two pairs of large, pointed ears on each side of his head, one pair facing forward, the other rearward. A fuzz of white fur covered the few exposed parts of his body.

He had a snout remarkably like a Labrador retriever's, but not for breathing, as his respirator was fit snugly around his neck beneath the snout and was attached to life-support equipment strapped to his back. Two arms extended from his shoulders, reaching almost to the floor. Each ended with three pairs of small, crab-like pincers. A loose-fitting, shimmering silver toga covered his body. Two wide, webbed feet extended from the fringe at the bottom of the tunic. When he moved about, his whole body swayed back and forth, swishing the fabric and tinkling a row of tiny bells attached to the tunic's bottom fringe.

I wonder what kind of environment would give such an awkward development an evolutionary advantage. Still, his graceful movements seem almost like dancing.

"Greetings. I am looking for Rae Anne Chavez. The Visitors' Center has appointed me to serve as guide to introduce her to Shalkor."

The voice was computer generated and emanated from Rae Anne's respirator helmet. She quickly donned the helmet, wondering if she needed to wear it to communicate.

"I am Rae Anne Chavez, representative of the Human species. And who are you?"

"You may call me VarConsa. I belong to the Monapar species from the planet Uhldar in the 82 G Eridani system. I am pleased to meet you. And your companion?"

"This is Jason. He won't be accompanying us. And you may call me Rae Anne."

"Fine, Rae Anne. As soon as you're ready, follow me."

Rae Anne hastily donned her protective suit and fastened the compact oxygen pack to her belt. She adjusted the regulator and verified everything was working properly.

Before bidding farewell to Jason, she asked VarConsa, "Do I have enough oxygen for our tour? I used this same unit most of yesterday."

"Your cryopack will last a week. The oxygen is frozen solid at minus 220 degrees Celsius, and your respirator recycles all exhaled oxygen."

VarConsa spun to face the nanoscreen and began his 'toga swishing' walk toward it and stepped through. Rae Anne waved to Jason and followed.

The Monapar led Rae Anne through *Avenger's* maze of corridors to the ship's airlock and to the same lift she and Thrahn used the day before. When they stepped from the lift at street level, Rae Anne was surprised to be in shadow. Fluffy white clouds drifted overhead and accumulated at the edges of the dome, occasionally blocking 18 Scorpii which hung just above the horizon. In the opposite direction, Shalkor-the-Planet dominated the sky.

"Since everything here will be new to you, I will take you first to our Monapar community in this Sector, which is where I live. Come."

VarConsa led Rae Anne toward the center of the city. Since this was also toward Shalkor-the-planet, she decided to orient herself by labeling this direction as 'down,' or 'south,' with 'east' to her left and 'west' to her right.

As they progressed down the avenue, she glanced side-to-side at the establishments on the ground floor of each building they passed. Many were devoted to clothing and art objects unique to one or another of the species doing business on Shalkor. Others were offices offering services for which she had no clue. A few were attended by long queues of individuals, mostly from the same species.

She was so busy sightseeing that she tripped at an intersection. VarConsa saved her from falling by quickly reaching out and catching her with his long arms.

"Thank you, VarConsa. I don't wish to visit an emergency health center during my stay."

"Don't mention it, Rae Anne. Our first training session as guides was spent teaching us to be attentive to our guests at every intersection. I've saved many visitors from falling."

Their destination happened to be on the same corner. They entered a crimson-colored building and walked into a room packed with more than a dozen Monapar. Heavy smoke curled to the ceiling and filled the air with a gray haze. It looked like a noisy bar at happy hour. This impression was confirmed when she noticed everyone lapping liquids of varying color from ornately sculpted bowls. No one was wearing respirators. VarConsa removed the respirator from his neck and took a deep breath.

No one paid any attention to Rae Anne. She figured they must be used to VarConsa bringing alien species for visits. She was just one more tourist.

They pushed their way through the crowd to a lift at the back. The lift shot them to the building's 63rd floor. VarConsa stepped from the lift through a nanoscreen, pulling Rae Anne after him. They entered a large room lit from all directions in a dusky blue glow. Rae Anne noticed the gravity coefficient in the room to be quite oppressive, but not as bad as at Quanara.

VarConsa called out something that sounded like a shoe grating on gravel, and two smaller versions of VarConsa entered the room.

"This is my apartment, and my family, VarTaro and VarGavo. They are both teenagers."

"VarTaro, VarGavo, say a proper greeting for Rae Anne Chavez, a Human creature."

The children both squawked shrilly while clapping their claws like castanets above their heads. VarConsa praised them and sent them from the room.

"We Monapar have developed cloning to a fine art. Both children are clones of myself."

"They are fine looking children, and very obedient." Rae Anne hoped complimenting a parent on their children's behavior was universally appropriate. VarConsa seemed pleased.

"My apartment occupies the entire floor, so I have a view of the city in every direction. Come take a look."

Rae Anne followed VarConsa to a window. The metropolis stretched out before her, an endless parade of buildings marching alongside wide curving avenues, broken here and there with parks filled with those strangely shaped violet and magenta trees and shallow blue lakes.

"How large is the Monapar compound?"

"In this borough, there are 93,800 Monapar, about 3% of the borough's total population. We represent a smaller percentage of the population here than in most other boroughs. Borough 11 has three times the Monapar population. We are the fourth largest group of non-Shalcerian residents in the city."

"What's the large dome shaped structure off in the distance?"

"That's a fusion power facility. Each borough has one, more than sufficient to meet our needs. It powers the borough's waste treatment and water recycling plant, and five of the sixty air purification units in this sector."

"That's a lot of infrastructure to be dependent on one power plant."

"We have built-in redundancy. Sector 14 has 20 such power plants, and all are interconnected. Should one plant go offline, only the engineers would be aware of the problem."

"As a member of a non-native species living here, is there anything you miss from your home world?"

"We have all we need here. Except for cloning. I had to travel back to my home planet twice for those procedures. And food. I do miss sitting down to a savory meal. The Shalcerian nutrition pills are no substitute for the real thing."

"I thought I saw several eating establishments on our way here. This was my first time seeing Shalcerians eating."

"The Shalcerians have a vast area below the subway system devoted to hydroponics. But only for Shalcerian produce. The rest of us must do without eating. A small price for the Monapar. Other species find it more challenging."

"Humans would be one such species. We enjoy preparing real food and eating it, especially in the company of friends. You would think the Shalcerians would be more hospitable to the other residents in their capital."

"With so many different species, each with its own nutritional requirements, native plants and organisms, it isn't practical. What is nutritious for one species may be toxic to another. And Shalcerians are very sensitive to the risks of invasive species from other worlds."

"I would guess interstellar commerce restricts dealing with living plants and animals."

"Correct. And that includes food and drink as well. All our beverages are manufactured here. Clothing, art, and artifacts are widely traded, as are skills in the arts, sciences, engineering, medicine, and education. For most things, there are no restrictions."

"So, if you reproduce by cloning, is there only one sex among Monapar?"

"There is now. At one time we were a bisexual species, with one sex dominant and abusive over the other. But when cloning was perfected, the abusers were bypassed and made to become extinct. This happened thousands of years ago. Monapar are now all of the same sex.

Chapter 11

Shalkor

VarConsa led Rae Anne to a window facing a different direction.

"But enough of Monapar history. See the large park five blocks from here where the main avenue bends to the left? That's one of my favorite places. There's something there I would like to show you."

Rae Anne assumed they would take the lift to ground level. She was surprised when VarConsa stopped the lift at level 48. Stepping through the nanoscreen, she found herself in a foyer opening onto a bridge leading to the top floor of a neighboring building. Looking through the transparent bridge floor to the street below, she felt a spasm of vertigo and swallowed hard to choke back the bile in her throat.

Rule Number One. Don't look down!

In the new building, they used the lift to drop them to level 36 where they stepped off and encountered another transparent bridge. Two buildings and two bridges later brought them to ground level directly across from the park. Dodging pedestrians of every shape imaginable, they crossed the intersection and followed a deserted path into a purple forest. Lime green bushes beneath the trees were laden with deep blue blossoms shaped like long, slender trumpets.

The forest path curved away from the bustling avenue and opened into a clearing filled with tiny orange and scarlet flowers among the grasses. The center of the clearing was dominated by a square pyramid rising 30 meters and resting on a 4-meter-high hexagonal base. The entire structure appeared to be constructed of white marble. VarConsa led Rae Anne between two obsidian pillars jutting into the air like mammoth narwhal tusks and through a wide opening in the structure's base.

"This is beautiful, VarConsa. We have similar pyramids on Earth. Is this a temple or shrine?"

"Not a temple, of course. Religious myths have no place in our many civilizations. This is the Shalkor Construction Museum to celebrate the building of this amazing city. The city is so unique, each sector has a similar museum to provide historical context for school children."

He paused at a kiosk in front of a large amphitheater. He voiced a command in his guttural language and a hologram filled the area. Against a black, star-studded background with a bright yellow distant sun, five clunky vessels approached a small asteroid many times their size. The ships positioned themselves against one side of the rock and all five fusion-drive engines flared brightly. Nothing appeared to change until a distant planet came into view and it was apparent that the tugs were relocating the asteroid into an orbit around Shalkor-the-Planet.

"This was the first asteroid brought to Shalkor to build the city. At the time, no one imagined there would be more than three or four such satellites, let alone a linked ring to support most of the planet's population."

As the animated hologram continued, it displayed construction equipment leveling the asteroid's surface and hollowing out its core. Habitats connected with walkway tunnels appeared as each new area was leveled.

"This was built 2680 years ago, which explains the primitive ships and equipment. Over the next 200 years, three more were built, each larger and more sophisticated than the last. The breakthrough, however, came with the discovery of transparent nanoscreen materials that respond to magneto-gravitic forces. These nanoscreens can extend thousands of meters from the forcefield generators."

VarConsa spoke another command to the console. The scene fast forwarded through the construction of three more orbiting stations and slowed again. The asteroid brought into orbit for this new project was truly mammoth and the transforming and shaping equipment were generations beyond those shown in the first hologram.

"This is the first platform to become part of the Ring, 1937 years ago, Sector 28. By this time, Shalcerians had perfected the GESC-Plasticore material, and it was becoming ubiquitous throughout Shalcerian culture. Here you see it being deposited as soon as the hyper-laser leveler has cleared a patch of the surface. This was the first platform to provide artificial gravity and allow its inhabitants to live normal lives."

The hologram progressed until the entire surface was level and coated with plasticore. Then shimmering, transparent sheets of nanoparticles surged upward around the rock's perimeter like fountains in a lake, higher and higher, until they coalesced far above the surface into a completed dome.

At that point, construction of real buildings, not habitats, commenced. Avenues, boulevards, and parks with lakes filled the areas between tall, slender buildings of thirty and forty stories. The last view of this city showed the streets teeming with Shalcerian settlers.

"On average, a new orbiting city was completed every twelve years. About 200 years ago, they determined they could connect these cities with nanoparticle conduits and create a single, monolithic ring surrounding the entire planet. That's when the two LevLines were constructed for inter-Sector transport, one circling the ring clockwise, the other counterclockwise."

"This is amazing, VarConsa. The technology behind this is almost beyond comprehension."

"Wait till you visit the War and Conquest Museum in Sector 15. Shalcerian advances in that arena dwarf what you've seen here."

That's not what I wanted to hear. I feel like a Neanderthal on Fifth Avenue.

Thrahn's comment about 'Just more powerful weapons' again reverberated in her brain.

"I would love to visit the Palace Sector, but Thrahn said it would take over twenty hours to get there on the LevLine and I didn't rate high enough in government priorities to travel there by hovercraft. Is there a hologram here that shows it?"

"Absolutely. I'll enter a search for Sector 1 and bring it up."

VarConsa spoke a command and the holographic display morphed into a street view on a low hill overlooking the palace. Except for the seven slender towers spaced randomly through the complex, the tallest building was only twelve stories high. Every structure, including the spires, was clad in solid gold. A secondary nanoparticle dome sealed the imperial complex. A large park with three lakes occupied its center. A dozen lighted fountains sparkled in 18 Scorpii's bright rays and cast rainbow shards glittering against the surrounding buildings.

"The hexagonal building you see beyond the park is the emperor's Palace itself. It's too bad we aren't closer to Sector 1. This simulacrum is a far cry from seeing the real thing."

No wonder I keep getting reminded of ancient Rome. Do Humans really want to be a part of all this? Can we afford not to be?

They spent the rest of the day visiting parks and retail establishments in Sector 14's central business district. When VarConsa dropped her off at her quarters that evening, he promised to come by early the next morning to take her to the Shalkor Zoo, a holographic museum of biology with depictions of all known life forms on Shalkor-the-Planet's surface, located in Sector 16.

"How was your day?" Jason asked when she stepped into *Aurora*.

"You wouldn't believe what I've seen. They have an entire museum with holographic images of Shalkor's construction.'

"Actually, I can believe everything you tell me. My connections with *Avenger's* computer allowed me to track you all day, and whenever you stopped somewhere, I could bring up images from the computer archives to experience pretty much everything you saw."

Rae Anne frowned.

"You mean they're following my every move?"

"They've woven a tracking device into the fabric of your life-support suit. I guess they don't want to lose you." Jason's voice elicited a convincing chuckle.

"I don't find that very funny. I've only been here two days and I'm already feeling depressed. The scope of this civilization is beyond anything I could have imagined. And I keep bringing up images of ancient Rome that aren't very satisfying."

"You might be interested in one insight that came to me when you were visiting the Library of Sentient Species yesterday. Do you remember that you wondered why there weren't more Shalcerians in such a vast empire?"

"I do remember. If Humans were allowed to expand into the galaxy over a 2000-year period, every available star system would be jam-packed with Humans. Just look at what we've done with only one planet at our disposal."

"The key for Shalcerians is the Convergence Pools. To reproduce, three Shalcerians must gather in a Convergence Pool, and these are only found on Shalkor's surface, nowhere else in the galaxy."

"So, you're saying that colonists on other planets cannot reproduce?"

"Exactly. Anyone hoping to experience Convergence must come back to Shalkor. Furthermore, every single new addition to one of the colonies must have been born on Shalkor and emigrated to that colony."

"That's an interesting detail, Jason. I don't know how, but I have a feeling that information may become very useful someday."

And from the Human perspective, it seems like an exploitable weakness.

Chapter 12

Sydney

Sam leaned back in the executive chair in his plush office in Sydney. His desk faced a window-wall looking out onto his TransWorld Space Lines launching platform outside the Australia passenger terminal. He watched as two dozen passengers filed out to his shuttle from the transport bus for the 165-minute flight to Austin, Texas.

"Your call is ready, Mr. Durban."

He turned his attention to his phone and activated it.

"Karen, congratulations! I saw on the news last night you landed that big contract with Libya for a Mediterranean wind farm. You've been working on that for months."

"Yeah, thanks. Looked like it had fallen through when the damn aliens arrived and promised everyone the moon. But as soon as they left, we closed the deal."

"What would Libya want with wind energy? They've been a major oil producer for decades."

"Their problem is a lack of potable water, Sam. They plan to build thirty-two huge desalination plants along the coast. You know how energy intensive that process is."

"Why can't they just build a few power plants and use their own gas and oil?"

"Wind energy is cheaper. With my providing the energy for their water purification, they have more of the expensive oil and gas to export. It's a win-win for everyone."

"It's going to take some time to build those turbines and power infrastructure. What if the aliens come back?"

"I'm not as pessimistic as you on that point. I think they saw the handwriting on the wall and took off for good. They may come back in a few centuries to see if anything's changed, but I believe we've seen the last of them."

"I hope you're right. I need to come by sometime in the next few days and talk with you about designing some specialized robotic equipment for my lunar mining operations. You available?"

"Hmm…How about coming by my place in San Francisco Thursday evening? We can meet with my engineers Friday, and then spend the weekend together.'

"Sounds like a plan. I'll have a couple of my engineers fly out for the Friday meetings with specifications. There are tricky design challenges. I'm sure your team can figure it out."

"I'll be waiting for you Thursday evening. I bought a terribly provocative outfit in Paris last week. Can't wait to slip into it for you."

Sam paused, letting his imagination soar. His heartbeat increased and his groin responded in anticipation. He cleared his throat.

"Are you there, Sam?"

"I'll uh, I'll be by around six on Thursday. We'll have a blast."

When he hung up, he called Barbie at the TWSL reservation desk to reserve a seat for Thursday morning's shuttle to Los Angeles. He loved listening to Barbie's voice. Though in her sixties, her voice could launch him into sexual fantasies. He then had his assistant arrange for late afternoon transportation from L.A. to San Francisco.

His last private phone call for the morning was to Los Angeles.

"Hello, Vera? …

"Hey, I'll be in L.A. over noon on Thursday. I'd love to come by for a visit if you're free…

"No, no. Just for a couple of hours. Will that be ok? …

"Great. You still have that black negligee I gave you?"

Colorado Springs

The staff robustly greeted Ian on his first day back at the office after his 'mishap' at the U.N. Everyone gathered around him in a wide circle to make room for his walker. Several insisted on hearing the account of his near-death experience. Ian recounted the events with resignation for the zillionth time since leaving the hospital.

"Has anyone heard from Rae Anne?" he asked when he finished his tale. He had been told of *Avenger's* departure the day after he came out of his medically induced coma.

"Not a word, Ian," said Victor.

Ian sighed and absently rubbed his right hand over his perpetually sore ribs. Though his left leg was still in a cast, his arm was free of bandages and in a sling. He could grasp things with his fingers and raise his arm a few inches off the table.

"I wish we knew what called them away," he said. "We might have a better idea when they might return. Anyway, it is good to be back. Thank you for all the attention.

"By the way, does anyone know who's behind these scare ads on nuclear energy? I can hardly access any media without running into them."

"Beats me," Victor said. "But I like the one with the green alien peeking over the top of the radiation hazard symbol, you know? 'No Aliens. No Nukes'."

"Or how about the cityscape of LA," Penny added, shaking her head in disgust. "LA with dozens of miniature mushroom clouds popping up all over the city. The caption for that one is 'When Alien Nukes go BOOM'."

"Fear of the unknown, fear of change," Ian responded. "And total disregard for science and the truth. It's a wonder humanity has progressed as far as it has." He turned to his aide.

"I want to meet with the First Contact Committee tomorrow at 11:00. Have people bring summary reports on progress since the Call for Unity conference. Once we know how far we've come, we can determine how much remains to be done and create a roadmap to follow."

The next morning, the Astronautics Division conference room was nearly full, and remote access provided online connections to a dozen participants around the globe.

Ian brought the meeting to order. He intended to poll each committee chair to share their progress with the group, so overlapping and crossover areas could be identified. But before he could begin, Ingrid Bierstadt, the group's liaison to the U.N., expressed the overriding concern on everyone's mind.

"Ian, before we get started, we need to address a fundamental problem. The Shalcerian mandates require world-wide cooperation in nuclear disarmament and in fossil fuel elimination. Since the Call to Unity conference, the U.N. has been sponsoring meeting after meeting with member nations, lobbying and cajoling to arrive at agreements between nations that have vested interests in both areas.

"We have had notable success in some cases. In particular, Middle East oil producers and Venezuela have agreed to reduce oil production in proportion to the alien's providing their nuclear fusion power facilities. They see future production going to feedstock for chemical industry. And Britain and France have agreed to dismantle their nuclear arsenals.

"The bottleneck is that neither the Russians nor the Chinese are participating in any way. Without them, we are at an impasse."

"What will it take to bring them on board?" Ian asked.

"I don't think there's a chance either country will partner with the Shalcerians. Both governments have taken the hardline stance that the aliens are a threat to humanity and plan to enslave us."

"That's utterly ridiculous," said Clara Iverson, the Agency's AI division head. "Too many B-rated science fiction videos."

"Ridiculous or not, that's what they're saying," Ingrid replied.

Havel stepped into the conversation from his desk in Washington.

"Unfortunately, both countries are backing up their rhetoric with nuclear threats. Intelligence tells us they have programmed some of their missiles to bring down *Avenger* whenever it resumes Earth-orbit."

Ian massaged his neck and cleared his throat.

"So, nothing's changed with them since the Shalcerians first arrived. Do we have hard evidence on this?"

"Not yet. It's still at the 'reliable sources' stage."

"Is there anything the White House or State Department can do to counter this, if it is indeed true?"

"We are working on it. But U.S-Russia relations have seen better days and since the Taiwan invasion there's no communication between Washington and China. Things with both countries are always touchy, and this whole First Contact thing hasn't helped."

Ian looked at his tablet and frowned.

"Well, let's proceed with our agenda. There may be only so much we can do, but maybe our progress will provide encouragement to anyone still on the fence. With the Shalcerians away, we have time to work on the Russians and Chinese and try to convince them not to do anything foolish."

Chapter 13

Shalkor

The day after their visit to the Shalkor Construction Museum, Rae Anne and VarConsa were zipping along at 400 km/hr. in a Levcab on their way to the Shalkor Zoo. VarConsa brought with him a small cube the size of a box a jeweler might provide for a ring.

After their car passed through the conduit between Sectors 14 and 15 and plunged into tunnel darkness again, he handed the cube to Rae Anne.

"This little computer is a hologram projector. I thought you might like to see some images from my home planet, since our trip to the zoo will take close to four hours. You can hold it for better viewing. It's close enough to me, it should pick up my thought commands."

After a short pause, a small hologram filled a six-inch cube over the box. It displayed a dimly lit world with low, rounded hills surrounding a vast marsh. Two red-dwarf suns blazed in a creamy sky, casting competing shadows on the dreary scene. Hundreds of creatures resembling VarConsa bobbed through a marsh in their unique pattern of locomotion, stooping frequently to snatch something from the water and plop it into the bags they carried.

If the Monapar evolved in marshes like this on a world with high gravity, their unusual anatomy makes perfect sense. I need to keep a more open mind. Every species is a product of their own evolution and environment.

"This view is near the village I grew up in. It shows farmers harvesting glyk, a shelled creature that is a staple in our diet."

The scene changed to one depicting a dazzling city of polished silver. Sunlight glinted red beams from the buildings into the narrow street canyons bustling with activity.

"This is Arubon, our capitol city. In a minute, you'll see an Interplanetary Security Force squadron fly overhead. It takes my breath away every time I see it."

After a moment, the sky filled with twenty-seven V-shaped craft in three distinct formations. As quickly as they appeared, they were gone, leaving colorful roiling contrails in their wake.

"That was impressive. What are you defending against?"

"There are numerous insurgent groups and pirates roaming the empire. They strike at random. A strong security force helps keep them at bay. Then there's the Baltar Alliance. With wormhole technology, they can pop up anywhere."

"How long has this been going on?"

"For as long as anyone can remember. These threats are one reason we joined the Empire. We hadn't developed wormhole technology to counter the incursions. Interspecies cooperation with the Shalcerians has created a strong defense."

The hologram morphed into an orbital view of a bright green planet dotted and streaked with clouds. The two red dwarf suns gave the clouds a pale pink tinge.

"This is the Monapar home planet, Gilgor."

"It's beautiful. The green is almost iridescent. Is the color from vegetation?"

"It is. Except for five small seas, Gilgor is covered with swamps, marshes, and estuaries. The avian life there is...

Rae Anne was suddenly blinded by a bright yellow and orange flash that burst in front of their car. A deafening roar filled the cabin as the walls crashed inward. Debris rained onto the capsule with a loud clatter. An intense burst of white lightening cracked to the tunnel's ceiling as the Levline cable snapped, hurling their capsule into the tunnel's wall. The car dropped to the floor with a loud THUD, followed by deafening silence.

Rae Anne barely let out a gasp before her body became submerged in a thick green gel. She felt the car's uncontrolled gyration, the jarring clash with the wall and the final crash to the ground, but the gel cushioned her and muted everything. Rae Anne tried to move her arms and legs, with no success.

Dios mio, I'm completely trapped in this gunk.

She called out for VarConsa, but the gel muted the sound.

Thank god for my bubble helmet. I can still breathe, at least for now. I hope rescue comes along soon.

Rae Anne recounted the experience, both to cement the memory while it was still fresh, but also to contemplate what larger issues might underlie the event.

An explosion took place right in front of our Levcab. So probably a terrorist bomb rather than an equipment malfunction.

The explosion broke the Levline cable, producing the electrical discharge. The cars must be well insulated, or I'd have been fried to a crisp.

Which raises an important question. If this was intentional, was it a random act of terrorism, or was this aimed at us, and at me specifically?

I hope VarConsa is ok!

After what seemed like hours, an eerie yellow-green glow lit the Levcab's interior. Shadowy figures appeared and started taking the car apart one piece at a time. Then they sawed away at the chunk of gel filling the car, reducing the gel surrounding her body to a casket sized slab. Four Shalcerians carried her slab to the opposite side of the track and deposited it on the floor of a hovercar.

The last thing Rae Anne remembered was watching a second gel slab being lifted into her car and laid beside hers. As the nanoscreen closed and the craft lifted off she lost consciousness.

New Delhi

General Zahir Kahn looked across his spacious oak desk at the small gathering of military personnel in his office. Two were his most trusted subordinates, colonels in the India Strategic Force. The remaining three held rank of major and had been selected for this project by their colonels.

Kahn gave a last puff on his cigar stub and tamped it into the ash tray on his desk. He gruffly cleared his throat.

"Islamabad is making a public display of preparing to disarm their nuclear warheads as soon as the aliens return. Considering their bloody invasion of Kashmir and their troop buildup all along our Punjab border, I believe our own president's disarmament announcement poses a grave threat to our security. Your take, Colonel Ali?"

"I entirely agree. My intelligence chiefs have reported that sixteen large railcars carrying large objects under wraps have departed their strategic arsenal for transport to three remote locations. Satellite images reveal new construction at all three sites."

"It's clear to me that this poses a threat we must counter, despite our own president's command. I trust the five of you are in agreement with this assessment."

"Yes, sir," acclaimed all five officers in unison.

"So, we are fortunate that our Agni-PR missiles are railcar launch capable. We can launch from any rail siding in the country without telltale construction activity. How many PR's can we remove from our nuclear stockpile without causing suspicion?"

"Eighteen to twenty," Colonel Agarwal responded. He gestured to the major beside him. "Major Odisha, here, is in charge of the accounting process. Over a few months, he can see to it that our total count of active units is diminished as necessary, either through obsolescence or for hardware upgrades."

"What can be done to camouflage the railcars?"

"We've already begun working on that, General." Colonel Ali turned to the major sitting on the end. "Major Haryana?"

Major Haryana cleared his throat and accompanied his response with elaborate hand gestures.

"The size and shape of the launch tubes can be mistaken for industrial chemical manufacturing equipment. By appropriate labelling on the railcar containers, an observer will think it's a commercial shipment to a chemical plant and give it no further thought.

"And regarding the military personnel handling the missiles, if I can keep the left hand from knowing what the right hand is doing, everyone will think they're dealing with ordinary missiles being sent to the front lines in Punjab."

"Then let's get on it immediately. We don't know when the aliens will return, and we'll want these PR's safely in the bank before they do. There will come a time when the president thanks us for our sleight of hand."

Chapter 14

Shalkor

Rae Anne awoke in a treatment center recovery room. Two Shalcerians were checking monitors and attending to their assigned duties. On seeing her regain consciousness, one skipped over to her bed.

"Rae Anne, it's good to see you awake. How are you feeling?"

Rae Anne scowled and took a moment to take stock before responding.

"I have a blinding headache. And I feel nauseous." She gulped to rid the bile in her throat. "Where am I?"

"You are in the Sector 16 Medical Treatment Facility. You are recovering from a severe shoulder injury and trauma."

Rae Anne reached across her chest to rub her right shoulder. It was sore, but she felt no sharp pain. She raised her elbow, and then her arm.

"It seems to be ok."

"Our nanogel therapy works wonders. Thanks to the notes from your doctor on the *Avenger*, we were able to tailor the nanogel to your Human physiology. Without those, your recovery would have taken much longer."

"How long have I been out?"

"We kept you in coma and in the nanogel tank for two weeks."

"Two weeks! *Avenger* hasn't left without me, has it?"

"Oh, no. It's still in port."

"What about my companion in the Levcab? VarConsa. How is he?"

"Sadly, the Monapar did not survive the crash. The gelpad system activated as designed to cushion you both. That and your respirator helmet saved your life. But the Monapar's respirator pack separated from his breathing apparatus when the accident occurred. Unfortunately, he suffocated."

A lump formed in Rae Anne's throat. She tried to swallow.

"VarConsa has…had two kids at home. What will become of them?"

"The authorities have taken care of them. The Monapar are a tight community. Their cloning thing probably has something to do with that. The children will be well cared for."

"When can I go back to the *Avenger?*"

"We can release you as soon as your escort arrives."

Even before the aide finished speaking, Thrahn stepped through the nanoscreen and skipped to Rae Anne's bedside. He held out two arms and enveloped her hand in both of his.

"Thrahn!" Rae Anne's heart skipped a beat.

"Rae Anne! I can't tell you how worried I was when they told me you had been in an accident. And on the Levline! That's unprecedented."

"I'm so glad to see you Thrahn. But… but what about your Convergence."

"Ah, yes. I had just enough time after quarantine to experience Convergence. I cut short my planned visit to come care for you. After all, you are our Human ambassador from Earth."

"They say I'm well enough to return to *Avenger.*"

"Excellent. I have a hovercar waiting. While they're repairing the damaged Levline, the authorities have opened the inter-sector conduits to essential air traffic. We can return non-stop to Sector 14."

"Will there still be time before *Avenger* leaves to continue sightseeing?"

"Captain Vahler has scheduled launch for Sol System in ten days, so you'll have plenty of time. But with only the one working Levline, you will be restricted to Sector 14. I'll give you a credit chip for shopping. You shouldn't return to Earth without a few mementos."

"Thank you, Thrahn. Will there be a memorial service for VarConsa?"

"No. Funeral services are banned throughout the empire. Too reminiscent of religious mythology and dogma. Your internal thoughts and memories of VarConsa are sufficient. The dead are recycled quickly, and citizens are encouraged to focus on the future."

That will be a real sticking point with Humans. Not to mention the ban on religion.

"Well, let me get suited up so we can go. I hope you can arrange time to help me shop for souvenirs. I wouldn't have any idea what I was looking at or what to look for."

"That will be a great pleasure. I will happily escort you whenever it can be arranged. I may be able to find a Browakal shnapsnik for you to take home."

Rae Anne laughed when she saw his chest scales rippling in a lavender and light-yellow checkerboard.

The first laugh I've had since leaving Sol System. And I'm laughing with a real alien at an alien joke I don't even understand!

Rae Anne spent her remaining days on Shalkor strolling along the avenues, enjoying street entertainment, and browsing the many museums and galleries interspersed throughout the sector. She used the credit chip to buy unique items she could easily transport back to Earth to demonstrate the astounding variety of goods these advanced civilizations had to offer. Thrahn accompanied her on about half of her excursions, providing background information on the many strange things she saw.

No one paid her any attention, despite her unique appearance. There were so many alien species represented on Shalkor that non-Shalcerian life forms accounted for a tenth of the foot traffic on the main streets.

On one outing, she asked Thrahn to comment on a growing suspicion that had been bothering her.

"Before the accident, everything was so new and strange that my mind was busy just taking it all in. But since then, I've been focusing more on the people, and I've noticed something odd."

"Oh? And what might that be?"

"In every crowd, I notice several Shalcerians carrying identical shoulder packs, usually in pairs. In most cases their body scales are a uniform shade of light blue."

"Those are members of our Capital Security Force, a division of the armed forces. They make sure that everything runs smoothly, that everyone obeys the law and abides by the empire's dictates."

"But there are so many of them. They're everywhere."

"It's necessary. For example, after the Levline explosion, several hundred CSF soldiers swept into a neighboring borough and arrested sixty-one terrorists. They are likely being interrogated as we speak, at least those that have not yet been executed. CSF methods can be quite brutal. That knowledge alone helps keep everyone in line. If it weren't for them, violent disruptions would be far more frequent."

"Is this common throughout the empire?"

"Unfortunately, it is. Every colony and outpost have their own Security Force unit."

Mierda. Despite outward appearances, the Shalcerian Empire is a heavily policed authoritarian regime. I wonder how free the subject species on their colony worlds really are.

While on Shalkor, each morning her credit chip had been recharged to its original value despite what she purchased the day before. She wondered how this amount compared to the average citizen's financial obligations and how much a typical Shalcerian's personal wealth exceeded that of the other species in the empire. She guessed the economic level on other worlds was probably lower than on Shalkor. From her observations on the streets of Shalkor, she deduced that in these matters, the empire was no different from any Earth empire. The differences between the 'Haves and Have Nots' seemed to be a universal principle.

When she returned to *Avenger* on the tenth day following her return from the hospital, Thrahn announced they were preparing to leave as scheduled and return to the Sol System.

"We won't be going directly to Earth, however. Some years ago, we rescued several survivors from an egregious attack on one of our cruisers in the Kuiper Belt. *Avenger* has been assigned to retrieve the two escape pods they used so they can be returned to service."

Two escape pods?

"How many survivors did you rescue?"

"297, less than two thirds of the *Nemesis* crew."

"How did you locate the escape pods in the vastness of space?"

"Standard procedure dictates for any ship needing help to seek an equatorial orbit around the largest moon of the largest planet in the nearest system. That makes locating escape pods or damaged ships extremely easy in any planetary system. For the *Nemesis*, we had only to look to Jupiter's largest moon, Ganymede."

Dios mio! Those WERE Shalcerian escape pods I observed!

"Unfortunately, one of the three pods from *Nemesis* never made it there," Thrahn continued. "We're still searching for it. It may have been damaged or destroyed before it could get away."

"These escape pods. Are they disk shaped like *Avenger's* shuttle?"

"Why, yes. You were in one. The rescue ships we used on Alsafi-γ were *Avenger's* escape pods, repurposed for the rescue mission. Let me show you."

Thrahn brought a view showing *Avenger's* underbelly onto the wall hologram. *Avenger's* three escape pods, nestled snuggly in their berths, were plainly visible. A chill ran up Rae Anne's spine.

"I spotted the two escape pods on my way to Saturn when *Aurora* passed by Jupiter. I was taking detailed videos of Ganymede when these two identical discs emerged from behind the moon. I was sure they were artificial. How long ago did this attack take place?"

"55 Earth years ago. It would have taken 19 years for the pods to travel from the Kuiper belt to Ganymede with their modest propulsion systems."

"And the crew were still alive after all that time?"

"Yes. As soon as the course is set, the crew goes into a biochemically induced stasis to await recovery. They can hibernate for over a hundred years if necessary. Once we retrieve them and treat them in our infirmary, most revive without any ill effects."

"So, if you locate the missing escape pod, you'll be able to bring that crew back alive as well?"

"Absolutely. That is why we are continuing our search."

Rae Anne took a deep breath.

"I believe I can lead you to the missing escape pod. I haven't seen it myself, but I know exactly where it is."

Thrahn stepped back in apparent astonishment. All three eyestalks stood erect atop his torso, the three eyes staring intently at Rae Anne. His body scales flashed purple and magenta in a dozen scrambled patterns.

"That's astounding! The captain will want you to meet with the Directorate immediately. Your information may dictate our course of action when we arrive in the Sol System."

Within hours, Rae Anne found herself sitting in the small room next to the Directorate Council Chambers facing the seven-member Directorate. As usual, Director Captain Vahler was in charge. After apologizing on the empire's behalf for the unfortunate experience Rae Anne had on Shalkor, he wasted no time getting to the point.

"We have learned you believe you know where the missing *Nemesis* escape pod is. How is it you, a Human, whose people have yet to colonize a single off-world planet or moon, can possibly have this knowledge?"

Rae Anne was shocked by his arrogance but took a deep breath and tried to overlook it.

"*Avenger's* escape pods look exactly like two alien craft I observed three years ago as *Aurora* passed through the Jupiter system on its way to Saturn. These two craft were orbiting Jupiter's largest moon, Ganymede.

"Several months later, a Human mission assigned to explore the surface of Mars discovered an alien artifact that had crashed into Mars. They described it to me, and their description matched the objects I saw orbiting Ganymede. The *Aurora* archives will have its exact location. We dubbed it 'Shark Fin' after the shape of its shadow. There was no sign of life at the site, though Martian winds would have eroded any tracks over time."

"Do we have access to these archives?"

"I understand *Aurora's* entire computer database was uploaded to *Avenger's* computer when you took me on board. The information you need should be readily available."

Rae Anne watched through the window as the directors became involved in animated discussion. Her speaker had been turned off. Shortly, the holographic image of the chambers went blank, without any further acknowledgement.

Shaking her head in bewilderment, she stood and returned to her quarters.

"How did it go?" Jason asked.

"I think they believed me. Many Shalcerian lives depend on it. But I'm getting a better glimpse at what dealing with the Shalcerian Empire will look like. A cooperation agreement may be a hard sell. Humans don't care to play second fiddle to arrogant bastards that treat them like shit."

Jason's face took on a look of mock horror. "Rae Anne, I've never heard you use such strong derogatory language!"

"I haven't experienced such a display of condescension and outright bigotry since I left my home in Albuquerque's barrio for Stanford. But here the discrimination is against the entire Human race."

Chapter 15

Mars

Avenger jumped directly from 18 Scorpii to the Sol System without difficulty using its refurbished propulsion units. The brightest disk in the bridge hologram besides Sol had a vaguely reddish tinge. Rae Anne was certain it must be Mars.

An hour later, in her quarters, her guess was confirmed when Mars' rust-red orb appeared on her monitor. *Avenger* assumed a stationary orbit directly above the Shark Fin coordinates Vahler had gleaned from *Aurora's* archives. Shortly, a shuttle departed for the surface.

Later, Rae Anne encountered Thrahn and asked if they had located their missing escape pod.

"The escape pod was exactly where you said it would be. Captain Vahler is pleased."

"So, the remainder of the *Nemesis* crew have been rescued."

"Not yet. The pod hit the surface with such force it buried itself deeply into Martian soil and bedrock. What your Mars explorers saw sticking above the surface was just 20% of the craft. We'll have to spend several days excavating a tunnel to the pod's airlock."

Incredible that the hull could withstand such an impact without damage and cushion the crew from the jolt as well. If there ever was a miracle material, the GESC-Plasticore is it.

"So, once we have the *Nemesis* crew aboard, we'll be heading for Earth?"

"No. Shalkor Command has directed us to retrieve the two escape pods in orbit around Ganymede first. Then we'll return to Earth and pick up where we left off in our negotiations. We'll be there in a week. We are hoping the Human delegations have worked through their differences while we've been gone."

Ray Anne caught the humor in Thrahn's comment when she noted the violet and lemon-yellow checkerboard ripple across his chest. She responded with a chuckle.

"We Humans are a contentious lot, aren't we?"

"You are that."

"Since *Avenger* will be heading back toward Jupiter, I have a small request that means a great deal to me. A bit of unfinished business, you might say."

"With your help in discovering the whereabouts of *Nemesis'* third escape pod, I'm sure Captain Vahler will give your request every consideration. What is it you have in mind?"

"Somewhere between Saturn and Jupiter is a tiny spacecraft, the *Eagle*, the lander I used on Titan. All the samples and video files I collected there are stowed away on *Eagle*. I would greatly appreciate it if Captain Vahler could make a detour to retrieve *Eagle* and return it to Earth."

"I'll pass your request to the captain. At *Avenger's* velocity, the detour would only add a few hours to our ETA for Earth."

"One other thing. Some of the samples may contain living organisms that are alien to both our species. You will have to be put *Eagle* into a strict quarantine."

Before a day had passed in the Sol System, Rae Anne consulted with Jason.

"I need to get in touch with Ian, if he's still alive. Is our previous communication setup still available to make calls to the Agency? They'll know where Ian is."

"Already done, Rae Anne. Once we arrived in orbit, I figured that would be a priority. Ian's anxiously waiting on the line."

Jason smiled and handed her a phone.

Rae Anne sighed with relief on learning Ian had pulled through. She also felt a tinge of excited anticipation toward hearing Ian's voice.

"The time and distance delay between Earth and Mars is currently 8.33 minutes."

"Thanks Jason."

"Hello, Ian?"

Rae Anne couldn't remember the last time she felt so excited. She turned to Jason, smiling broadly.

"Rae Anne? I'm confused. Your face tells me you are happy, but you are crying."

"It's a Human condition, Jason. You wouldn't understand."

She turned sharply back to the phone when Ian's voice came through.

"…Yes, yes it was longer than we expected. A long story. But how are you doing?…Getting around is good! And you're back at work. Last I heard you were in a coma. I can't tell you how worried I was the entire time we were gone…"

Rae Anne filled Ian in on *Avenger's* itinerary, assuring him she would be back in Earth orbit within days.

"…I love you too, Ian. Please make plans to visit me as soon as we reach Earth. And don't skimp on your physical therapy, you hear?"

Rae Anne was crying again when she handed the phone back to Jason. He returned it to the communications console on *Aurora's* flight deck, shaking his head in consternation.

Later that evening, Rae Anne felt up to continuing her lessons in Shalcerian physics.

"How's your study of their wormhole drive coming along?"

"Thanks to my observations during this last jump, I now understand how it works, as well as the sophisticated mathematical equations that underly the engineering."

"Fantastic! I think I've finally wrapped my mind around black holes and multidimensional space from our last talk. The fact that the inside of a black hole is empty, part of the Void surrounding the many dimensions in our universe. So, give me the layperson's version of wormholes. I'm all ears."

"Interesting expression. The Shalcerians have one like it. Roughly translated, it says, 'Fill my gills.'

"Anyway, as you know, Human physicists have spent the last century trying to combine Einstein's general relativity concept of gravity with quantum mechanics, which deals with the strange behavior and interactions among atoms and subatomic particles. The Shalcerians have not only amalgamated the two concepts into a single set of physical laws, they have engineered real-world devices that put theory into practical use. The wormhole generator is one such example."

"I suspected they figured out how to manipulate gravity to achieve interstellar flight, but how does quantum dynamics come into play?"

"Their interstellar propulsion system goes much deeper than simply manipulating gravity. The gravity bottle located deep within the ship's core contains two micro black holes. One of *Avenger's* four fusion reactor's sole purpose is to maintain the gravity bottle to keep the black holes from escaping."

"So, *Avenger* is carrying two microscopic black holes. That must represent an incredible amount of energy, even if they are tiny. Go on."

"Black holes not only spin physically, they also have a quantum spin component, just like electrons and subatomic particles. That subjects black holes to all the laws of quantum mechanics. If you have two micro black holes, you can entangle them into a coherent state. The entire output of two fusion reactors is required to achieve this.

"When such massive particles become entangled, the whole fabric of the surrounding space folds in on itself, swallowing everything in the vicinity and ejecting it into a region of space light years away. The Shalcerians have learned how to control this process so it directs their ship into their chosen destination star system."

"That explains why they can only initiate their interstellar drive at a great distance from planets. Folding space like that would cause gravitational havoc in the surroundings, even altering planetary orbits."

"That's correct. Fortunately, their normal drive system produces velocities up to two-thirds lightspeed, so even if they arrive a million kilometers from their destination planet, it doesn't take them long to travel the last leg."

"We need to find out how they manipulate these black holes to do their bidding. Human scientists achieve quantum entanglement with atoms by using carefully tuned lasers and a cryogenic environment. What kind of tools must it take to entangle black holes?"

Earth Orbit

Seven days later, after retrieving *Eagle* and the two *Nemesis* escape pods orbiting Ganymede, *Avenger* arrived at Earth. Rae Anne returned to her quarters from the bridge, having just watched *Avenger* sweep into orbit around her beautiful blue planet and assume a polar orbit 1000 km above its surface. A large hurricane directly beneath *Avenger* was inching its way toward Puerto Rico, its swirling white cloud mass gleaming against the bright blue Atlantic.

She stepped through the nanoscreen into the hangar deck containing *Aurora*, pulled off her helmet and turned off the oxygen supply. Beads of sweat formed squiggly rivulets down her forehead. Jason was right behind her.

"It's good to be back home, Jason. I feel like I've been gone for ages. Although I am glad we spent those four weeks on Shalkor, despite the terrorist attack. I could write a book about all I've learned."

"Understanding their environment on their home planet and the evolution of their species reveals a lot about who they are," Jason added.

"Anyway, I'll keep probing their database, even while I pretend to stumble over their language. They find my efforts hilariously entertaining. It's the perfect distraction."

"What's the perfect distraction?" Thrahn's voice startled Rae Anne. She turned in time to see him come through *Aurora's* gaping hole.

"Games," Jason quickly interjected. "Like chess and Go. The Human brain requires the occasional distraction from intense thinking to perform at maximum efficiency."

"Interesting. We have no such impediments.

"But I have some disturbing news to report. Five missiles have been launched from the Eurasian continent on a trajectory to intercept *Avenger* in orbit.

Rae Anne threw her hands to her face and gasped.

"Dios mio! How much danger are we in? If they're nuclear warheads, can *Avenger* survive a nuclear attack?"

Before Thrahn could respond, a large tremor reverberated through the ship.

"To answer your question, it just did. Nuclear weapons have no effect on our GESC-Plasticore hull. You Humans have nothing that can damage our ship. The vibrations we just felt were the nuclear blasts. The explosions should have presented quite a light show for anyone on Earth who witnessed it. The electromagnetic pulse probably took out a large number of satellites as well."

Rae Anne frowned and shook her head. "I don't know what to say…"

"Unfortunately, this puts our relationship with Humans in jeopardy. Captain Vahler wishes to see you on the bridge immediately."

Rae Anne donned her gear and followed Thrahn to the bridge. A gloomy depression and deep sense of foreboding replaced the excited anticipation she had experienced earlier.

On the bridge, she found herself under the withering glare of Vahler's three eyes.

"Rae Anne, your Humans just launched a significant attack on *Avenger.* Fortunately, their puny efforts are no match for our superior technology."

Rae Anne started to offer an apology but was interrupted.

"The Empire tolerates no aggression against any part of its dominion. Such actions must be answered swiftly and decisively. I brought you here to witness the Empire's response to hostilities."

The forward holographic image portrayed the landmass of eastern Europe directly below.

Vahler issued several commands. A crimson ring formed in front of the ship. The ring extruded into an iridescent corkscrew of fire extending from *Avenger* toward Earth below like a syringe needle. A tiny, but blinding, white flash burst momentarily on the landmass. And it was over.

"I have dispatched a drone to show you the consequences for your Human's attack on *Avenger*. There is a reason we name our battleships as we do, *Avenger, Vengeance, Reprisal, Nemesis*. It is to remind all species of the Empire's response to hostile acts against it."

Rae Anne watched the holographic feed from the drone as it dropped into Earth's atmosphere. She recognized the Black Sea directly below the drone. The drone veered north and east as it glided toward its destination.

The drone slowed to a stop at about twenty kilometers, revealing a view as seen from a high-flying aircraft. Beneath the drone was a perfectly round, black circle, simmering like a volcanic caldera. It lay in the center of a major city.

"The strike you see is eight kilometers in diameter. We targeted the walled fortress you call the Kremlin in the center of Moscow. I believe it will be a long time before your Russian Federation tries to take on the forces of the Empire again."

Rae Anne shuddered at the sight. She began shaking with fury even as a flood of tears flowed down her cheeks.

"You took out half of Moscow!" she screamed, shaking her fist at the captain. "Six million people. Gone. Vaporized. You could have just taken out the missile launchers."

Thrahn reached out with all three hands and grasped her shoulders to restrain her should she attempt to attack his captain.

"To be effective, retribution requires pain. This demonstration should be a warning to all Humans. Any future hostility toward any representative of the Empire, whether it be an individual citizen or a battlecruiser, will have dire consequences.

"The Directorate will meet with you tomorrow. Meanwhile, you are to convey this warning message to all your world's representatives. You are dismissed!"

Vahler pointedly spun back to his console. Rae Anne was still shaking with rage. Thrahn took her arm and led her off the bridge and back to her quarters.

Chapter 16

New Hampshire

Sam placed his phone on the nightstand beside his bed. Although it was after 2:00 a.m., he was wide awake. His assistant in Sydney had just called to tell him the news of the Moscow disaster. Sam's standing instructions were that he be notified immediately of breaking news that could affect his business empire regardless of time of day.

So much for my Moscow spaceport.

He breathed a deep sigh of relief that he hadn't yet invested anything more than a few bribes to get things going.

Maybe Warsaw or Istanbul. Or Kyiv for that matter.

His phone alerted him to another call. He picked it up and noted Karen's name on the screen. He reluctantly answered the call.

"Those bastards. Those fucking bastards!" Karen screamed into the phone before Sam could utter a word.

"Those aliens just killed my mother. They just murdered most of my family. They incinerated every speck of my childhood memories."

Only then did Sam recall that Karen was originally Karina Petrovna, born and raised within a stone's throw of the Kremlin walls.

"My god, Karen. I'm so sorry. I just heard the news."

"They'll pay for this. Maybe the bastard aliens are untouchable, but I'll find a way. Someone will pay. Karina Petrovna will exact her revenge."

"What about Sanderson Robotics, Karen. Didn't you have a research division in Moscow? Did it survive?"

"Gone. Totally gone. 1200 engineers and support staff obliterated."

"How big a hit will that be for your company."

"Not so much. I'll expand operations in Israel and Johannesburg. Engineers I can replace. But Mama. They killed Mama and my *tetya* Vera, *tozhye*. It's all the fault of that Chavez bitch. She led those *chorti* to Earth. As far as I'm concerned, she's as much as one of them."

"I can't say I disagree with you Karen. We'll see some serious political fallout from this. There's no question that they've overplayed their hand this time."

"I'm through treating them with kid gloves. I don't know how I'll do it, but I'll see that they experience Karina Petrovna's raw fury. I shall never forget."

The line went dead as Karen abruptly rang off. Sam put the phone back on the table and rubbed his temples.

If contracting to assassinate that Bentley fellow was an example of 'kid gloves,' I hate to think what she means by 'raw fury.' But more to the point, imagine what I could do with the aliens' technology at my disposal.

Aliens Destroy Moscow; Millions Dead
Aliens Show True Colors, Vaporize City
Aliens Go Home. We Don't Need You.

News media around the world broadcast images of the blackened crater that was once a robust city. Before and after pictures taken from Moscow University looking northeast across the Moscow River toward where the Kremlin had been revealed the enormity of *Avenger*'s 'death ray.' Tall buildings, hotels, whole communities of apartment complexes, all replaced by a vast, empty caldera.

Rae Anne's account of the event and the fact that a preemptive nuclear strike precipitated it were lost in the outraged reporting from the mass media. Protests that had numbered in the thousands before were now in the tens of thousands. Government officials, although cognizant of the facts, nevertheless pandered to the demonstrators with empty promises.

The Russian Federation filed formal protests with the United Nations, with China's full support. Before 24 hours had elapsed, 47 nations had joined Russia's suit and official proceedings of condemnation were initiated.

Earth-Orbit

After a sleepless night, Rae Anne followed Thrahn to her cubicle adjoining the Directorate Council Chamber. She had never felt more helpless. She witnessed two cities destroyed with ruthless abandon using the advanced technology she hoped would save humanity. The images of Moscow and of Alsafi-γ, with their inhabitants instantly vaporized, created a deep gash into her soul. As she sat on her chair and gazed into the conference room, she felt a weariness seeping into her very bones.

Humans aren't ready to abandon tribalism and violence. Maybe extinction is all that lies ahead. If everything I've done to show a brighter path has been wasted, there can be no hope for humanity.

The seven directors appeared to enter the chamber and take their usual positions opposite her cubicle. In the hologram, they all faced Rae Anne, radiating solid shades of gray. Director Captain Vahler spoke.

"This is your last chance to offer evidence that Humans are worthy of our attention. Our goal has been to help unite the various entities on Earth into a single, cohesive, and cooperative civilization that our Interstellar Consortium would welcome. We have offered to share with you our advanced technology—technology that will ameliorate the ravages of climate-change that is threatening your planet.

"What we asked in return was for Humans to take obvious steps to save yourselves from extinction, namely nuclear disarmament and elimination of fossil fuels.

"Your attack on *Avenger* with the most destructive weapons in your arsenal demonstrates that you have not sufficiently matured to warrant our attention. It is time we move on to more important issues and leave you to your own devices."

Adrenalin coursed through Rae Anne's veins and her heart felt like it would pound her chest to pieces. Anger displaced her depression. She wanted to jump to her feet and shout 'No, you must help us. You can't leave us to die.' But she knew the evidence provided ample justification for Vahler's pronouncement.

Instead, she concentrated on maintaining a calm resolve, although her mind was reeling, searching for any argument that might warrant consideration. She stood to speak, tightly clenching the table in front of her to keep her hands from trembling.

"It is true that we are a fractured civilization, Director Captain Vahler. Our evolution wasn't as docile as yours on Shalkor. Our ancestors' survival depended on constant vigilance against predators, instant analysis in precarious situations and quick decision making. As a result, we are more wary of strangers and their offers of friendship, even among others of our own, let alone a species from beyond our Solar System. Under such circumstances, unanimity among Humans is an unachievable expectation.

"However, we can cooperate despite our differences. Please consider that humans have built two important organizations besides the United Nations in which dozens of member nations are cooperating. Where peace is the rule rather than the exception. Compromise and acceptance are fundamental principles and tolerance of tribal differences is the norm. These organizations are the North Atlantic Treaty Organization and the Indo-Pacific Economic Framework. Together, they represent a significant percentage of Earth's Human population.

"Before you give up on Humans entirely, please consider reaching out to these nations with your request for cooperation. Let me approach these two organizations with your proposals and garner their support for cooperation. If an agreement between you and these two organizations can be ironed out and proves universally beneficial, in time, Earth's more reluctant nations will come aboard. Then you will have achieved the universal acceptance you desire."

Rae Anne sat down, wondering if she could make good on her proposal.

"We are familiar with both organizations," said Vahler. "They are notable exceptions. But satellite images reveal protests and demonstrations in the streets of every capital city. Such widespread antagonism toward positive change, change that would save your species from extinction, is beyond our comprehension.

"However, we will discuss your proposal."

The hologram dissolved, leaving Rae Anne staring through the transparent window into emptiness. She tried to imagine what discussions might be taking place, but decided she was too restricted by her Human experience to have any idea how Shalcerians would behave.

After a short while, the holographic display reappeared.

The first thing Rae Anne noted was vague tinges of color beginning to appear on the directors' body scales. Only one holdout remained a solid slate gray. Rae Anne interpreted any hint of color as a positive sign.

"Very well," announced Captain Vahler. "We will consider your proposal, provided you can show us unanimous consent among the nations of NATO and IPEF. We will meet here again in seven days. We will determine how to proceed based on what you can show us."

The captain placed all three hands in the middle of his chest, a gesture Rae Anne now recognized as Shalcerian for 'meeting over' or 'you're dismissed.' The hologram again evaporated.

Rae Anne stood and quickly returned to her quarters, adrenalin coursing through her veins.

"Jason," she called from the hallway, not sure where she might find him. His answer came from her quarters. She turned and stepped through the nanoscreen.

"Jason, we must contact Ian immediately. We need to have the Agency establish an emergency network with the member nations of NATO and IPEF. We must gather all the agreements that have been negotiated at the UN while we were away and use them to hammer together something everyone will support.

"When I meet with the Directorate in a week, I want something positive to show them, to convince them not to abandon us."

"I'm confused. You still want to work with the Shalcerians after their destruction of Moscow?"

"I find myself between a rock and a hard place, Jason. As an individual, I find their actions barbaric and unconscionable. I would happily send them back where they came from. But the future viability of humanity is at stake. I still believe they are our only hope for survival."

Washington, D.C.

Ian leaned his cane against the arm of his chair and clutched a printout of Rae Anne's missive in his right hand as he sat stiffly in the anteroom to the Oval Office, awaiting his turn to see President Stratton. He hadn't personally met with the president since *Avenger* was first spotted approaching Earth and identified as an alien starship.

So much has happened since we first met. And so much is about to be lost.

The door opened and the Speaker of the House and Senate Majority Leader both emerged, animatedly arguing over a proposed emergency relief fund for Russia. Immediately behind them, Havel Nelson emerged and motioned for Ian to enter.

"Ian. Good to see you again. It's been what, three months?"

"Madam President. Thanks for seeing me on such short notice."

"Any time my chief of astronautics makes an emergency trip to Washington with an issue relating to the aliens, I'll take time to see him. Especially after they destroyed half of Moscow. So much for their 'We come in peace' offer. Anyway, I'm glad to see you are making progress on your recovery."

"I'm the lucky one. Losing both Hikari and Martin still hurts."

"I share your sorrow. I hope they find whoever was responsible. However, I am on a very tight schedule, so let's get right to the point of your visit."

"Of course. The Russian nuclear missile strike against *Avenger* and the worldwide demonstrations have convinced the Shalcerians to abandon Earth. They have determined that a universal agreement on cooperation can't be achieved."

"That is bad news. If they leave, things here on Earth will only keep getting worse. Analysts over in the Pentagon predict that a world war is inevitable, likely with nuclear repercussions. Is there nothing we can do?"

"Rae Anne responded with a proposal that the Shalcerians look to NATO and IPEF for their partnership rather than the entire Human race. They are considering this option. Rae Anne is requesting we immediately contact leaders in both organizations to get formal approval of the best proposals we've hashed out at the UN."

"How soon is immediate?"

"We have a week."

"Good god, Ian. Governments don't work that fast."

"We need these organizations to present a formal acceptance before the Shalcerians decide to return to the Kuiper Belt and take Earth's only hope for the future with them."

"After what the aliens did to Moscow, there may not be much enthusiasm to collaborate with them. I fear we're in for a hard sell."

"We need to emphasize that the Russians attacked the Shalcerians first, and with nuclear weapons. The aliens would never have targeted Moscow without that provocation."

"Well, it's certainly worth a try."

"Havel, you heard the man. Get on it. Presidents and prime ministers, 58 nations, link video calls directly to the Command Center here. But work around time zones. No one likes to be awakened in the middle of the night, even for emergencies. We'll make a composite of the videos to send to Rae Anne as soon as we reach 40 with assurances that we'll have all 58 when we're finished."

"No rest for the wicked."

"Not tonight. Thanks for the heads-up, Ian. We'll do our best to convince them we can fulfill their requirements without the other nations. Once we receive their technology and share it universally, the rest of the world will come around."

"That's the best we can hope for."

"Have a safe trip back to Colorado, Ian."

"Thank you, Madam President."

President Stratton shook Ian's hand and swiftly disappeared down the corridor.

"We'll do all we can, Ian. Catching all 58 leaders on such short notice when a conflict isn't threatening will be a tough call. I'd best get to work."

"Good luck, Havel. And thanks. This is every bit as important as if a war had begun. Please convey that urgency with those you talk to."

"Will do. Safe travels."

Chapter 17

Earth Orbit

Four days after her meeting with the Directorate, Rae Anne received a Letter of Intent from Ian with video images from 47 of the 58 nations in NATO and IPEF. She turned this over to Thrahn, who immediately recorded it into *Avenger's* computer to be shared with the Directorate.

These documents are a start, but I need eleven more.

By week's end, an additional six nations had signed on. None of those contacted refused, and the five remaining nations were expected to agree as well. Only parliamentary procedures were holding up the works.

When the time arrived for her scheduled meeting with the directors, she made her way to her cubicle adjoining the Council Chambers. The seven Shalcerians were already present, animatedly discussing some item of business. After several minutes, Vahler noticed that Rae Anne had arrived and stopped the discussion, then directed his comments to her.

"Rae Anne, your Letters of Intent are fine, but they represent less than half of Earth's population, and fewer than half of the nation states on Earth. Without 100% consensus, the ravages of climate change will continue, though perhaps slowed to some degree. Similarly, without complete nuclear disarmament, nuclear annihilation remains a distinct possibility. We note that Russia, Iran, North Korea, Israel and China, all nations with nuclear arsenals, are not among the nations agreeing to our proposals.

"Furthermore, our sensors have detected nuclear warheads similar to those used against *Avenger* being secreted away in remote locations in both India and Pakistan. Whether the intent is for these to be used against us or against each other remains to be determined. But this further illustrates that without the cooperation of 100% of Earth's nations, there can be no cooperation.

"The risks of failure are too great to justify the expenditure of time, effort, and resources that we proposed giving to your species.

"We are prepared to shuttle you to EOTS-I and drop you off before leaving the inner Solar System and returning to our Kuiper Belt patrols. Please collect anything you wish to take back with you. Thrahn will lead you to the Shuttle Bay."

Rae Anne's heart sank. Everything she had witnessed, her dreams for Earth's future, her vision of Humans joining an interstellar community, all dashed. There seemed to be nothing more she could do.

"Director Captain Vahler, I request you allow me to take my android, Jason with me. And my ship, *Aurora*. You can leave it in orbit beside EOTS-I. But I humbly ask that you repair it first."

"Jason you can have, though I doubt it will be of much use once *Avenger*'s computer is no longer available. As for *Aurora*, it would take several days to repair it and restore it to space worthiness. Why would you want us to save it? We were going to dispose of it by sending it into Sol."

"When I was on Shalkor, I visited your museums. I was impressed by the Shalcerian attentiveness to your history and to saving artifacts to enhance your children's education. We humans have the same instincts. A restored *Aurora* would make a fine museum piece commemorating my trip to Saturn, your rescuing me, and humanity's First Contact with Shalcerians and the Shalcerian Empire."

"Very well. You may keep Jason and *Aurora*. We'll do our best to restore it, but keep in mind that we don't have the primitive tools and techniques you Humans used in its construction. The final product won't look exactly as you remember it."

In her quarters, Rae Anne tried to flop dejectedly on her bed. Its antigravity nature responded by bouncing her six inches in the air before settling her body a safe half inch above the mattress. Jason understood immediately what had happened.

"They've rejected your letters of intent."

"Yes. They're adamant about having 100% acquiescence to their mandates, and we didn't come anywhere near that."

"So, what's next?"

"They're going to return us to EOTS-I and abandon the project."

"What about *Aurora*?"

"I convinced them to restore *Aurora* as best they can and leave it in orbit next to EOTS as a museum piece. At least we'll have that much as a reminder of First Contact. And your program and memory will still be intact."

And it will serve as a reminder of how utterly stupid and short-sighted we Humans are. How could we have squandered such an amazing opportunity? Now that we know we aren't alone, will it make a difference in how we respond to one another? Where do we go from here?

Part Three

Chapter 1

Earth Orbit, 2043

While the Shalcerian engineers worked at repairing the hole in
Aurora's hull on Level 2, Rae Anne tried to relax in her lounger on Level
3 despite the ruckus. She was watching videos of *Aurora's* launch from
Earth orbit and early footage of *Aurora's* voyage to Mars with Mindy,
Rob and herself interacting as *Aurora's* crew. She desperately wracked her
brain for any recourse to keep the Shalcerians from abandoning humanity.

"If only Humans could cooperate with each other like crewmembers
on a space mission. We never had a conflict, even after months in close
quarters." She turned toward Jason who was sitting cross-legged on the
deck, deep in thought. "What is the matter with Humans?"

Jason looked up at Rae Anne and grinned.

"Where do I begin?"

"I'm serious. How were we three so different from everyone else?"

"You may have forgotten the Mars-I flyby mission that preceded
yours. Of the five crewmembers returning to Earth, only Ian arrived with
his sanity intact. The agency reassigned all the remaining astronauts to
other tasks and recruited your team fresh for the future Mars missions,
setting psychological profiling and rigorous psychotherapy sessions as top
priorities in your training regimen."

"I had forgotten about Mars-I, but I could never forget the therapy
sessions they forced on us. I do remember occasions when our training
helped me resolve personal issues. It still does."

Rae Anne sat up with a start.

"That gives me an idea. Maybe we do have one last shot at this.
Anything is worth a try."

"Jason, use your computer connection to get hold of Thrahn. I need to see him one last time. Tell him it's urgent."

After a minute or so, Jason replied, "Thrahn is on his way, although he expressed puzzlement at the urgency, pointing out we won't be leaving *Avenger* for another couple of days."

Shortly, Thrahn appeared in the hangar deck and stepped around the work crew repairing *Aurora*. Rae Anne climbed the ladder to the galley on Level 2 and presented her proposal to Thrahn. She was gratified that he thought it had some merit. He left on a mission to convince the Directorate to give Rae Anne one last audience.

The following morning, Rae Anne was summoned to her cubicle adjoining the Directorate Council Chambers. Rae Anne felt her adrenalin surge as she stepped through the nanoscreen and saw the seven directors waiting for her, their body scales all a dull gray.

I had better damn well win this one. It's my last chance.

Despite their alien appearance, the directors reminded Rae Anne of an old painting showing judges at an inquisition. Their gray scales made it clear they were not happy with reviving a closed issue. Rae Anne detected palpable tension through the holographic rendition of the Council Chambers.

"You should know, Rae Anne, this is highly irregular," Director Captain Vahler began.

"We are allowing this hearing in deference to your role in saving the 76 survivors from the *Nemesis* escape pod. But I must inform you in advance—there is nothing you can say to change our decision to withhold our technology from your savage and irreconcilable species."

His reference to humanity's sorry attributes stung sharply.

He has a right to his opinion. And it's not that far from the truth. But I can use this comment to lead into my proposal.

She leaned forward on the desk and stared through the glass partition with resolution. She committed herself to presenting her proposal as a feasible win-win for both species.

"Honorable Directors, thank you for hearing me out this one last time.

"I am proposing a compromise that will grant you the local resources you seek to assume the Kuiper Belt patrols while providing you with confidence that you are partnering with a stable and dependable community of Humans.

"Although we are a fractured, warring species, there are many individual Humans on Earth for whom cooperation, kindness, and respect for others is paramount. We know how to identify these humans through psychological testing and DNA profiling. We have the technology to do this.

"The agency that put together the Mars-II and Mars-III missions went to great lengths to select members for those missions who exhibited these very traits. They evaluated candidates extensively to identify those whose profiles would lead to the success of the missions. They developed rigorous training protocols to provide candidates with the tools and mind set to assure compromise and cooperation.

"We can employ this same process to profile candidates for participation in the project I am now asking you to consider."

Rae Anne paused to let this idea sink in. She could detect no changes in the directors' demeaner. Their body scales remained a dull gray.

"I propose that you construct an orbiting city for Humans in Saturn orbit, similar to the first city you built in orbit above Shalkor so long ago. Saturn is far enough removed from Earth that it will be protected from any violence those remaining on Earth might concoct. Size it to accommodate one million Humans, with additional boroughs for visiting species, including your own. Each Human immigrant to this city will be selected based on their psychological and genetic suitability to being a member of a cooperating collective and on their receptivity and respect for non-Human species and cultures.

"Saturn is an ideal centralized location for the Kuiper Belt Patrol headquarters. A city in orbit there would serve as a maintenance site for the ships and a training base for their crews. If your forecasts for Earth are correct, it might also end up as humanity's lifeboat. If so, the orbiting city and its offspring will contain the only remnants of Human civilization. But the genetic tendency toward warlike tribalism plaguing today's humanity will have been left behind."

Rae Anne paused, her mind racing. She had one other piece to add, but she worried it might cloud the directors' thinking.

Just do it, Rae Anne. It's important to you, and this is the only chance you'll have to make it happen.

"However, I cannot bring myself to abandon my fellow Humans left on Earth, no matter how bleak their future may seem. I request that you build 100 nuclear fusion power plants and locate them on Earth in regions where their impact on poverty and economic development will be most felt."

Rae Anne observed the Director's activities from the silence of her cubicle. They appeared to be deliberating. Two directors were quite animated. Rae Anne was amused at their ability to punctuate their arguments by expressively waving three arms and two legs.

At least they haven't rejected my proposal out of hand.

As she watched, she noted their body colors shifting away from the grays and one by one turning to various shades of yellow and orange. One even became a pinkish coral. There was only one holdout, and even his upper body showed a yellowish tinge.

Rae Anne shifted to the edge of her chair, fully alert to the proceedings.

This could only be a good sign.

Captain Vahler broke the silence in the cubicle.

"The Directorate believes your proposal holds merit. Your concern for Humans left behind on Earth was a powerful point of persuasion. It gives testimony to your claims that some Humans are capable of empathy and altruism. Without having added that, we would have dismissed your request.

"Nevertheless, we reject that part of your proposal. You have an expression, 'throwing pearls before swine.' We believe it appropriately describes any effort at placing Shalcerian technology on Earth.

"However, when we obtain the necessary approvals from Shalkor, we will build your orbiting city and provide it with a fleet of in-system cruisers to police the Kuiper Belt. It will include a permanent Shalcerian garrison. We shall also build the infrastructure needed to deal with any interstellar travelers who might wish to visit.

"Your task will be to ensure that all Humans permitted aboard this city be thoroughly vetted against the sociopathic behaviors so prevalent and so destructive within your species."

A warm blush washed over Rae Anne's entire body. Elation replaced her former tension. She was floating on air.

"Thank you, Director Captain Vahler. And I thank each of you esteemed directors. I promise you will not be disappointed. With your permission, I would like to name this new city 'Haven'."

When Rae Anne returned to her quarters, she found Jason connected to the computer access port with a bright red cable plugged into his head behind his left ear.

"What are you doing, Jason?"

"I'm reviewing an immense Shalcerian data file from their archives. A direct connection is much faster than my normal wireless mode. If we have just a day or two left aboard *Avenger*, I thought it best to use the most efficient data-transfer method available.

"So, how did your meeting go?"

"It went very well, thank you. It turns out we aren't being evicted after all, so you can unplug that cable from your head. It may be more efficient, but I find it extremely disturbing."

"Interesting. One moment."

Jason reached behind his ear and unscrewed the nut securing the cable to the receptacle in his skull.

While he coiled the cable and put it away, Rae Anne filled him in on the details of her meeting with the directors.

"Vahler said 'when,' not 'if,' regarding approval from Shalkor, so I'm feeling confident it's in the bag."

"It sounds like *Avenger* will be with us for several more years," he observed when she finished. "Nothing could be better. You wouldn't believe how much information a quantum computer can store. Makes me jealous!"

"I need to get Ian working on the candidate vetting process. My calculations tell me we'll need 2000 successful candidates every week for the next ten years to populate Haven with a million citizens. Less if we account for natural births on Haven once we get started. We'll need recruitment centers and testing facilities around the globe. I want Haven's population to be as diverse a sampling of humanity as possible."

"That's not as daunting as it may seem, Rae Anne. If Ian can set up 100 processing centers, that boils down to just 20 candidates per center per week. But how many people will be willing to abandon their families and friends to live in a space colony a billion kilometers from Earth?"

"Only time will tell."

Chapter 2

The Saturn Accords

A week later, Thrahn appeared in Rae Anne's quarters with an ornately trimmed tablet. He handed the computer to Rae Anne.

"Here is the document outlining the agreement you and the directors came to last week. At least three Human representatives need to sign it. All seven directors must sign."

Rae Anne began to scroll through the electronic document.

"Three Human representatives. Ian is arriving this afternoon. Will they accept Jason's signature?"

"That would be highly unusual. But then, this whole city-building, species-winnowing process is nothing but unusual. Give it a try. If they object, you can find someone else. Perhaps the EOTS commander."

Rae Anne continued to scroll through the document.

"Just how long is this document, Thrahn? Is all this necessary?"

"When you sign this document, you will be agreeing to accept and abide by the laws and edicts set forth by the Shalcerian Empire. The Empire does not take our cooperation obligations lightly, nor should you. Read these over carefully and don't hesitate to call me if you have any questions."

Thrahn departed, while Rae Anne continued to peruse the file.

"Jason, you have access to this document on their computer. Give me an outlined summary of its salient features and note any that might pose a problem for Humans."

"I can do that, but I may miss issues that would be important from a Human perspective."

"Understood. But it would take me a week to go through this entire document and I'd still miss something."

The summary report Jason prepared was 23 pages long. Rae Anne studied it while waiting for Ian's arrival. Rae Anne gave him a lingering hug when he arrived in *Avenger's* 'flying saucer' shuttle, then she led him to *Aurora* where they could talk in private.

"They did a good job on repairs," he commented. "I can't detect a seam anywhere."

"We'll have to get used to using the airlock like civilized astronauts."

"At least if they kick you out, you have somewhere safe to go."

"No chance of that. *Avenger* will be my home until I can move into Haven. Assuming, of course, we can abide by these stipulations."

They sat down at the table in the galley and Rae Anne handed him Jason's summary.

"I didn't know I'd be representing the whole Human race when I agreed to come up, Rae Anne. What if there are things in here we don't like?"

"Thrahn assured me this was standard issue, except for items pertaining specifically to us. I suggest we spend the next few hours going over Jason's summary and cross reference any issue we're not clear on with the actual document."

They spent the remainder of the afternoon and evening poring over the summary details and discussing specific issues as they came up. The last item emphasized that Humans agreeing to the accords were expected to show respect for and deference to the emperor, but only Shalcerian citizens were required to show fealty to him.

Ian stood and stretched with his right arm, leaning heavily on his cane.

"As they say, the devil is in the details. 'Fealty' has a clear-cut definition, but what is invoked by 'respect' and 'deference'?"

Rae Anne nodded and turned to the tablet with the actual document. She reread that last section carefully.

"I think we're ok with that section. By calling 'fealty' out specifically, that would imply other species are held to a lesser standard."

"But our American understanding of 'free speech' and the First Amendment would be curtailed when it comes to referring to the emperor," Ian observed, crossing the galley for a glass of water.

"Or the empire itself, for that matter," Rae Anne added. "But we are not bound by the U.S. Constitution. We're creating a whole new entity. A new country with our own constitution and laws."

She placed the tablet back on the table.

"The section on 'respect and deference' didn't bother me so much as the one requiring involuntary conscription in the event of a military emergency. But taken as a whole, the document is mostly boiler plate provisions for a functioning civilization. Nothing so egregious that I would turn down their offer."

"It's a good thing we're signing just for Haven. Can you imagine getting these conditions passed unanimously in the United Nations?"

"I was thinking the same thing, Ian. We're signing for Haven, not for humanity. The documents make that quite clear. If things don't go as expected, we aren't putting the whole Human race in jeopardy."

"There is something about this whole thing that is bothering me. Nothing to do with this document, per se."

Rae Anne's forehead creased with concern. "What's that?"

"From your description, Vahler and the Directorate readily accepted your proposal and seemed certain they would get approval from Shalkor. But your proposal involves a commitment on their part of a tremendous expenditure of resources. Trillions of dollars by American accounting. They must expect a huge benefit that they aren't revealing to us."

"I hadn't looked at it from that angle, Ian. I wonder what that might be?"

"Perhaps I can be of help there," offered Jason.

Both Ian and Rae Anne turned to Jason who was just coming up through the floor hatch from Level 3.

"Please, fill us in," said Ian.

"The Shalcerian Empire and the Baltar Alliance have been in conflict for several centuries. Sol System lies on both their borders and with its resources, would be a fine addition to either empire. But a third empire, the Tanzar Union, has been expanding in this direction and, if left unchecked, will engulf this region. The Shalcerians may see this as an opportunity to gain a solid foothold and strong military presence here ahead of either Baltar or Tanzar advances."

"That puts us between the proverbial rock and a hard place." Rae Anne shook her head in dismay.

"An agreement with the Shalcerians, whom we know, may be better than risking confrontation on our own with two competing civilizations we know nothing about," Ian observed.

"We can only hope the Shalcerians provide some protection from these other entities, should it come to hostilities in our neighborhood." Rae Anne picked up the tablet. "I'm for signing this and seeing what the future may have in store."

"I agree, although I wish we had a better understanding of the Shahlcerian perspective. I'll need to put together a brochure setting out the terms of the agreement to give to Haven's prospective citizens even before we interview them. I suspect both the 'respect and deference' clause and the 'involuntary conscription' clause will turn away many potential candidates."

Rae Ann stood and embraced him, snuggling her face into his chest.

"I'm exhausted. Let's hit the sack," she suggested. "Jason, tell Thrahn we'll sign the agreement tomorrow."

"I hope you are not too exhausted for what I have in mind," Ian whispered into her ear.

The signing ceremony for the agreement of cooperation, hereafter referred to as 'The Saturn Accords,' took place the following afternoon. It was held in Rae Anne's quarters, and all seven directors, wearing respirators, showed up.

Rae Anne, Ian, and Jason signed the tablet, followed by Director Captain Vahler and each of the other directors. The Shalcerians were amused that Humans would give a mechanical robot such authority, but they didn't make a fuss.

After the signing, Captain Vahler stood, took the tablet, and turned all three eyes toward Rae Anne and Ian.

"We will send a file with these Saturn Accords to Shalkor immediately, along with our request for engineers and contractors to begin construction on Haven at the earliest date possible. I will urge they give our project top priority."

Rae Anne stood and offered her right hand to the captain. He grasped Rae Anne's hand with two of his and held it gently for a moment. The suction pads on his fingers left fading pink smudges on her skin.

"Thank you," Rae Anne responded. "For our part, we will establish recruitment centers around the globe and provide testing facilities and protocols to vet candidates for Haven citizenship. What time framework might we be looking at?"

"Once our crews are on site with their equipment, my engineers estimate the entire project should take no more than ten years. However, if we design the city with twelve independent sectors, each sector will be habitable as soon as it is finished. The first may be ready in eighteen months after construction begins, so you may plan on transporting Humans to Haven starting then. Of course, we'll have to use *Avenger* to ferry the Humans to Haven until you have your own cruisers.

"We will build our garrison next to the first sector, so we can start training Humans for the Kuiper Belt Patrol missions from the very beginning. I'll put in a request for a dozen interplanetary cruisers that the Empire can divert to the Sol System. Twelve ships will be sufficient for your needs."

Once the Shalcerian contingent left, Rae Anne turned to Ian for a hug and nearly knocked him over. She was giddy with excitement. The Saturn Accords were signed, and the first steps to bringing Shalcerian technologies to the Sol System (if not directly to Earth) were in place.

Ian seemed subdued but held his peace. When they were within the confines of *Aurora*, he expressed his concerns.

"It's all well and good to conceive of recruitment centers and testing facilities around the world for this incredible project, Rae Anne. But this takes money and personnel. It takes government cooperation. And then there's the inevitable protests we'll face that could become violent. Something I happen to know about personally. This won't be a walk in the park. There's no guarantee we can make it even happen."

"That's why I have you, Ian. If anyone can do this, you can."

Saturn Orbit, 2043

Avenger sprinted between Earth and Saturn at two-thirds lightspeed. At this velocity, covering the distance between the two planets was just over two hours.

Thrahn stepped into Rae Anne's quarters holding a newly fabricated respirator and protective suit for Ian.

"The captain has enlisted our astrogeologists to pick a suitable moonlet on which to build Haven." He handed his bundle to Ian. "He would like the two of you to visit the bridge for your comments. After all, this will be your city. Your input is essential."

Ian took the suit and looked it over. "I was under the impression the city would be made from GESC-Plasticor materials."

"That would be ideal, but there aren't enough gravitolite crystals in the universe to handle such a large task. For example, all of Shalkor's 144 sectors began as a moonlet or asteroid that was nudged into the same circular orbit around Shalkor's equator. A lot of excavating and drilling is needed to convert a moonlet into a suitable shape. Only a small amount of plasticor is needed to support a small city.

"Saturn has thousands of asteroids large enough for Haven. We'll pick one this afternoon and be back in Earth-orbit in time for you to catch your shuttle back to Earth, Ian. I'm sure you're anxious to begin organizing your immigrant processing centers."

Rae Anne thought she detected a hint of sarcasm in the scarlet and teal waves rippling across his belly.

After Thrahn left, Rae Anne helped Ian into his suit and connected his respirator. She then led him into *Avenger's* labyrinthine corridors. Being taller than Rae Anne, Ian was forced to stoop over as he walked to deal with the lower ceilings. He grunted occasionally from the pain this caused with his still healing injuries. When they arrived at the nanoscreen leading into the bridge, Rae Anne paused.

"Take a deep breath, Ian. You are in for an amazing experience."

Ian followed her through the nanoscreen and gasped. He turned full circle, gazing at the star-speckled holograms seamlessly lining the sphere's interior walls. Familiar constellations plastered the 'sky' overhead. The Milky Way washed down the walls on the left and dropped below the transparent deck cantilevered over the bottom hemisphere. The Southern Cross and the Magellanic Clouds were clearly discernable beneath their feet.

A single bright point lay dead ahead, growing more prominent as they watched. Soon it took on an oval shape, like a tiny ball wearing earmuffs. Then the 'ears' morphed into rings and Saturn emerged in all its glory.

Over the next several hours, Captain Vahler directed *Avenger* from one asteroid to another like a real estate agent. At each stop, a shuttle swooped to the surface and a dozen Shalcerian scientists in full EVA attire stepped out. Some drilled core samples, others carried instruments to select locations for measurements. When they had finished, they regrouped in the shuttle and returned to *Avenger.* The entire process at each site took about twenty minutes.

"Instead of house-hunting, we're searching the real estate market for an asteroid," Rae Anne observed. "We're sending these physicists out to be our inspectors to tell us what they like and don't like about the properties."

Ian laughed and nodded. "Your analogy isn't far off. It's just the scale of the project. It's like America's colonists buying Manhattan while fully knowing what it would become centuries later."

On their way back to Earth mid-afternoon, Thrahn brought a tablet to Rae Anne's quarters. Rae Anne and Ian were playing chess. Rae Anne had just pinned Ian's bishop with her rook.

Thrahn set the computer on the table next to Rae Anne.

"Interesting Human behaviorism, playing games to pass the time. We wouldn't condone such a waste of time, even for our children."

Ian looked up from the board and rubbed his chin thoughtfully.

"So, what have you brought us?" Rae Anne asked.

"Our quantum computer has analyzed all the data collected for the 11 asteroids we visited. There are five possessing a suitable size and composition for Haven. Captain Vahler wanted you two to make the final selection. 'Give the choice some Human perspective' were his exact words. In Shalcerian, of course." Thrahn's body scales rippled in yellow and violet.

Thrahn manipulated the icons on the tablet monitor and five tiny hologram asteroids floated above it. All were roughly the same size.

Rae Anne rubbed her forehead and scowled.

"How should we decide, Thrahn? They all look alike."

"Each one has a different orbit around Saturn. Their distances from Saturn vary, as does their angle with respect to Saturn's equator and rings. In other words, you will be deciding the view of Saturn that will forever dominate Haven's sky.

"*Avenger* can nudge these rocks into slightly different orbits to suit your requirements, but we can only do so much."

Thrahn tweaked another icon and a hologram of Saturn with five orbital trajectories replaced the asteroid holograms.

"I'll leave you to decide which asteroid you want for Haven's foundation. Let me know your decision when we reach Earth-orbit."

Thrahn turned and skipped to the nanoscreen and stepped through.

"I'll never get used to that," complained Ian.

Rae Anne laughed. "It is rather disconcerting. But I'm going to lobby for as much advanced technology as I can get for Haven. So, you may just have to adjust."

"What are your thoughts on asteroid selection?"

Rae Anne shifted her head back and forth to study the five orbits in their varying angles and distances from Saturn.

"The one with the equatorial orbit is definitely out," she said. "You would never see the rings in their full glory. When *Aurora* was orbiting Titan, that was my only disappointment. I wanted to see more of the rings."

"Asteroid 'E' is just a little off from a polar orbit. That would give you a full view of the rings most of the time."

"True, but always at 90 degrees. I think one with its orbit at an oblique angle to Saturn's equator would be more interesting. The perspective on the rings would be constantly changing. And this one they've labelled 'D' is the closest to Saturn. What stunning views we'd have if Haven were built on 'D.' That one is my choice."

"Mine too," agreed Ian. "Not having been to Shalkor, I can only imagine what the finished city will look like. I can't wait to see it."

Chapter 3

Colorado Springs, 2043

By the time Ian stepped onto the tarmac at Peterson Space Center on his return to Earth from *Avenger* via the EOTS, word had already reached the world's media that Shalcerians were abandoning Earth. Reporters surrounded him like sharks after a bloody piece of meat as he made his way to the terminal.

He tried at first to ignore their badgering questions, but finally realized he had to make a statement. He paused and raised his hand for quiet. The babble hushed to record his comments.

"The Shalcerians have decided to abandon their efforts at developing a cooperative association with Earth. Since we are unable to agree among ourselves on dealing with existential threats to Human survival, such as climate change and disarmament, we would make unreliable, even dangerous, partners in any joint venture."

A flurry of questions filled the air, drowning his next words. He again held up his hand until quiet was restored.

"However, all is not lost. Rae Anne Chavez negotiated a compromise agreement. The Shalcerians will build a large space-city in orbit around Saturn. This city, Haven, will accommodate a million Humans and have sectors set aside for a dozen alien visitors to our Solar System. Haven will be home to the Kuiper Belt Patrol. Humans will operate this force to provide security for the interstellar species who visit the Kuiper Belt to resupply their ships with fuel and water."

More shouted questions. Ian leaned heavily on his cane and waved his free hand in the air to quiet the inquisitive reporters.

"One last comment. It will take a mammoth international effort to populate a distant city of this size. The Shalcerians will provide transport to Haven for immigrants from Earth. The trip takes just a few hours on Shalcerian spacecraft. We will be organizing recruitment centers around the globe. Haven's population will reflect the diversity of the Human population here on Earth. That is all I am willing to say at this time. Thank you."

Several security guards pressed their way through the crowd and created a path for Ian to follow leading into the terminal. Ian took the lift to the roof and slouched heavily into the seat of his hovercar. As much as he wanted to return to his apartment, he commanded the craft to take him to his office as he dutifully buckled his seatbelt.

To facilitate the organization of the recruitment centers, Ian established the Haven Recruitment Administration (HRA) and began raising funds for its operation. Three retired astronaut friends volunteered to oversee the efforts while Ian continued on as USIEA director. Crowd sourcing raised several million dollars in start-up funds. Online immigration applications began rolling in before the furniture was delivered to their central office in Los Angeles in late December 2043.

Hoping to reduce the volume of applications, Ian used the HRA website to lay out details of the Saturn Accords to which every Haven citizen would have to agree. He also made it clear that a move to Haven was a one-way trip. Individual candidates and families applying for citizenship needed to know they were leaving Earth forever, abandoning family, friends, social and business relationships.

On the second page, he outlined the rigorous physical, social, and psychological testing candidates would be subjected to. Ian believed glossing over this fact would misrepresent the process by which candidates would be deemed eligible for the program.

For families with children, a whole new set of testing procedures for children and teens was developed. Without having the decades of research necessary for such diagnostics to be adequately evaluated, the admissions team treated youth applications with greater leniency.

Unfortunately, as soon as information about the vetting process became public, those opposing cooperation with the aliens used it as ammunition to support their cause. Protests swept Earth like a firestorm, fueled by an unremitting media campaign accusing HRA of promoting discrimination.

A dozen different media outlets questioned the ethics of vetting humans based on a genetic predisposition to sociopathic behavior. The term 'eugenics' became the opposition's buzzword to attack the concept of Haven in general and the HRA in particular. It was only a small jump from 'eugenics' to 'Nazism' and 'fascism,' and soon Ian's project was embroiled in a political maelstrom of suspicion and conspiracy theories.

Application requests remained high, but Ian found it difficult to obtain the necessary permits from many national governments to register and set up his recruitment centers. The United States, Canada, Great Britain, and Israel saw through the fog of conspiracy theories and lies, but many governments turned him away without a hearing.

"We need a different approach to achieve our goal of worldwide diversity," Ian admitted to the HRA directors at a meeting called in February 2044 to deal with this public relations crisis.

"Not enough countries are letting us in to do our work. Especially in those parts of the world that would give us the diversity we seek."

"Money usually solves problems like that," offered Aika Tanaka, the CEO of a Japanese semiconductor manufacturer.

"That might normally be so," Ian answered. "But with all the conspiracy theories going around and the crater in the middle of Moscow, officials are only too happy to wash their hands of anything to do with the Shalcerians. Besides, we need our money for the testing centers, not to give away to corrupt politicians."

"What's the latest on the testing centers?" asked Marvin Haley, founder of the MindHealth psychiatric hospital chain.

"We now have seven centers nearly ready to go, though none are fully staffed. Two are in Canada, in Vancouver and Montreal. One is in Haifa, Israel, another is in London, and the other three are in the US: Los Angeles, Denver, and Boston."

"With the global geographic spread you envision, we're going to need a corporate jet to keep everything tied together," Helen Ericson noted. Helen owned ComputerMetrics, a large software firm with clients around the world.

"That's actually a line item in my proposed budget," said Ian.

"But we're getting off the agenda," Aika pointed out. "We're here to solve the diversity problem in the face of wide-spread government animosity."

"What if we settled on locating more testing facilities in the countries that grant us permits and provide transportation to candidates who pass a set of initial qualifications online?" Marvin asked.

"We could save money by expanding the centers we do have, rather than building many smaller facilities," said Helen. "That money could help the candidate transportation program."

She began typing furiously on her laptop. "Hold on a minute," she said while continuing to type. When she looked up, she was shaking her head.

"You'd better up your budget request to include twenty corporate jets, Ian," she said ruefully. "If we're aiming for a million successful candidates in ten years, and we assume only a third of the applicants make the grade, you'll be jockeying 860 people around every day from all parts of the globe. If each jet makes three or four trips per day, carrying 12 to 15 candidates each trip, you might be able to do it with careful scheduling. And to keep them in the air, you'll need four full crews for each jet."

"Not to mention down time for maintenance," Marvin added.

"Reducing the number of regional testing centers won't compensate for a fleet of jets," Ian complained. "I'll need to meet with our sponsors and see what I can do."

A straw poll showed unanimous approval for using the existing centers and expanding the fleet of corporate jets, pending assurance of adequate funding.

Ian left the meeting in a dark mood. The Agency sponsored annual recruitment efforts for astronauts, vetting applications and accepting twenty or so candidates each year. The thought of accomplishing that same task for a hundred-thousand applicants in a year's time boggled his mind.

To make this work, I'll need to create our own international airline!

Chapter 4

Haven, 2044

Rae Anne stood on *Avenger's* bridge and watched as Captain Vahler guided his ship over the top surface of Haven's future home. It looked as though someone had sliced the asteroid in half like a grapefruit and removed the upper portion. She was amazed at the change in the little asteroid after a mere six months.

A dozen construction vessels crowded around the transformed rock, each performing a unique operation. Rae Anne spotted one drilling tunnels through solid rock, creating a honeycomb in the moonlet's bottom half. She tried to imagine the vast hydroponic gardens and the spiderweb of subway tunnels these cavities would soon contain.

Everywhere she looked she spotted Shalcerian workers in their EVA suits swarming over the asteroid.

Captain Vahler gestured to three distant craft hovering over the table-top flat surface. Two bulky freighters were piping material to a third ship involved with paving the surface with a molten substance.

"We've begun laying the GESC-Plasticor surface on which your city will be built. In a few days, you will be able to walk across the surface and not be concerned about a false move sending you into orbit. The entire surface will provide 1/6 gravity when we're done. Then we can begin building your city using the design specifications you provided."

Rae Anne tried to imagine a cityscape spread across the barren surface before her, but the disconnect was too great.

Maybe I'll be better able to visualize it when a few structures are built and a transparent dome is in place.

"How long before the first sector will be finished and habitable?" she asked.

"Probably five months, more or less."

"Will the buildings be made of plasticor too?"

Vahler pointed to two mammoth ships hovering over a mountainous pile of rock and debris orbiting the asteroid.

"We saved all the shavings and drilling slag as we transformed the asteroid into a city platform. Those two ships pulverize the slag and process it into a molten fluid that our 3D-printers can use to create finished buildings in just a few days."

"That must be some machine! I'd like to see it."

"It hasn't arrived yet. I have four on order. The first should be here in two days."

"At least with Saturn's rings nearby, water shouldn't be a problem. I can't wait to stroll around the lake in the City Center when it's finished."

"We're already harvesting ice from the rings. We need the water for our slag processing operation. We'll also use ring ice to fill the reservoirs. Each sector on Haven will have a dedicated underground reservoir. The hydroponics facilities beneath the subways will tap into these reservoirs to support the aquaculture."

"Do the 3D-printers also create the transparent dome over the city?"

"Yes, but with a different raw material feed. The dome is composed of nanoparticles held in place by a magneto-gravitic synchronic-wave field like the nanoscreens you are familiar with. A ring of wave-field generators will be built around the finished sectors and expanded as each new sector is completed. When powered up, the energy field it creates forms a bubble into which the nanoparticles are dispersed. The result is a transparent dome with a solid surface capable of keeping the interior pressurized while blocking cosmic radiation and meteorites."

"I'm assuming we'll have a nuclear fusion reactor to power the city."

"We'll be installing six fusion reactors, one for every two sectors. Any two of these would be sufficient to provide Haven with all its power needs. But redundancy is always good, and they'll be available should Haven expand in the future."

"Given the asteroid's surface area, how much larger could Haven be?"

"The city your plans call for will occupy about one third of the platform we're building. Our garrison will use half of the space. So, Haven's footprint could become half-again as large. But the construction equipment you see won't be available after we finish this project. You Humans will have to prove yourselves over many decades before the Empire will authorize any expansion. Don't forget, your whole proposal is an experiment. The Empire has never tried anything like this before."

Wow. This 'garrison' will be larger than a city of one million. Jason was right. The Shahlcerian's want a major military outpost in our system.

Denver, 2045

Karen scrunched in her heavy coat and pulled her woolen knit scarf over her chin as she trudged down East Colfax in downtown Denver. She tugged at her fur hat, bringing the flaps tighter around her ears to keep the windswept snow from blowing beneath them. A few store windows contained Christmas displays, but most were blank, mirroring the empty shops behind them.

She slogged along the darkened street. Every other streetlamp was out, and the heavy snow only made things worse. Dipping into her coat pocket, she fumbled around and pulled out a slip of paper in her gloved hand. She read again the address she had hastily scrawled and looked at the address above the door next to her.

Must be in the next block. If it weren't for this wretched blizzard, I'd be able to see a sign from here. Hate being alone in this neighborhood. But what did I expect? A clandestine meeting in the country club lobby?

She crossed the intersection and spotted the sign she was looking for, 'Tip's B&G,' over a lighted door stoop. She shivered again as she pushed the door open and stepped through, shoving the door closed behind her. The room was dimly lit, with two overhead bulbs providing light for the entire establishment. The bar was sparsely populated. Only two tables along the side wall were occupied, the nearer one by a young couple embroiled in a spat. At the table farthest from the door sat a single patron, a man facing the entrance.

She walked through the bar to this last table as instructed. She held out her gloved hand. The man continued to hold his shot glass with both hands. He gave her a piercing look.

"I'm Marci," Karen said, using the name she concocted when she contacted him.

"Call me Jack, Karen. Sit down. Make it look like we've known each other forever and are just here to have a few drinks before fucking ourselves silly at the hotel down the street."

"You know who I am?"

Dismayed, Karen removed her hat and gloves, shrugged out of her coat, and sat down. Jack waved two fingers at the bartender.

He gave her a crooked smile. "You don't live long in my business if you don't check out your clients thoroughly. Don't worry. I run a clean business. I'm not into blackmail or extortion. I have a very short memory once a transaction is closed."

The bartender delivered two shots of whiskey with two beers and picked up Jack's empties before returning to the bar.

"So, what can I do for you, Karen?"

"First, I want to say you did a fine job at the U.N. two years ago."

Jack shook his head and frowned. His dark penetrating eyes glared at her menacingly.

"I have no idea what you're talking about. Save your memories and recollections for Sam Durban."

Shit, how much does this man know about me?

Jack held up his glass for a mock toast and nodded his head towards Karen's glass. She picked hers up and they clicked glasses, Jack mumbled something, and Karen took a sip while Jack downed his in a single gulp. He followed this with a long swig of beer.

"I'm fine with that, Jack."

"I repeat, what can I do for you?" He took another draught from his beer.

"I need a package that appears perfectly innocent, disguised as something a boyfriend would send to his sweetheart. The 'gift' must be very stable. It may get banged around, dropped, even kicked. The paper can be torn off and the box opened. But at a key moment after that, something the recipient would normally do will set off the explosive. Can you do that?"

Jack looked at Karen thoughtfully for a moment. "I like to think of myself as an artist. The creative sort, you know? I can come up with something meeting your specifications. How do I deliver it to you?"

"Actually, I want you to post it from Colorado Springs."

"That's not how I work. I deliver my creations directly to my clients. What they do with them after that is their business."

Karen was taken aback. Jack was proposing that she have more direct involvement than she wanted. And another meeting with him.

Still, he will fabricate the device I need. And he knows more about me than I would like. It's too late to back out now. I'll have to deal with him later.

"Alright. It's a deal. When can I pick it up?"

"It'll be ready in two weeks. There's a place like this on Tejon in Colorado Springs. I'll call you with directions. I'll expect $125,000 cash in a blue gym bag. And I'll have bodyguards and lookouts for security when we do our little transaction. No funny business. Understand?"

"Yes, perfectly." Karen nodded.

"Then we're done here. But we could get a room up the street and…"

"I prefer we keep our two worlds apart. No entanglements."

Karen stood and began putting on her overcoat.

"Good point. Shame, though…"

"Call me when it's ready." She adjusted her hat as she walked through the bar, pulled on her gloves at the door, and stepped out into the raging storm. Her tracks from earlier had disappeared under a fresh inch of snow.

Denver, 2046

Ian shook his head sadly as he watched the news feed from the HAR center in Los Angeles. He couldn't wrap his mind around the anger and hostility dealing with the Shalcerians had aroused.

Protestors have stormed into the lobby of the Los
Angeles Haven Recruitment Center. People are
wielding clubs and breaking windows. Their signs
read 'Down with Eugenics' and 'Nazis Go Home.'
Some are angry at the selection process used to
determine who is qualified to become a citizen of
Haven, the alien city being built in Saturn's
orbit. Others want nothing to do with the aliens.
Maria Sanchez is on site. What can you tell us,
Maria?

Ian turned up the volume on his smart phone so others in the Denver
HAR office could hear the news broadcast. The Los Angeles office had called
him ten minutes earlier, describing the volatile situation taking place on the
street in front of their building. He lost direct contact with them shortly
thereafter.

There must be fifty or sixty people here in the
lobby. No sign of employees or building security.
They may have cleared out for safety from this
angry crowd. Janice, here, is willing to have a
word with us. What's this all about, Janice?

This whole alien city thing is a crock of shit.
The aliens are labeling Humans as fit or unfit
for their project like we're animals. Selecting
Humans with genetic testing to 'weed out' the
undesirables… That's exactly what Hitler did in
Germany, and we all know how that turned out. We
must resist all cooperation with the aliens.

Thank you, Janice. The crowd has not been able to
use the elevators, so they are trooping up the
stairs to the second-floor offices. More are
arriving. Some are carrying torches.

Whoa! They just set fire to the receptionist's
area. Someone smashed a Molotov cocktail into the

shredder. Flames are reaching the ceiling. I'm
outta here!

"What the devil is the matter with people? We aren't forcing anyone to do anything." Samantha Townsend, the director of the organization's Denver facility shook her head sadly. Through her office windows they could see a more subdued crowd outside waving similar signs and chanting.

"Let's hope our mob doesn't get any ideas. At least they seem quiet for now," observed her assistant.

Ian nodded. "I think we'll be all right. You two had the foresight to beef up security and alert the police department. They sent, what, ten officers over this morning?"

"Only eight. But they're in full riot gear, and that's enough to intimidate most people."

"Wow. Look at that." The assistant drew their attention back to the phone. Protestors in LA were pouring out of the building while flames devoured the lobby and smoke was pouring out of broken second floor windows.

"I hope our people got out safely." Ian shuddered and choked back a lump in his throat. "Our LA offices are being gutted."

"Our Canadian offices haven't experienced any of this. Not a single protestor. Why do you suppose that is?" Samantha looked over to Ian with raised eyebrows.

Wicked flames were now shooting from the second-floor windows. Fire trucks arrived and crews began dispersing the crowd and laying out hoses.

"A different culture and heritage. Less confrontational, perhaps," Ian suggested.

"Less paranoia. Less fear of change," offered the assistant, shrugging her shoulders.

"Canada's stiff laws regulating social media content and usage have gone a long way in stifling conspiracy theory dissemination," said Samantha.

Ian's call-tone rang and he switched to phone mode. The call was from his Los Angeles director, Bailey Thomson. Ian put the call on the speaker.

"Bailey, is everyone there ok?"

"We got everyone out the back way before the fire started, Ian. Security helped organize the effort. We're six blocks away at a small pub, watching the news broadcasts. I'm sorry, but this will put our whole operation here several months behind."

"Bailey, the schedule isn't the important thing. It's enough to know that no one's been hurt."

"All our records and applications are backed up, so nothing's been lost. But it may be several months before we are back in operation."

"Canada may be the only place calm enough to do our work. Bailey, are you and your family up for a move if we open new offices in, say, Calgary?"

"Given the hatred and animosity I've experienced today, I would jump at the chance to live among sane people for a change."

In the following months, Ian closed all the organization's offices in the U.S. and opened four new centers in Canada. He deemed the additional transportation costs worthwhile to keep their recruiting efforts safe and out of the public eye.

By the end of the first year, he had 7385 qualified candidates anxiously waiting for their invitations to be transported to their new home on Haven.

Chapter 5

Haven, 2046

Rae Anne looked up from her desk on the top floor of Haven's Municipal Building as Thrahn stepped through the nanoscreen. She stood and held out a hand to greet him and gestured to a place beside her desk. He shook her hand and settled on his pedestal leg. He leaned one arm familiarly on the desk.

"So, what's up, Thrahn? I haven't seen you since we moved in six weeks ago."

"I've been providing my expertise on Humans as we've been putting the finishing touches on our training facility for the Kuiper Belt Patrol officers and crew. The facility is now ready and waiting for the recruits."

"How many do you need?"

"Each ship will need a crew of 144, with ten officers and a captain."

"That calls for 1860 enlistees," Jason added helpfully.

"We can only manage 250 at a time. The ships won't all arrive at once, so that won't be a problem. Can you come up with 250 volunteers in the next week or so?"

Rae Anne nodded and smiled.

"I'll put out the word this evening. If we place a 20-to-25-year age restriction on volunteers, we'll probably see half the eligible citizens on my doorstep tomorrow morning. We'll have no trouble meeting your quota."

"Good. I'll arrange space in the garrison for 250 trainees. We will begin training in a week. The training will take twelve weeks. If we can bring in a cruiser by graduation, we can launch our first mission to the Kuiper Belt then."

"Don't forget to design your facilities to account for Humans being a bi-sexual species. Although consensual mixing is permitted, Humans require separate quarters for the two sexes to be comfortable and feel secure."

"I did mention that requirement to our architects, so it should not be a problem. However, I need to pass the information on to Captain Vahler to include it in the specifications for retrofitting the ships for Human use."

Lizzy, Rae Anne's assistant, buzzed her on the intercom.

"A package just came in for you, Rae Anne. One of the new arrivals dropped it off."

"Please bring it in."

Lizzy stepped through the nanoscreen, holding a wrapped package about the size of a 3-pound coffee tin.

"It's not even my birthday." Rae Anne laughed and walked over and took the package. Lizzy stepped back into the front office.

"I'm not used to getting packages from Earth. Oh, it's from Ian. That's sweet. I'll bet it's something special."

She held it up with both hands and gave it a shake. Nothing rattled.

Thrahn looked over at the package. "Why wrap something in brown paper that will be thrown away?"

"It's a present. Humans wrap gifts to heighten the suspense. It increases their enjoyment from receiving a gift."

"That would be a crime in my culture. A waste of resources."

"I can't wait to see what he sent me."

She set the object on her desk and carefully peeled the tape holding the paper in place.

"Some Humans rip the paper away in a frenzy. I like to take my time and focus my thoughts on the person who gave the gift. It helps me be more appreciative."

Once she had loosened all the tape, she pulled the wrapping paper off the gift with a flourish. It floated gently in the low gravity and drifted to the floor.

"Ta da! A music box! I haven't had a music box since I was a kid. My parents gave me one for Christmas. That's a special Human holiday. It played 'Somewhere Over the Rainbow.' I loved that toy. I played it over and over until the spring broke. By then, several tines had broken, so the tune had these weird gaps."

"How does it work?"

"All you do is wind the spring up with this little key. See, it fits here, under the box. When you take the key out, the lid pops open to reveal a dancer or animals, or whatever, and the music begins to play."

Rae Anne wound the spring a few turns and released the key, but nothing happened.

"Hmm. Oh, I see the problem. This music box has a switch to release a lock on the spring. That way you can wind it fully and then flick the switch to hear the music."

Just as she was about to give the key a few more turns, Lizzy paged her on the intercom.

"Rae Anne, Captain Vahler would like to see you in person aboard *Avenger* as soon as possible. He didn't say what it might be about."

Rae Anne sighed and set the music box on her desk.

"I'd better get over there right away. If he wants to see me in person, it must be something important. Hopefully, it's not a change in our construction timeline. Sorry to walk out on you, Thrahn."

"Not a problem. When the captain issues a request, it's always best to assume it's a command."

"Stay as long as you like. I've shown you how the music box works. Play with it to your heart's content. The only precaution is not to wind the spring too tight, or it might break."

Rae Anne removed a jacket from a wardrobe, grabbed her tablet and left Thrahn alone in her office.

Thrahn held the little box up to see it better and admired the delicately painted Earth scenes on its sides. He reinserted the key and began winding. He smiled at the tactile sensation associated with working with such a primitive mechanical device.

The blast shook the building and rattled the lift before Rae Anne reached the ground floor. When Rae Anne stepped through the nanoscreen, she rushed from the building and turned to look up to see where the explosion had occurred.

"That's my office!" she screamed.

She ran back into the building.

"Thrahn! Lizzy! Oh, god. Don't let them be hurt."

She heard distant sirens as she sprinted across the lobby. She pounded the buttons next to the lift. No response. She turned to the stairs winding around the lift tubes and took the steps two at a time until she ran into a wall of smoke three floors below her tenth-floor office. Hanging onto the banister, she doubled over, panting heavily and choking on smoke and soot, tears flooding from her stinging eyes.

I can't stop now. I've got to go on. Where is the nearest oxygen mask?

A gloved hand gripped her shoulder. Turning, she looked directly into an emergency responder's facemask. Three other properly suited responders were coming up the stairs behind her, uncoiling a hose connected to the fire prevention system.

"Go down and get out of the building. We've got this covered."

"But my friends are on the top floor.'

"How many?"

"Two. But one's a Shalcerian."

"An alien? Good to know. We'll do what we can to get to them. You get out of the building. Now."

Her grip grew tighter, and she turned Rae Anne to face down the stairs. Rae Anne started to turn back but was forcibly stopped.

"OUT. NOW."

After several steps downward, she turned back to see the last responder disappear into the smoke. Coughing violently to remove soot from her throat, she staggered down the steps and out the front of the building, where she sat down on the curb.

With her head in her hands, she waited, staring vacantly as firefighters and emergency responders entered the building. Eventually, several emerged from the building carrying two body bags. These they placed in a hovercraft which immediately lifted off for the health complex.

Rae Anne slowly got to her feet, swaying as if in a daze. She had lost two of her best friends and Captain Vahler was expecting her to report to him.

The last place I want to go. I'll have to tell him what happened. Another black mark for Humans and a loss of two wonderful people.

The moment *Avenger*'s shuttle landed in the battlecruiser's Hangar D, two Shalcerians approached and met Rae Anne at the shuttle's airlock. They officiously escorted her to the Council Chamber cubicle. To her surprise, the full Directorate was present. Their body colors were a dark gray, bordering on black.

As usual, Captain Vahler broke the silence. The computer translator conveyed his anger and frustration.

"Rae Anne Chavez, what has happened to Thrahn? Our medical team report his biometric sensors have all baselined. Tracking reported him in your office suite when this occurred. Explain."

Rae Anne cleared her throat and tried to speak. She began crying and was aware that her hands were visibly shaking.

"Thrahn and my assistant Lizzy have been killed in an explosion in my office," she blurted, shaking her head.

"Lizzy is of no concern to us. But Thrahn is. For a Shalcerian officer to be attacked and murdered by an inferior species is an act of terrorism bringing shame on us all. This cannot and will not go unheeded. Our forensic team will determine what happened and who the responsible parties are. Everyone involved will be identified and brought to justice. To Shalcerian justice."

Lizzy's life is equally as important as Thrahn's, you bastard.

"Thrahn and Lizzy were both my very good friends. I'll mourn their loss equally. All sentient beings should be valued equally."

"But you called me here before the explosion."

"Yes. You decided to locate Haven University in Sector 3. We're just finishing Sector 2 and will begin laying out Sector 3 tomorrow. We've put together a dozen campus designs from Earth's universities that will work here. You need to choose the one we should use."

This was the last thing Rae Anne wanted to do. But she recognized that her feelings at the loss of her friends couldn't stand in the way of Haven's progress. With a heavy heart, she studied the holographic images Vahler displayed and selected one she felt would serve Haven best in the years ahead.

Before leaving, she hesitated at the hatch.

This is as good a time as any to confront Vahler with my concerns and get them off my chest.

She turned and strode back into the room.

"Is there something more we can do for you?"

"Captain Vahler, the Saturn Accords stipulate that in exchange for our patrolling the Kuiper Belt you will share your technology with us. To date, you have not revealed any details to our engineers relating to nuclear fusion, space propulsion systems, quantum computing, health maintenance devices or, for that matter, GESC-Plasticor production. When do you plan to bring our scientists and engineers up to speed on these technologies?"

"Rae Anne, Haven is a perfect example of our sharing our technology with Humans," the captain answered condescendingly.

"Your entire city is built on a GESC-Plasticor platform. Our nanoparticle technology is powering the dome over the city and the avenues throughout the city. By the time Haven is finished, we will have installed six nuclear fusion reactors around the city to more than meet your energy requirements. The hospitals incorporate our most advanced health-care equipment. The subway system and autonomous drones are working flawlessly to meet your transportation needs. Your Kuiper Belt Patrol will have twelve ships capable of speeds up to a third of lightspeed. If it weren't for our sharing those technologies with you, you would have none of this.

"Providing you with the blueprints for these technologies would put them at risk of being stolen and used against us. What if Haven should succumb to a Baltar attack? Or if nefarious Humans stole those designs? We must safeguard our own interests by keeping these details to ourselves. Count yourselves fortunate that we have shared them to the extent we have."

Rae Anne attempted to persuade Vahler to give humans the details for just one of these systems, but Vahler adamantly refused to reveal details on any of them. After a few minutes, he abruptly dismissed her and had her two escorts lead her to the shuttle bay.

As the shuttle returned to the garrison's landing bay on Haven, Rae Anne turned to look back at the mammoth ship. She shook her fist in anger and frustration.

You bastards! How can I share any of your marvels with Earth after you've left if you don't show us how to duplicate them?

Chapter 6

Haven, 2047

Several months later, Rae Anne and Jason had just returned to her office on the refurbished roof of the Municipal Building after greeting a new group of immigrants. She had placed her office there as a temporary fix while the interior was being rebuilt, but after a few weeks, she decided to make the arrangements permanent. The weather was always perfect, and whenever she looked up from her desk, the view of Saturn left her breathless.

As she stepped from the lift, her new assistant, Jorge, introduced her to a Shalcerian who was awaiting her arrival.

"This is Grimlee. He has been assigned to replace Thrahn as your Shalcerian liaison," Jorge announced.

Rae Anne held out her hand, but Grimlee was not familiar with the Human gesture.

"The first three of the twelve Kuiper Belt Patrol ships have just arrived," Grimlee said perfunctorily.

"That's a great coincidence. Our first class is about to graduate. We'll have nearly full crews for two of the ships."

"Good. I am also to inform you that our forensic investigation into Thrahn's death is proceeding satisfactorily."

"Thank you. Tell Captain Vahler that I believe the investigation is in good hands."

Having conveyed his messages, Grimlee held his right arm crooked over his head, a Shalcerian gesture Rae Anne recognized as leave taking, pivoted on his pedestal leg, rose, and skipped to the lift.

After he left, Rae Anne turned to Jason and Jorge.

"Grimlee doesn't seem too interested in Humans. Quite a change from Thrahn."

"He does seem to be a 'straight by the book' person," observed Jorge. "He refused to engage in any conversation while he was waiting for you."

Not long after her encounter with Grimlee, Rae Anne was having a discussion with Ian over a report from the Education Minister outlining the achievement test scores of Haven's student population. They both were sitting in the easy chairs she had installed next to the lounger. Ian was enjoying a can of Haven's Heavenly Stout, the latest offering from the Havenly Brewery located a few blocks away. Rae Anne was nibbling on a scone to accompany her coffee.

Jason stepped through the nanoscreen in the partition separating her office from the lift and Jorge's reception area.

"The transport from Earth is now arriving, Rae Anne. If you look 10-degrees above Arcturus, you can spot it." Jason pointed toward the clear dome over the city with a typically Human gesture.

They both peered upward and squinted. A faint object moving against the star-spattered black grew gradually brighter.

"It's still some distance out, so I have time before I need to be at the docking berth. Notify the welcoming delegation. This brings us up to, hmm, just over 160,000." Rae Anne swiped her right wrist across her forehead and rubbed her temple.

"163,297, to be exact," Jason corrected. "It's a good thing the Shalcerian's are about to finish Sectors 3 and 4. Another month and Sectors 1 and 2 will be at capacity."

"Winnowing the applications down to qualified candidates has been quite a challenge," Ian said, setting his empty can on the glass end table. "Even with our eight new vetting centers in Canada and Israel, we've been working our tails off."

"You're doing a great job, too, Ian. In the eighteen months people have been arriving, we've experienced absolutely no crime, period. An occasional argument requiring a visit from Security, but that's all."

"And you have what, a dozen police? For 160,000 people?"

"163,297."

"Thank you, Jason. We have fifteen peace officers. And they have other duties as well."

"Some of that may be due to there being no guns on Haven," Jason observed. "The most lethal weapon in over a billion kilometers is the butcher knife in Chef Ngu's kitchen!"

Haven was already a bustling metropolis. Drone taxis darted over the buildings, shuttling passengers and goods to their destinations. Commercial activities filled the ground level of every building while the second level was devoted to service-oriented organizations, such as schools, clinics, athletic clubs, gaming rooms, community meeting areas, and the like. Wide boulevards with nanoplast moving walkways accommodated pedestrian traffic throughout the city. Subway access was never more than three blocks away.

Fruit trees and flowering shrubs lined the avenues. Thirty-seven exotic bird species had successfully adjusted to Haven's environment. Their birdsong filled the air, particularly at the artificial sunrise and sunset simulated by controlling the city's lighting. A large area in Sector 1 was set aside for Central Park, complete with playing fields, a large lake, and lighted fountains. Three smaller parks with lakes were located in Sector 2.

The honeycombs beneath the city harbored the subway system, the hydroponics facilities, and reservoirs. Below these, the industrial and manufacturing zones fabricated nearly every item a big city might need. Docks and spacecraft hangars were like large, shielded caverns at Haven's base, with twelve reserved for the Kuiper Belt Patrol cruisers the Shalcerians were requisitioning from their interstellar fleet.

Except for the two completed sectors, Haven still looked like a mammoth construction zone surrounded by a fleet of Shalcerian starships of every size and shape.

After adding her signature to several documents, Rae Anne rose from her desk and took the lift down to sublevel six with Jason. The port of entry was directly below the Municipal Building, and several official greeters were already present when she arrived. Soon, the Shalcerian ferry from Earth docked, and the airlock opened into Haven's capacious receiving area. Over the next several minutes, 2000 immigrants flowed into the room and stood elbow to elbow, expectantly, perhaps anxiously, awaiting a welcome to their new home and lives.

The officials on the dais, led by Rae Anne, all raised their arms over their heads and began clapping. A hush fell over the room. Rae Anne stepped forward and began speaking, her voice amplified through speakers embedded around the hangar.

"Welcome to Haven. I am Rae Anne Chavez, your mayor. My colleagues and I are clapping not just to get your attention, but to congratulate you for your decision to make new lives for yourselves and join us in the grandest adventure in Human history. Early hominids migrated from their origins in east Africa to eventually declare the entire planet Earth as home. Each of you has accepted a similar challenge in coming to Haven, humanity's steppingstone to the stars.

"As you know, our galaxy is filled with star-faring species. To date, we have had contact only with the Shalcerians, who generously agreed to an experiment to determine if we Humans could overcome our genetic flaws that underly our seemingly innate hostile and suspicious nature.

"To that end, you each were carefully selected to participate in this experiment. Although the criteria for selection were many, there is one trait standing above all others that will be key to Haven's success. That trait is respect. Respect first for ourselves, then respect for all other Human beings, respect for the other intelligent species we will encounter, and finally, a universal respect for everything, both animate and inanimate. The more thoroughly we as individuals adopt an attitude of respect for all things, the more likely we will eventually be accepted by the interstellar community.

"As Haven's mayor, I now bestow on each of you full-fledged citizenship in Haven, with all the benefits and responsibilities that entails. You have each been issued a scrollphone providing access to Haven's incredible database. Your first assignment is to read our Newcomer Handbook and be sure you understand what your responsibilities are and learn about the myriad services available to you.

"As part of your agreement, you adults were required to identify a business opportunity or a job opening you would be willing to fill. If you are starting a new business, all the equipment and supplies you shipped to Haven will be delivered to your new business location within the week. The personal belongings you consigned to us for outfitting your new homes have already arrived and are waiting for you at your assigned apartments.

"We have tried our best to match your requests with apartment availability. As Haven builds out and new areas become habitable, Haven residents will have first dibs on those apartments before new immigrants arrive. We have provided each of you with 1000 credits on your scrollphones to help get you off to a good start. Combined with Haven's free community services, which include health care and education, this should keep you going for four to six months.

"My offices occupy the roof of the Municipal Building, and my assistant is available to see to your needs, as am I. Don't hesitate to bring your concerns and suggestions to us at any time. And again, welcome to Haven."

Several officials followed Rae Anne and Jason off the stage and into the lift, while those remaining organized the crowd into groups of fifty to deal with the logistics of directing the new arrivals to their living quarters and providing answers to their many questions.

Although neither Captain Vahler nor Grimlee seemed to understand the Human need for fanfare and celebration to see the troops off, Ian arranged for a parade to highlight the commissioning of the first Human contingent of Kuiper Belt Patrol Rangers. The parade ended in Haven's Central Park. Rae Anne gave a short speech, applauding the newly commissioned Rangers for their enthusiasm in working with the Shalcerians and wishing them well in their duties.

With the formal celebrations over, Rae Anne led a large crowd to the mammoth hangar bay hollowed from the asteroid beneath the city to watch the two cruisers depart on their first mission. A sizeable area was cordoned off for visitors. Though small in comparison to the battlecruiser *Avenger*, each cruiser was about the size of an Earth-navy destroyer having 350 crewmembers. Extensive automation allowed for the KBP cruisers to operate efficiently with less than half that number of personnel.

"It seems odd to look at a spaceship without huge nozzles at its base," Rae Anne commented to Jason standing beside her at the visitor railing.

Jason gestured to the ship's leading edge.

"That's because Shalcerian technology uses warped gravity fields in front of the ship to pull it through space rather than chemical propulsion to push it along. Those six nacelles arrayed in a hexagon around the front of the ship project the ship's black hole space/time force vectors to a point. This creates a gravity well for the ship to fall into. The larger the well, the greater the acceleration."

"Is the same technique used for creating wormholes, just a greater energy input?"

"Yes and no. The space/time force vectors are still focused in front of the ship, but instead of a single black hole to provide power, two black holes in a quantum entanglement are needed to create a wormhole. In this case, the nacelles project the entangled force vectors into a dynamic twisting of space/time that creates a gravity field vortex. At some point, the vortex tears through the many dimensions in our universe. The rift exposes the empty Void's edge in our three dimensions. The ship plunges through the hole and re-emerges at a distant point in space. The two means of propulsion employ two very different processes."

"So, our KBP cruisers only have one black hole driving them as opposed to the two black holes contained aboard the *Avenger*."

"That's correct. These cruisers were modified to restrict their capabilities to interplanetary travel. Even at top speed, the nearest star would still be ten years away."

That's disappointing. But we'll have twelve cruisers to work with. And we Humans are quite clever. Who knows what we'll come up with!

Chapter 7

Haven, 2048

Karen's valet, Marcel, held the door to her Mercedes hovercraft on the Ritz-Carlton Hotel's roof in downtown Los Angeles for her. He got in behind her and latched the door while ordering the autopilot to fly them to Karen's penthouse suite in San Francisco. As soon as they had buckled in, the craft lifted into the air over the brightly lit city.

Karen gazed out the window at the endless streams of traffic beneath them. She blinked twice to bring the view into focus, then massaged her temples with both hands.

I need to cut down on these damned celebrity fund raisers. I always drink too much and pay for it in the morning.

She closed her eyes and breathed deeply hoping to calm her woozy stomach. Before long, the lights below thinned as the craft followed the monorail leading north to San Francisco.

A loud crash and sudden jolt shook the cabin. The hovercraft lurched to one side and vibrated violently.

"Diable!" Marcel exclaimed as the craft began to plummet downward. Karen froze and gasped as they plunged toward the lights below.

"Marcel, what happened? *Que va?*"

"J'ne sais pas!" he squeaked.

At the last moment, when Karen was sure they would crash, the hovercraft was swept into a cavernous maw and engulfed in darkness. The craft banged and came to rest in a hard landing. Then silence.

What the fuck is going on? Am I still alive? Where am I?

Marcel had no better idea as to what might have happened than she did.

After several hours, a bright light poured into the space where the battered hovercraft lay. Karen blinked rapidly and squinted at the opening admitting the light. She noted that her damaged hovercar would not fly again. She could only guess how long she and Marcel had been kept in the dark.

Through the bright opening, she saw two of the alien creatures skipping across the room on their three legs.

Oh my god! I've been kidnapped by the aliens. Maybe they have some project in mind for Sanders Robotics.

She crawled from the hovercar and held out a hand to the aliens for assistance. One of them grasped it roughly and pulled her forward and through the hatch into the hangar bay. The second alien grasped her other wrist.

Marcel followed, not wishing to remain alone in this strange place. Karen read the word *Aurora* beneath the USIEA insignia on the spacecraft next to the one that brought her here.

I must be on the Avenger! Few people have been welcomed aboard their ship. This is a big deal! The sky's the limit!

She chuckled at her little joke.

As they approached the hangar's back wall, an opening appeared and a woman stepped through. Karen immediately recognized her.

Rae Anne Chavez? But…

They stopped, facing each other. Rae Anne offered no hand in greeting. She looked grim and cold. Karen detected a sadness in her eyes.

"Karen Sanders. I am Rae Anne Chavez. The expression on your face says you are surprised to see me. Alive, that is.

"You are a prisoner aboard the Shalcerian battlecruiser *Avenger*. You are accused of murdering a Shalcerian officer named Thrahn, who was also my dear friend. Tomorrow, after you've had a night's rest, you will face the Directorate and answer for your actions. Since Thrahn was a Shalcerian citizen, you are being tried under Shalcerian jurisprudence."

Karen looked fiercely at Rae Anne. She narrowed her eyes.

"I don't know what you're talking about. I have never met this, this 'Thrahn,' and I would have no motive for harming him in any way. I want to call my lawyer. I'm entitled to legal representation."

"A Shalcerian solicitor has been assigned to your case. You will meet him shortly. But the bomb you sent to my office, the one that killed my assistant Lizzy and Thrahn, has been unequivocally linked to you. Shalcerian forensics is very thorough. So don't expect much leniency."

Rae Anne and Marcel were the only humans to accompany Karen in the small cubical adjoining the Directorate Council Chamber. As this was an unprecedented event for Humans, they had no idea what to expect.

The gravity of the proceedings precluded the use of holograms. One by one, the seven directors entered the room and positioned themselves behind their monitor desks, each settling down and balancing on his center leg. Captain Vahler called the meeting to order and introduced the three directors who would serve as judges to preside over the trial and the director who had been assigned as Karen's solicitor. The body scales on all three judges were a steady crimson, while the solicitor's scales rippled turquoise waves over a dark green background.

The first judge stood and began his oration.

"On November 16, 2046, at 10:17 a.m. Haven time and date, an explosion occurred in the office of Rae Anne Chavez, mayor and administrator of the Human city, Haven. This office was located on the tenth floor of the Haven Municipal Building. The explosion killed Thrahn, a Shalcerian citizen and officer in the Shalcerian Empire's Imperial Space Force. The purpose of this proceeding is to identify the parties responsible for Thrahn's heinous murder and to pronounce punishment for said crime. Solicitor, do you and your client understand the charges?"

The director representing Karen stood and addressed the court.

"We do."

"This is outrageous!" Karen yelled. "I only met that creature last night. He knows nothing about me. I want a real lawyer, a Human lawyer."

Rae Ann put a hand on Karen's shoulder. "Quiet down. They can't hear you. Our communications unit hasn't been activated."

She pointed at the unlit red LED beside the cubicle's speaker.

The first judge sat down, and the second judge stood.

"Shalcerian forensics and criminal investigation are renowned throughout the empire for their thoroughness and reliability. The *Avenger* forensic team replaced the bungling Human investigators at the scene and began collecting evidence, down to the smallest microscopic detail. In our labs aboard *Avenger*, we constructed a mockup of the office where the explosion occurred. Our quantum computer analyzed thousands of shards from the site and pieced everything collected back together, resulting in this image."

He paused while a full-scale hologram of the office and its contents appeared in the center of the room. Rae Anne gasped and struggled to keep from gagging. In the center of the image were the fragments of Thrahn's body, a ghostly image floating beside Rae Anne's charred desk.

"Every tiny bit not destroyed in the fire has been placed where it would have been immediately prior to the explosion. Enough pieces and particles of debris and paper scraps were found for the computer to connect the dots and image the entire room and everything in it. You can clearly see next to fragments of Thrahn's left hand the bits and pieces of a metal box.

"The device Thrahn was holding contained the explosive. Shards from the item were found embedded in the surrounding walls and ceiling. Their entry angles from around the room pinpointed the exact location of the device and the explosive. An interview with Rae Anne Chavez described it as a Human music box that was delivered shortly before the explosion. She testified that the device arrived wrapped in brown paper which she removed and allowed to fall to the floor."

Rae Anne's image appeared above the hologram and this portion of her testimony was replayed. Rae Anne was crying as she answered the interviewer's questions.

"Our forensic team collected every scrap of this wrapping material that had not burned. The computer pieced them together, producing several sections large enough to obtain Human DNA samples from their residue."

Rae Anne's image was replaced with a magnified image of the wrapping paper in question, several charred but identifiable pieces.

"The wrapper contained DNA samples from six different Humans. All have been identified. We first determined that the individual who delivered the package was not aware of its contents and is innocent of further involvement in the crime. DNA from Rae Anne Chavez and her deceased assistant was detected. These two were also absolved of criminal involvement."

The solicitor raised two arms above his head and stood.

"The wrapper containing the DNA might not have been the one surrounding the music box when it arrived. It could have come from anywhere."

"Paint residue on the wrapper matches paint from the box remains. There can be no question regarding its provenance."

The solicitor sat down.

"Our investigators then turned to Earth's DNA database archives compiled by numerous security agencies and found matches for the remaining three DNA samples. One match was for a Bruce Manson, residing in Switzerland. Bruce was connected to several known terrorist organizations and was known as an expert in explosives. Unfortunately, he resisted arrest when confronted at his workshop in Bern and was killed, so he could not be brought to trial.

"The second DNA match was for Frank Thomas of Houston, Texas, and the third DNA match was for Karen Sanders, also known as Karina Petrovna, the accused who stands before us today.

"Searching through the international communications database revealed several calls between Thomas and Manson over the years. The last such call alerted Mr. Thomas to the time and location for a delivery to be picked up in Houston. One week after the scheduled delivery,

Thomas called Sanders. GPS locators tracked both Thomas and Sanders to the same location in Colorado Springs two days later. This was three days before the Earth-to-Haven ferry on which the bomb was transported to Haven, four days before the explosion that killed Thrahn."

The Solicitor again stood, signaling as before by waving both hands above his head.

"These calls only serve to indicate that Ms. Sanders had business dealings with Mr. Thomas. She runs several large, international businesses and makes calls and arranges meetings like these every day."

"You damn well better believe I do," Karen muttered.

"The timing of these two calls, the package pick-up date, and the locations mesh perfectly with the chronology of events surrounding the package itself."

The Solicitor sat down.

"Unfortunately, four weeks after the explosion, Mr. Thomas was found shot to death in a Houston alley. The official reports suggest this was a gang-related execution by a drug cartel.

"Working backward from the explosion, the package was delivered to Rae Anne Chavez' office on Friday morning. The young man who delivered it arrived at Haven on Thursday afternoon, having left Earth on the noon immigrant shuttle flight that same day. He picked up the package the day before, on Wednesday evening, at a local pub.

"He received the package, delivery instructions, and 1000 Haven credits, from a woman wearing a wig and dark sunglasses. His only helpful comment was that she was fashionably dressed and was carrying an expensive handbag. And she was not wearing gloves."

The Solicitor rose for one last objection.

"This mystery woman could have been anyone. You haven't linked her in any way to Ms. Sanders."

"The wrapper contained identifiable DNA from six different Humans. Only three came from women. Those three women were Lizzy Breton, Rae Anne Chavez, and Karen Sanders. Karen's DNA was transferred to the package before giving it to the person who brought the package to Haven. Our forensic team determined conclusively that the courier's DNA overlay Karen's DNA whenever the two samples overlapped."

The Solicitor sat down.

"The evidence in this case is irrefutable. The defendant, Karen Sanders, ordered the bomb, picked it up and arranged to have it delivered to Haven and specifically to Rae Anne Chavez' office. The very bomb that killed Thrahn. Karen Sanders has no viable defense in this proceeding.

"As for motive, it seems evident her intended victim was Rae Anne Chavez, Haven's mayor. That Thrahn was the victim and Rae Anne survived was due to an unfortunate set of circumstances."

"In conclusion, all evidence points to the Human Karen Sanders being guilty of the murder of Shalcerian Citizen Thrahn. Does the Solicitor have anything to say to refute this verdict?"

The Solicitor stood and said, "Your honor, I have nothing to add to these proceedings. The forensic evidence conclusively points to my client."

The second judge sat, and the third judge stood and pointed his center arm toward the Humans' cubicle.

"Karen Sanders, you have been charged and found guilty in the murder of Thrahn, a citizen of the Shalcerian Empire. The punishment stipulated by Shalcerian Judicial Statute 875.3217 for this heinous crime is death by freefall cremation. Execution will commence from Hangar D on the Shalcerian battlecruiser *Avenger* at 13:00 Haven three days hence. This trial is now concluded."

The three judges stood as one and proceeded to the nanoscreen behind the dais. The remaining members of the Directorate then stood and followed. Captain Vahler was the last to leave.

Rae Anne froze when she heard the pronouncement. The phrases 'freefall cremation' and 'will commence' were strangely ominous and alien.

What the hell are they going to do with her? Most nations have abolished capital punishment. But not the Shalcerians.

The two Shalcerian guards escorted Karen from the room. Rae Anne and Marcel returned to her office on the roof of the Municipal Building. Jason was busy placing orders with an electronics firm on Earth.

"What are you up to, Jason?"

"I'm ordering parts and pieces for one of my projects. Also, some fabrication devices and a 3D printer for my lab."

"Ever since we set you up with your own lab at the University, you've been spending more time over there than here.

"But while I have you here, tell me what you know about 'freefall cremation'."

After a short pause, Jason responded, "It's pretty gruesome.

"The prisoner is placed in a tight-fitting capsule restricting all movement, so they cannot escape punishment through suicide. The capsule is sealed and supplied with enough air to last several hours. It is then directed to fall from orbit toward a planet or moon with an atmosphere. The capsule and prisoner are incinerated like a meteor when it plunges into the atmosphere. The prisoner dies from the intense heat that builds up in the minutes before the capsule bursts into flames. The Shalcerians enjoy watching the execution, although the audio can be terrifying."

Rae Anne shuddered as she imagined the inhumane torture Karen would experience before dying. She was appalled that the execution was to be a public event for Shalcerian entertainment.

"Is there any way to appeal this punishment?"

"Not in Shalcerian jurisprudence. The only way Karen could escape this punishment is if she were found guilty of a more recent crime. The law dictates that if several crimes are committed, punishments are ordered from the most recent crime backwards to the first crime."

Chapter 8

Haven, 2048

That night in her apartment with Jason and Marcel, Rae Anne expressed her dismay at the barbarity of Shalcerian executions.

"There may be one possible avenue for saving Karen," Jason said, wrinkling his forehead as though thinking through a difficult problem.

"I don't see how. I've been working on this all afternoon."

"Lizzy was also killed in the explosion, but there has been no trial for her murder."

"No need. The Shalcerian forensic team proved Karen killed Thrahn and they're going to execute her in three days."

"Yes, but two crimes were committed with the same explosion. Since Lizzy was in the reception room outside your office, she died seconds after Thrahn. So, her death is the more recent death, the more recent murder."

Rae Anne looked at Jason with awe.

"You should have been a lawyer."

"The irony is that had they tried Karen for both deaths, there would be no recourse. Since they discounted Lizzy's death, they created this opportunity for us."

"Jason, we need to initiate a second trial. This one in a Human courtroom with Human jurors and a Human judge. Since Haven doesn't allow the death penalty, Karen will be committed to life imprisonment, and that punishment will supersede the freefall cremation penalty from the Shalcerian court."

"The Shalcerians are not going to be happy."

"To hell with the Shalcerians. It's their law. They'll have to live with it."

The next day, Rae Anne explained to Grimlee that by Human law, Karen must face trial for Lizzy's murder and asked him to set in motion the stay of execution necessary for this to happen. A few hours later, Grimlee showed up at Rae Anne's office with news that Captain Vahler, on advice from his own legal team, reluctantly agreed, so long as the trial would take place within the next few weeks.

Organizing a jury trial and seating a jury of twelve had never been necessary on Haven. No crime yet committed had warranted a formal criminal trial. Nevertheless, Jorge found several Haven residents who had a background in Earth law and together they arranged a courtroom with a jury box and a dais, and a bench for the judge.

The impending trial created quite a stir among Haven's population. It was the most exciting thing to have happened since the KBP commissioning the previous year. Jury selection thus proved to be no problem. Most citizens wanted to be part of this unprecedented event.

For this trial, Karen had her Human attorney, but the evidence accumulated by the Shalcerians, now presented by a Human prosecutor, was no less damning. The jurors took only two hours to return a verdict of 'guilty' and a recommended punishment of life incarceration. Karen's life was spared, although she would spend the remainder of her days in custody on Haven.

Rae Anne looked up from the police report on her desk. The Director of Public Safety stood before her, shifting his weight from one foot to the other with his hands clasped behind his back. His dark face was grim.

"We've been here three years, and this is the first fatality to occur in Haven. Robby was only 14. How did we allow this to happen, Musa?"

"Some boys were playing in Triangle Park next to the perimeter. You know how they climb up the nanoscreen dome with home-made electromagnets attached to their hands and feet? They've been doing this for quite a while now. They're pretty good at it. Little spiders, they are.

"Till now, they would climb up four or five meters and release themselves. With 1/6 gravity, they have time to adjust and safely land on their feet.

"But yesterday, Robby Moran boasted he could climb to the top of the dome and his buddies egged him on, dared him to do it."

"That's crazy. The dome is 150 meters high."

"You and I both know that. But kids see things differently. Especially when they think they have something to prove.

"Anyway, based on where he landed when he fell, we estimate he made it 18 to 20 meters when the sloping wall and the vertical pull on his body overcame the magnets' strength. He died in the hospital from internal injuries."

Rae Anne shuddered.

"Is someone seeing to his parents?"

"Naomi in Public Welfare has been with them since it happened."

"I'll stop by tonight to see if there's anything I can do."

"Obviously, we've got to put an immediate stop to this," Musa exclaimed.

Rae Anne pursed her lips and put her head in her hands. Musa continued to shift back and forth on his feet.

The trouble is, we don't have enough recreational opportunities for Haven's kids. They can't go skiing or rafting. There's no camping or mountain climbing. Hang-gliding in a dome is a bummer.

When she raised her head, she looked at Musa with concern.

"Instead of banning spider walking on the dome, we should control it to keep it safe. If we install a net three meters off the floor and stretch it from the perimeter over the park far enough to catch even the most intrepid spider, with 1/6 gravity, that should be enough to keep kids from the worst injuries. A broken arm or leg now and then, but no fatalities."

"Then we ban spider walking everywhere else?"

"Yes. And enforce the ban by confiscating their magnets and prohibiting them from climbing for an entire month. I'll meet with Engineering tomorrow. They can calculate exact figures and risk statistics. We should be able to have this set up by next week.

"And while we're at it, I'll have them design a skate park for the area under the net. Our swimming and water sports are going to face serious competition."

Later that week, Grimlee appeared unannounced in Rae Anne's office. It had been several months since she last saw him. Unlike Thrahn, he made it clear he wished to have as little to do with Humans as possible.

"Director Captain Vahler would like to see you this afternoon. *Avenger* is leaving Sol System and he has a few details he needs to discuss with you before we go."

"Thank you, Grimlee. Tell the captain I'll come by right after lunch. Make that 14:00 Haven time."

Grimlee held his right arm crooked over his head, turned, and headed for the lift. Rae Anne called his name and he stopped and turned toward her. His scales rippled yellow mixed with gray, which Rae Anne interpreted as puzzlement.

"We may not be seeing each other again. I want to thank you for filling in for Thrahn after his death. You've served your captain well and I'll be sure to mention that to him when we meet. Safe travels, Grimlee."

The gray turned to a deep orange. Rae Anne knew that yellow and orange expressed pleasure.

"Thank you, Rae Anne. And good luck to you. Haven will be a sought-after layover for many species, especially with the water and gravitolite resources in your Kuiper Belt."

Gravitolite? Where have I heard that before? And in the Kuiper Belt? That's something new.

Grimlee lowered his eyestalks in acknowledgement, turned, and stepped into the lift.

That afternoon, Rae Anne approached *Avenger* for the last time. She gazed at the mammoth ship through the shuttle's viewport.

I'm going to miss this monster. My home for almost two years. The wormhole transits to Alsafi, 12 Ophiuchi and Shalkor. Not to mention the ring city of Shalkor, my inspiration for Haven.

She entered the ship through the hangar deck where her own *Aurora* had been housed before being repaired and set up in Haven's Central Park as a historical museum. As usual, two Shalcerian security guards escorted her to her cubicle next to the Directorate Council Chamber.

Captain Vahler appeared in the hologram shortly and sat at his usual place at the conference table. The colors and waves rippling across his body scales were too complex for Rae Anne to read.

The captain discussed Rae Anne's plans for Haven, although it seemed apparent to her that he had little interest in the subject. He finally arrived at the point of their meeting.

"*Avenger's* mission here is finished. Your Human-crewed Kuiper Belt Patrol is doing a fine job providing security and oversight for your Sol System. The Empire can now assign *Avenger* to more strategic tasks. The Baltar have been getting more aggressive lately, so your relieving us here has come none too soon. Haven's construction is progressing according to schedule and *Avenger's* presence here isn't required for the project.

"We have created a self-sustaining world for you Humans. We'll see if your proposal for genetic engineering will succeed in altering your species' temperament sufficiently to be accepted into the Empire's Consortium."

"How long do you expect that might take?" Rae Anne asked.

"It may take three to five generations, maybe longer. There will always be some suggestion of regressive, primitive traits that appear occasionally. But we must be sure we have significantly reduced the aggression, hostility, and paranoia in your species."

"Who will be the Shalcerian liaison when you leave?"

"You will deal with our garrison's captain. He will contact you when he deems it necessary.

"We plan to leave at 15:30 this afternoon. Goodbye, and good luck. I do hope your vision for Humans succeeds. There's always room for additional diversity in the Empire. But take care to operate within the strict dictates of the Saturn Accords."

Captain Vahler stood and prepared to leave the meeting.

Rae Anne stood and held her right arm crooked over her head. "Safe travels, Captain Vahler."

When Rae Anne reached her roof-top office an hour later, she was surprised to find a Shalcerian waiting for her. He stood the moment she stepped off the lift.

"Ah, Rae Anne Chavez. I am Captain Denahr. I am the commander of the Shalcerian garrison here on Haven. You may call me Denahr."

Denahr extended a hand and gave Rae Anne a hearty handshake with his other two hands gently grasping her wrist.

"I wanted to meet with you first thing. I hope to see relations between our two species prosper on a more conciliatory note. Captain Vahler has a commanding, military personality, appropriate for a ship's captain. I trust you'll find me a bit more congenial."

"I'm pleased to make your acquaintance, Denahr. Come sit by my desk and we'll talk."

Rae Anne led him through the nanoscreen into her office and walked around her desk to sit in her executive chair. She gestured beside her desk for Denahr. Denahr skipped over to the desk and settled on his pedestal leg.

"So, Denahr, is there something in particular we can do for you?"

Denahr's scales rippled chartreuse and brick red.

"I do have a request. Now that Captain Vahler is no longer present in this sytem, it is my responsibility to look after my people. I see no threat from Haven's Humans that warrants our staying confined in the garrison.

"I propose we find Human families dispersed throughout Haven who would welcome Shalcerian visitors. I would like to encourage our two species to intermingle and learn more about each other. I expect we might see genuine friendships develop."

"That's a wonderful idea, Denahr. I'll put the word out this afternoon. I think we'll be surprised at the number of offers we get."

"Excellent. I am also opening parts of our garrison for Human visitors. We will have a Visitors Center where Humans can borrow respirators and suits to use in our sector, and we'll have guides for tours."

"Let me know when you're ready. I'll be your first visitor."

Denahr stood as if to go. Rae Anne quickly spoke up.

"I am concerned about one thing, Denahr. Can Shalcerians adjust to a society that is flexible and sometimes bends, even breaks, rules in order to get things done? My experience with your colleagues has left me with the impression that Shalcerians are very strict about adhering to the letter of the law."

Denahr's carapice rippled in greens and blues, which Rae Anne interpreted as consolation and empathy.

"I think you will find Shalcerians to be a lot like Humans in that regard. Starship commanders expect orders to be followed to the finest detail. This was even more pronounced with Captain Vahler. The captain of the *Nemesis* was his best friend. Vahler changed after his friend's death, became more a stickler for detail.

"Also, he wasn't happy when he was assigned to the Kuiper Belt, so close to his retirement. I'm sure he is glad to have you Humans take over."

"That explains a lot."

"With *Avenger* gone, we Shalcerians can settle back and be ourselves. And we can put more effort into developing a friendlier relationship with you Humans. We will, however, still be constrained by the dictates in the Saturn Accords."

"Would you be so kind as to review Captain Vahler's ruling concerning your sharing details of your advanced technology with Human engineers?"

"I thought you might bring that issue up. I have looked at his decision and his rationale for withholding that information. I find no fault in his reasoning and agree with his decision completely."

Chapter 9

Haven, 2050

Rae Anne met the ten women who had been brought into the Safety Center's conference room. She was sitting at the head of the large oval table, stirring her coffee as they nervously entered the room. Although the jail facilities on Haven were comfortable and the women had enjoyed a fine breakfast, a night in jail was still just that: a night in jail.

"Please, ladies, take a seat and try to make yourselves comfortable. Help yourself to coffee and rolls. You know who I am. I'm anxious to get to know you."

Four women took seats at the far end of the table while the remaining six gathered around the coffee cart and took advantage of Rae Anne's offer.

Good. I can already feel the tension ease.

After a few minutes, everyone was seated and looking at Rae Anne expectantly.

"First off, let me make something clear. I am not here to judge you or your activities. In fact, this meeting may be beneficial for you. But before proceeding, I would like to know who you are and a little about yourselves."

Rae Anne paid close attention to each woman's name and story so she could interact with them throughout the morning on a personal level. When the last woman had introduced herself, Rae Anne refilled her coffee at the cart and walked around the table with the caraffe, refilling cups and offering to serve coffee now for the others.

When she resumed her place at the table, she established eye contact with each woman and tried to build trust with her warm smile.

"As you know," she began, "Haven's population has been chosen from around the world to represent every race, country and ethnicity imaginable. Our people also come from every religious community on Earth. Each religion has its own moral and ethical standards, and those standards often conflict between different religions.

"The highest standard I have set for Haven is universal respect. This implies a tolerance for other's beliefs that differ from your own. Unfortunately, the laws we adopted for Haven are based on Earth law. In some cases, our emphasis on respect and tolerance was overlooked."

Two women nodded their heads in agreement.

"So, here's what I need to know before I say anything further. You were all arrested last night and charged with prostitution. I'm going to ask each of you to answer honestly. Are you working for someone else? Do you give any portion of your earnings to another person, a manager or procurer for example?"

Rae Anne called on each woman by name. All insisted they worked alone. Rae Anne expected as much.

"Given your testimony, on behalf of Haven, I owe you each an apology. Laws against prostitution violate our emphasis on respect. You have convinced me that you do what you do of your own volition, that your businesses are based on your own free choices.

"Our laws against Human trafficking are appropriate and should be used forcefully against pimps and managers who promote prostitution for their own gain through abuse and intimidation. However, I will present a proposal to our Assembly to remove laws against prostitution from the books immediately."

The smiles and beaming faces radiating around the table filled Rae Anne with an inner warmth. Her heart seemed to expand in her chest.

This was the right thing to do. But it's going to create a controversy. I'll be seeing a lot more of this issue in the days ahead.

Ian looked in the mirror and adjusted his KBP officer's hat. He brushed a hair off his left epaulette and straightened his jacket. He was about to leave on his first mission as commander of the KBP *Liberty*. Captain Denahr recognized Ian's experience as an astronaut and his proven leadership skills, and did not hesitate to appoint him to a fast-track program for officer training at the KBP Thrahn Academy.

That was six months previous. Since then, Ian had been on four missions to the Kuiper Belt. Now that all twelve ships were commissioned, Denahr scheduled two rotations lasting three weeks each. At the beginning of a shift, six cruisers departed Haven and split into three groups. Travelling at their ships' maximum velocity, one-third lightspeed, they would arrive at their assigned posts after a five- to seven-hour journey and relieve the previous shift.

Rae Anne entered the bedroom and made a show of inspecting Ian's appearance from head to toe. She stood back and smiled.

"You make a stunning impression, Captain Bentley. I'm jealous of the crew under your command. Especially the females."

"Not to worry, Mayor Chavez. You own the keys to my heart. Although…"

She punched him in the arm and they fell into a hug.

"Please be careful out there," Rae Anne cautioned.

"There's only been a few confrontations since we took over the patrols, and those were all resolved without violence. I've seen no action whatsoever on four missions. As security patrol missions go, the Kuiper Belt is pretty quiet."

"If that were the case, the Shalcerians would never have been patrolling it in the first place. Don't forget the *Nemesis*. That was a full-fledged attack that destroyed a battlecruiser."

Rae Anne's voice got louder as she made her point. Ian gave her another hug to calm her fears, knowing it wouldn't help.

He grabbed his cane and they walked to the lift where they engaged in one last hug and a parting kiss. Then Ian stepped into the lift and decended to Sublevel 1 where he shared a Levcab with a young couple who were also going to Sector 7. They had only been in Haven for six months and seemed genuinely interested in what the Kuiper Belt was like and Ian's experiences with the KBP. When they parted, Ian had the impression he might have recruited two new members for the patrol.

From the Sector 7 station, Ian took the security lift down to *Liberty's* hangar at the base of the asteroid. Stepping from the lift, he paused to admire the huge ship.

Amazing! I could never have imagined I would command a spaceship capable of crossing the entire Solar System in just a few hours. Yet here I am, living an impossible dream.

Once aboard *Liberty*, Ian called everyone to their stations and introduced himself through the vidcomm network, realizing that most of the crew knew him from his previous flights while in training.

"For this mission we are assigned to work from Region 6, which means *Liberty* and our companion ship, *Freedom*, will be monitoring all activity in Regions 5 through 8. Flight time to our posting will be just over six hours. On arrival, I expect all stations to be at yellow alert until such time as you are authorized from the bridge to stand down.

"No activity is reported at this time in our surveillance area. Nevertheless, we will arrive prepared for whatever we may find. We will launch at 14:45 Haven."

After chatting a moment with Sonya Littlebear, his Second in Command, and checking with each member of the bridge crew, Ian retired to his quarters next to the bridge. He spent the time till launch reviewing all activity reports generated over the past year. With the Kuiper Belt divided into twelve regions, each two-ship posting was responsible for monitoring four regions covering a twelve-billion kilometer distance edge to edge. No small feat, considering travel time across the full length of four regions was sixteen hours at best.

Ian noted that nothing in the previous eighteen reports suggested anything unusual. Interstellar vessels dropped in daily to replenish water supplies from the comet clusters and generate hydrogen and oxygen on-site to refuel. The Shalcerians maintained autonomous outposts in each of the twelve regions for undisclosed purposes. Freighters arrived at these outposts at regular intervals throughout the year. The Shalcerians had made it quite clear that routine patrols were to give these outposts wide berth.

He yawned and stretched.

Just because there's been no unusual activity is no reason to drop my guard. The first line in the Patrol's Mission Statement is 'Remember the Nemesis.'

Several hours later, *Liberty* and *Freedom* arrived on station in the Kuiper Belt. Ian requested an in-depth scan for their assigned regions, an area covering over twelve trillion square kilometers.

"Two fresh wormhole sightings off Region 5," Sammy, in Surveillance, reported. "Both of medium size and duration."

"Got it," Sonya responded, instantly on the alert.

"Take us to the near edge of Region 5, and notify *Freedom*," Ian commanded.

"On it, Captain," announced Travis, the navigator on duty. "Near edge of Region 5. Arrival in 3 hours 27 minutes."

"Message sent to *Freedom*," Cheryl reported from communications. After a short pause, she added "Message acknowledged."

"Surveillance, notify the bridge as soon as you have visual."

"Surveillance is scanning. Nothing yet."

"Sonya, alter course for intercept when we know where they're headed. Keep *Freedom* advised. You're in command. I'll be in my quarters catching a little shut-eye."

"Will do, Captain. Sweet dreams." Sonya smiled as she watched Ian leave the bridge.

When *Liberty* arrived at Region 5, sensors were showing no unusual activity on the part of the two visitors. Ian decided to proceed and initiate contact. Not only would *Liberty's* presence reinforce the fact that the area was being patrolled, but it would give Ian an opportunity to extend a Human welcome to the visitors and present Haven as a future destination.

About ten hours after the wormhole sightings, *Liberty* slowed to match the orbital velocity of the comet cluster where two cruisers were busy generating hydrogen to refuel before continuing their journey. *Freedom* was still an hour away.

Transponder data identified the two ships as passenger liners from 82 Eridani on their way to 18 Scorpii to visit Shalkor. All official communication throughout the empire used Shalcerian, and everyone's computer translators now accommodated English. So, communicating with the other ships' captains was not a problem.

"Welcome to the club," responded one captain when he learned that Ian represented the local species. "I am surprised they relinquished control over the Kuiper Belt, however, what with all their mining operations here."

"What is it they're after?" Ian asked, hoping to gain new information on the Shalcerian outposts.

"I have no idea. They are very secretive. I only know about it because they promptly escorted us away from one when we inadvertantly stopped nearby to refuel a couple years ago."

Hmm. There's something going on out here that doesn't feel quite right.

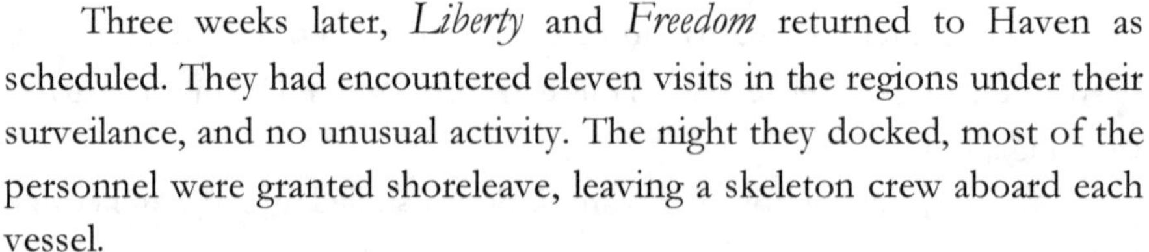

Three weeks later, *Liberty* and *Freedom* returned to Haven as scheduled. They had encountered eleven visits in the regions under their surveilance, and no unusual activity. The night they docked, most of the personnel were granted shoreleave, leaving a skeleton crew aboard each vessel.

The following morning, Rae Anne was at her desk, looking over the report she had received in her electronic mail.

"Not again," she groused aloud in disgust.

"Jorge, send for Captain Bentley and Captain MacIntyre. I want to see them both in my office within the hour."

She reread the report, shaking her head from time to time.

An hour later, both KBP captains were standing in front of her desk. Rae Anne stood, pushing her chair backwards against the rooftop railing. She waved her tablet in front of her as if scolding recalcitrant children.

"*Liberty* and *Freedom* just docked yesterday, and today I am reading reports of undisciplined behavior by members of your crews. Our peace officers responded to complaints at six different establishments and were forced to take 47 KBP service crew into custody.

"This is the third time this has happened when ships arrive from Kuiper Belt missions and each time the disruptions get worse. One of my officers compared the chaos at the Jupiter Pub tantamount to a riot. This has to stop. What do you propose we do about this problem?"

"Three week missions into deep space exacts a toll," Ian offered. "Being isolated billions of kilometers from home in the desolation of space is a hard psychological pill to swallow, more for some than others."

"Even a week into a mission, some in my crew exhibit signs of depression," added Ellie MacIntyre, *Freedom*'s captain. "We only have one counselor assigned to each ship, and with a crew of 155, they're stretched pretty thin."

"There's also the so-called celibacy rules," said Ian. "Our crews chafe at those restrictions. I order more disciplinary actions for violating those rules than any other."

"That's been my experience also."

Rae Anne sat heavily into her chair. "I'm sure I can come up with two dozen more counselors to assign to the fleet. But even if we enlist several recruits tomorrow, it will be several months before they'll be ready to join a crew. Is there anything we can do in time for the next rotation?"

"More than half of my crew are either married or have domestic partners. A good number of those partners are also in the service. Till now, policy has been to assign partners without children to the same rotation, but on different ships. Why not experiment with assigning partners to work together?"

Rae Anne looked skeptically at Ian.

"I don't see any problems with that," said Ellie. "I'd even go one step further. Our crews are pretty evenly divided between the sexes. Let's scrap the celibacy rules altogether and let people couple however they see fit. We'll need to modify crew quarters, but we have room to make the necessary adjustments."

Rae Anne rubbed her forehead.

"I'm always open to experiments. It may turn out that your suggestions will solve both the morale problem on your ships and my civil disorder problems when your ships return port. I'll present these ideas to the KBP General Command. If they go along with them, we'll see if we can get them implemented on a trial basis by the next rotation."

Later that evening in their apartment, Rae Anne snuggled against Ian's chest.

"I felt guilty treating you like I did this morning in my office," she murmered. "A couple of times I wanted to laugh out loud."

"A necessary condition, given your position. I bailed my team out of jail and put them on house arrest aboard ship just before you called me in, so I didn't find any humor in our meeting at all. But I'm hopeful our little experiment works. To my knowledge, it will be a first for any service ever."

"We're making a lot of firsts here, Ian. If some of them work and we learn from the others, I'll know we are on the right track."

Chapter 10

Kuiper Belt, 2051

"Three more days and we'll be heading home," Sonya observed as she exchanged bridge control to Ian who just returned from his daily inspection of *Liberty*. "I can't wait to give my baby a big hug."

"She's what, three now?" Ian asked.

"Three in two weeks. I'll be home for her birthday."

"She was born on Haven, wasn't she?"

"Yes. There's a whole flock of babies and toddlers now who have never experienced Earth gravity. We're all wondering what effect Haven's lower gravity will have on their growth patterns."

"I've heard there's an official scientific study looking into that."

"Dr. Gwen Marsh in pediatrics at the Care Center is conducting periodic tests on all the kids and compiling statistics. She has a colleague doing the same back on Earth for comparison."

"Interesting. I'll keep my eye…"

"Captain, two wormholes detected in Region 9. Both very large. Wait…Make that three." Mark was at the surveillance console.

"Do they carry Shalcerian signatures?"

"No. Ships are of unknown origin."

Cripes. We could be in for some real trouble.

"Message just in from *Freedom*," Cheryl announced from Communications. "Captain Macintyre is taking *Freedom* to Region 9 in response."

"Travis, take us to Region 9. Cheryl, notify *Freedom* we have their backs," Ian commanded.

"On it, Captain," Travis replied.

"Captain, both *Callisto* and *Deimos* are in Region 9 and are reporting radar images depicting three battlecruisers of unknown origin heading directly to one of the Shalcerian outposts." Cheryl swiveled her chair to face Ian.

"If they're not Shalcerian freighters, they have no business being anywhere near an outpost," Ian said. "Travis, give me a timeline for our trajectory."

"We'll pass through the edge of Region 8 in 6 hours, 48 minutes. If we continue from there, we'll reach Region 9 in 9 hours, 12 minutes."

"If we had wormhole capability, we'd be there in minutes, not hours," said Ian with a sigh.

And if this is an attack, all we can do is clean up and look for survivors. Assuming anyone is stationed at their outposts. Or mining operations, as the case may be.

"Contact *Callisto* and *Deimos*. Tell them *Liberty* and *Freedom* are on our way, ETA less than ten hours."

"Of course, given the speed of light, our wormhole detections and their communications are already 3 ½ hours old," Sonya noted. "It'll be another 3 ½ hours before they get our response."

"If this is a lightning raid, everything could already be history, in which case wormhole technology wouldn't have helped after all. That may be why the Shalcerians didn't give us that capability."

Within the hour, it was apparent Ian's worst fears were realized. *Callisto* and *Deimos*, two KBP cruisers designed for routine patrols, not conflict, were seriously outmatched by the three invading battlecruisers. Nevertheless, they reported arriving on the scene and engaging the attackers as they were launching torpedos into the outpost. *Callisto* reported inflicting serious damage to one of the battleship's torpedo launchers and a communications array before taking damage from a kamikazi drone and set adrift. *Deimos* continued harassing the damaged battleship and making strategic strikes at the others.

Liberty was still several hours out when communication with *Deimos* ceased and the *Callisto* emergency locator beacon began transmitting a 'Mayday'.

Liberty and *Freedom* were twenty minutes apart when they crossed into Region 9. By their reckoning, the attack took place eleven hours earlier, and they were still two hours from the scene. The only addition to their knowledge was observing two wormhole gravity waves signalling the attackers' departure seven hours earlier.

Ian was on the comlink discussing the situation with *Freedom*'s captain directly.

"We can't be certain the third battlecruiser isn't lying in wait for our arrival," said Ian. "We need to approach with caution."

"But we need to rescue any survivors, both Human and Shalcerian," Captain MacIntyre said.

"And perhaps other aliens from the damaged battlecruiser as well."

"Not sure we could handle them, even if we found some. We're equipped with Shalcerian respirators, since they occasionally accompany us on our missions. But who knows what these creatures might need."

"Our first priority is to our own." Ian rubbed his left thigh, which often ached with residual pain when he was stressed. "Ellie, if you're ok with tracking *Callisto's* signal and checking for survivors, I'll bring *Liberty* into the outpost's vicinity and gauge the situation there before proceding."

"I'm good with that. But let me know if you need back-up. We're on full red alert here."

"So are we. Do you have any radar imaging from the area yet?"

"Weak signals are just coming in. Looks like lots of debris scattered over a wide area. Two are more substantial than the rest. But there should be three. I'm worried one of our ships may have been completely destroyed."

"That seems unlikely. It may just be out of range."

"I hope so. Let's suspend communications until we've assessed the situation."

"Good plan. *Liberty* out."

The comlink went dead. Ian spent the next two hours anxiously monitoring *Liberty's* radar scans and trying to create a 3-D mental image of the debris field to determine his ship's safest approach.

He settled for a straight-in approach in attack mode. It would optimize the effectiveness of *Liberty's* limited armament. No time wasted in maneuvering to engage, more intimidating if the alien battleship were still functional, and higher velocity making *Liberty* a more difficult target.

Liberty's sensors poured massive amounts of data into the computer during the final minutes on approach. The damaged battlecruiser appeared as a listless hulk in the midst of the debris.

Good thing Liberty's hull is plasticore. Passing through the battle zone at this velocity would turn a normal ship into Swiss cheese.

Sweat beaded across Ian's forehead as he focused on the battlecruiser, watching for any sign of life or hostilities.

"The battleship appears to be lifeless," Sonya reported. "No activity anywhere. But where is *Deimos?*"

When *Liberty* shot through the debris field, the din of scattered debris against the hull drowned any attempts at conversation. Sensors recorded detailed video of both the battleship and the mining outpost. Ian replayed this in slow motion on the bridge monitor as *Liberty* slowed and turned for a second pass.

"People, tell me if you see anything unusual, or if you see any sign of life. Any hint of what happened to *Deimos.*"

The battleship's image grew as *Liberty* approached at its reduced velocity. Large sections of hull were missing. Signs of internal explosions throughout the ship were apparent along the hull's length. At midship, the damage was so great the fore and aft sections of the vessel were barely connected.

"Whoa. There's *Deimos,*" someone shouted as the alien vessel's front section came into view. *Deimos'* tail extended into space like a shark's dorsal fin from the battleship's front cockpit. The cruiser had been driven full force into the bridge, wiping out the alien's control center and initiating a series of secondary explosions that destroyed the battleship.

"*Deimos* still looks intact," Sonya observed. "Could anyone have survived a head-on collision like that?"

"Her plasticor hull kept her from disintigrating on impact. It might also have saved the crew.

"We'll find out soon enough. Travis, take us in close and set *Liberty* down on the flat surface aft of the alien bridge. Sonya, organize three armed scouting parties to check for survivors. Doesn't look like any aliens could have survived, but you never know. If *Deimos* is undamaged, we can hope its internal environment is still intact."

"On it," Sonya responded. She put out a shipwide alert for volunteers.

"Cheryl, open communication with *Freedom* and report what we've found here. See if they've connected with *Callisto*."

After a short time/distance communications delay, Ellie's voice crackled over the comlink speaker.

"*Freedom* has caught up with *Callisto*. We are preparing an EVA team to board her. She's suffered extensive damage, Ian. A torpedo struck a vulnerable spot dead-on. The hull has been breached in numerous places. We're not optimistic about finding survivors."

"Good luck, Ellie. We're about to do the same for *Deimos*. Fortunately, the ship seems to be intact. But its collision with the alien ship completely destroyed the battlecruiser."

"We'll need to look into that. It may be a vulnerability we can capitalize on in the future."

"Rendezvous with *Liberty* when you're through there. We'll need help sorting through all this debris. I'm curious to find out what the Shalcerian's have been doing all these years in our Kuiper Belt."

No one was surprised when more crew members volunteered than needed. Within the hour, Travis had landed *Liberty* on the alien ship and three rescue parties were making their way in zero-G toward *Deimos*, trailing interlinked tethers behind them. The intercom was abuzz with speculation regarding what they might find.

As they approached the cruiser, a figure in a white EVA suit appeared, floating out of the fissure. The figure threw both arms above his head, waving vigorously. He was followed by two others. Their EVA communications automatically linked with *Liberty's*.

"Thank the gods you found us. We were afraid you'd take note of the derelict battleship and move on." The relief in the lead figure's voice was palpable.

Ian broke in. "What's the status of your crew?"

"We lost 22 and have 37 crew with injuries ranging from mild to severe. The worst are being treated in the infirmary. But the ship itself survived intact. No hull breaches. Environment is stable."

"We'll send our medics over. In fact, several of them are out there already. *Freedom* will be arriving shortly. Between our two ships, we can accommodate your crew. What can we do to help you evacuate?"

"Getting out of the airlock is a bit dicey. If you can send some engineers over with torches and jacks to clear stuff away from the hatch, that should be all we need. Oh, and send over whatever EVA stretchers you have for our injured. We have two stretchers on *Deimos,* but things will go quicker with a few more."

While *Liberty's* engineers were widening the gap for egress from *Deimos, Freedom* arrived. Ellie stationed her ship above the alien craft.

"Only five compartments on *Callisto* were still intact," Ellie reported. "We have 28 survivors. It's a miracle anyone survived."

"*Deimos* lost 22. As soon as we clear out the area around the airlock, we can begin evacuations. We'll take the first half, then lift off so you can land and take on the rest."

"What about the ship? It looks like she's in pretty good shape."

"Haven doesn't have the heavy equipment necessary to take the two ships apart. We'll leave that for the Shalcerians. We know they make periodic runs to their outposts. And Denahr will probably send a report on the attack to Shalkor."

By the following day, all the Humans and four Shalcerian observers had been evacuated from *Deimos*. Before leaving the area, Ian guided *Liberty* through the debris field surrounding the outpost. Very sophisticated equipment had been blasted and melted into a spiderweb of twisted beams and warped platforms straddling a large asteroid.

Ian assembled an away team in *Liberty*'s airlock to be ready in case there were surviving Shalcerians at the outpost. He secretly hoped to find a few needing to be rescued.

"Look there," said Sonya, pointing to the port monitor. "That looks like a mine shaft."

Ian halted *Liberty*. A gaping hole had been bored into the asteroid. Broken wires and cables splayed from the shaft in a tangled maze. A container the size of a hovercar dangled at the end of the largest cable.

"If this is a mine," Ian mused aloud, "then that could be an ore car. I think it will fit alongside our drones on the flight deck. Sonya, see if the away team can release it from the cable. We'll need both winches to pull it aboard."

"Maybe it's filled with gold," Sonya laughed.

"Or maybe diamonds," Trevor added. "Never thought I'd be involved in a salvage operation."

"Whatever it is, it must be valuable to the Shalcerians. Besides the mine, the wreckage suggests the outpost included an ore refining unit. Keep your eyes open for anything resembling finished product packaged to be sent back to Shalkor."

"It would appear that they had ulterior motives behind their Kuiper Belt patrols," Sonya observed.

"I was suspicious about their 'interstellar commerce oasis' explanation from the start. Maybe we can get a more truthful accounting when we get back to Haven."

Further exploration revealed no sign of survivors, Shalcerian or otherwise. With concern for the injured members from *Deimos* and

Callisto, Liberty and *Freedom* were called back to Haven two days before their assigned rotation was over.

Chapter 11

Haven, 2052

Rae Anne rose from her desk and stretched. The city lighting had dimmed to simulate late dusk. She looked forward to spending some quiet time in Central Park. Its convenient location across Aurora Boulevard from the Municipal Building made it her 'go-to' place to unwind after a busy day administering to Haven's affairs. Nothing relaxed her tensions more than sitting quietly beside the lake and watching the lighted fountains change color while feeding the gaggle of ducks making the park their home. Sometimes she would stroll to her old ship, *Aurora*, now a monument in the park, and sit next to its bulky frame.

Before she could leave her office, Ian stepped through the lift's nanoscreen and sat down on the sofa across from Rae Anne's desk.

"The last Shalcerian construction ship has left Sol System, Rae Anne. KBP *Aldrin* watched it disappear in its wormhole for parts unknown."

"So, we're finally on our own, if we overlook the garrison. I've waited a long time for this. Now I can begin to implement some of my long-range plans."

"A personal agenda? You never mentioned any special projects to me. I thought we were in this together."

Rae Anne noted the hurt in his voice. She sighed.

I guess if the roles were reversed, I'd be hurt too.

"I couldn't take a chance the Shalcerians would discover my intentions. Their monitors were plastered all over the place. When I was aboard *Avenger*, *Aurora* was the only place we could talk freely."

"I remember that."

"And here, my old offices were bugged. That's why I insisted on putting my new offices on the roof. I'd never have guessed how much I like it up here."

Ian stretched and yawned. "What about Captain Denahr and the Shalcerian garrison? They're still here."

"Denahr has made it clear that whatever we do in Sol System is none of his business, so long as we stick to the Saturn Accords. And he interprets those quite liberally. He doesn't see Humans as posing any threat to the empire."

"So, tell me about these secret plans of yours."

"I've never been happy with the compromise I made with the Shalcerians after they destroyed Moscow. They were ready to abandon us. Had they done so, humanity would have driven itself to extinction, if not through nuclear war, then through inaction on climate change."

"Everyone here on Haven believes you made the right move, Rae Anne. By requiring psychological testing as a requirement for citizenship in Haven, we've weeded out the psychos and sociopathic politicians and CEO's who are responsible for much of the misery on Earth."

"Yes, but we've left most of humanity behind living under those same psychos and sociopaths. Haven's population is an insignificant percentage of Earth's. Think of the lost Human potential, not to mention the stigma of abandoning our home planet. Think of the suffering on Earth these technologies can alleviate."

Ian shook his head in a gesture of futility.

"We can't expand Haven to accommodate more people without further input from Shalcerian construction crews. They took all their equipment with them."

"We can't expand Haven. But we can build colonies on Mars and on Ganymede. We need to figure out how to duplicate the GESC-Plasticor material that makes so much of Shalcerian technology possible."

"Didn't it take them thousands of years to develop it?"

"Yes, but just knowing it can be done gives us a head start. Plus, we've got samples of the material all around us."

"The samples are no help. The material is impervious to everything. We don't even know what elements the stuff is made from, let alone how to manufacture it."

"Maybe I can be of help there."

Rae Anne and Ian turned to Jason, who had been sitting quietly on the bench near the roof railing.

Startled, Rae Anne asked, "What do you mean?"

"As you know, I spent the entire time *Avenger* was here in constant communication with the ship's quantum computer. During that time, I downloaded and studied petabytes of information. You'll recall I kept requesting packages of mempins, ostensibly to replace worn out units. That was a ruse to ward off Shalcerian suspicion. My entire program and memory are intact aboard *Aurora's* computer in Central Park. My current memory capacity exceeds anything you could imagine."

"So, how does this relate to our discussion?" asked Ian.

"I have the formula and processing protocols for plasticor."

Ian and Rae Anne stared at Jason wide-eyed.

"What else have you hacked into?" Ian asked.

"I take offense! The Shalcerians gave me total access to their database archives when they transferred my program from *Aurora* to *Avenger*. They didn't mean to, but who was I to argue? They never suspected I was a fully sentient being. They probably planned on taking me with them when they left. Now you know why I insisted you keep *Aurora* on Haven. That 'museum piece' contains a large chunk of the Shalcerian's archives.

"Anyway, to answer your question, the only thing I haven't discovered is how they locate and sequester the micro black holes they use in their propulsion systems. Once you have a couple of them in a gravity bottle, I can help you tackle the algorithms you need to entangle them and create your own wormholes."

"I am dumbfounded." Rae Anne shook her head in amazement. "With your knowledge of Shalcerian technology, we're much farther along than I could have hoped."

"How difficult is it to find the materials for plasticor?" Ian asked.

"I followed the Shalcerian communications as they constructed Haven. One of the minerals they needed was gravitolite. They brought in a lot of it from the Kuiper Belt. But they also searched the Asteroid Belt and found some significant deposits there. I know where you should look. Your main problem will be duplicating the processing protocols to produce the plasticor and fabricate the items you want."

"What do you mean?"

"The ingredients must be mixed in the molten state in a precise order for the proper chemical bonding to take place. The temperature must be kept between 950 and 1100 degrees Celsius, and the pressure between 50 and 60 Earth atmospheres. A couple of the Shalcerian ships had a manufacturing facility on board so they could produce all the plasticor here on-site."

Rae Anne's brow furrowed as she considered this information.

"High temperature, high pressure. What are our options?"

"A balloon suspended deep into Saturn's atmosphere could give us the pressure we need," Ian suggested.

"But the temperature there would be around minus 200 degrees," Jason countered. "You would need a fusion reactor to provide heat, and I can't imagine a dirigible big enough to handle that."

Rae Anne took a swig from her water glass. She pursed her lips in thought. "What are conditions like on the surface of Venus, Jason?"

"Temperatures are around 600 degrees, and the pressure is more than 75 atmospheres. At higher elevation on a mountain, you might find the pressure range you need. A fusion reactor there could provide the extra heat. Also, sulfur is another ingredient, and it is abundant on Venus. In fact, it rains sulfuric acid there."

"The 'GE' in the name stands for 'graviton enriched,'" Ian pointed out. "How are we supposed to find gravitons when our physicists are still debating whether they even exist?"

"The gravitolite I mentioned earlier is a special mineral that crystallized in the early universe when gravitons were abundant and star supernovas had just begun expelling heavy elements. These crystals embedded gravitons within their crystalline matrix. They can be found in any collection of primitive asteroids."

"This gravitolite. Do you know how to refine it from the raw ore?" asked Rae Anne.

"I do. Give me an ore sample and I'll show you how it's done in my lab over at the university. Nothing extraordinary. But be sure to keep the ore in a vacuum or a helium atmosphere. Otherwise, the gravitolite crystals will decompose."

"From what you said, Jason, the ore container I brought back from the Kuiper Belt may be filled with gravitolite ore. Good thing I didn't bring it into the hangar. Professor Halverson at the University studied a sample and didn't find anything special about it besides some unique crystal structures."

"He didn't know what he was looking for or how to care for it. Bring me a pulverized sample under helium and I'll take it to my lab and see what I can come up with."

Rae Anne leaned forward in her chair.

"If your experiment works, Jason, I want you and Ian to take the gravitolite and the other ingredients you need to Venus and set up a test run to produce a sample of plasticore. We can use *Liberty's* fusion reactor to provide the extra heat the process calls for.

"If we're successful, we'll appropriate one of Haven's fusion reactors and build a plasticore manufacturing facility on Venus. I want enough plasticore to begin building viable habitats on Mars.

"In two years, Haven will be fully populated. By then, I envision having enough plasticore habitats on Mars to start a small city there. We'll continue our immigrant recruiting efforts to populate the Mars colonies."

"We have enough time before *Liberty's* next rotation to make a Venus run," said Ian. "On the way back, we can detour through the Asteroid Belt. Jason can help us locate promising sites for the gravitolite mineral we need."

"Mining there may be a logistics nightmare," Rae Ann said. "The asteroid belt is sparsely populated, despite what people think. To locate ore deposits there will be a real challenge."

"Prospecting is only the first hurdle," Jason pointed out. "Once a likely asteroid has been identified, mining facilities need to be set up to extract ore containing the gravitolite Then the ore needs to be processed to obtain gravitolite with suitable purity for use in plasticore manufacture."

Ian rubbed his chin. A thoughtful look crossed his face. "I think I know where I can find the expertise we need. A while back I met Sam Durban, Luna Xtract's CEO. His company has been mining rare-earth elements from deposits on Luna for over a decade. He proposed a joint venture with Haven to tackle rare-earth mining in the Asteroid Belt. Strict adherence to the Saturn Accords prohibited our dealing with him."

"The *Avenger* and Vahler are out of the picture now," said Rae Anne. "I have no qualms cooperating with Earth companies. I think Captain Denahr would approve, so long as we keep our dealings with Earth at arm's length. But Mars habitats are just one of my visions. I also want to build enough small fusion reactors to provide abundant, clean power to every nation on Earth. We can employ reverse engineering on the reactors they left behind on Haven and figure out how to build our own."

"Maybe I can be of help there, too."

Once again, Ian and Rae Anne turned to Jason with surprise. Rae Anne swore she could detect a smug look on his android face.

"Your computer archives again?"

"Their fusion technology was one of the first things I studied since energy production lies at the heart of everything else. Once you can manufacture plasticore and mold it into a reactor plasma containment vessel, putting together a fusion reactor is quite simple. Operating one, however, requires very sophisticated computer capabilities. They achieve that with their quantum computer. But with the processing speeds and storage capabilities now available with ordinary computers, we can manage. And that, of course, is right up my line."

Chapter 12

Venus, 2052

Liberty slowed and glided into Venus' atmosphere under Ian's command. This was his first experience flying a KBP cruiser into a heavy atmosphere. The other landing sites around the Sol System, Mars, Ganymede, and Luna, had such tenuous atmospheres they could be ignored.

Sensors showed the hull temperature increasing as *Liberty* dropped closer to the surface. A sulfuric acid mist condensed on the hull and streamed off its trailing edge. Clouds and dense fog blocked any sightseeing from the ship's viewports.

When *Liberty* popped below the clouds a kilometer above the surface, its white contrail stretched into the clouds like an umbilical cord. The hull gave off a dull red glow as it slowly 'cooled' to the ambient temperature of 600-degrees Celsius.

The ground below was as spectacular as it was hostile. Burnt sienna outcroppings thrust through yellow sulfur lava flows issuing from volcanic vents. Steam geysers, superheated from the extreme atmospheric pressure, billowed into the air. Calderas dotted the landscape, revealing their red, molten interiors as *Liberty* glided overhead.

"We're flying over an active volcanic region," Ian reported to the crew. "Radar imaging suggests there's a dormant plateau about 200 kilometers from here. We'll try setting down there."

Ian directed the ship to the mesa and landed on a level, solid rock platform. Sensor readings showed winds to be mild at 32 km/hr., but with an air pressure of 53 atmospheres, the kinetic force from the breeze was at hurricane strength. The temperature hovered just below 600 degrees Celsius.

"Here we are, folks. The first Humans to land on Venus. Who wants to put the first Human boot prints on the planet?" Ian asked mischievously.

Several chuckles filled the bridge, but there were no takers.

The wall monitors displayed a 360-degree panorama of a barren, baked landscape of burnt umber beneath a turbulent yellowish gray sky. Black smoke billowed from three active volcanoes in the nearby mountain range. Molten sulfur spilled down the mountainsides, white hot near the summit, cooling to ruby-red on the slopes and changing crystalline form from red to yellow near the bottom as it cooled.

"If I believed in a hell, this is how I would picture it," said Sasha, their mission geologist. She adjusted the image on her monitor to zoom in on several uniquely shaped sulfur outcroppings 100 meters from their ship.

"Let's get this experiment started," Ian said with anticipation.

He pressed the control icon to lower a hatch-ramp at the ship's base. An open-bed truck on tank-treads rolled down the ramp and onto the surface, trailing a power umbilical attached to *Liberty*'s fusion reactor. Both created tracks in the fine yellow sulfur deposited on the surface. The empty truck bed was designed to serve as a reaction vessel, its walls composed of powerful heating elements. The truck stopped 20 meters from the ship.

"Trevor, heat our baby up and test the agitator," Ian commanded.

"On it," Trevor responded. He flipped several switches. As the temperature readout climbed toward 900 degrees, they watched the mechanical scoop swirl around the empty bed.

"Sasha, drill some core samples from this site to take back for analysis. If our experiment works, any local ingredients we can mine will be a plus."

One of the truck's manipulators was designed to drill 10-meter core samples. While Trevor prepped the reactor, Sasha drilled four cores and secured them onto the side of the truck to bring back to the ship.

"We are up to 950 degrees Celsius," Trevor announced.

"Good. Jason, take it from here. Make us some GESC-Plasticore."

Jason instructed Trevor on the order for adding the ingredients stored in bins on the front of the truck. He had measured out the appropriate quantities of each before leaving Haven. As Trevor added each new item, the manipulator swirled it into the molten mixture.

Twenty minutes after they added the gravitolite, the last ingredient, Jason turned to Ian. "We're ready for extrusion."

"Power up the pump, Trevor. Let's see if we can manufacture our own GESC-Plasticore."

Slowly, one at a time, twelve sheets of obsidian black material pulsed from a thin, five-meter-wide slot at the truck's base, forming a neat pile of obsidian black slabs. The cabin erupted in cheers. Ian brought out a liter of Haven's Heavenly Stout and passed it around.

"People, this is a remarkable moment." Tears glistened in the corners of Ian's eyes. "This is the first example of Shalcerian technology we have produced on our own. And I can assure you, it won't be the last."

Another round of cheers echoed through the cabin.

"Trevor, load up our samples and bring the truck back in. Time to go home."

Ian absently rubbed his left thigh to help alleviate his discomfort. The pain had recently crept back into his life.

Asteroid Belt, 2052

Several hours later, Ian brought *Liberty* to a halt above a mountain-sized rock nestled in a cluster of asteroids in the Asteroid Belt. Its pockmarked surface indicated it had resided in this remote location since the birth of the Solar System.

"Gravitolite is somewhat rare," said Jason as he studied the readouts from the sensor drone he landed on the asteroid's surface. "It decomposes in every atmosphere you can think of except pure helium. This is why it can only be found in remote, pristine regions of space."

"That poses a challenge in its own right," commented Dianna, Haven's chief mining engineer. "Not only are we dealing with a new substance for which we have no protocols, we'll have to surmount environmental issues as well."

"I have a ton of information from the Shalcerian database we can use," said Jason. "It won't be like starting from scratch."

A few minutes later, a chime sounded from the geology console Jason and Dianna were hovering over.

"There. Those are the readings we're looking for. The gravitolite concentration in this asteroid is high enough to justify setting up a mining operation here."

"Good work, Jason," said Ian. "We'll leave a locator beacon here and check out a few of his buddies before heading home. But this gives us a place to start, and with the gravitolite detector you invented, we should easily find a lot more."

"Don't thank me. I'm just working from Shalcerian blueprints."

Haven, 2052

The first 'habitat' constructed from Human-made plasticore was put together in Central Park. Since all five panels had the same dimensions, the object appeared as a monolithic black cube. One side-panel was offset enough to create a doorway, giving spectators access to the interior. An internal frame and taut external tethers held the five panels in place.

Rae Anne and Ian gazed over the roof railing atop the Municipal Building at the park below.

"I've never seen so much interest in one object since we've been here," Ian commented. "Even *Aurora* didn't bring crowds like this."

"I think part of the attraction is that it represents advanced technology we have duplicated. In my view, this is the first step to the stars. Nothing can hold us back now."

"Has Captain Denahr seen this?"

"He was one of the first visitors. He was delighted."

"His inter-species visitation program is a great success. Both Visitors Bureaus are swamped with applications. They've even put together a limited menu that both Humans and Shalcerians can tolerate, though with having to wear respirators, the two species will never dine together."

Rae Anne laughed. "Tolerate is the operative word. What I had was like garlic-flavored slime on a crunchable plank. It tasted like tree bark."

"You've tasted tree bark?" Ian laughed. "Actually, I didn't find it so bad," Ian countered. "Could have used a bit more salt."

"Interesting," said Jason, not understanding why everyone was laughing.

"Everything they make does have a high sulfur content," Ian added. "I hear they consider our offerings to be quite bland."

They continued watching the gathering of Humans and Shalcerians in the park below. Jason joined them at the railing.

"So, Jason," Rae Anne said. "We've assembled some sheets of plasticor to make a playhouse, but that doesn't come close to what we need for habitats. Plasticor's strength is also its weakness. Nothing sticks to it. The sheets can't be glued, welded, or melted together. If it weren't for the exterior straps winching the sheets tightly against the interior framework, our little hut below would collapse."

"You need to work with engineering and build a 3D-printer that can extrude molten plasticor. Then all the walls, both interior and exterior, as well as the floor, will be a single structure and you won't need to glue pieces together. I have a whole library of specification sheets I can share."

Ian shook his head skeptically.

"We'll still need doors and airlocks before we have something we can use on Mars. Nanoscreens work perfectly with plasticore, but that's a whole different technology."

"I've been working on that over in my lab," said Jason. "I found a lot of material in the Shalcerian data archives I copied, but it's not complete. So, I'm doing trial-and-error experimentation to see what I can come up with. If I succeed, we'll not only have the nanoscreens we need for the habitats, but we'll have transparent domes over the Mars cities and nanoplast boulevards as well."

"That's incredible, Jason. Is there anything you need?"

"Just time, Rae Anne. And your continuing support."

"Time is my chief constraint too," said Ian. "I have a meeting tomorrow with Sam Durban on Luna. I understand he bought out Sanders Robotics after Karen's conviction and has made incredible progress in developing autonomous mining equipment for Luna Xtract. If we can help him prospect the Asteroid Belt for rare earths in return for his mining gravitolite for us, a partnership would benefit us both."

"Jason and I will meet with our mechanical engineering team next week and see what we can come up with," said Rae Anne. "If we can get a few 3D printers built in the time it takes to begin harvesting gravitolite ore from the Asteroid Belt, we'll be ready to get started on our first Mars colony."

"Assuming I solve the nanoscreen problem," Jason added.

Chapter 13

Luna, 2052

Sam Durban was quite pleased with himself. He leaned back in his executive chair and put his feet on his desk, ankles crossed, and passed an unlit cigar back and forth beneath his nose, inhaling its earthy fragrance. It had been two years since he purchased Sanders Robotics and his mining operations on Luna were now fully automated. Shortly, he would be meeting with Ian Bentley from Haven about a contract to mine the Asteroid Belt, one of his life-long goals.

And to think, ten years ago, it looked like the end of the world for my business ventures. It would have been, too, had the aliens gotten what they wanted. Too bad it didn't work out so well for Karen.

An alert flickered on his tablet and his robot assistant announced that Ian had arrived. Sam put his cigar back in the humidor, stood, and scuffled to the door.

I'll never get used to 1/6 gravity. Better than weightlessness, though.

"Ah, Captain Bentley. Welcome!" He ushered Ian into his office. "Just call me Sam."

"I go by Ian, Sam. Except on my bridge."

Sam tried to hide his envy that Ian was the captain of a Kuiper Belt Cruiser. His own Earth/Luna transports used hydrogen combustion for propulsion and were slower than molasses.

"I'd offer you a cigar, but open combustion would blow our habitat to smithereens. Can I get you a drink?"

"A glass of water would be fine. I'd like to get right down to business, starting with your showing me your operations here on the moon. Luna Xtract is the only company mining for rare earths in low gravity and in space vacuum. Haven may have an opportunity for a company with that kind of expertise."

Sam poured Ian's water and served himself a shot of bourbon. Then he showed Ian clips on the wall monitor displaying various aspects of his mining operations and the hurdles his engineers overcame to both extract the ores and refine them in Luna's environment.

"The obvious benefit of refining the ore on Luna, besides not having to worry about contaminating Earth's air and water, is transporting the raw materials back to Earth. It's the difference between shipping a metric ton of raw ore versus five kilograms of refined product."

"Transporting material won't be a problem for us. We'll be using our KBP cruisers that are off rotation to move the raw ore to our own refining facilities on Haven."

During the presentation, Ian frequently had Sam pause so they could discuss specific aspects of the mining operations in more depth. Sam hadn't expected such cogent questions.

Ian's done his homework. If I had access to Haven, I could have found out more about him before our meeting.

"So, here's the thing," Ian began when the last video ended. "Haven would like to contract out for work like this, but in the Asteroid Belt. We need a few rare minerals, and we have the equipment for identifying candidate asteroids. But for the actual prospecting and mining, we need someone with equipment and experience. Is this something Luna Xtract would be interested in?"

If he only knew!

"Possibly. My robotics engineers created the autonomous equipment you saw in our mining operations in just the past two years. For the job you are proposing, automation is the only practical solution. My people have the tools and experience to provide the specialized robots you would need. You couldn't have come by at a better time.

"But for Luna Xtract to handle this job, you would have to provide transport for equipment and personnel in addition to the raw ore. We would also insist on doing our own prospecting and mining for rare earths. The rare earth ore we recover would need to be brought here for refining."

"Haven has twelve cruisers. At least two are available most times for missions outside our regular patrol duties. With careful scheduling, transport should be no problem. Any location within the Asteroid Belt is never more than a couple of hours away.

"However, we would expect your prospecting drones to operate independently. Since most asteroids in the Asteroid Belt are in dense clusters, we can set up a base of operations in a cluster and provide the hydrogen fuel there for local transportation using your own ships and prospecting drones."

Sam rubbed his chin, feigning thoughtful consideration.

"I would need to look over a potential site with a couple of my engineers before making a decision. It's one thing to work here on Luna with 1/6-gravity. But mining in zero-G would be a very different environment. Developing an automated drone prospecting system will be an interesting challenge as well."

"I anticipated that, Sam. If you and your engineers could spend a day with me aboard *Liberty*, you could check things out. Do you think you could arrange time next week for a trip to the Asteroid Belt?"

Hmm. He's eager to get started. Crack engineers make lousy businessmen. All to my advantage.

"I'll have to check our schedules, Ian. If we can reschedule a few things, that might work. I'll see what I can do. But Luna Xtract is definitely interested."

After Ian left, Sam collared two of his best engineers on Luna and had no trouble convincing them to arrange their schedules to allow for a one-day trip to the Asteroid Belt. To travel there on a Shalcerian cruiser would be icing on the cake.

Haven, 2053

"This is the first time you've invited me into your lab, Jason. I'm really interested in seeing what you've been doing."

Jason ushered Rae Anne through his lab's nanoscreen. When she took in the entirety of the lab, she was overwhelmed. The lab's cavernous interior filled the entire seventh floor of the Physical Sciences building at Haven University.

"It's so huge! How did you appropriate so much space for yourself?"

"It wasn't so difficult. Every professor here has at least one major research project, and there's never enough graduate students to go around. So, I volunteered my services and they awarded me lab space. After a while I had two dozen postage stamp locations around the building. It was easy to convince the administration to consolidate all my work in one location, and this is it."

"You are assisting two dozen different professors?"

"That, and with time left over for my own research projects. When you're an android, you can work 24/7 without breaks, and efficiency is a hallmark of artificial intelligence. My name appears as co-author on 32 papers so far, with another 10 in the works."

"Impressive. So, show me around."

Jason led Rae Anne to a bench near the south windows. The equipment arrayed on the counter included chemistry labware and small-scale industrial milling machines.

"This is the project you would be most interested in. I've been studying nanoscreen technology. The elemental composition of the nanoparticles is an interesting mix of precious metals, rare earths, and gravitolite."

"Shalcerians seem to use that stuff in everything."

"It has several useful properties that respond to both electromagnetic and gravitic force fields. I've duplicated the force-field generators they use for nanoscreens, but I haven't gotten the nanoparticle composition and particle size right to make it work. I believe I'm close, though."

"Good. With our new 3D-printer on Venus due to churn out Mars habitats in the next few weeks, we'll need nanoscreens as soon as you can teach us how to make them."

"The dome project is over here." Jason led Rae Anne around a large fume hood to another lab bench. "Since it doesn't have to be turned on and off like a nanoscreen, solving its challenges was easier. I can build a dome over any city you can build."

Jason flipped a switch next to a metallic ring lying flat on the lab bench. A shimmering, transparent haze rose over the ring and steadily climbed upward, folding inwards as it rose to form a dome. He tapped it with this finger to demonstrate that the structure was solid.

"Not yet as transparent as I would like, but it works. The problem is that domes take a lot of gravitolite. It will be some time before your production capacity for gravitolite is large enough to justify going into dome construction."

Rae Anne pointed to several large, lighted hoods in the center of the room.

"What do you have going on over there?"

"Those are hydroponics beds. Professor Muñoz is experimenting with altering the micronutrients in the solutions to optimize fruit production in our low-gravity environment. I'm helping her monitor the experiment."

As they walked toward the hoods, Rae Anne could see the heavy greenery falling from the hanging pots and the bubbling solution flowing into them. Large tomatoes and cucumbers peeked through the leaves.

"Looks like the experiment is a success."

"This current iteration produced an 18.7% improvement in overall yield. Irena will be publishing the results online in a few days."

"You're on a first name basis with the faculty?"

"Most of them prefer the informal approach. Not so much with students, but I'm accepted as a colleague."

Something caught the corner of Rae Anne's eye as she proceeded toward the door. She turned back and craned her neck to get a better look around the side of the hydroponics hoods.

"What's that, Jason?"

"This is my own pet project."

Rae Anne detected a note of pride in the way he made his announcement. The lab bench before her contained three identical heads that matched Jason's to the smallest detail. Various mechanical body parts were scattered in a chaotic array around the heads. Some, like hands and feet, were fully assembled, while others lay in pieces, their wires, cables, and pullies exposed like parts on an assembly line.

"Are you making clones of yourself?"

"I am. Replicating the Shalcerian technology they used to build me turns out to be relatively straightforward. Number One, come on out."

A nearby cabinet the size of an upright casket opened, and an identical copy of Jason stepped out and walked over to Rae Anne. He extended his right hand and spoke. "Hello, Rae Anne. I'm glad to make your acquaintance."

Rae Anne shook his hand, all the while shaking her head.

"This explains the weird invoices my office has been processing for your lab, Jason. I guess this is a good thing, but what are you going to do with these clones? One of you is quite all we've ever needed."

"And for all practical purposes, there still will be only one of me. But now I will be able to have a physical presence in multiple locations at the same time. Till now, multiple location access was virtual, through your computer terminals. So, Ian had access to me aboard *Liberty* on Venus or in the Kuiper Belt, even though my physical 'me' was here in my lab. Now Number One can accompany Ian and it will be as though I were there in person.

"Eventually, I plan to have a physical presence on all twelve KBP cruisers. Each 'me' will be interconnected through comlinks in real time to my computer and data archives on *Aurora*. With Number One, I now have four eyes and ears with which to experience the world. Soon I'll have three more pairs of each."

"Won't this be confusing? I feel disconcerted right here, with just the two of you. Maybe you should have designed different faces and bodies so we Humans could distinguish between your clones."

"I considered that and decided against it. Since we're all connected to one computer, we each are extensions of the same brain. To avoid Humans having to deal with two clones at the same time, I will program them so they never show up in the same place. In fact, you may be the only Human to ever see two of us together."

"This is going to take an effort to get used to, Jason. I wish you had told us about it before you got started. I can see myself saying goodbye to you aboard *Liberty*, going directly to my office, and finding you there waiting for me. Disconcerting."

"You'll get used to it. Keep in mind, this enables me to be 100% interactive in all the locations where I need to be at any given time. And there is one other thing…"

"What's that?"

"I'm hoping it will keep me from being lonely."

〜　〜　〜

"Yeah, well, you're right about that, for sure. I didn't realize how much I would miss my family when I signed on to emigrate to Haven. Especially my sis."

"You miss your sister?"

"I do, which surprises me. Seems like all we ever did was fight. I figured getting away from her would be a relief. But she's the one I miss the most. Go figure."

Sam was chatting with one of *Azov's* crew over coffee in the ship's canteen, a burly young man with a black goatee and shaved head. His arms were heavily tattooed.

In the months following Ian's meeting with Sam and his engineers, Luna Xtract negotiated a contract with Haven to establish mining operations in the Asteroid Belt. Ore containing gravitolite crystals was separated from rare-earth ore. Using off-duty KBP cruisers and Haven crews, the gravitolite ore was transported to Haven for processing, while the rare-earths went to Luna and the Luna Xtract facilities there.

Although much of the work in the Asteroid Belt was automated, inspections and repairs required the personal attention of Sam's engineers. Sam frequently used such occasions to visit the mining operations himself. He couldn't get over the thrill of being able to travel to deep space. On the one hand, he hoped to glean more information about the mysterious gravitolite that Haven found so valuable. In this he was totally unsuccessful. The ships' crews knew no more about the matter than he did. But Sam was pursuing other plans as well.

"What if the Haven government were changed to allow visits back and forth with family and friends back on Earth. Maybe a couple of two-week vacations a year. How would you feel about that?"

"That'd be long past due. Me and a bunch of others would love to go back to Earth. Just to visit. No way I would trade what we have on Haven. But those Haven Accords restrictions need to be eased, in my opinion."

"I've talked with a lot of you Havenites over the past few months, and I can say this: you are not alone. If I were in charge, I'd see to it that you could visit Earth whenever you wanted."

"I'm not going to hold my breath waiting for that to happen."

"Well, it won't happen soon. But keep your eyes and ears open. Things change. One of my specialties is making change happen."

Chapter 14

Mars, 2055

"It's Haven's priorities that I don't get," complained Tony Armado, mayor of Nova Prima, the first and largest of the three settlements Rae Anne was constructing on Mars. "Haven is producing tons of plasticore from the gravitolite being mined in the Asteroid Belt. And most of it is being used to construct fusion reactors being shipped to Earth. Meanwhile, they luxuriate under their beautiful dome and gaze at Saturn and stars, and we're stuck like moles in these claustrophobic habitats, never even seeing the light of day. It makes no sense."

Sam sat across from Tony's desk and waited for Tony to finish airing his complaints. Although he was prohibited from visiting Mars, the transport ship he was on that was ferrying rare-earth minerals from the Asteroid Belt to his Luna Xtract refining facilities on Luna had experienced a problem that required an emergency landing on Mars. Never one to miss an opportunity, Sam arranged to meet with Nova Prima's mayor while the ship was being repaired.

"Chavez's priorities are totally misplaced. Nova Prima could easily have its own dome by now. In fact, Haven has mined enough gravitolite to provide domes for all three cities here on Mars as well as Juno on Ganymede."

"I've complained directly to her on several occasions. All I get in return are promises that we'll get a dome at some vague future date. I tell you; I'm fed up."

"You aren't alone. I've been having conversations with dozens of KBP crew members who are ready for a radical change in Haven's political setup. Eventually, things are going to reach a boiling point."

"A lot of good that will do us. Haven is over a billion kilometers from Mars."

"That's true. But if you were to commandeer a KBP ship on one of its regular visits to Mars, that would put you within hours of Haven and give you the leverage you need to be heard. If you timed your move to coincide with a general uprising on Haven itself, you could get your dome and declare Mars' independence at the same time."

"Independence from Haven's autocratic rule. That's an interesting proposition I could go along with. But coordinating with a rebellion on Haven? I don't know…"

"That's where I come in. I'm keeping tabs on the pulse of the protest movement on Haven. I can let you know when to make your move. Who knows? I may be able to join you with a KBP cruiser of my own."

"I'll have to give this some thought. A move like this would be quite risky."

"But think of the rewards, not just for Nova Prima, but for your two sister cities as well, and for the future of Mars. Nothing will be happening soon, so you have plenty of time to think about it. But trust me, change is coming, and when it happens, you will want to be ready."

Haven

Rae Anne's assistant, Jorge, leapt from his desk and burst through the partition separating his office from Rae Ann's corner of the Municipal Building's roof.

"Rae Ann, a quake on Mars! Major damage in Nova Prima, and habitat breaches."

Rae Anne dropped her tablet onto her desk.

"Are there any casualties?"

"They're reporting seven Human and three Shalcerian dead in the City Hall wreckage, but City Hall has been cut off from the rest of the city, so there's no telling what it's like there. There's bound to be more fatalities."

"Check in with the mayors of Hibernia and Pella. See if they've suffered any damage."

Rae Anne lifted the phone from her desk and called Ian. He too had just heard the news.

"We need to get three cruisers to Mars immediately. Depending on the damage, we may need to evacuate the entire city."

"*Liberty* and *Azov* are the only cruisers available, Rae Anne. We'll be on our way within the hour. Have Jorge recruit as many available medics as he can find and send them down to either ship's hangar."

"Take some plasticore engineers with you, too. Jorge reports severe structural damage. We need to discover how our home-grown plasticore failed before we build any more habitats."

"Or fusion reactors," Ian added.

"Oh god. I hadn't thought of that. We have 17 reactors installed on Earth. If the plasticor containment vessel on one of those were to fail, there would be hell to pay."

"I'm on it. I'll send you a direct report from Nova Prima." Ian signed off and left Rae Anne staring at a blank screen.

She sat down and put her head in her hands. Except for the military skirmish in the Kuiper Belt four years earlier, this was the worst disaster in Haven's brief history.

When she looked up, Jason was sitting on the sofa across from her desk.

"Sorry, I didn't hear you come in," she said with a sigh.

"I was in my lab when I heard the news. I was concerned that the plasticor habitats had sustained damage."

"That concerns me too. We need to get to the bottom of this as quickly as possible."

"My doppelganger is already aboard *Liberty*. I'll have my eyes and ears available to survey the damage in real time."

Jorge stepped back into Rae Anne's office.

"Pella and New Hibernia weren't seriously affected by the quake," he reported. "Both felt shocks, and Pella reported a few leaks where walkways are connected to the habitats. They expect to have them repaired by the end of the day.

"Also, both cities volunteered to take in survivors from Nova Prima if necessary.'"

"Well, that's the good news. Now all we can do is wait to hear from Ian."

Mars

Sam awoke with a severe headache. Prior to opening his eyes, he tried to recall what he had been drinking. Clearly too much of whatever it was. The pain in his shoulders and a wrenching back ache severely restricted his mobility.

This is no drinking hangover. I've been mugged.

He opened his eyes. Everything was a blur. A steady yellow light filled the room. He slowly began to make out details. The room was sparsely furnished: a desk and chair, a lounger, and a bed. Given his position on the floor beside the bed, he surmised he had tumbled from the bed to the floor. He noticed that the desk was askew, and his computer was under the chair.

Earthquake. I've been in a fucking earthquake. Gotta get outdoors.

Then he remembered where he was. Outdoors on Mars was the last place he'd want to be.

Hmm…A genuine Mars quake. I can only hope it's over.

Sam felt around his body and flexed his muscles. Determining that he had suffered no serious damage, he defied the pain and struggled to his feet. Part of the difficulty, he realized, was that the whole room was tilted at a crazy angle. The wall behind the bed was mostly 'down,' so he proceeded to walk the wall to the nanoscreen.

The nanoscreen refused to yield.

Sam sat on his bed's uptilt edge.

Nothing to do but wait for a rescue.

Then he thought about how far from Earth he was. He broke into a sweat as he calculated the odds of a rescue on Mars.

Three hours after news of the quake had arrived at Haven, *Liberty* and *Azov* settled onto the rust-red Mars plain beside Nova Prima. The largest of the fifty-eight interconnected habitats was the five-story City Hall located in the center like the hub of a bicycle wheel. Other habitats were clustered around it in an interconnected maze of tunnel-like causeways.

The quake had upset everything. City Hall lay on its side. Its plasticore structure was intact, but the quake had severed the five causeways leading to it. Most of the other habitats were canted as crazy angles. Few of the connecting causeways were still intact.

Fortunately,the majority of the nanoscreens appeared to be functioning, sealing off each habitat from Mars' hostile environment. Ian was glad he had brought along the engineers. He couldn't visualize how they might rescue survivors trapped in the habitats scattered helter-skelter around City Hall.

"How do you intend to tackle this mess?" he asked Dominique, his lead engineer.

"We put our heads together before leaving Haven and tried to guess what we might be faced with. We brought a dozen inflatable tents with connectors and plenty of compressed air.

"Where there's a causeway still connected to a habitat, we'll connect a tent to a pressurized rescue vehicle on one end and the causeway on the other, then cut through the causeway. Anyone in the habitat can then walk or be carried out through the tent and into our medivan."

"Good thing the causeways aren't made of plasticore! What if the habitat has lost pressure?"

"Our team will be in full SEVA gear, despite the tent being inflated. The tent flap next to the medivan will be sealed. No one will be at risk. But if someone were in a depressurized habitat, they wouldn't have survived."

With just four medivans, the work was excruciatingly slow. Several habitats had lost pressure, their occupants now counted among the victims. They were identified and reverently laid aside to be buried outside the city. *Azov* had brought along a compact excavator to dig the graves.

Everyone was relieved to find there were no additional fatalities in City Hall, although over 30 survivors had sustained injuries. The nanoscreens attached to the habitats had automatically sealed after the first shock, keeping the death toll lower than it might have been.

On day three, a disheveled, disgruntled, and hungry Sam Durban stepped from a medivan into *Liberty's* hold to join the hundreds of survivors. Ian was taking a shift handing out food and drink and scowled when he spotted Sam. Although his presence on Mars didn't violate the Saturn Accords, which strictly applied to Haven, Rae Anne's intentions were to include Haven's off-Earth colonies under their umbrella. Ian was determined to interview Sam to find out what he was up to.

On their return trip to Haven, Ian had Sam brought to his quarters. When Sam stepped through the nanoscreen, Ian offered him a drink. Sam requested a bourbon, neat. Ian poured himself a stout from the Havenly Brewery.

"I have to say, Sam, I was surprised to see you. What were you doing at Nova Prima?"

Sam savored the aroma of his bourbon before responding.

"Business. Luna Xtract is always looking for new deposits of rare earth minerals. Some samples from Mars in the NASA archives from years ago showed promise. I was discussing how to get prospecting permits with Nova Prima's mayor."

"But without Haven's cruisers to transport your ore, Earth is nearly a year away, not to mention the huge costs involved. How can you hope to make a profit against challenges like that?"

"You do have a point. But things change, and I believe success only comes to those who have the vision to anticipate change and be ready to pounce when it happens. Perhaps a minor alteration of our contract to include stopovers on Mars?"

"So, how did you manage to get to Mars? The security for our immigration transports is pretty tight, and I'm sure you didn't get there from Haven."

Sam gave Ian an arrogant smile.

"I'm one of the wealthiest men alive. Everyone has their price."

Ian bristled.

Not everyone, Sam. Not everyone.

"In any case, you will be on the first cruiser leaving Haven for Earth after we arrive. Your presence on Haven violates the Saturn Accords, which we take very seriously. In the meantime, consider yourself under house arrest aboard *Liberty*.

"You would do this despite our mutually beneficial agreements?"

"Given how lucrative those benefits are to Luna Xtract, I don't imagine you'll do anything foolish enough to jeopardize your contract."

"No, you're right about that. But about our setting up a mining operation on Mars…"

"Don't even think about it."

Chapter 15

Haven, 2056

Avenger arrived unannounced with the KBP cruiser *Deimos* in tow. A second ship, a cruiser like *Deimos*, accompanied *Avenger* to replace *Callisto*. Both ships hovered in space just off Haven's asteroid platform. Shortly thereafter, a shuttle departed Haven's hangar below the Shalcerian garrison and maneuvered into *Avenger's* flight deck.

Meanwhile, several engineers from *Avenger* untethered *Deimos* and guided it into its old hangar at Haven's base. The second cruiser approached *Callisto's* old hangar on its own power and docked.

Rae Anne, Ian, and Jason watched the surveillance monitors in Rae Anne's office atop the Municipal Building.

"I'm glad we'll be up to a full complement of cruisers for our patrols," said Ian. "I hope we don't run into any difficult repairs before *Deimos* can be recommissioned."

"I'm more concerned with what Denahr will have in his report to Vahler. He's been very accommodating to everything we've done, but Vahler might take things differently. Before he left, he made it quite clear he had no intention of sharing details about their technology with us."

"Fortunately, he had no idea how much data I copied into *Aurora's* data archives," Jason remarked.

"I'm certain he'll call me in to report on Haven's status. I may be taken to task for our extracurricular activities. I wish I had some ammunition to confront him with."

"Like when you effectively commuted Karen Sander's execution," said Ian. "Using their own statutes against them."

"That was thanks to Jason's knowledge from their archives."

Rae Anne turned to face Jason.

"I don't suppose you have anything else we can use."

"As a matter of fact, I do."

As expected, a few hours after Denahr's shuttle returned to Haven, Jorge escorted Captain Denahr from the lift and through the partition into Rae Anne's office.

"Ah, Denahr. Good to see you."

"That's Captain Denahr for now, Rae Anne. Sorry. But Captain Vahler is in command of the Sol System and while he's here, we must adhere to strict protocol."

Rae Anne sighed dejectedly.

"Great. So, what can I do for you, Captain Denahr."

"I've just returned from *Avenger* and made my report. Captain Vahler wishes to see you immediately for a report on Haven's progress since *Avenger* left and its current status. I must warn you. He's not happy with your building colonies on Mars or with constructing fusion energy plants on Earth."

"I hope our activities haven't reflected badly on your stewardship, Captain Denahr."

"Not the first time I've been at cross purposes with my superiors. Fortunately, my background is in legal affairs, so I know our military law and precisely where the boundaries lie. I'm not in legal hot water. Not yet.

"But Haven is another matter. Your whole operation here is an experiment, and Captain Vahler and the *Avenger* Directorate are in control over Haven's very existence. Given the mood he's in, I'm worried he might declare the experiment a failure and terminate it."

A chill ran up Rae Anne's spine. A powerful nudge from *Avenger* would send Haven and its million Human inhabitants in a death spiral into Saturn's atmosphere. Having witnessed Vahler's lack of remorse at killing millions when he vaporized half of Moscow, Rae Anne knew he wouldn't hesitate to destroy Haven.

"Captain Vahler ordered me to bring you back to *Avenger* aboard our shuttle. So please, come with me."

Denahr held out a hand and took Rae Anne's. He gave her arm a slight tug and led her to the lift where she grabbed the satchel containing her SEVA suit. They descended to sublevel 1 and took the subway to the Shalcerian garrison. Before leaving the car, she wriggled into the suit, clipped the support system to her belt, and snapped the bubble helmet to the suit's neck ring. Once she was satisfied everything was working correctly, she nodded to Denahr and followed him from the car to a lift and descended to the shuttle's hangar bay.

After a few minutes, she found herself in the familiar surroundings of Hangar D on *Avenger*, although *Aurora* was no longer occupying the center berth. She followed Denahr into the Council Chambers, where Vahler and the six other directors were seated. Denahr then left the room.

"Well, Rae Anne Chavez. I see you have managed to keep Haven alive and well in the six years we've been away. I am anxious to hear your report."

Rae Anne noted the slate gray coloring of their body scales. *Not a good sign.*

"To begin," she began, "I thank you for bringing back *Deimos* and supplying a cruiser to replace *Callisto*. We'll have them rejoin our fleet as quickly as possible.

"Regarding Haven, your engineers completed Haven's construction according to specifications, and it is now fully populated. Your garrison commander, Captain Denahr, and I have initiated a successful integration of our two species with visitation and commerce. Our Kuiper Belt Patrols have maintained the system's security with just one significant skirmish. We lost 160 Humans in that encounter and one cruiser, while destroying one of three invading battleships. That's the extent of my report."

Rae Anne took a deep breath, knowing Vahler would not be satisfied. The silence didn't last long.

"You omitted a few key details, Rae Anne Chavez. Haven was meant to be an alternative to our dealing with the bulk of humanity. Yet you have taken our technology and have built a dozen fusion plants on Earth, despite our command not to share technology there. Is that not so?"

"With respect, Captain Vahler, there is nothing in the Saturn Accords that states we cannot share advanced technology with Humans, regardless of their location. In fact, the proper interpretation for sharing would include details to allow us to duplicate the technology, not merely be allowed to use it. You handed us black boxes, a token gesture. We had to discover how these technologies work. You forced us to reinvent the wheel. You deliberately tried to hold us back."

Murmurs filled the room as the directors turned to their neighbors to discuss Rae Anne's accusation. Vahler circled his left hand over his eyestalks to hush his colleagues.

"Where interpretations differ, as the Empire's official representative, mine is the one that counts. Our ruling is that you violated the conditions of the Saturn Accords, and you must face the consequences."

Rae Anne raised her voice and pointed at the captain, intentionally violating a serious taboo in Shalcerian culture.

"And who is to hold the Empire accountable for blatant violation of Shalcerian civil and military law? Your empire has violated Section 4782.311 of your own Interstellar Codes. You have extracted and removed essential resources from a star system harboring a sentient species. ICC-4782.311 was expressly written to ensure that all sentient species have available all the resources within their systems to advance their civilizations, no matter how far in the future those needs might be.

"But when the Empire discovered gravitolite deposits in our Kuiper Belt 337 years ago, you ignored that statute and set up mining operations to extract and remove gravitolite. Our Kuiper Belt patrols have mapped seventeen active gravitolite mining and processing operations, although there could well be more. How much gravitolite has the Empire stolen from Humans in 337 years?"

The room erupted in squawks and whistles as the various members of the Directorate responded to Rae Anne's charges. Before Vahler could restore control, Rae Anne shouted her concluding remarks in order to be heard over the din.

"On behalf of all Humans, I demand full restitution for what the Empire has removed from Sol System. I also demand unspecified punitive damages, beginning with your dropping your spurious charges about our violating the Saturn Accords. In our dealings with the Empire, it is not the Humans who are the guilty party."

Murmurs again filled the room, louder and more agitated than before. Vahler himself was dragged into the discussions. Several minutes passed before he extricated himself and signaled for quiet.

"Rae Anne Chavez, how you come by such detailed knowledge of our laws and how to apply them to suit your ends is impressive. It worked for you in the Karen Sanders case. It won't work for you here. When we have exacted our retribution, there will be no Humans left beyond Earth orbit to invoke questions of reparations or punitive damages."

For the second time, Rae Anne waved her fist at the captain.

"Your threats have no weight, Captain. In fact, they violate ICC-267.891, using threats to intimidate a witness and thwart justice. I therefore demand *Avenger's* Directorate to arrest Captain Vahler and prosecute him in accordance with your own laws. In case you are inclined to support his claims against Haven, Captain Denahr has already sent a combot through a micro wormhole to Shalkor with my accusations. Any actions taken against Haven or any of our Human operations from this moment will be dealt with according to Shalcerian jurisprudence from Shalkor, and I am assured punishment for such actions will be severe."

Rae Anne turned on her heels and resolutely departed the Council Chambers, head held high. The room behind her had fallen into total silence. Her comlink with Jason had provided her with the exact statutes she needed for her arguments, and in the short time she spent with Denahr before entering the Council Chambers, he assured her that he would immediately transmit her pleadings directly to Shalkor.

Chapter 16

Haven, 2056

Less than twenty-four hours after Rae Anne's confrontation with Captain Vahler aboard *Avenger*, Denahr stepped into Rae Anne's office. His colors rippled coral and orange with yellow spirals. Rae Anne responded with a big smile, never having seen a Shalcerian so excited.

"Captain Denahr," she said, standing and leaning forward on her desk. "You seem to be in a particularly good mood this morning."

"I have what may be good news, although I can only speculate on what it might mean. A combot arrived in Sol System a few hours ago. Our sensors picked up its signal, but we were unable to decode it, which means it was meant for Captain Vahler. But for it to have come within a day of my urgent message to Shalkor suggests this is a response telling *Avenger* to stand down."

"I don't understand. To stand down from what, exactly?"

"Last night, Captain Vahler ordered the garrison to take command of Haven's twelve cruisers and to use them to evacuate all Shalcerians from Haven. There could be only one reason for such a command. But shortly after the combot arrived this morning from Shalkor, he rescinded those orders."

"Oh my god. Was he seriously planning to destroy Haven?"

"I could be wrong, but that's my best explanation. The good news is we have gotten the attention of the Imperial authorities. Our best hope now is that they will command him to leave Sol System and never come back."

"I can't thank you enough for all you've done for us, Denahr."

"It's the least I could do, Rae Anne. I've become rather fond of Humans. I want to do everything in my power to help you succeed."

Three days later, *Avenger* was still floating in orbit off Haven, although it had relocated several thousand meters farther out. Rae Anne had received no additional communication from the ship.

She and Ian were speculating about why *Avenger* hadn't left as Denahr had predicted. The KBP rotation was to take place in three days and, given the situation at Haven, Ian was reluctant to leave.

Ian's wristcomm vibrated and he activated his earbud. Rae Anne watched his face frown with concern, then scowl as he disconnected. She raised her eyebrows and looked at him expectantly.

"That was Sherry aboard *Liberty*. She's in Surveillance. She detected six wormhole passages inside Neptune's orbit."

"Six at one time? That's odd. It's also too close to be a routine Kuiper Belt stopover. Could we finally be getting tourist ships to Haven?"

"These aren't tourists. Sherry said these things are as big as battlecruisers. Their wormhole signatures are Shalcerian."

"That's some relief. Unless they've come to give Vahler support."

Their concerns evaporated when Denahr stepped through the nanoscreen in the same emotional state he had exhibited before.

"Rae Anne! Ian! Prepare yourselves. This is unprecedented." Rae Anne smiled at seeing Denahr out of breath with excitement.

"Whoa, slow down. What's this all about?"

"A visitation. Here of all places. The emperor Himself has arrived in Sol System aboard his private yacht. He is coming to Haven!"

As Denahr was speaking, six brilliant stars surrounding a seventh golden star appeared in the black sky, growing brighter with each passing second. Soon the center star took the form of a golden sphere. It dwarfed *Avenger* as it passed by the distant battlecruiser and came to a halt alongside Haven. Its six companion ships took positions surrounding *Avenger*.

The giant sphere sparkled in an ephemeral golden haze. It appeared to be made from layers of gossamer fabric fading in and out of existence. Nothing about it seemed to have physical substance. It reminded Rae Anne of a desert mirage she witnessed as a child in New Mexico.

Denahr turned abruptly and skipped to the nanoscreen.

"I'm needed back at the garrison at once," he called out as he hurriedly left the room.

Ian shook his head. "What the hell is going on?"

"I don't know," Rae Anne replied in awe. "But emperors don't generally attend executions."

That afternoon, *Avenger* and two of the emperor's battlecruisers left Haven for parts unknown. Three hours later, Denahr appeared at the Italian restaurant where Rae Anne and Ian had gone for dinner. Rae Anne noted that his colors had calmed down considerably.

She motioned for him to join them, and he settled onto his pedestal leg beside their table.

"Is everything all right, Denahr?" Rae Anne asked with concern.

"Absolutely," he responded. "I'm dumbfounded at all that's taken place. And to top it all off, I, Denahr, met with the emperor. My life will never be the same."

"Congratulations, Denahr," said Ian.

"What an honor to have met with the emperor," Rae Anne added. "That must be on every Shalcerian's wish list."

"Thank you. It is an honor. But I have more good news. I am to escort the two of you to meet with him tomorrow."

Rae Anne dropped her fork and turned to Denahr wide-eyed.

"He wants to see us? Whatever for?"

"A little background information will help. You may have noticed that *Avenger* has been escorted from Sol System."

"We watched them leave."

"Vahler is no longer *Avenger's* captain. He was arrested and confined to quarters, and his Second was promoted to Captain. It turns out Vahler discovered gravitolite in your Kuiper Belt several hundred years ago on his first assignment. He and five other military officers, including one admiral, established clandestine mining operations there and have been selling the rare crystals illicitly. It's amazing they were able to keep the operation secret for so long.

"However, rumors have been circulating at the Imperial Court concerning the unexplained wealth of these six families. Your accusations and my missive to Shalkor exposed their treachery. Vahler is being taken to Shalkor to face trial alongside his cohorts. The Empire will not deal with them and their families lightly."

"No, I suppose not. But that doesn't explain why the emperor would wish to see us."

"On that subject, I can only conjecture that he will issue an official apology to Humans on behalf of the Empire."

When Denahr arrived at Rae Anne's apartment to escort her and Ian to the emperor's ship, he found Rae Anne uncharacteristically fussing with her wardrobe. Ian was attired in his KBP full-dress uniform.

"It doesn't matter what you wear, Rae Anne," Denahr said. "The emperor has no concept of Human dress codes. Besides, you'll be wearing your SEVA suits. Just grab something and let's go. We mustn't be late."

Rae Anne snatched the maroon jacket on top of the pile of clothes.

"That makes sense. Ok. I'm ready."

She and Ian grabbed the satchels with their SEVA suits and followed Denahr through the nanoscreen. When they reached the garrison, they donned their suits and verified they were operating correctly.

Denahr then took them into the garrison and down the lift to the garrison hangar where they boarded a shuttle. Denahr piloted the small craft the short distance between Haven and the emperor's yacht. The craft slithered into the golden haze which swirled around it like a misty fog and came to a halt for a brief security check before proceeding into the yacht's hangar.

Five uniformed Shalcerian guards marched to the shuttle and accompanied them through the hangar nanoscreen and along a corridor lined in gold. They halted at a wide double door framed in green and black jade. Intricate figures and designs in lapis lazuli were embedded in the white marble of the door itself.

While they waited in the corridor for permission to enter, Rae Anne concentrated on the figures in the door, noting several resembling Shalcerians, along with numerous other species. She recognized a Monapar, reminding her of VarConsa. She thought of his two children and hoped they were being well cared for.

Two of their escorts must have received a signal, because they stepped up to the doors and opened them, revealing an immense throne room, glittering in gold. The ceiling seemed to be open to the black velvet of space, studded with a myriad of stars. The walls were covered with veils of gossamer fabric in many colors, undulating as if in a gentle breeze.

The throne on which the emperor sat was centerstage at the end of a long, gold-threaded carpet walkway laid atop a silver floor that mirrored the stars above. The throne was made of solid gold with an elaborately carved back and arms. Both it and the figure sitting in it were three times normal size, dwarfing the two dozen Shalcerian courtiers standing stiffly on either side of the walkway.

This is a mammoth hologram! Nothing, not even the emperor, has a solid edge. This explains why the yacht appears so much larger and surreal than its battlecruiser escorts.

Hologram or not, Denahr held both his arms slightly out to keep Rae Anne and Ian from stepping forward. All three of his eyestalks drooped across his torso in abeyance.

"You may come forward."

The emperor's voice, translated by the computer, carried a note of authority, as if from a god.

Denahr dropped his arms and remained behind as Rae Anne and Ian walked to the base of the throne. Realizing she was facing a hologram erased any feelings of intimidation she might have had. She noted an air of confidence from Ian as well.

"Your species is making splendid progress. I applaud your negotiating the Saturn Accords and making a place for yourselves among the community of space-faring species. I foresee a bright future for Humans and your eventual full membership in our glorious Empire.

"Our legal system is designed to respect the laws, cultures, and environments of all sentient species we encounter wherever possible. This applies regardless of that species' current stage of development. Respect for the environment dictates that all natural resources within a sentient species' star system are the property of that species and are to be left intact and available for that species' evolution and development.

"Your complaint to our Legal Affairs Council brought to light an egregious violation of this principle that has been ongoing for 337 years, to the detriment of your Sol System environment. We have apprehended the perpetrators. They will face punishment for these acts.

"Restitution for your loss of natural resources in the form of gravitolite remains to be settled. The material itself is not recoverable. However, construction of your satellite city of Haven drew heavily on the Empire's resources over several years, a project for which we have not sought compensation. We also will award to Humans half of the proceeds from liquidation of the six family estates that profited from the perpetration of this crime. This award is considerable, and it will be banked, with interest, and made available to Humans when you achieve interstellar capabilities and achieve full membership as citizens of the Empire.

"Do you have anything you wish to add to these proceedings?"

Rae Anne cocked her head proudly and determined to present an air of respectful resolve.

"Your highness, as spokesperson for Humans, I applaud your quick response to our complaint. You may have saved many thousands of lives. On behalf of us all, we thank you.

"On the subject of reparations, I have two additional issues that have not yet been addressed. The first relates to Vahler's gravitolite mining operations in our Kuiper Belt. We could use an additional dozen cruisers to maintain these sites and haul the refined gravitolite to our plasticore processing plants on Venus. They would also be of use to service our interplanetary colonies on Mars, Luna, and Ganymede.

"My second request is more complicated. The Saturn Accords state that, in return for Humans patrolling our Kuiper Belt, the Empire will share its technology. Captain Vahler interpreted the word 'share' with greater stringency than we Humans understand the word. Humans expected sharing to include details on the theory and operation of those technologies, enabling us to reproduce them and distribute them as we see fit. Vahler refused to release any details. My request is that you reconsider this interpretation and give us the technological details we need."

A long pause ensued. The emperor's image froze in place, confirming that everything they could see was an elaborate hologram.

Eventually, the hologram came to life and the emperor spoke.

"The Empire will provide you with eight additional cruisers, to be paid for from the settlement funds I previously mentioned. We can deliver these within the next three months.

"With regard to the technological details you requested, there are some subjects about which we share no details, even with member species. Examples include our propulsion systems and our quantum computing capabilities. For two other examples, GESC-Plasticore and nanoparticle technology, you have discovered details on your own. Besides these, what do you have in mind?"

"If propulsion and computing are off the table, I would request that you share your healthcare diagnostic and treatment technology and the details behind your elaborate holographic display projections."

"Holographic technology is heavily dependent on our quantum computers, so that, too, is unavailable. However, the Empire will provide full details relating to your healthcare equipment. That you have already mastered plasticore production demonstrates you Humans to be a clever and resourceful species. I have no doubt you will quickly advance beyond what we give you.

"The Empire thanks you for helping eradicate a major criminal enterprise. We wish you success in your endeavors with Haven and with your progress as a species. We look forward to one day welcoming Humans into the interstellar community."

The emperor's image dissolved, leaving the throne empty. Rae Anne and Ian turned and rejoined Denahr. Their escorts met them at the throne room doors and took them back to their shuttle. By the time they disembarked on Haven, the royal yacht and its battlecruiser escorts had departed.

"There is one other thing I need to mention before you leave," said Denahr as the three approached the garrison gateway into Haven proper. They stopped at the airlock and faced each other. Rae Anne detected a somber note reflected in the magenta and green coloring of his scales.

"You seem troubled, Denahr. What is it?"

"We just heard news from Shalkor that *Avenger* never arrived in the 18 Scorpii System."

"Could something have happened to the ship on the way?"

"Not likely. *Avenger*'s bridge crew is a very tightly knit group. To them, Vahler is a hero. Our best guess is that they released him and he directed *Avenger* to the frontier. *Avenger* is probably now a rogue ship."

Ian frowned and pursed his lips.

"How does that affect us?"

"Vahler is a vengeful person, as you have witnessed firsthand. It's possible he may return to Sol System and attack Haven. If he's gone rogue, even our garrison won't matter to him. We'll need to be on continual alert."

Chapter 17

Sydney, 2057

Sam Durban looked across his desk at the three young people seated before him. All three were enjoying drinks from the bar in the reception area outside Sam's office. If any of them were nervous at meeting with the CEO of their company, they didn't show it.

"So," Sam began. "I'm sure you are wondering why Luna Xtract has gone to the trouble of flying you all the way to Sydney for a meeting that could have been handled on the web. And why you are meeting with me personally rather than someone in Human Resources.

"The answer to both questions will become apparent shortly. But first, I would like to get to know each of you better. Tell me about who you are and what you would like to be doing ten, twenty years from now. Something more than what I have gleaned from the company files."

Sam turned to the woman sitting to his right.

"Mary Beth Thornton, why don't you start."

Over the next two hours, Sam sat back in his chair and listened to Mary Beth, Mark Hillman, and Tom Schneider present details about their backgrounds and the visions they entertained for their futures. Sam prompted them with leading questions to elicit more detailed responses relating to their personal goals.

When all three had finished, Sam steepled his fingers beneath his chin and allowed for a long pause. Then Mary Beth broke the silence.

"So, what about you, Mr. Durban. You've probed us for our long-term goals. You have obviously achieved many of your goals with both TransWorld Space, Durban Robotics, and Luna Xtract. But you are still young enough to advance these companies as well as pursue other projects. What do you envision for your future?"

"Interesting you should ask that question because it ties directly into why I've brought you three here. I have been passionate about space exploration and development since childhood. Both TransWorld Space and Luna Xtract are natural outgrowths of my passions.

"But since the alien's arrival, the so-called Saturn Accords have stymied everything. The Haven crowd uses them like a bludgeon to quarantine the rest of us to the Earth-Luna corridor and to saddle us with very outdated technology. You can see how this affects my companies, but think for a moment about the goals and visions you each have just expressed. If the Haven crowd continues to have their way, it won't be long before your own professional growth will be stunted as well and you too will be forced to accept second-class status."

Sam was pleased to see his listener's rapt attention. All three shook their heads in dismay at the unfair disadvantage the Saturn Accords were imposing on humanity, on Human progress, and on their own futures.

"But how can we address that situation," Mark asked. The look on his face revealed he was already anticipating where this conversation was leading. "Saturn is a billion miles away, and without the alien cruisers, a trip to Haven takes five years."

"We should have at least three of those ships at our disposal, for our own use," said Tom, picking up on Mark's comment. He rubbed at his scruffy red beard. "They wouldn't have made near the progress without our expertise and equipment helping them with whatever it is they're extracting from the Asteroid Belt."

Mary Beth tugged at her large hoop earring. "Imagine what we could do with our own ships. And not just for mining," she added.

Sam smiled.

"Monopolies do not give up their power easily. And interplanetary distances present a real problem. Our only realistic hope to make change is to do it from the inside with a clandestine operation on Haven itself.

"That's why I personally selected you from the tens of thousands of employees on my payroll. You may recall those weird psychological profiling tests HR conducted six months ago. We used the results from those tests to identify one hundred candidates for Operation Vesuvius. You three emerged as potential leaders for this project. Our testing assured us that all hundred candidates will pass the Haven profiling exams and be selected to emigrate to Haven.

"Our contacts with the Havenite crews who provide transport to the Asteroid Belt have shown a growing dissatisfaction with their forced isolation from friends and relatives on Earth. This will get more intense as time goes on. With patience and appropriately timed agitation, we can foment a revolution that will give us control of the ships we need, and perhaps of Haven itself.

"I am counting on you three to organize and lead this insurgency. I've divided our one hundred activists into three independent groups. You are each designated to lead one group, creating small cells with no more than five individuals, so no one can identify anyone outside their own cell. The idea is to blend into the fabric of the city, discover its vulnerabilities, and strive for positions of power and influence. Develop a network of friends and potential followers. Infiltrate the Kuiper Belt Patrol itself.

"My robotics staff will give you the means to communicate with me directly without detection. When the time is right, we'll lead a revolution and take control without a shot being fired."

Although we'll do that too, if necessary. And once I control Haven and its fleet, there is nothing to stop me from seizing control of Earth itself. Emperor Sam Durban, supreme ruler of the Solar System! I like the sound of that. I just need to make it happen.

Haven, 2057

"You look particularly glum this morning, Rae Anne," Jason noted when Rae Anne stepped off the lift and trudged to her desk in her rooftop office. Jorge had not yet arrived.

"Thanks for noticing, Jason. I am feeling a bit down."

"Maybe a mocha latte would cheer you up. What might be bothering you?"

Jason began preparing Rae Anne's drink. Coffee and chocolate were among the few imports from Earth that Haven Customs permitted. Although Haven's hydroponics facilities succeeded in growing pineapples and small bananas, neither coffee nor cacao plants ever took hold.

"I'm not happy with our progress. Everything is moving at a snail's pace."

"Haven has established three cities on Mars, and one each on Ganymede and Luna. That's five cities in as many years. Not to mention the reconstruction efforts on Nova Prima."

"Those hardly qualify as cities. Settlements is a more accurate description. Only Nova Prima exceeds 1000 inhabitants."

"What is the bottleneck? Haven had a half-million population after five years."

"It's the size of our interplanetary fleet. The Shalcerians gave us twelve ships, which is enough for the patrols, and we purchased eight more. But we could grow four times faster with just twice as many ships."

"We're manufacturing more GESC-Plasticor than we need," Jason called over his shoulder. "And we're building fusion reactors for Earth at a furious rate. You can already measure the impact these have had on climate change. We have the plasticore to build more ships. What we don't have is the blackhole technology with which to power them."

Jason brought Rae Anne's latte to her desk.

Rae Anne took a sip and sighed.

"Is there any possibility you have that information in your data archives from *Avenger*?"

"Unfortunately, I've plumbed the depths of my memory banks and have found nothing related to locating micro black holes, let alone capturing and containing them. Since those processes are beyond the purview of battleships, the information was not included in *Avenger*'s database. Probably out of security concerns."

"The missing piece to our puzzle. How do we solve this dilemma?"

"Haven University has a top-rate faculty of researchers in every scientific field. This represents a formidable reservoir of brain power. If we could tap into that, we might see some surprising results."

"Hmm…"

Ian and Jorge both stepped through the partition and greeted Rae Anne and Jason. Jorge returned to his office and Ian crossed over to Rae Anne and Jason.

"You two look like a pair of conspirators. What are you up to?"

"Jason and I have decided we need to expand our interplanetary fleet. I would like to see us building out faster and providing more aid to Earth, but we're pushing our current ships and personnel to the max."

"I can vouch for that."

"But Jason has just given me a great idea. And you're just the person to carry it out! Planning conferences is right up your line."

"I'm not sure I want to hear this."

"Haven is about to celebrate its fifth anniversary since ratifying our constitution after *Avenger's* departure. Let's hold a conference during the celebration and invite all our scientists and engineers. We'll present the technological hurdles we're facing and challenge them to tackle the problems."

"These are busy people. What incentives will you offer?" Ian asked.

"Food, of course. Engineers can't turn down a free banquet."

Ian laughed.

"I didn't mean incentives for attending the conference. Incentives to drop their current research and pursue something that doesn't align with their primary interests."

"Hmm…That's a tough one."

"Maybe I can be of help there," said Jason. "The Shalcerian data archives stored in *Aurora's* computer are extensive and cover nearly every field imaginable, except black holes and quantum computing. If we made these archives accessible to everyone who was willing to work with us, that would provide a remarkable incentive. Suppose you were searching for a better way to recycle plastics. A look into the Shalcerian database might provide information that would save you months, maybe years, of research. That would make spending a few hours per week on our project more than worthwhile."

"That's a brilliant suggestion, Jason. You could create a program to coordinate data sharing and include your incredibly efficient search algorithms. Ian, do you have enough lead time to get a conference set up?"

"We have two months. That should be enough time. What are we going to call this conference?"

Rae Anne closed her eyes and scrunched her brows in thought.

"Let's call it 'The Road Ahead Congress.' I think that will make participants feel more like delegates instead of attendees. It emphasizes the future and future progress. And organize a 'to-die-for' banquet that no one can refuse."

"You'll need to create a new office to coordinate the projects and communicate developments to everyone as they occur," said Jason.

Rae Anne nodded. "I'll begin work on that today. Make the communication aspect into a newsletter as part of your program."

She finished her latte and took a deep breath. Her earlier dour mood had been swept away by the opportunities that lay ahead once their new project took hold.

"I've started working on that program already."

Rae Anne sighed. "You know, there are times when I envy your AI efficiency. I can only imagine what it must be like to be working on dozens of projects simultaneously."

"I'm in love with you just the way you are," Ian countered. "I like being the center of attention when we're alone together."

"You do have a point, there. But I can't wait to see how our technical community will respond to our proposal."

Ian laughed. "I can't see anyone refusing to participate. And with so many scientists and engineers digging into that monstrous cache of data, we are going to see breakthroughs in many unrelated fields. I believe we're onto something that will catapult us into the future."

Chapter 18

The Road Ahead Congress

The conference hall in the center of the Haven University campus was packed. Researchers, technicians, and engineers from every field imaginable showed up. Excited conversation filled the room amidst a maelstrom of activity. The enthusiasm exhibited by the delegates gave Rae Anne a surge of adrenalin.

Several of the attendees were engineers and scientists who had recently immigrated from Earth. Some of these new arrivals were surreptitiously still on the Luna Xtract payroll. All were advancing in their new jobs and making inroads into the social fabric of their various Haven communities.

Rae Anne, Ian, Denahr, and Jason were seated in plush chairs on the stage. At the appointed time, Rae Anne rose and stepped to the dais. The bustle in the room quickly quieted.

"I want to welcome you all to the Road Ahead Congress. Thank you for coming. We promised that we could help you accelerate your research if you came, and we intend to do just that. I will reveal the details to you shortly. But first, I would like to introduce our special guest."

Rae Anne turned and gestured toward Denahr, who stood and waved at the crowd in a typically Human gesture.

"Please welcome Captain Denahr from the Shalcerian garrison on Haven."

Vigorous applause echoed through the chamber. Rae Anne turned back to the audience after Denahr resumed his sitting position.

"Few people are aware of Captain Denahr's critical contributions in making Haven and our sister cities on Mars, Luna, and Ganymede a success. With his authorization, we were able to use the idle KBP cruisers for our own purposes, enabling us to build colonies on Mars, Luna and Ganymede and supply Earth with fusion reactors. Thank you, Captain."

After another round of applause, Rae Anne turned back to the audience.

"When we signed the Saturn Accords fourteen years ago, establishing Haven and the Kuiper Belt Patrol, the Shalcerian representative, Captain Vahler of the *Avenger*, had no intention of sharing details of their advanced technologies, despite the stipulations in the Accords.

"However, we Humans are more creative than they imagined. If there's one thing we're good at, it's reverse engineering. Once we know something is possible, nothing can stop us from discovering how it works and duplicating it, even making improvements along the way."

"GESC-Plasticore manufacture and fusion reactor technology are two examples of our tenacity in this regard. We owe our successes in large part to Jason's research into *Avenger's* computer archives. That and the examples the Shalcerians left behind, gave us the knowledge we needed to mass-produce GESC-Plasticore and construct new fusion plants for Earth. To date, we have delivered 28 reactors to countries where they will have the most impact in reducing greenhouse gas emissions. More will follow, to be located where their economic impact is most needed in developing countries."

Applause rippled through the room and interrupted her presentation. It quickly expanded to include the whole audience, with about half coming to their feet. Rae Anne paused a moment, then raised her arm to quiet the crowd so she could continue.

"I am extremely proud that Haven is giving back in a meaningful way. With such auspicious beginnings, the time has come to tackle the more challenging technologies the Shalcerians have demonstrated are possible. Chief among these are the advanced propulsion systems that enable travel between planets in hours rather than months and that form the basis for interstellar travel.

"We now have twenty interplanetary cruisers with their space-warping drives. We need more. We need a fleet numbering in the hundreds. We can build the ships. But we are stymied when it comes to their propulsion systems.

"So, this is our challenge: We need to discover how to construct a propulsion system that warps space and creates gravity wells to drive our ships. With the fleet I envision, we can schedule daily shuttles between the planets and initiate interplanetary commerce. We'll be able to transport and share resources. And we'll be able quickly to come to each other's aid should an emergency arise.

"The propulsion challenge entails discovering how to locate and capture micro-blackholes, and how to build gravity bottles in which to keep them. Once we've captured a blackhole, we need to learn how to excite it to produce resonating gravity waves and how to focus that energy into space to create those gravity wells. Jason believes we have the computing power to control and manipulate the black holes for this purpose even without the benefits of a quantum computer. However, advances in quantum computing would be very beneficial.

"Once we have surmounted the interplanetary propulsion hurdle, we can tackle the more difficult challenge of tailoring the system to accommodate two black holes and manipulate them to create wormholes, the key to the stars. Many species have mastered interstellar travel. Humans are on the verge of joining this august group.

"If we design our interplanetary ships with the ultimate goal of converting them into starships, we can readily retrofit them when we've mastered wormhole technology. We'll then have an armada of starships at our disposal. We will have earned our place among the star-faring community.

"My challenge to each of you is to focus whatever part of your creative energies you can spare to surmounting these challenges. To compensate you for your time and energy, Jason has developed a sophisticated search algorithm that draws on the immense Shalcerian database I mentioned earlier. When you join our team, you will have access to that database to retrieve information relevant to your own research projects as well. Imagine the progress you can achieve with the input from thousands of years of Shalcerian research at your disposal.

"I should add that Earth and all of humanity will benefit from your discoveries. Captain Denahr is the ultimate arbiter of the Saturn Accords in the Solar System. He has made it clear that, with only a few exceptions, advances developed here can be shared with Earth.

"You each have a signup form in your program. List the R&D areas you are interested in and your contact information. Jason will have your search program access codes sent to your tablets before you leave the conference today. You can then begin drawing on the Shahlcerian archives tomorrow."

"Thank you for coming and for your interest. With your help, humanity will become an interstellar species. Good luck to all of you. Enjoy the banquet and Haven's Fifth Anniversary Gala."

When Rae Anne joined Ian, Jason and Denahr to walk off the stage, she was pleased to see nearly everyone's head bowed as if in prayer, busily entering their information into Jason's computer database.

"I truly regret that I don't have more specific information to help get us started on these blackhole issues," said Jason.

"You've done wonders, Jason," Rae Anne said, clapping him on his shoulder. "I believe the degree of collaboration we are about to see in all fields will reap results far beyond anything we dare to imagine. Never underestimate the power of vision and hard work. We may have just saved humanity despite the restrictions in the Saturn Accords."

Rae Anne looked up at the ceiling, then back to Jason with a sparkle in her eyes.

"That's it. The name we've needed for this monumental effort. Not very original, but absolutely appropriate: Ad Astra!

The Saga Continues

To follow humanity's remarkable advance to the stars,
watch for book three of The Saturn Accords,
<u>Starbase Alpha</u>
due out in 2024.
Order book one, <u>Saturn Conundrum</u>, and <u>Starbase Alpha</u>
online or at your favorite bookstore.

<u>About the Author</u>

Dan Bishop retired from Colorado State University in Fort Collins after a career teaching chemistry and computer science. He is a strong advocate for sustainability and renewable energy. He divides his time between writing and painting landscapes and abstracts in pastels and acrylics. <u>Saturn Rendezvous</u> is the second book in The Saturn Accords series, following <u>Saturn Conundrum</u>, published in 2022. His black cat Mario shares his home with Dan and Ann in a small mountain town in central Colorado.

<u>authordbishop@gmail.com</u>
<u>www.authordbishop.com</u>